Also by Vincent Canby

Living Quarters

UNNATURAL SCENERY

UNNATURAL SCENERY.

by

VINCENT CANBY

Alfred A. Knopf   NEW YORK   1979

THIS IS A BORZOI BOOK
PUBLISHED BY ALFRED A. KNOPF, INC.

Copyright © 1978 by Vincent Canby

Grateful acknowledgment is made to the following to reprint
previously published material:

The University of North Carolina Press: Excerpt from
The History and Present State of Virginia by Robert Beverley,
edited by Louis B. Wright. Published for the Institute of
Early American History and Culture, Williamsburg.
Copyright 1947 The University of North Carolina Press.

Library of Congress Cataloging in Publication Data

Canby, Vincent.   Unnatural scenery.

I. Title.
PZ4.C215Un 1978   [PS3553.A4894]   813'.5'4   78–7562
ISBN 0–394–50148–9

Manufactured in the United States of America

Published January 22nd, 1979
Second Printing, February 1979

To Robert C. Ascher

ON MEETING A SAVAGE AT THE HOME OF A MUTUAL FRIEND:

"I asked him concerning their God, and what Notions of Him were? He freely told me they believ'd God was universally beneficent, that his Dwelling was in the Heavens above, and that the Influences of his Goodness reach'd to the Earth beneath. That he was incomprehensible in his Excellence, and enjoyed all possible Felicity: That his duration was eternal, his Perfection boundless, and that he possesses everlasting Indolence and Ease. I told him, I had heard that they Worshipped the Devil, and asked why they did not rather Worship God, whom they had so high an opinion of, and who wou'd give them all good things, and protect them from any Mischief that the Devil could do them? To this his answer was, That, 'tis true, God is the giver of all good things, but they flow naturally and promiscuously from him; that they are shower'd down upon all Men indifferently without distinction; that God do's not trouble himself with the impertinent affairs of Men, nor is concern'd at what they do: but leaves them to make the most of their Free Will, and to secure as many as they can, and of the good things that flow from him. That therefore it was to no purpose either to fear, or Worship: But on the contrary, if they did not pacify the Evil Spirit, and make him propitious, he wou'd take away, or spoil all those good things that God had given, and ruine their Health, their Peace and their Plenty, by sending War, Plague and Famine among them; for, said he, this Evil Spirit, is always busying himself with our affairs, and frequently visiting us, being present in the Air, in the Thunder, and in the Storms. He told me farther, That he expected Adoration and Sacrifice from them, on the pain of his displeasure; and that therefore they thought it convenient to make their Court to him. I then asked him concerning the Image, which they Worship in their *Quioccasan*; and assur'd him that it was a dead insensible Log, equip't with a bundle of Clouts, a meer helpless thing made by Men, that could neither hear, see nor speak; and that such a stupid thing could no ways hurt, or help them. To this he an-swer'd very unwillingly, and with much hesitation; However, he at last deliver'd himself in these broken and imperfect sentences; *It is the Priests—they make the people believe, and*—Here he paus'd a little, and then repeated to me, that *it was the Priests*—and then gave me hopes that he wou'd have said something more, but a qualm crost his Conscience, and hinder'd him from making farther Confession."

—Robert Beverley, *The History and Present State of Virginia*, published in London in 1705

"I've got out of going to Switzerland thank heavens, it is a blessed relief to feel that I've escaped those snow-capped peaks. Like my hairdresser, when I said why do you hate Switzerland, '*Ah les montagnes,*' was all he could say in a sort of groan. I so agree don't you—I think natural scenery is THE END."

—Nancy Mitford,
in a letter, December 1930

UNNATURAL SCENERY

1

Tatterhummock County has always been at least two and sometimes three or more places in my mind simultaneously. Each is of
equal importance. There are no visible contradictions. As in a
dream there are no differences in time, no confrontations for
space. One house may be several settings, one person two. Someone many years dead is the child of parents not yet born. Logic
bends. Tatterhummock County is Wicheley Hall, the central section of which was started in 1659 by Sir William Wicheley, who
later became the royal governor and used the Hall as his summer
residence when he wanted to escape the heat of Williamsburg and
the importunities of its society. Wicheley Hall is unique, being the
only surviving clapboard manor house in Virginia. Its classic lines
describe in flammable white-painted wood the style of the later
brick manor houses called Georgian. The main house now has
thirty-two rooms, including a ballroom attached to the west wing
and a third-floor dormitory that once slept as many as thirty
bachelors who came for hunting weekends and dances during the
early decades of the eighteenth century. The house is more or less
in charge of a splendid view north and east across the Tatterhummock River, six miles wide at that point, to Lancaster County and
the southern perimeter of the region known as the Northern Neck,
which gave us George Washington, the Lees (Francis Lightfoot,
Light-Horse Harry and Robert E.), "King" Carter, some of the
early Byrds, as well as DeKoven Crozier. The Hall, occupied

briefly by Cornwallis on his journey to Yorktown, raided but not sacked by a British naval party in 1812 and missed during the Peninsular Campaign by the Yankees (who turned left instead of right at Four Corners), has been owned for the last twenty-five years by a Pittsburgh-born New York stockbroker who summers in Maine and winters in Palm Desert. It's not a house with a family of its own—it's changed hands two dozen times in 300 years—but its decay is seemly. Today it looks no different than it did more than thirty years ago when I was a student at St. Matthew's School for Boys and explored the grounds and the house that, though possessed, was seldom occupied. Among its treasures are a ceiling designed by the Adam brothers, some nineteenth-century hand-painted chinoiserie wallpaper with willow trees that look like fountains, a rose garden that still blooms after three centuries, box hedges as tall as hickory trees. There are also a four-bedroom guest house and another substantial house that serves as the farm manager's cottage, when there is a farm manager, 250 acres of once fertile tobacco land, a swimming pool and, where Queen Anne Creek flows into the Tatterhummock River, a deep cove protected by bluffs that makes a fine hurricane anchorage. One million seven hundred and fifty thousand dollars will buy the works, all of its furnishings, including some said to be original, a disputed Peale portrait of Mrs. Douglas Wormley of Philadelphia, two tractors and other assorted farm machinery, a 1935 two-door V-8 Ford, a 1961 General Motors pickup truck, a rotting oyster boat that could, with love, be made seaworthy, fishing gear and nearly a dozen forgotten umbrellas.

Ancient Wicheley is the present and future of Tatterhummock County. The past is life at Lewis's Landing, the Lewis family farm, as remembered by Lockie, my Lewis grandmother, who was born there, and by Ma, who was born and raised in Chicago but spent long periods of time at Lewis's Landing playing out her maidenhood. When I was small Lockie and Ma created picture postcards in which the big, comfortable but perfectly common-place farmhouse, put up in the eighties and without connections to history, became a landmark to equal Wicheley. They recalled life at Lewis's Landing as something that was aging-in-the-wood, getting richer with time—an unending series of brilliantly sunshined mornings, tranquil afternoons, gay evening parties, with gut-busting feasts on Sundays and holidays. They gave me memories of warm family feelings and of cousins of ages to suit any child's need for companionship. Cousins especially appealed to me since my brother Tom was four years older and never a true companion until death did us join. I had no real cousins that I knew. Ma was an only child and my father's two brothers, though they had children, lived on the West Coast and hadn't been close to my father even Before the Fall. After his disgrace I'm sure they stopped exchanging Christmas cards. My only cousin is Cousin Mary Lee Carter (née Moulton) who, when I was a boy, lived at Lewis's Landing with her widowed mother and spinster aunt. But Cousin Mary Lee, whom I'm still fond of, was ten years older than I and a second cousin twice removed at that.

Ma and Lockie never remembered sitting on a porch at Lewis's Landing. It was always the north, south or east veranda. The living room was a drawing room heated by log fires in the fireplace, not in the Franklin stove that actually dominated the room. When Ma and Lockie slept, it was in feathers that geese don't grow any more, in a softness that rendered insomnia more rare at Lewis's Landing than leprosy. The scent of roses and honeysuckle hung over the house like a pea-soup fog, year-round. Retainers were born, raised and died at the Landing in the service of masters they adored and fussed over twenty-four hours a day, ever heedless of manumission. Lockie and Ma turned themselves on reminiscing about a place they created out of whole cloth. Ma would get so carried away that before we knew it we'd be up to our asses in out-of-state "ah declares" and "you alls."

The county that I first came to know was a drear, worn-out place cut off from civilization. One saw an occasional lumber schooner tacking its way up the Tatterhummock River, but aside from the oyster boats the river looked unused. There still is no railroad within twenty miles of the county. It would have cost a nineteenth-century railroad baron as much to build the dozen or so bridges necessary to span the rivers as it did Cornelius Vanderbilt to connect New York to Chicago.

Though neither Lockie nor Ma spent much time at Lewis's Landing in later years, they held onto it as if it were an essential compass point. They also held fast to the name of Lewis. Lockie, having been born a Lewis, remained Mary *Lewis* Kemper in marriage. Ma was Mary *Lewis* Kemper, Jr., before she married my father. My brother Tom, who was supposed to be a junior, was named Thomas *Lewis* Henderson, while I, named for my father's father, the crooked judge, was Marshall *Lewis* Henderson. From all this you might have thought the Lewises to be an exotic breed, the Bourbons of Tatterhummock County. Not exactly. There were Lewises all over the county and all over Virginia, Kentucky, Indiana, Ohio and any other state you can name in half an hour. Some are kin, some not. There were so many Lewises that they would have been the Joneses of the county if there weren't already so many real Joneses there. Whether Anglican Lewises, as we were, or Presbyterian Lewises, as many of the others were, they all claimed kin to Meriwether Lewis and to Thomas Jefferson, who had no sons. The Lewises and the Jeffersons had so relentlessly intermarried through several generations that there has been speculation that what Jefferson called "the hypochondriacal affections" of Meriwether Lewis were among the results. There has also been suspicion that others affected included the two Lewis boys, Lilburne and Isham, who one night in 1811, in a fraternal spree, skinned alive and dismembered a seventeen-year-old slave boy named George. That's a story that Lockie and Ma didn't remember, but it's no surprise since they didn't make it up.

"I declare, Mary," Lockie said to Ma in front of Tom and me, "both of them are looking more and more like Lewises every day." I was ten and Tom fourteen. We were in Lockie's Packard, Tom and I sitting on the jump seats, Ma and Lockie on the back seat with the center armrest down, Garrett, in full livery, at the wheel, speeding us along at perhaps twenty-five miles an hour. It was in the period After the Fall when Lockie, usually unannounced, would turn up at the Henderson hovel in Barrington (where we'd been exiled from Lake Forest) to take us on an outing that had to be clandestine. Boo, Ma's father, believed that Ma and Tommy had to get out of this thing themselves. He frowned on favors if not family intercourse. "They are Lewises and that's all there is to it," said Lockie. Tom was not the brightest of children but he could identify a fallacy when an attempt was made to present it to him as a gift. "How can we both look like Lewises," said Tom, "when we don't even look like each other?" Which was true. Tom was even-featured, blond and blue-eyed, muscular, with the kind of thick skin that immediately turns dark gold in the summer sun. He was the image of Our Father, Handsome Tommy Henderson, the Celebrated Society Embezzler. I was always too skinny. My hair was black, wavy, my face long like Ma's, with her green eyes and white skin that, unless it's methodically oiled, burns and peels a half dozen times before it accepts color.

"Well," said Lockie, "not all the Lewises look alike. You look like my Uncle Henry Lewis who was killed in the war." "The Civil War?" said Tom. "Yes," said Lockie. "What a handsome man— he was only twenty-three. He did have a small problem with the ladies, though." "What sort of small problem?" I asked. "He was very ardent," said Lockie. "He liked to play in other people's back yards." "Oh, mother," said Ma, tsking. "It's the truth," said Lockie. "That's what they called it in those days." "If he died in the Civil War," said Tom, "how can you remember what he looked like when you weren't even born yet?" "There's a portrait of him at Lewis's Landing, just outside Cousin Annie Lee's room. And Marshall looks like his great-grandfather Lewis." Tom: "Great-grandfather Lewis must have looked like a creep." "He was a most attractive man," said Lockie. "He was a poet and he looked like a poet." "I thought he owned a general store," said Tom. "He did," said Lockie, "but he also wrote some poems." Tom: "Why do you always say we're Lewises? I'm a Henderson. If I'm a Lewis, I'm also a Kemper like Ma and Boo, and a lot of other things—a Smith or a Jones or a Rappaport," which was the name of Lockie's favorite pharmacist in Lake Forest. "You're certainly not a Rappaport," said Lockie. "I did have some Jones cousins in Albemarle County, but only by marriage." Tom: "My father never talks about the Hendersons the way you and Ma talk about the Lewises. Boo never talks about the Kempers except to talk about the business, and Boo *is* the business." "Don't show off, darling," said Ma. Lockie's laughter was full of love. "You're a Lewis, dear, and a Tatterhummock Lewis at that." Tom's spontaneous victories were the ones I resented most.

I'm a Yankee by birth and in all my sympathies, a Lewis by name and by blood, and I'm forever connected to Tatterhummock County by chance, joined at the hip, so to speak. In 1940 at age seventeen, while I was a boarding student at St. Matthew's School for Boys, two miles downriver from Wicheley, eight miles downriver from Lewis's Landing, I had an accident that cracked my spinal column in two places. For all intents and purposes I'm paralyzed from the waist down. In the course of my years of therapy I first learned how to get about with one of those four-legged walkers in which old people creep around upper Broadway toward death, often irritably, knowing they are slow but going as fast as they can. Later I graduated to crutches I handle so adroitly that no matter how expensive the leg braces—and I do have the best—and no matter how careful the maintenance, the braces clank and squeak for need of 3-in-One oil at the end of an active day.

For many years after the accident I avoided Virginia and the Tidewater, a lonesome territory of high, flat peninsulas that reach from the center of the state down to the Chesapeake Bay, fingers of land separated by those broad blue rivers whose languor is deceptive, their movements not of this world, having been ordered by the moon. While my friends and classmates grew up to fight in World War II, I was starting over from scratch, learning how to crawl, to walk, to run my own life and to value my talents. My disadvantaged state, I fear, did not make me a better man, but I've held on.

Though I could not walk as others do, I learned how to fly. A detour of sorts. I once financed and participated in an expedition to prospect for gold in Alaska. I developed a continuing passion for Egyptology, have set up and abandoned residences in Lake Forest, New York, Paris, East Hampton and Luxor, married twice and had several serious affairs, one of which (with Jacqueline Gold of Queens) has lasted longer than either of my marriages.

Yet there have been only two constants in my life. The first, an ever-renewing interest in the rituals, records and literature associated with the heresy of the Albigenses in the eleventh and twelfth centuries—papal bulls, manifestos and other public documents, private correspondence that passed between Popes Innocent, Gregory and Marius and their representatives in southwestern France, the military logs of the Albigensian Crusade, instructions to inquisitors, manuals on methods of persuasion, final testaments of prominent heretics whose only purpose, as a rich cloth merchant of Toulouse put it, was "to clarify God and to identify the good and evil within the Personality that Mani taught us is dual." Not widely known is the existence of a large number of Albigensian ballads, thought by Rome to be inflammatory still—the translation of which has become my lifetime's work. I also own a small but priceless cache of pornographic literature, produced in Rome under papal instructions, designed to discredit the Albigenses' claims to perfect chastity—material discovered in a château near Languedoc by a mad old Alsatian priest named Klein, a backsliding Jesuit and a true subversive who shares my obsession. I have two convictions: that during the two centuries when Rome was suppressing the high- but muddle-minded Albigenses, civilized lunacy attained a refinement never since equaled in western culture; and the haunted one that Tom, so long dead, is responsible for the unbuttoned condition of the lower half of my body.

I've only 10 percent use of my legs—and this percent limited to my upper thighs—but I've been spared the worst traumas of paraplegia. I'm in full command of my bowels and my bladder and, more important, of my cock, which at a bitter moment in recent American history, I considered having cast in a suitable alloy—bronze, probably—to donate to the county as a public monument. As I like to say when I've been especially rotten and am in need of instant absolution, I know I'm not *always* a nice person.

"You're a bastard," Utah said to me—this was in 1962 or '63. Though she said it gently, she elocuted it so perfectly she might have been taping a radio show. She was presenting me with a private investigator's report that described how I'd had her telephone bugged. I'd suspected, wrongly as it turned out, that Utah, my second wife, was having an affair with a hairdresser at Bergdorf's. "You're suspicious and mean." Utah didn't like to waste her acting abilities on real-life scenes so the words were spoken with no more than an earnest cheerlessness. "I don't understand you," she said. "I never have." "I know I'm not *always* a nice person," I said then as always.

It's cant and I recognize it as such, but cant has its functions. It reassures. It imposes order. "From shirtsleeves to shirtsleeves in three generations," Lockie would say when she heard of someone's reversal in fortune, even if he were a Romanov. "Horses sweat, men perspire and ladies are all aglow," said Ma, who thought it rude to glow except on the hottest day of the year. "It's easy to get your name into the papers," said Boo. "The trick is keeping it out." The inspiration for this last was my father's arrest in the early 1930s, an event that for two days was treated by the Chicago newspapers as if it were a local Teapot Dome. Though I was aware of the unpleasant aspects of the disclosure, I was not displeased to find the family could make front-page news when the facts warranted. Boo was profoundly distressed when he came upon me in the kitchen of Chantilly, the Kemper castle in Lake Forest, meticulously clipping the afternoon newspaper stories about my father and pasting them in a scrapbook labeled: "Souvenirs of My Life—Marshall Lewis Henderson, Nine."

Because Boo was sincere in his belief that anonymity was a virtue second only to profit-taking, he should never have married a Lewis. The Lewises have pride in family and put great store by form but at least once a generation they somehow call for the attention of the world. Meriwether Lewis, tracking west with Mr. Clark, brought honor to the name. Three years later, suffering what his benefactor Jefferson called "the hypochondriacal affections" in a way station in the Natchez Trace, a place run by a certain Mr. and Mrs. Grinder, Meriwether Lewis embarrassed everyone by putting one bullet into his head and another into his chest.

In the summer of 1976 I made my decision to buy Wicheley Hall for reasons that were not entirely nice.

2

It is July 15 of the Bicentennial Year. Unable to move easily I sit stuck to the leather of what at one time was an expensive (for Jackie), finely balanced Eames chair. After so much use it tilts to the left as if it had suffered a series of small strokes and I worry it may be doing further damage to my spine. As is my habit I close barn doors and cry over spilt milk. It is a dreadful night, hot, dripping with moisture but not with rain. The windows are open. From West 88th Street nine floors below comes the manic horn music of transplanted San Juan, Ponce, Bayamón and Cataño. Every four minutes the community-owned Harley Davidson takes off eastward across Amsterdam Avenue on 88th Street, its roar blanketing the music for a few seconds. It turns right on Columbus Avenue, races south to 87th Street, comes west on 87th Street to Broadway, up Broadway to 88th Street, turns right again and dives toward the landing pad in front of Hector's Self-Service Laundry. The trick is not to overshoot, to speed until the last, then to stop without injury. Around and around all evening, middle-aged men, boys, teenagers, to the approval of children on the sidewalks and women in the windows above. The riders are all sizes, shapes and dispositions, but on the Harley, wearing the white helmet, their faces shadows behind clear plastic, exercising power not yet paid for, they are one person who marks his terri-tory with sound.

I am aware that an unusual sensitivity to odors is one of the early symptoms of schizophrenia, but as I sit here I can smell perfume so thick and sweet the scent could be drunk as a liqueur, followed by a wave of body deodorant that protects against offense by so puckering the nostrils one cannot smell anything. I look across the roof of the tenement opposite, which, thank God, is only five stories high (the poor shouldn't have to climb any higher, said Ma), where this afternoon during a heavy thunder-shower I saw the old lady, the owner of a parrot she airs on the fire escape on hot days, hanging out the window to hold a red

umbrella over the birdcage. The parrot, who speaks only gibber-
ish, was frightened and annoyed. It fluttered wildly around the
cage unaware of the love that was being offered. Beyond the tenement I can look into another building much like our own, a large,
substantial, rent-controlled island of bourgeoisie surrounded by a
sea of immigrants. On the ninth floor of that building, a full city
block south, I see behind windows locked against the heat, young
women and young men in tights and leotards, stepping high, arch-
ing their bodies, leaping as if in a dream but in uneasy concert,
disappearing for a moment in their flight to the other end of the
room, reappearing in a window further along. In air-conditioned
comfort they lumber back and forth like turkeys attempting to fly.
What must it be like to live below that place, someone's dance-
studio-in-the-home? A cottage industry of New York's Upper
West Side. I am fascinated by the students' purposeful endeavor.
Secretaries? Clerks? Messengers? A free-lance copy editor? A
mail-order radical? A junior executive who subscribes to *The New
York Review* but reads *Screw* first? They work ceremoniously.
They want to dance but they also leap to keep their stomachs
flat.

A page is turned with authority. I glance across the room to
the couch where Jackie lies lengthwise, wearing a dress that seems
to have been made from a railroad engineer's red bandanas but
probably cost a fortune. She is reading R. D. Laing the way other
people dance or do Royal Canadian Air Force exercises, but she is
ready at the flicker of my eyelash to reassess again our not quite
permanent arrangement. She reminds me of a bedspring that's
been tentatively uncoiled. She is long and slim but I'm aware of
the extraordinary tensile strength. When she is not prone, she is
tall, five foot eleven, almost as tall as I am, which is one of the
things I like about her though, when we first met, she stooped,
was round-shouldered, something that had less to do with her
height than with her being Jewish. With me now she walks erect,
strides really, proud of what I call her desert origins even though
all her grandparents came from Minsk, and of that profile no
surgeon has improved, her ass clenched so firmly that she could
lift a Manhattan telephone directory were it properly attached.

When we first met she was pretty in a common way. Over the years she has become a beauty. Tonight she is sullen but ravishing. I stare with pleasure at her long, bare, tanned feet that have pale nails and are ringed with a narrow line of white skin next to the soles. She's the only woman I've ever known who has become more beautiful with time. Too suddenly for me, she catches my eye.

"What *are* you doing?" said with boredom and annoyance.

"Preparing some papers for Jimmy Barnes. He has to notarize them and send them on to Ma's lawyers."

"Couldn't you have done it in East Hampton?"

"No—they must be in the mail tomorrow, at the latest."

Pause.

Jackie: "I am—I think—exceedingly bored."

"I'm sorry. You could have gone out to East Hampton by yourself."

"I didn't want to go out by myself. You know I don't like it by myself. It's your house."

"It's *our* house."

Jackie: "This is *our* apartment. The house in East Hampton is *your* house." Pause. She turns back to R. D. Laing and says to the book, "Maybe I will go out tomorrow, or some place. . . ."

Jackie blinks slowly—it's her silent sigh—and continues to read. It's not been a successful evening or day or week or month or year. Tonight she celebrated her graduation from a ten-day total immersion course in Szechuan cuisine by cooking an eight-course meal, each course of which tasted exactly like every other. Duck, chicken, fish, shrimp, lobster, beef, pork—I couldn't tell one from the other, a fact I felt compelled to mention since she'd asked me to be frank, and since she knows quite well that I don't like any kind of Chinese cooking and have a special antipathy for Szechuan. Jackie once took a Cordon Bleu course in the interests of her career but has never succeeded in constructing a single edible quenelle. Dear, sweet, determined, beautiful Jackie. I'm starved but I dare not go into the kitchen for, as she said in warning, "Margaret can clean it up in the morning. That's what she's paid to do."

In one capacity and another Margaret has been with me for twenty years. She came on board as a cook when Higgenbotham, my first wife, walked out on me, stayed on as a housekeeper and forewoman during Utah's tenure, when there were never less than four people on the staff, people that Utah called servants but who were no more than strangers underfoot. In twenty years, though, Margaret has never been paid to clean up the chaos created by someone's unsuccessfully experimenting with an eight-course Szechuan meal whose two basic ingredients were shredded iceberg lettuce and several pounds of ginger cut, sliced, diced and minced in a blender.

Margaret is an old lady, in her seventies. She's stood by me through the unacknowledged failure of my second marriage and through Jackie. Margaret would live in. There's room enough in this labyrinth if Jackie would permit it, but Jackie says no. She doesn't believe in servants, particularly black servants, though she sees nothing wrong in working them on an intensified daily basis at the lower weekly rate to do tasks that Jackie has no interest in. I suspect it has something to do with Jackie's terrible guilt about having grown up middle class in Queens. She's capable of being rude and sharp-tongued to anyone as long as the person goes home at night, but she has no idea how to deal with someone who shares her life. As a result Margaret lives in a posh East Side co-operative, bought and maintained by me, with a terrace overlooking the East River, twenty-four-hour doormen, Nelson Eddy and Jeanette MacDonald singing nonstop in the elevators, and the honored promise of complete tenant control of all apartment sales, none of which, needless to say, is enjoyed by Jackie and me. The arrangement is not quite as expensive as it might be. I would pay for Margaret's taxis to and from the East Side but New York taxi drivers frighten her. They drive badly and Margaret has read stories about a ring of taxi drivers who mug passengers going to and from fashionable East Side addresses. The few times she has agreed to take a taxi home late at night, she's been disguised as a wondrously black Hungarian peasant, her handsome head wrapped in an old babushka, her Gucci purse hidden at the bottom of a Sloane's shopping bag topped with trash, her feet in

carpet slippers even in winter. Margaret prefers the crosstown bus
and shanks' mare. Very thoughtfully every morning she brings me
the *Daily News* so that, if we are alone, we can discuss the obitu-
aries and the alarmingly early ages at which people seem to be, as
Margaret says, "passing" these days.

Jackie slams R. D. Laing shut. Part of the problem, I know, is
that having finished a long and not very challenging piece for *Esquire* about alimony for ex-husbands, she has no new assignment
to prepare for. Her agent is on vacation and her analyst is about to
go. All she has is me.

Jackie: "*I'm* going to bed."

I say nothing. I mime absorption in an inventory of securities
representing a system I once told Jackie I didn't believe in. She
made the inevitable comment, to which I replied, "Of course I
accept the income. It's mine. How else would I live?" She no
longer pounces on what she sees to be the contradictions between
what I say and what I do. As I remember the conversation I
shrug. There's no easy way to tell someone she's being dense. But
I have a sudden change of heart. She puts the book aside and
stands up.

"*I'm* going to bed," she says again, frowning. I attempt to
smile but I know it's the graceless smile of the self-interested.

Obviously she's going to bed—she's told me twice—but after
all that R. D. Laing she'll need to decompress by watching some
barmy-brained talk show or late-night movie, listening through
giant, foam-padded earphones that make her look like a Mouseke-
teer. I once forced her to keep them on while I attempted to fuck
her but we began to laugh so that both the earphones and the fuck
were put off. Tonight she's in no mood to laugh. She could be
talked into a fuck, but now I'm not in the mood.

What am I doing? I'm not sure yet. Ma asked the same question when I reached her this afternoon at the house in Harbor
Point.

"I think it's a good investment," I said.

"It's a great deal of money, darling," said Ma, "and I can't see
you as a farmer."

"I'll let somebody else do that. I've gone through all the reports. It almost pays for itself."

"I can't believe that," said Ma. "No one has seriously worked that place for years."

"I want to buy it," I said. "That's all. I can do it on my own but I'd like your help."

"What does Jackie say?"

"She thinks it's a marvelous idea," I said, though I haven't mentioned a word of the plan to Jackie. Then, as is my way, I was unable to let one lie fly alone. "She wants to live down there."

"What about the house in East Hampton?"

"I'm selling it," I said, which was true. "I've had two extremely good offers," which wasn't true.

"All I can say," said Ma, which usually was a preface to a ten-minute monologue, "is that it all sounds terribly *peculiar* to me. You don't even like the county. You never go down there."

"I went down there last spring. . . ."

"For the first time in years. . . . Maybe you should talk to your father. He knows about this sort of thing. . . ."

"I'm not going to talk to him," I said. "For Christ's sake, Ma, it's my money, and besides, he's senile. I told you the last time I talked to him he kept calling me Tom."

"I'm getting old, too, darling. . . ."

"But you aren't senile *yet*."

Girlish laughter. "Darling, that's the nicest thing you've said to me in years."

"Oh, Ma. . . ." Was I five or fifty? It was at such times that everything inclined toward confusion, often ending in a bitter fight and someone's slamming down the telephone receiver. "Oh, well," said Ma, "why not? Lockie would be pleased. But make sure you get some good advice from somebody. How much will you need?" I told her and said I'd send on the papers tomorrow.

I look up from a lawyer's letter that has the appearance and sound of an international trade treaty though it was written by someone I've known since I was a boy. Jackie stands in the living room door wearing nothing but a white silk robe, brushing her hair, her tits at the ready.

"Are you coming to bed soon?" says Jackie. "I wanted to talk."

"I've got to get through these papers. Louise" (my secretary) "is coming at nine."

Pause.

Jackie: "Your study is a mess. . . ." Brush, brush. "Why did you have that old steamer trunk brought up?"

"There are some things I want to go through."

"Why do you keep it locked?"

"I don't keep it locked."

Jackie: "It was standing open when I came home this afternoon and now it's locked."

"I don't like people poking around. I don't want Margaret tidying things up."

Jackie begins to give her hair the ten final, most furious strokes.

"I thought you'd like to know," she says, a pained expression to match each stroke of the brush, "I've made a reservation to fly down to Fort Lauderdale. . . ."

"That's nice."

"Tomorrow."

I control my temper. "Fine," I say. She's made her point. She knows that I don't like surprises that exclude me. "Have a good time."

"I will," she says. "Goodnight." She comes over and kisses my cheek with an ice cube.

Voices knife up from the bodega on the corner of Amsterdam and 88th. Angry? Probably not. Old friends in an embrace, not having seen each other in the twenty minutes since one left the other in the bar.

If the air conditioning were not bust I might drink myself blind. It's too hot. Under other circumstances I might seek a pacifying fuck, but that's out of the question now. I'm not going to make things pleasant for Jackie just before she takes off for Fort Lauderdale with the prime purpose of irritating me. I cling to the documents in my lap. Money and property.

Sooner or later all peoples pass—with their civilizations, institutions, languages, scandals, customs, indispositions. Peoples are

entitled. So be it. Attempts to reconstruct lives from tiny fragments of bone or pottery or petrified shit keep us on our toes. The
will—the impulse—to contain the present by knowing the past is,
I'm afraid, more important—more enduring—than what we
learn, which we quickly confuse by making our own sense of. May
the Etruscans continue to guard their secrets that we will perse-
vere.

The Tatterhummock Trail, the two-lane blacktop that idles its
way up through the center of the county to connect Walden's
Point, on the Chesapeake, and Fredericksburg, sixty-eight miles
northwest, should be called the Poropotank Trail in the interests
of historical accuracy, if accuracy were in the interests of history.
The highway follows a path said to have been made by the Poropotanks, who were never in a hurry to get where they were going,
and later usurped by the Tatterhummocks, the Indians who
hunted the peninsula at the time John Smith set up his colony
at Jamestown. How the Tatterhummocks dispossessed the Poropotanks is a matter of speculation. Perhaps in war, though
that seems unlikely. Maybe by tacit agreement, or by making the
Poropotanks feel unwanted. Whatever the method they succeeded,
but then in less than 100 years the Tatterhummocks themselves
had all but vanished. Contemporary accounts report there were
very few Tatterhummocks among the county's Indians by the time
Nat Bacon, a kinsman of Sir Francis and the man who gave his
name to this land's first substantial insurrection, launched his
systematized slaughter of the Indians against the governor's orders. This was in 1676. Bacon's Rebellion wasn't much but it was
a start, a seminal forming of the lines. On one side, the governor
and the Indians, linked by their common interest in the tobacco
trade; on the other, the poor colonists whose every farm was a
frontier and who had to labor beyond ordinary endurance to
achieve a subsistence level. Elegance and sophistication versus the
self-styled representatives of law, order and the Christian god.
Bacon and his men had been provoked, of course. One spring
morning the heirs of Opechancanough had risen up throughout
the colony to murder the settlers they loved and, in some in-
stances, were breakfasting with. Even though an economic im-
balance had created the class struggle, it's not easy to interpret

Bacon's Rebellion in Marxist terms. The whites were red. In the course of his small adventure Bacon died, not in battle but of colic.

I doubt that Bacon's army slew any Tatterhummocks. By 1676 there were no more than a dozen or so in the county, and these few misfits, drunks, eccentrics or professional guests—token savages invited to dinners or weekends to certify a host's humanitarianism. I have very little information about the Tatterhummocks but the little I have draws me to them. They were not a hardy race. Long before there were serious confrontations in battle their numbers had dwindled. Not from hunger or disease. Being in the vicinity of white men they languished. A people of delicate taste, sensitive to the mediocrity of the mercantile nation, the Tatterhummocks swooned into extinction.

3

Just one week after I'd made up my mind to buy Wicheley and had set in motion the machinery by which cash can be made to flow from vaults all over the country, the lawyer for the Pittsburgh-born New York stockbroker telephoned Jimmy Barnes, my lawyer, to tell Jimmy that the stockbroker is now having second thoughts. Jimmy Barnes told me not to worry, that something would be worked out. In the meantime the stockbroker is investigating new channels whereby Wicheley can be presented to the state of Virginia as a public trust and a private tax write-off. "Oh, shit," I said to Jimmy Barnes, a fellow who'd been in my class at the Bell School and to whom I throw a bone now and then. "That's that," I said. "Not at all," said Jimmy. "He's tried to give the place to the state before but the state doesn't want it. They don't have the money to maintain it. Just sit tight."

Sitting tight is not something I'm good at. Jackie has been gone a week, the only word from her being a postcard, one of those that Jackie calls a don't-come-here postcard. It shows the vast empty parking lot of the beautiful, exclusive new Fort Lauderdale Ramada Inn. The message: "The humidity is unbearable. All is about as expected but at least there have been no new cases of cancer reported since breakfast. Dad is trying to find another lawyer. Mom and I spend our afternoons visiting shopping centers. We don't buy. We're comparison lookers."

That's somewhat reassuring. I know that Jackie must be going out of her mind in that retirement village where every lot is on the waterfront and where last fall the waterfront made them a surprise visit, coming up from the bottom through the fully applianced home's genuine imitation Spanish terrazzo floor. For a week Mr. and Mrs. Gold slopped around in 1 inch of polluted canal water. When they went outside they sank up to their ankles in mush that's trade-named Sherwood Forest Turf and has been crossbred to be resistant to salt water. Nevertheless it turned brown and died. Mrs. Gold in a letter to Jackie: "It isn't too hard on me. I just wear my platforms but Dad has to go barefoot." There was also the danger that every time they switched on the TV, they'd transform their matching Barcaloungers into matching electric chairs. They refused to move without full and immediate compensation, which was not forthcoming. Naturally they filed a suit, the progress of which has become the sole subject of the weekly letters-from-home that Jackie has recently begun to file in a desk drawer after skimming the first and last paragraphs.

I feel a new, precarious kind of loneliness during this absence of Jackie. This one is unlike the others. Something is going very wrong. To fill the time I kept Jimmy Barnes on the telephone much longer than was necessary this morning. I even asked about his family, boring people I couldn't care less about. This morning I also dictated twenty-three letters to Louise, including one to the *Times* pointing out the hypocrisy contained in an editorial that feebly lamented the existence of massage parlors (one should be either FOR or AGAINST massage parlors), as well as a letter to Gordon Felix containing a $500 check for the St. Matthew's Alumni Association. I was very frosty in that one. I don't want that little hermaphrodite on my back again. Each letter was urgent, I told Louise, and insisted that she stay and type them so they'd be ready for my signature when I returned from my daily workout at the River Club. Louise, who has grown from being a bride to a grandmother in my employ, is worth her immense salary by being discreet and compliant and having a personality she wears like her slip, so that it seldom shows.

As Margaret was serving dinner tonight she reminded me that she starts her vacation next week and asked if I'd like her to delay it. "Go, go," I said. "Everybody gets a vacation except me, and I pay all the bills." She knows me well enough not to become upset by that sort of thing. She was only a tiny bit peeved when she brought in the coffee. "I won't go if you don't want me to," she said, measuring the contents of the scotch bottle as if she were a bartender. "No, of course not," I said, wondering if I possibly could ask her to stay, but she's going on that bloody North Cape cruise and even I couldn't interrupt that.

I've been certain that Jackie would telephone after dinner. She's due. I wait in my study, staring at the great battered steamer trunk, the companion of my youth. It stands open in the center of the room occupying what Jackie might once have called "the conversation area." Diaries, photograph albums, defunct deeds, old dictionaries, histories, letters, scrapbooks, including "Souvenirs of My Life—Marshall Lewis Henderson, Nine," and one that remains unmarked and that contains most of what is public record on the life of Prud'homme Shackleford, Baby Pru, my natural son.

When Jackie calls, we'll make a plan to go away somewhere. I owe her that much even though she knows there are no places I want to go any more. I can't even look at the packet of material I received from Father Klein today—Xeroxes of six newly authenticated letters written by Simon de Montfort, leader of the Albigensian Crusade, to the heretic Bishop of Anvers, his first cousin. Instead I turn the pages of one of those idiot magazines that Jackie contributes to all too frequently. It makes me feel out of touch, one hundred years old. Could the Primal Screamers or the people at Esalen revive my interest in tourism? I doubt it. I'm a classicist. If that didn't work, nothing will.

When I go to bed I take both telephones off their hooks. If she calls—which I doubt—*she* won't be able to reach *me*.

. . .

Nightmares all through the night. One is set in my old digs on East 67th Street, a handsome, palazzo-like building but a ridiculous house to live in. Five stories high, with an elevator, but only six rooms so that it was impossible to get away for a little peace within it. When Higgenbotham kicked me out of our bedroom I was forced to sleep in the library before moving to a hotel. In the dream Higgenbotham is giving one of her parties for lots of well-known people who don't know us and lots of classy leeches and hustlers who do. Carole Lombard is there, looking older but little the worse for having been so long dead. Myrna Loy is also there, very pretty and delicate and intelligent, the way she is today. On the first floor of the palace where, in real life, there had been a small ladies powder room, there is, in the dream, a Roman bath the size of Caracalla. I open the door and come upon an orgy. In one tub of bubble bath I see a beautiful young woman, standing, being entered from the rear by a male-model type as Higgenbotham, who isn't participating, tells everyone to come witness this remarkable union. I know that Higgenbotham would think me tiresome for objecting to such goings-on in the midst of an otherwise respectable party. It is Higgenbotham's way of insulting the famous guests she wants to know but never will. In the worst nightmare I am with Utah, but where I've no idea. She says, "When I was in town today I ran into ***** who told me that Mary had committed suicide. . . ." I awoke without knowing which Mary.

4

I must be absolutely honest: I'm not the easiest person to live with. I think of the day this spring when, after waiting six months for a decision, I received a letter from my friend at the Princeton University Press informing me that they had decided not to publish "Songs of Faint Praise: An Introduction to the Literature of the Albigenses (Medieval Dualism) 1000–1275 A.D." The board of editors, he told me with the casuistry typical of academe, felt that although I'd done my work well and had, indeed, uncovered much new material, and, further, that my translation of things heretofore available only in Old French was first rate, much of my research was not sufficiently substantiated by other recognized scholars. "This results," he wrote as if he were a dean of admissions, "in certain weaknesses in your speculations relating to the possible origins of some of your material in the Gnostic literature of the first and second centuries." Briefly translated, he was saying that I'd had the poor taste to turn in an outline without one footnote in ancient Greek. In the smarmiest paragraph of all, he told me they believed my planned work appeared to be too slim for publication by itself ("You might do well to organize the material into a paper first. . . .") unless I included more historical data on the relationship between the Bogomils of Yugoslavia and Bulgaria and my Albigenses, ground already covered thoroughly, he pointed out, by Steven Runciman, "an English historian whose works you might be interested in consulting."

As if I weren't perfectly aware of Runciman! As if, at one point, I hadn't carried on an extended correspondence with him that concluded with his encouraging me and saying he was sure that no one else, to his knowledge, was as well equipped as I to pursue this particular research. I could produce the letter if I had to, but I won't. I refuse to kiss the asses of a bunch of ambitious, small-minded academicians interested only in money and tenure. Of course my volume will be slim. That's the whole point. It's an introduction, for Christ's sake, not the collected fucking works. This was a blow, obviously, but not entirely unexpected since Oxford, Yale, Harvard and California had already declined. I refused to become paranoid, though. If I had been Jackie I'd have immediately suspected that the long arm of Rome were in some way involved, trying to squash an inquiry into a scandal 1,000 years old. But that, I realized, was nonsense. It was simply a coincidence. Or was it? Who is Klein? Could it be that I was Klein's "case"? *His* life's work? For a few hours I thought I might be going out of my mind. Instead, I took Jackie to the Côte Basque.

It was not a great evening. For the first hour, as we dawdled over cocktails, Jackie was apparently sympathetic.

"Well," Jackie said at last. Having given me the first sixty

minutes of prime time, she was taking over the second. "I've something to tell *you*."

"What?"

"I've been asked to do a book."

Me (wary): "What sort of book?" It didn't seem the ideal
news to spring.

"Well, not *write* a book exactly, but . . ." and she mentioned
the name of a schlock publisher who specializes in confessions of
secondary interest, ". . . has expressed interest in publishing a
collection of my interviews, you know, as a sort of profile of our
time. . . ."

"Our time!" I howled. "You're kidding!"

"What's wrong?"

I stared at the murals. I had to find the right words.

"What kind of profile of our time?" I said.

"Well, a sort of chronicle of the people who were making the
news in the first half of the seventies. . . ."

"Who," I said, "Ho Chi Minh? Nixon? Golda Meir?"

"Of course not. . . . People I've interviewed, you know, Mick
Jagger, Clint Eastwood, Tatum O'Neal, Elizabeth Taylor, Abbie
Hoffman, Margaret Trudeau. . . ."

"Oh my God. . . ."

"What's wrong?"

"That's just the kind of thing you shouldn't do."

"Why not?"

"It's garbage."

"It's not garbage."

"No. I'm sorry." That wasn't the right approach. "It's not
garbage, but it doesn't belong in a book."

"I don't agree."

"The pieces aren't good enough. I mean, they're fine in a
magazine, as journalism, but they're the kind of pieces that look
silly in a book. Besides, for your first book you don't want to be
published by someone like that."

"What's wrong with him?"

"He publishes crap. When he publishes you, you become crap.
I trust you told him that you aren't interested."

"Well," said Jackie, who was becoming irritated, "I didn't tell him anything, but I *am* interested."

I burped, causing a few heads to turn our way, but I know exactly how rude I can be without permanently alienating the management. Crutches help. So does money. Burps aren't something just anyone can get away with at the Côte Basque.

"You are becoming very unpleasant," said Jackie.

"I think I'll have another drink," I said, "instead of the wine. Wine will upset my stomach."

Jackie sighed and looked away, thus turning to me her magnificent profile. With her hair pulled back in an elaborate bun, exposing a sexy bit of nape-neck, she was the most desirable woman in the room. I was terrifically proud of her. "Why," I said, "are you wearing those awful earrings?"

They were long, dangly things, sapphires and rubies set in gold, vaguely Aztec, which I'd bought her several years before at Buccellati's, earrings of a sort she'd never worn before she met me but which I liked.

"You gave them to me." She was frowning in a way that could be nurtured into tears either of hurt or of fury.

"I'm all too aware," I said. "They cost a fortune, but I was wrong. They make you look like a hooker."

Very deliberately she removed the one from the right ear, then the one from the left ear—gestures of promise (when you're going to bed) or of boredom (if they're pinching the earlobes). She put them away in her purse.

"That's better," I said. "You should be careful not to overdo things. You have that tendency, you know."

We ate in silence for most of the meal. Jackie only nibbled at the food and refused to finish even one glass of wine.

Jackie (finally): "I'm sorry you are jealous."

This was a new line. At least, she'd never had the guts to say it out loud before. It was also a low blow.

"Jealous! Jesus Christ! Jealous of what?"

"I mean. . . . I know you were disappointed about the Princeton Press thing. It wasn't the best time for me to talk about doing a book."

"Why do you keep saying 'doing' a book? One doesn't 'do' a book. That's the whole point. Publishing a bunch of pieces of old journalism is just that—'doing' a book. Books should be written, not 'done.' "

"They'll give me a five-thousand-dollar advance. . . ."

"That's peanuts. You can get more than that for a couple of decent magazine pieces."

"I'd like to have a book. . . ."

"And I'm not jealous of you . . . in connection with books or anything else."

"What's that supposed to mean?"

Me (sweetly): "That I trust you."

"Perhaps you shouldn't. . . ."

"I know you can trust me, so I trust you. You know that I do trust you?" She shrugged. I was suddenly feeling expansive. "Since we've been together, I haven't seriously looked at another woman. That's not nothing."

"I'm sure," said Jackie.

"You fulfill all my most fundamental needs and all my wildest desires. It's true."

"Maybe you're getting old."

"That's not very kind."

"You do want me to be frank, don't you?"

"Of course."

"For one thing," said with a calm I'm not too keen on, "I've never really believed you were the satyr you claimed to be before we met. You may have taken a lot of women out, but you didn't exactly sweep me off my feet. My God . . . three months. I was beginning to think you were impotent after all. . . ."

Sudden memory: It is early afternoon on a sub-freezing, resplendently clear winter day. I am in my car, sealed, being driven home from the River Club, proceeding north on Park Avenue when we stop for a red light at 72nd Street. I look up to see Jackie crossing from east to west, wearing her long, loose sheepskin coat that has a hood but no real buttons to keep the coat fastened. The hood is thrown back, her hair streaming out behind. One hand clutches the folds of the coat together. As she strides along she holds her face up into the brilliant sunlight, eyes squinting against the glare, her cheeks flushed. She seems to be smiling with happiness. If I'd seen her one second earlier, when she was on the sidewalk, I would have hailed her, but I was lucky. I hadn't. It would have spoiled a privileged moment. She looked so well, so invigorated, so full of life. I had no idea where she was coming from, nor where she was going, though I knew she would eventually be coming to me. I cherish this memory. When she arrived at the apartment later I saw her again for the first time. I couldn't believe my good fortune and she couldn't understand my high humor. I pinched her ass, grabbed a tit and pulled her into bed. I didn't tell her what had done the trick. Though I'd watched her sleeping many times and am always moved (when she isn't snoring, which she does do), this was the first time I'd ever seen her when she was without me. I'd glimpsed the other side of the moon.

Bitch.

5

True scholars do not need public acclaim. Fuck the Princeton University Press and all who publish there. In Jackie's absence I push on. A most eccentric communication this morning from Father Klein, postmarked Belgrade and written on what appears to be a German typewriter. Umlauts everywhere. The name and the return address on the envelope are new: Peter Weingarten, 14 Montague Mews, London, S.W.2, which is apparently the old boy's latest ruse to confuse Rome's secret police. Poor Klein. I fear he's nearing the edge, but at least he's not boring and he has been remarkably effective in obtaining rare materials for me, including some originals but mostly copies of things I thought existed only in private collections or under lock at the Vatican. Of course, he may be one of the greatest con artists who ever lived, but he works so diligently that he deserves compensation as well as appreciation. Jackie, who loathes him (a feeling that is returned in a distracted sort of way), would be fascinated by this latest letter that, as usual, asks for money in the hustler's manner

that mixes whine with threat: ". . . I don't know to what extremes
I shall be driven should you either be incapable or disinclined to
dispatch the above-mentioned sum (£100) to me (Peter Weingarten) at my new address (14 Montague Mews, London,
S.W.2), soonest. Sometimes I feel you don't understand the true
import of our work nor do you honor our long and close relationship in the fashion that has become, for me, a sacred responsibility. . . ."

Our "relationship" has been long—nearly three decades—but
no closer than a half dozen meetings in Paris over the years. I'm
not even sure how old he is, but I estimate he must now be over
eighty if he was in his forties at the time he was packed off to
Auschwitz in 1942. Jackie is convinced that he's a fraud and that,
in fact, he is a Jew who converted to Catholicism to avoid the gas
chamber, which, I suppose, could be true. It would explain the
ease with which, for reasons never explained, he changes identities
so often. Yet it needn't be true. Klein is a perfectly common Alsatian Catholic name, and I'd think it highly unlikely that a Jewish
Catholic convert at Auschwitz, if there ever were any such things,
would have had the time and energy after liberation to pursue
orders in the Society of Jesus. Nevertheless there is about him
something that Jackie has correctly and delicately described as
"extremely ambiguous."

We met in 1950, the year Higgenbotham and I spent in Paris
in a flat we had sublet on the Île St. Louis. Higgenbotham was
attempting to find herself, studying painting with a stud from
Omaha, while I began my research into the life of Esclarmonde,
the heretic princess of Foix. It was a gray, damp January afternoon and I was having a slight disagreement with a clerk in the
medieval reading room at the Bibliothèque Nationale when Klein
offered his help. Klein stepped in, studied the card I'd filled out
and which the clerk refused to honor, changed one letter in the file
number (apparently from memory) and dismissed the clerk to
fetch my book. Klein was a most impressive figure in those days,
so memorable-looking I can't imagine he would have been much
good to the Resistance that, he told me later, had led to his "mis-
fortune" with the Germans. There was no place where Klein
would not attract attention. He was something over six five or six

six, with a huge, sculptured head that gave him the aspect of a
gryphon. The rugged, still handsome features were made fierce
by far-sightedness he refused to correct with spectacles. He had
every hair he'd ever grown but they were cropped to look like the
bristles of a military brush. His hair was the only thing about him
that looked neat. Below his neck he was grossly untidy, the cassock stained with years of thin monastic soups (I assumed) and
about 5 inches too short so that his orange ski boots, worn with
the white American sweatsocks he fancied that winter, became,
after his eyes, the focus of attention. One found oneself repeatedly
studying his feet. He was the most peculiar-looking priest I'd ever
met. The great tarnished crucifix he wore around his neck was not
a cross. It was a blunt instrument.

Klein was also somewhat deaf. He introduced himself to me
very loudly, in heavily German-accented English, repeated my
name several times as if to find associations that were not there,
then said, "You think I am English?" I said no. "I'm always being
taken for English," said Klein, "because I studied at Oxford in the
twenties . . . the Middle Ages, hah! Hah!" Instead of periods, loud,
humorless "hahs" punctuated Klein's sentences. One of Klein's
traits, I've learned through the years, is that he is never mysterious
or surprising in ways he believes he is, while he is absolutely im-
penetrable about certain basics. He was then traveling on a Costa
Rican passport, a detail he never made any attempt to hide or to
explain. He spent the whole of that first afternoon expounding on
the fascinating parallels between a small, little-known Paulician
sect, whose members worshipped the serpent in its role as temptor,
and thus as the enemy of the Old Testament's wicked Jehovah,
and a collective of mass murderers whose trial in Boise, Idaho,
was then very much in the Paris newspapers. I worried at first that
he was a certified loon, but quickly gave in to his talk, which was
nonstop and allusive, full of intimate references to the subject that
was becoming my life's work. When the library closed, we moved
to a nearby Dupont and, when it was clear that I couldn't easily
shake him, to the Île St. Louis flat which, I must say, impressed
him so much that he kept quiet through most of dinner. Higgenbotham, small and pretty and bored, was rude in polite ways that
completely escaped his notice. Though he had drunk nothing at

the Dupont or before dinner except mineral water, he drank a full
bottle of wine at table and nearly an entire decanter of brandy
afterwards. At one point when Higgenbotham left the drawing
room, he said, "Are you happily married?" "Yes," I said. "I'm
not," said Klein, "a bother. Hah." There was no serious way to
respond to much of what he said.

Higgenbotham made two exits to go to bed, returned each
time for a last cigarette and finally, by saying that both she and I
had to be up early, convinced Klein that he should depart. Before
he left he suddenly sobered up enough to offer me a fourteenth-
century copy of the *Chansons de la Croisade*, which I didn't then
know existed. "Well, dear chap, it does, it does. On the open
market it would fetch several thousand pounds. I might be able to
obtain it for you for no more than ten thousand Swiss francs.
Should you be interested." I said that I might. "Think about it, my
boy. No need to make a snap decision. Shall we have a luncheon
engagement? I think that would be convenient. . . . Yes, it would."

As I walked him to the lift he paid no greater attention to my
crutches than he had earlier in the day, which I first took to be
politeness, then decided he was simply self-centered. I'm sure that
if he were asked today he wouldn't know whether I used crutches
or not.

The lift rose lazily to us, making those soft, kindly sounds I
associate with elevators in very expensive Paris houses. "I sense,"
he said suddenly, "that I shall be the instrument of your salva-
tion." Then, noting my surprise, he laughed in his horrendous
way, "Ah hah, hah, hah." He caught his breath. "That's rich," he
said. "Rich, rich, rich." I said that I didn't think I'd make a very
serious convert. "Ah hah," said Klein, "but a convert to what?
Hah. That's the question, my dear chap." He entered the lift, the
door closed and he descended into hell.

When I came back into the flat Higgenbotham was clearing up
some of the mess of cigar ash and spilt brandy that defined the
perimeters of the area Klein had been occupying since dinner. She
opened the balcony doors and waved them back and forth to coax
the smoke out. "I hope we don't have to see *him* again soon," she
said.

"What's wrong? Like all deaf people he's noisy, but I have a feeling he's a very unusual man."

"I don't trust him," said Higgenbotham, "and besides, he has b.o."

In twenty-six years I've probably paid Klein close to $200,000 to help in my research and to obtain various manuscripts, including the papal pornography and a twelfth-century Cathar Bible produced by Herman of Valenciennes, a sad, fragile little volume that some scholars believe once belonged to Esclarmonde herself. In that same time I've written to him as Father Rudolph Klein in the care of a hostel run by Jesuits near Lyons, as Robert Rudolph at the Hôtel Gare du Nord in Paris, as Pierre Gardner in the care of Mme Hélène Gardner at a post office in Savoy, and now as Peter Weingarten in London. This morning I sent him the £100 I owe him for the latest Xeroxes, plus an extra £100 to grow on.

I was twelve and making my way through the *Encyclopaedia Britannica*, starting with Volume One, when I first came upon the fundamental facts of the Cathar conspiracy that, because of the exemplary administration of Barthélemy of Carcassonne (after he was transferred to Albi in 1167), became forever known as the Albigensian heresy. What drew me to those good, foolish souls? My imagination might have been pricked by a tenet which held that Jesus had entered Mary through her left ear and nine months later, when her time had arrived, made his exit through the same orifice. "Blessed art thou among women, and blessed is the fruit of Thy Ear, Jesus!" Yet many early Christians believed the same nonsense and I've never been much attracted to them. All that non-fucking seems so dreary, and their emphasis on life-after-death turns me off. Dualism is something else. It's not even Christian, strictly speaking, since, to the dualist, Christ never came to earth as a man. He only *appeared* to come to earth as a man. He was simply a manifestation and, to some, not even a first-class one at that, being no more than one of the higher ranking eons. Though dualism is quite as confused as any Christian sect, and though its brief springtime in southwestern France was as much the result of the excesses of the clergy as it was of the nationalistic fervor of the locals, high-born and low, it came to appeal to me through the elaborate, often witty way it attempted to answer fundamental contradictions within Christian dogma that Augustine so ponderously glossed over. How is it possible that a good, loving, kind, all-seeing, all-knowing god could have fabricated a world so full of neon, wrong-headedness, carbon monoxide, misleading advertising and noise? The dualist answers directly: God didn't. The world was not created by God but by the Demiurge, sometimes called Old Scratch, who, as he went about his vile business, accidentally allowed some tiny divine spark to lodge in man. It was to free this spark, and to salvage God's good name, that the dualists contrived their philosophy, which mixed common sense and poetry in equal proportions. God was not responsible, thus they didn't expect him to meddle. It wasn't His table. The Demiurge was the fellow they had to reckon with—sloppy carpenter that he was.

Because the chief aim of any life was to return the divine spark to God as clean and wrinkle-free as possible, the heretics determined that man should attempt to live as far away as practical from matter, which, for the strong of purpose, could mean all sorts of prohibitions. But the Albigenses acknowledged the world and worldliness; they recognized evil, which was not to embrace it. Hell, they taught, was life on earth. They gave no promise of life after death, only the hope that one's divine spark might return whence it came. The begetting of children was frowned upon— each new child containing one more divine spark that would have to be reassimilated. They understood, though, that carnal relations were beyond reasonable control, so they worked to fit sex in. "It's impossible to sin with any part of the body below the navel," wrote (I think) Henry of Le Mans. The ultimate goal of all this: race-suicide. In the meantime, life was to be lived, property acquired, families protected, businesses maintained, honor upheld, injustices corrected. The heresy spawned its share of nuts, as has Christianity. It's generally agreed that Clementius of Bucy, a peasant who gained notoriety as a holy heretic, sponsored orgies at which perversions lamely called "unspeakable" were performed. The word "buggery" comes to us from "Bulgar," for the

Bogomils, whose teachings—carried to France by rug merchants and doctors—originated in Bulgaria.

The Albigenses were literate. They were patrons of the arts. They were patriotic, conscientious, thrifty. They were intimidated neither by Rome and its armies from the north, nor by the inquisitors who set themselves up in storefronts to save their souls. They denied the sacraments of Holy Communion, baptism, marriage. They disbelieved in the priesthood and ecclesiastical hierarchy, having bishops, who acted as administrators, and Perfects, a priestlike caste of men and women whose only authority was by holy example. They forbade worship of the Cross, teaching instead that it should be hated as the instrument of Christ's suffering. Because they had little use for the Old Testament, which they read as propaganda for the Demiurge, the heretics liberated women from the Garden of Eden. Women played as important a role in the history of the Albigenses as men. Constance, Queen of Aquitaine, was an early sympathizer. Esclarmonde of Foix, herself a Perfect, brought to them the fortress of Montségur, which had been part of her dowry and later became, for the doomed Albigenses, their Alamo. Esclarmonde was put to the stake, as were the dowager Lady Cavaers of Fanjeaux, the Duchess of Mirepoix and the five nieces of Peter of Navidals, who himself was burned to death later the same year. In less than 100 years, 20,000 went up in smoke, yet the heresy collapsed as an exhausted army rather than as a discredited religion. Leaders surrendered on battlefields, recanted and returned to their estates as chastened *hereticales*. As the foot soldiers were fined or executed, the Church reasserted its control through a reformed clergy and France moved closer to its destiny as a national state. In the course of time, belief that had been impervious to flames evaporated like dew. The age of the troubadours was beginning. After the fire, a song.

Before going to sleep last night I dialed Ma in Michigan but replaced the receiver before the first ring. Instead I called Cousin Mary Lee at Tatterhummock Court House to tell her the latest news in the Wicheley negotiations. After ten minutes of listening to her gurglings, including at least a dozen references to the Gen-

eral, I hung up, putting on quite an act about the phone's having
gone bad in such a way that I could no longer hear her though she
might still be able to hear me. I didn't want to talk. I only wanted
to know that I could establish a connection.

6

I never part with the memory of a betrayal without receiving a fair
price. The first time I visited Lewis's Landing, Lockie accompanied Tom and me—my first trip anywhere without either of my
parents. We traveled in the Packard, the demon Garrett driving as
if seeking a safe path across a minefield. We took a full week to
cover a distance my father would have driven in two days and a
half. But Handsome Tommy didn't stop in odd towns to look in
telephone directories for old friends who may or may not have
died, moved or changed their names, if they had ever lived there
in the first place. Lockie also made sure that we saw all the sights
along the route, and several, including the Cumberland Gap,
which weren't. In a town that interested her for one reason
or another we would always search out the local undertaking establishment since Lockie believed one could best judge the afflu-
ence of a community by the grandeur of its funeral parlor. I must
have been five or six—I was just learning how to read and write—
and I spent long hours as we drove through Indiana, Ohio and
Kentucky going through my collection of Big Little Books, sitting
on the jump seat or sometimes communicating with Garrett
through the intercom. God knows what Garrett, a taciturn old
Scot, and I had to talk about. I suppose it was only the act of
communicating that was important, not what was communicated.
Lockie and Tom sat on the back seat playing Pinochle or checkers
on a small table atop the armrest between them. One of my first
disappointments with the world was the state of Virginia.

The day before we crossed the border Lockie, after studying a
road map spread out over the checkerboard, decided that we
should spend the night in Charleston, West Virginia, so that Tom
and I would be wide awake and fresh when we first laid eyes on

the Old Dominion. All this was for my benefit, I guess now, because Tom had already visited Lewis's Landing several times with
Ma. Lockie possessed a sense of drama, but in this case it closed
out of town. We arrived at Charleston at 2:30 in the afternoon,
which meant that we had half a day and a night to kill in a city
that is for ennui what Port Said was once for sin. After registering
at the hotel and checking our luggage, Lockie had Garrett drive
us around the city but we saw all there was of it in less than an
hour. Lockie then thought it might be interesting if Tom and I
could be shown a coal mine; but the coal mines in that area
weren't owned by anyone she knew—and, I suppose, one just
didn't barge in on a strange coal mine. The Old Manners. In
desperation she finally took me to a movie while Tom stayed with
Garrett at the hotel to listen to a Cubs baseball game on a radio.

The lengthy layover in Charleston created an anticipation for
wonder that probably no state could have fulfilled. The following
day, at approximately 10:22 A.M., a few miles beyond the village
of Harmon, West Virginia, in a region of craggy, ugly hills that
weren't quite big enough to be called mountains, we entered the
state of Virginia. There was a signpost at the side of the road but
no customs inspection, no immigration check, no triumphal arch.
Though Lockie giggled and patted me on the back, encouraging
me to make note of this historic moment, I was profoundly disappointed. The Virginia side of the border looked exactly like the
West Virginia side. I had expected the Emerald City.

Before proceeding to Lewis's Landing we spent another day
and a half on the road, stopping in Charlottesville to be shown
through Monticello, at Westmoreland County to see Stratford, the
family seat of the Lees ("only very distant kin"), and Wakefield,
the birthplace of George Washington ("no kin whatsoever").
When we arrived in Tatterhummock County in mid-afternoon, we
went first to Wicheley Hall and because the front gate was pad-
locked, Tom and I climbed onto the fence to have my first look at
the Hall, a quarter of a mile down a perfectly straight, limestone
drive, the house partially hidden by the elms and the box hedges.
It did appear to be enormous.

Again Lockie's talent for the dramatic build-up failed, certainly for me, though I've no doubt she felt that she was saving the

best for the last. After Monticello, Stratford, Wakefield and Wicheley, Lewis's Landing looked like a large, square outhouse, one with porches. Garrett came close to breaking an axle on the rutted road that led from the highway to the farm. The house stood in the center of a large, weed-strewn clearing surrounded by a forest of loblollies and scrub pine. Behind the house were barns and other supplemental buildings in such disrepair the place seemed abandoned. Though the house was on high ground, it didn't even have a view of the river in summer when the trees were in leaf. To see the river, less than a half mile away, one had to climb to the third floor and peer through an attic window.

Tom, I think, eventually came to enjoy those annual summer visits to the Landing while, for me, they were always two weeks in limbo. Tom had the company of Cousin Mary Lee who, though six years older, was the sort of only child who could adapt herself to another child of any age. Cousin Mary Lee was a hugger, a squeezer, a toucher and a kisser. When she was with Tom and me she couldn't keep her hands off us, though she treated me as the baby she and Tom were responsible for. She deferred to Tom as the dad, allowing him to make up the schedule for the day, to set the rules of the games we played, to select the fantasies to be enacted. When Tom decided to make bows and arrows, Cousin Mary Lee was an enthusiastic, robust fifteen-year-old Maid Marian to Tom's nine-year-old Robin Hood. Sometimes I was Little John (I *was* little) or Friar Tuck or Will Scarlet. Whatever it was, it was always a supporting role. As long as Tom was alive, I was never more than a spear carrier in the spectacle in which he was the star.

Tom was very fond of Cousin Mary Lee but he also thought her a bit dopey, being suspicious of any girl that much older who took everything he said so seriously. Tom was fond of her while he exploited her. I was simultaneously furious with her—jealous of her affection for Tom—and head-over-heels in love. They always spoke of Cousin Mary Lee—often in front of her—as the prettiest girl in the county, which she was then and still is. A big girl with a tendency toward plumpness, Cousin Mary Lee was—is—pretty in a fashion that seems archaic today. Her figure was full-blown—I think of Goya's Maja, though she was never that voluptuous—and, more than anything else, soft. One wanted to lie on her, or rest against her, to be enveloped by her, to nest in her. Her face was perfectly oval, which was emphasized by the pronounced widow's peak of dark brown hair. The eyes were large and brown and warm—tirelessly responsive eyes—the skin milk-white as once was thought admirable, and the lips as red as cherry wine, even without lip rouge, which she wasn't allowed to use until some years later when Ma put her foot in. Cousin Mary Lee was the girl on the side of a box of Sun·Maid seedless raisins. All she lacked was a sunbonnet. Somewhere in the steamer trunk I have a snapshot, taken when she was sixteen or seventeen, showing her posed beside a Lewis's Landing rosebush, bent at the waist, sniffing a blossom. Extremely coy, of course, but still very much the real—the spontaneous—Cousin Mary Lee. She was a girl who would stop anything she was doing to sniff a rose, to be transported by the perfume as if experiencing a series of small orgasms. Though she was overwhelmingly maternal even as a girl, she was virginal, and so ripe it didn't seem as if she could last much longer on the vine. It seemed she might fall at any minute whether or not someone was there to catch her. But Cousin Mary Lee was much more strong-willed and determined than she appeared. She managed to hang on until she was almost thirty.

The rest of the household was a good deal less interesting to a small boy. Cousin Annie Lee Moulton, Cousin Mary Lee's mother, was a tiny, pretty, grayish woman with an unreliable heart who, after being a widow five years, continued to wear deep mourning, though Lockie said to Tom and me that widowhood was the best thing that ever happened to her. Cousin Whateverhisname had been a rake who passed early with a big assist from cirrhosis of the liver. Miss Mary Lewis, the only Lewis kin I ever met who still bore the name, was Cousin Annie Lee's younger sister, a tall, slim, severe-looking spinster who taught Latin and Greek in a girls' boarding school in Lancaster County and who I thought might possibly be a witch. She was never unkind or sharp with me, just vaguely disinterested, which can be more disorienting for a child than any amount of unreason. Lockie and Ma always talked about how brilliant Miss Mary was—how "smart-looking" in her skin-tight black evening dress that had long sleeves but was cut almost down to the navel in front. Miss Mary (don't ask me why one sister was called "Cousin" and the other "Miss"—that's just the way it was) intimidated Ma and Lockie, who felt she never approved of them, so they fell all over themselves trying to please her, which they did with only occasional success. Rounding out the ménage was Aunt Minnie, a thin, spare, ill-tempered slave who came in by the day (from where, I don't know) to clean, cook, serve, wash up, sew, garden and give opinions on any subject when asked.

There was no decent beach at Lewis's Landing, only a mudbank covered with fragments of oyster shells that cut bare feet. We could never really swim at the Landing. We'd wade around the end of the pier where, if the tide were high, the water would be 3 feet deep, but even that was unpleasant because of the clumps of seaweed one had to walk through—nests for scaleless toadfish, which have spikes along their backs and are inedible, and for crab, which pinch toes and are edible only for a few weeks in the spring. I was bored out of my mind at Lewis's Landing. The two weeks that Tom and I spent there each summer were lost. When years later the time came for me to be sent to St. Matthew's School for Boys, I didn't look forward to a return to the county, but with a record like mine—as long as your arm—I had no choice.

In his journal Henry Spelman, Jr., otherwise unknown to history, described his decision to leave England and settle in the Virginia Colony in 1609:

"Beinge in displeasure of my familye and frends and desirous to see other cuntryes. . . ." I suspect he was putting a good face on it even then.

St. Matthew's School for Boys was the ninth and last on the improvised list of schools I attended in the four-year period that ended in Tatterhummock County in September 1939. I was then sixteen and weary. Earlier Ma, my father and the inexorcisable ghost of Tom had started me off at the top. I'd been asked to leave St. Paul's in January, 1936, because I'd spent an unau-

thorized week in New York seeing the shows with a girl who went
to Brearley and who lived at home with a family that became
terribly curious about the identity of her fun-loving Daddy War-
bucks. She was fourteen, thought I was fifteen and dropped me
without ever saying goodbye when she learned the truth: I had
just turned thirteen. I finished that year in the Lake Forest public
school system, living with Lockie. The following September we
started over at Culver, where I stayed two weeks before it was
decided that I was emotionally unfit for military life, followed by
Boys Latin in Chicago, where I flunked, then back to Lake Forest
and Lockie, who found me good company and liked having me
around. In the next few years I passed through schools the way
other people go through bus depots, without looking. There were
Exeter, Pawling, Milton and, penultimately, Stonehenge, a school
that specialized in students with psychological problems.

Stonehenge's method was startlingly simple. It allowed its students to do exactly as they pleased, but that was a method that
didn't please me at all. Even then I knew that license is not liberty.
My desire was for an education in what might be termed the
religion of humanism. From a very early age I was cognizant of
what interested me and what did not. I was aware that I had no
desire to compete with the herd, and that because of singularly
fortunate circumstances, it made no difference. With care I was
preparing myself to live the good, ample, complete life. I was
interested only in what are called but seldom are the liberal arts,
in literature, languages, history, painting, music. I knew that I
wanted to prospect for gold in Alaska and so I applied myself to
geology and mineralogy. For a while I was interested in horses
and horse racing and thought I might like to have my own colors,
but I abandoned the idea when I read about Louis B. Mayer.
Horce racing had in the course of the continuing world revolution
become the sport of the nouveau riche. I wanted to fly my own
plane and was aware that to navigate it all I needed to know was
arithmetic and what log tables to use. I was not interested in
chemistry, biology, botany, algebra, solid geometry, trigonometry,
team sports or Sir Walter Scott, each of which, at one time or
another, provided difficulties. I was preparing myself to become a
nineteenth-century gentleman in the twentieth century, a fellow

who, being a rare breed, is not easily identified. At the age of twenty-one I would take possession of the trust fund of eight figures set up by Boo and Lockie, with even more money in the kitty should they have already gone on to their rewards, the amount depending only on how they—or whichever was the survivor— felt about Ma at the time of the actual writing of the final last-will- and-testament. If she had eloped with another bigamous officer of the law, as she had once done in Reno, she'd receive minimum beans and I'd get everything else. If she were being frightfully respectable, as she is at the minute, married to a minor English character, Sir Paul Plyant (real name: John Harcourt-Foster), who is a decent, not unintelligent old fellow in spite of his blind spot about Ma, she could wind up with steamer trunks full of the easily negotiables. Which is approximately what happened.

St. Matthew's was a last resort. When I refused to return to Stonehenge, Ma, who was then between mates, had the spur-of-the- moment idea of enrolling me at St. Matthew's while she caught her breath in temporary residence at Lewis's Landing with Cousin Annie Lee and Miss Mary, and with Cousin Mary Lee, who had reached twenty-seven unmarried and still in the process of becom- ing engaged or figuring out ways in which to become unengaged. My Mary—Ma (every woman in our family is named Mary, which is often confusing) shook up Lewis's Landing in a way it hadn't been shook up since the Civil War. Between us we did rather a job on the entire county.

Ma had another reason for sending me to St. Matthew's: David Prud'homme Devereaux III, the headmaster, which was all Ma needed to know to entrust the school with the care and instruction of her only surviving son. She hadn't known, nor did it much worry her when I reported it to her, that the school was a pedant's nightmare, an ecclesial joke, a hotbed of vice and a finishing school for misfits, so fiscally mismanaged that the Tatterhummock County Power and Light Company in early October turned off the electricity for twenty-four hours because Mr. Devereaux had not heeded the ten-day warning on the bottom of the last unpaid bill. Though the school was sponsored by the Virginia diocese, the diocese didn't exercise any apparent supervision. In the nine years that Mr. Devereaux had been headmaster St. Matthew's had become his private game reservation, a place where he could study outstanding or quintessential examples of local fauna in something like their natural habitats.

The school was a collection of ugly orange-brick buildings, put up at the turn of the century, plus a pint-sized reproduction of Mount Vernon that served as the headmaster's house and that, with a minimum of effort, could have been turned into a filling station. St. Matthew's was broke much of the time and survived the two semesters I was there, I'm sure, because of the donations that Ma and my father made, each having paid my tuition in full without the knowledge of the other. It need not have been that broke except that one-third of the thirty-nine students were on full scholarship and many of the rest on partial scholarship. With three or four exceptions the students were all Tidewater specimens that Mr. Devereaux fancied as if they were creatures of rare distinction instead of the pimply-faced, pockmarked, tongue-tied, pointy-headed animals they seemed to me when I arrived—sons of Northern Neck farmers with ancient names, scions of Tatterhummock oystermen and fishermen with accents that Mr. Devereaux was convinced were Elizabethan but that to me sounded simply Gullah.

Mr. Devereaux's love for people and place was genuine but his vision was his own. He didn't notice that the six masters he'd imported from other parts of the state for what amounted to room and board and the privilege to shape tiny minds were themselves barely literate. When Mr. Devereaux stood before the school body at morning assembly he saw not a human zoo, a collection of untutored monsters, but the vestiges of a confidential Eden. I often wondered how he would have reacted had he known that his special favorite, a shy, earnest, red-headed boy with an angularly misshapen face, a fellow named Deke Crozier, who came as close to scoring a touchdown as any member of the St. Matthew's football squad that year, was, at the age of sixteen, hopelessly lost to sheep-fucking. Deke Crozier's sheep-fucking was an act that I watched late one warm October night in Mr. Whabble's meadow, which separated the school campus, on the bluff, from the river a half mile away. Deke was not self-conscious about it. The other students made gentle jokes but never to his face. After all, Deke was the school's star football player and that gave him perquisites. If poor, simple-minded Gordon Felix had done it, he would have been abused cruelly. Deke was open and sincere and a good athlete, and during football training he limited himself to one fuck a week. On Friday nights, after the game. He enjoyed himself at will the rest of the year. He was not attached to one particular animal. Any sheep would do. Like all boys Deke Crozier had no concept of promiscuity. He was blessedly unaware of the adjustments he would have to make in later life.

Mr. Devereaux also was one of Ma's former suitors and, I suspected then (but not now), her lover in an era when nice girls didn't do it.

Ma speaks. When Ma speaks she assumes the accents fitting either the place she's in or the subject she's speaking about. In London where she now lives six months a year, Lady Plyant would give Edith Evans as Lady Bracknell reason to shut up. Recalling summers at Lewis's Landing she sheds time and slips into her Virginia belle-hoopskirt drag, never using a period when a question mark or an exclamation point will do:

"I declare, darling, he was the handsomest man I'd ever laid eyes on! Very tall, very slim, very very military and straight in his uniform with the high collar . . . you know what I mean? A sort of choker? They don't wear them any more. . . . Army officers? Do they? It was the summer of '17 and he was on leave? Before sailing to France? His father, old Doctor Devereaux, was the ladies' man of the family. Doctor Devereaux was on his third wife then. They all died, bless them. I guess he wore them out. You remember that awful poem? Of course, you do, darling. Cousin Mary Lee taught it to you? No? Was it Tom? 'Old Doctor Devereaux sleeping in his bed/His first wife's pillow underneath his head/His second wife's something something something/His third wife's coverlet laying on his hide/His fourth wife's something something dreaming by his side!' Oh, he was a wicked man, but so charming! And so crude! He used to scratch his privates in front of the congregation, on Sunday mornings? Stick the little finger of his right hand between the buttons of his cassock and just scratch away! They say that's why he was never made a bishop? All the other Devereauxs had been bishops . . . but David was shy. He looked like Gary Cooper, but taller? And skinnier? Sandy-blond hair slicked back, parted in the middle, and those pale blue eyes that were always so . . . severe? I think I mixed him up with Rupert Brooke, or was it Clive Brook? Not the actor, the poet? Am I losing my memory? Oh, he was a handsome man! We saw each other every day and every night for two solid weeks! And we were engaged for the last three days of his leave, though we didn't tell anyone about it? He gave me his U of V-A class ring and I wore it on a gold chain around my neck, so that no one would see it? But then it fell off and I lost the ring and he said I wasn't serious! Wasn't serious! I'd never been so serious about anyone in my entire life! I would have died for that boy! But then I knew I was too young to be *that* serious and I enjoyed going to parties and having beaux, and the future was so uncertain and all.

"I broke the engagement and cried my eyes out for a week! He wrote me several times from France? He was wounded, you know, and he spent months in a hospital in England. I don't know *what* was wounded, something *internal*, I assume. We sort of lost touch until the war ended . . . when I went back to Lewis's Landing for your great-grandmother's funeral? David was teaching in the public school in Queen Anne and coaching the football team, and we started all over again. That time it *was* serious. He gave me a real ring but I'd already met your father and then . . . and then . . ." (slow fadeout of Lewis's Landing as Lake Forest takes over) ". . . I don't know . . . Boo liked the idea of David's being a teacher and all, because of the business, but David didn't want to go into the business. He didn't want to see textbooks, and he didn't like my friends. He was out of his element in Lake Forest and it became . . . well . . . terribly *sordid*. I'm afraid I was very *mean*. I gave him one last chance to say yes to everything, and when he wouldn't, I returned his ring and married your father, which I guess I'd wanted to do anyway. . . ." Laughs. "I don't think I would have been very good as a teacher's wife, not that Odile is much of an asset. She drinks. . . ."

7

What of Gethsemane, my Hebe, my Helen, my black Aphrodite, my silent Circe, my Sappho of the loblollies? It now makes thirty-seven years. I caught my first sight of her late on a golden afternoon at the start of the September term at St. Matthew's. Earlier I had been in the community shower room, which I'd had to myself until the arrival of fat, unpleasant little Gordon Felix. Most of the student body would have been showering in the gym. They were the football squad that I'd been able to avoid by claiming a chronically inflamed appendix. I'd quickly come to treasure the privacy of those long steamy showers when I could put my thoughts in order and allow the most turbulent sexual fantasies free rein under the warming pressure of the old-fashioned shower nozzle, the only one of the eight nozzles in the community bath having the proper density to it. I had been standing there, eyes closed, experiencing the usual transports of adolescent pleasure, when I suddenly became aware of the arrival of someone else. Felix turned on the shower next to mine, drenching me in frigid spray. Although Gordon Felix was the water boy for the St. Matthew's football team, the position did not entitle him to shower in the gym with the active squad members. Too bad. A small privilege that would have given unspeakable joy. Felix was such an obvious toad, so dramatically disadvantaged in terms of brain, that one of the first things I'd learned at St. Matthew's was the story of his father. People felt they had to explain Felix's presence. His father, Osgood Felix, the mayor and justice of the peace of Queenstown-on-James, was a man of some fame in those days. He had pulled off the greatest public relations hustle since Harding had been elected president. One night, many years earlier, Mr. Felix had had a glorious dream. He had had a vision of Queenstown-on-James restored to its colonial glory when, before the completion of Williamsburg and after the abandonment of Jamestown, it had been for six months the capital of the Virginia Crown Colony. Rockefeller money financed the restoration project as well as

Gordon Felix's feeble stabs at degeneracy. But more about that later. In September 1939, Hitler was overrunning Poland and the lights were going out all over Europe but I was not yet destitute.

Thus was Felix standing in the community shower room, delighted, transfixed by something on my person somewhere between my knees and my belly button. With as much style as I could manage, I finished my shower, retrieved my towel from a rusting hook on the opposite wall and led myself down the hall to my cell, a cubicle separated from the rest, as they all were, by a wooden partition that was 7 feet high and varnished a sort of rectory-orange. My single, unshaded window on the dormitory's second floor looked across a patch of once-formal, now weedy garden, marked here and there by the tall, dry stalk of a dead hollyhock, to Mount Vernon, the Devereaux residence opposite. Even as I sat on the foot of my cot, carefully sprinkling Desinex powder between my toes (though I was never athletic to any important degree I was frequently host to the fungus), I could look down upon the garden that had been forgotten by Odile Devereaux in her bouts with booze and hysteria. I could also look directly into the second-floor bedroom of Jojo Devereaux, a raucous, spindly-legged Shirley Temple whose hair was mercilessly peroxided and permed by her mother whenever Odile got a load on. Jojo was not even seven yet her hair already had the exhausted look of an elderly fox terrier's. In the course of my pedal prophylaxis and while wondering what sights in the unshaded dormitory windows the spoiled Jojo most fancied, I saw Jojo walking toward the house, treading diagonally across what should have been flowerbeds, accompanied not by her mammy but by a large black construction worker who wore baggy khaki pants, a dark blue workshirt, what seemed to be the high, reinforced shoes that protect a fellow when he drops a steel beam on his foot and, the most eccentric touch of all, a New York Yankees baseball cap that sat squarely atop the bushy, unkonked hair. As my proud erection had led me from the shower room, so, in those days, did this curious hat appear to lead Gethsemane.

Jojo and her companion entered the house through the kitchen door by the garden and a few minutes later appeared in Jojo's room. That is, Gethsemane did. I was applying unscented talc to my body when the blinds in Jojo's room were suddenly raised and the window opened. There we were, in a manner of speaking, face to face. I was startled, to say the least. I'm not by nature an exhibitionist, though I suspect there is some exhibitionism in us all even if an impartial jury were to rule there was nothing to be exhibitionistic about. I remember wondering where the brat was. Taking a leak most likely. Jojo either had a malfunctioning bladder or was in periodic need of the isolation afforded by the toilet. David, Odile and Jojo took their meals in the school dining hall with the boys and never would a meal be successfully gotten through without Jojo's having to excuse herself to piss. Always once, sometimes twice. Gethsemane did not turn away, nor did I, though I was inclined to be shy about my physique, which, at a weight of 130 pounds, was skeletal. How long we stared I've no idea. Probably ten seconds. First I was aware of the tightness of her shirt, of the hidden delights just beneath, of big black tits, full and firm with large blue-black aureoles. Though her hips were large enough to comfort a bear, her waist was tiny. She was, I guessed, somewhat older than I and almost as tall. Then I saw her eyes. They were huge and dark and revealed nothing and, because of that, were incredibly sorrowful. The window having been opened, the blinds were abruptly dropped between us. It was our first sexual encounter.

In April of the Bicentennial Year I flew to Richmond where I was met by a hired car and a chauffeur, a neat young black man named Carroll Tucker, who spent three days driving me around Tatterhummock County revisiting the scenes of my folly. There is now a four-lane highway that takes one from Richmond to within three miles of Tatterhummock Court House with only two stops in between. The highway, constructed for the benefit of pilgrims going to Williamsburg and Queenstown-on-James, was most disorienting for me. When I'd gone to school at St. Matthew's the trip from Richmond took at least two hours in a private car and four hours in the Walden's Point bus. We drove it in fifty-five minutes. The towns and villages by which we measured our journey appear to have been removed. The highway is called a thruway though it doesn't go through anything. It passes forever outside, most of the time running in a straight line at the base of a finely cut grass culvert. The initial impression is pleasant, that of a soft green trench nobly free of billboards and the usual highway clutter, but then after a while the impression changes. One is going sixty to seventy miles per hour but seems to be standing still. It's so ascetic one could be dead. From time to time small, unobtrusive, tasteful road signs—probably chosen by garden club ladies—announce exits to those places I once knew so well: Bottom's Bridge, Providence Forge, Talleysville. But the signs could be directions to gravesites. I began to fear that when we reached Tatterhummock Court House there would be nothing but a flat, grassy plain and a state historical marker. I needn't have worried.

The county appeared largely unchanged. Walden's Point, at the foot of the county on the Chesapeake Bay, has become a haven for pleasure boats owned by people from Richmond, Norfolk and Newport News. I spent two nights at Walden's Point at a dreadful, stateless motor court of the sort one might find in South Dakota or California or on the Sunrise Highway. Though the county appears largely unchanged, there have been adjustments. I was astonished on the drive from Tatterhummock Court House to Walden's Point when, for several miles, we trailed a county school bus delivering black children as well as white to roadside mailboxes. That evening the manager of the motor court, a native of Pennsylvania, told me at great length that all was not serene in that particular area. "The niggers," he said, "are just laying low. They remember '64." "Were you here then?" "No, but I sure as hell heard about it. When they can, they pick up and move out of the county." I told him I'd heard that St. Matthew's now accepted black students. "That's different," he said. "They's African niggers, the ones who own all those oil wells. That ain't the same as county niggers."

Another thing I wasn't prepared for: the moist green beauty of the spring landscape. Ancient elms and oaks luxuriously bent with the weight of leaf. The sudden view of the Tatterhummock River from the highway a mile outside Queen Anne. Driving between fields planted with chickpeas, one comes over a small rise to see—beyond the rolling cultivated plain, beyond the grove of elms hiding Wicheley Hall—the breadth of that magnificent river that, in spring, is balm. It's a tender landscape, made so by the season and the accumulation of time.

Periodically during the autumn of 1939 when I was trying to play the game for Mr. Devereaux, at least to the point of pulling myself together enough to engage in some activity that wasn't entirely sedentary, I would go off on solitary afternoon hiking trips. I explored Wicheley at leisure, though I could never find a way into the main house. One afternoon I discovered a cache of nineteenth-century clay pipes embedded in the riverbank. On another afternoon I decided to find the source of Queen Anne Creek, which in the Middle West would have been called a river, being a quarter of a mile wide at its mouth. Starting at Wicheley, where the creek flows into the Tatterhummock, I walked upstream, following ever-smaller tributaries until I was walking along a stream that I could jump across as the need arose. After more than an hour I came upon a dark, concealed pool no more than 15 feet round. I could straddle the streams by which the pool was filled and emptied, and which seemed to have no bearing on the life of the pool itself. I suspect it was fed by its own spring. The pool was in a rocky pocket 6 feet below the level of the surrounding forest floor. Its waters were black, made dark, I suppose, by the lack of sunlight, which was shaded by the tangle of scrub pine and honeysuckle overhead. The ground was wet, so I sat on my haunches at the edge of the pool, smoking forbidden cigarettes and recalling the latest indignity I'd suffered at the whims of the troglodytes Mr. Devereaux called masters. That morning my form master had ex-propriated a set of Proust on the pretext that *Swann's Way* was unsuitable reading for anyone my age and, further, responsible for my flunking chemistry, as well as for my having told him to go fuck himself (on the blackboard in the lab, in handwriting I made no attempt to disguise). My degenerate literature had been locked up in Mr. Devereaux's office for the duration of the term or for whenever I began to pass chemistry, whichever came first. It seemed likely that I'd be separated from Swann and his gang until Christmas vacation at the earliest. I didn't mind that—I was finding it impossible to penetrate the prose beyond page 37—as much as I minded the politics of the punishment, the arbitrariness of the system of fines and rewards.

I was on my third cigarette and close to tears when I noticed a stirring in the pool and saw, for a second only, what seemed to be a great dark shape within. Like Ma in moments of superficial stress, I thought I might be losing my grip. I threw my cigarette into the pool and immediately a giant prehistoric creature, horned, bluntly shaped, at least 4 feet long, brushed up against the cigarette butt with its nose as the butt was carried toward the pool's exit. I stood. My knees weak and my stomach in the vicinity of my heart, I determined not to panic. I secured a log and began to probe the pool, which was, I estimated, about 4 feet deep at its center. As I probed, there were more stirrings and suddenly the creature broke the surface. He could have been a dragon. He was armor-plated, with blue-gray scales the size of 50-cent pieces. He had a mean mouth and a determined eye but he fought with the fury of someone drugged. His size was such that he could scarcely turn around in the place he had called home for who knows how long, perhaps 1,000 years. Though I was apprehensive, the fight was, at first, play. It was horsing around and I was curious. Then the play turned serious. As I tired, I became angry. Approaching fatigue created an obsession. We were Ahab and Moby Dick in a turpentine forest. My log was heavy, unwieldy. There was little space to wind up for a swing or to get a purchase for a perpendicular attack. Then, too, the water cushioned my blows even when they were accurate. The fight went on but in slow motion. As I neared exhaustion I became fearful of stumbling into the pool. The shore was booby-trapped with rocks and exposed roots of the trees growing above. But if I was nearing exhaustion and not exactly Captain Ahab in the splendor of my obsession, the creature was a miserable Moby Dick. He was sluggish and he was dumb. Little by little I maneuvered him into the shallows at the head of the pool when, suicidally, he made a leap onto the bed of the feeding stream, as if to escape me by wiggling his way, fully exposed, over and around the rocks to some dimly remembered pool further upstream. With a deliberation and dispassion that I can sometimes summon in myself, I beat him to death with my

log. When I'd finished, the head was a jelly of brains, scales, eye-
balls and blood.

The deed being done I worked the body up onto the bank and
then sat down, opposite it, to decide what to do. I was sitting
squarely on the ticky earth and not until I was aware that my ass
was wet did I realize that I could have sat on my Abercrombie's
suede jacket, a merry, $150, off-to-school (again) present from
my father and the sensible Claire. I removed my jacket and when
I'd finished another cigarette, stepped across the stream to my
victim. Carefully, so as not to touch the possibly venomous creature with my bare hands, I wrapped it in my suede jacket, knowing that the blood and the smell would henceforth be always a part
of my country wardrobe.

It took me two hours to walk back to the school. The creature
was heavy. As we traveled his odor rose, but as we neared the
campus my spirits also rose. I'd never done anything like this by
myself before. Perhaps, I thought, I'd discovered some link to the
past long considered to be extinct. Such things had happened. At
the very least it was a creature not previously known in Tatterhummock County. As I approached the dormitory I passed the
kitchen where MacDougal, our cook, a big, cheerful black man
who always wore his chef's hat on the back of his head and a
dishcloth tied around his neck to catch the sweat, was standing
outside the kitchen door, having a cup of tea that was generally
known to be bourbon and water. "MacDougal," I said, hearing
myself use a tone of camaraderie totally alien to my nature, "look
at what I've got."

He ambled over, belly pushed forward, the pinkie finger extended from the others that clutched the booze. "You're from
around here," I said. "Have you ever seen anything like this before?" I dropped my victim on the ground, opened the now
thoroughly soiled suede jacket and watched MacDougal's reaction. His eyes opened wide. He laughed and clapped me on the
back. "Gawd, boy," he said. "Gawd sakes, you got yourself a
granddaddy." I was pleased at his pleasure, but also disappointed
that he didn't seem surprised or mystified. I maintained my composure. "A granddaddy what?" I said. "Why, boy, that there's a
granddaddy carp, about twenty-two pounds, I reckon. Good eat-

ing, too." A goddamn carp, I thought. Who the fuck wants to eat a
22-pound goldfish! "We catch lots of them hereabouts," said Mac-
Dougal, swigging his cocktail. At which point Mr. Devereaux
joined us, accompanied by his old, none-too-bright, gun-shy bird
dog, Stonewall Jackson. MacDougal finished his tea in one gulp,
wiped his mouth discreetly and pointed to my coelacanth. "Look
what the boy done caught hisself—a beautiful granddaddy carp."

Except for the pinkness of his skin and the accusing blueness
of his eyes, Mr. Devereaux was steel-gray all over, virtually mono-
colored. Steel-gray hair, steel-gray flannel suit, steel-gray spectacle
rims, steel-gray socks (cordovan shoes). With his walking stick of
hickory (steel-handled and steel-tipped) Mr. Devereaux prodded
the fish here and there as Stonewall Jackson flopped on the ground
and sniffed at it with no interest. Mr. Devereaux smiled. I think it
was the first time I ever saw him smile, or maybe it was the first
time he'd ever smiled in connection with me. "Where'd you catch
him, Marshall?" I told him. "Well I'll be dogged," he said. "He's a
beauty. Good eating, too." He laughed. "MacDougal, I'd say
there's still hope for this boy, wouldn't you? When he can do
something like this?" MacDougal smiled and burped in agreement. Mr. Devereaux: "Yes, sir, Marshall, there's hope for you yet.
Your mother won't know you when St. Matthew's gets through
with you. A new man, that's what you'll be. . . ."

For a few days, anyway, Mr. Devereaux was convinced he
could transform me into a Huckleberry Finn or, better yet, a
DeKoven Crozier. As for me, I was forced to face something I
preferred not thinking about: under the right circumstances, given
the desperate necessity, I could kill and enjoy it.

Joke: "Mo, Mo, Mo," I panted. I shoved and pulled, thrusting
from one side of her to the other, seeking bases not yet touched.
"Goddammit . . . Mo!" I had my face buried between those huge
black tits, licking the sweat running down between them, every
now and then detouring to pop a nipple into my mouth. I was
aware that I was moaning. "Mo!" Gethsemane looked down at
me, laughing. "Mo'? My gawd, boy! There ain't any mo'. You
got all there is!" End joke.

Freud says that every man wants a woman as much like his mother as he can stand, which is what I found in Gethsemane. Mo had been my wet nurse and then had stayed with us until I was four. My father may still have some home movies taken the winter I was two, of me on old-fashioned, four-runner ice skates trying to push big, fat, black Mo, sitting in the kitchen chair in the middle of the ice of Otis Lake, outside Lake Forest. Mo wears her brown winter coat with the fur collar whose texture and camphor smell I can yet recall. I push and shove but the chair does not budge. Instead my feet slide backwards and I slowly slip to my knees, still working solemnly, trying to get that goddamned chair to move. Mo laughs, but she keeps a mittened hand cupped over her mouth, fearful that her dentures might jump out as they have a way of doing when the temperature drops below freezing.

I don't think I ever seriously wanted to fuck Ma, though I remember once when I was about fourteen getting a hard-on as she sat on my lap in a taxi we were sharing with some other people going from the Ambassador East to the Chicago & North Western Railroad Station. I was mortified, afraid that my cock would pierce my pants to impale Ma in front of friends who were no more than passing acquaintances. The more embarrassed I became, the more ready stood my tool, and the more Ma bounced around on my lap, exclaiming about how short a time it had been when things were just the other way around. That's Ma. On second thought, maybe there was a time when I did want to fuck her but not, certainly, after I got to know her. Mo was something else: food source, nurse, mother, friend, sex object. She finally left us to work for the Caffreys in Lake Forest and we lost touch. The Caffreys moved around a great deal but Mo somehow found her way back to attend Tom's funeral—a terrible day.

I was standing alone in the hall of Chantilly, Lockie's Lake Forest house, when the cab came up the drive and stopped in front of the double Norman doors that were open in the heat. A passenger I could not see took what seemed to be an inordinate amount of time fumbling with dollar bills and a change purse, then climbed out of the taxi sideways, though still being squeezed. She was enormous. I couldn't have described her before that second but as soon as I saw her I knew it was Mo, wearing clothes I never would have associated with her: a tent of fine, heavy black satin (though this was June and a very hot day), a matching black satin hat with a veil, pearls around her neck, black gloves on her hands. She was younger than I might have thought but her huge size made movement difficult for her. As with many obese people, her great shape suddenly narrowed at the knees, ending (or beginning) with tiny, slim feet encased uncharacteristically in black highheels that were probably unsafe. Mo lumbered, *en pointe*, through the open door. She stopped a moment to adjust her eyes to the shade, and then saw me. I maintained my usual reserve. "Marshall?" she said. "Is that you, boy?" "Yes," I said, very cool. She put her arms around me and I began to sob tears I didn't know were in me. "Baby, baby," she said. "It's all right now. . . ."

She led me to one of those big, fake-baronial chairs so often placed in entranceways of that sort, and she may have been the first person to sit down on it. The hall of Lockie's house was a place in which to be greeted, to be sent off from or to pass through. It was not a place for communion and comfort. Mo cradled me, cuddled me, though I was twelve and tall now for my age. The more comfort that was given, the more I cried. By the time Ma and Lockie came from the drawing room I was in what they described as hysterics. Mo rocked me from side to side, telling me that everything would be all right, stroking me, petting me, letting me smell the old nurse's scent which is far more erotic than anything manufactured by Balenciaga or Hermes. "Ah, ah, ah," I said, meaning "Mo, Mo, Mo." They didn't allow me to go to the funeral, thinking it would be too disturbing. They didn't realize I only wanted Mo.

8

Out of the steamer trunk: One of the souvenirs of my life at age nine is a clipping from the Chicago *Herald-American*, the Hearst afternoon newspaper, of June 20, 1932. Under a picture of my father, his face hidden behind a natty boater (one that, I remember, had around the crown a grosgrain ribbon of horizontally striped dark blue-red-dark blue, his team colors), there is this caption:

"Polo-playing Tommy Henderson, right, leaving Chicago Criminal Court Building yesterday accompanied by his lawyer after the judge hit him with the mallet of the law. See story on page 16." There was no Cholly Dearborn in those days but the article was apparently written by a reporter auditioning for the job:

Chicago business associates, North Shore friends and his teammates are still stunned 24 hours after receiving the news that Thomas Henderson, 35, known as "Handsome Tommy" in polo-playing circles here, had been arrested and charged on three counts of embezzlement of funds amounting to almost $200,000. That's the sum allegedly missing from the till of Marlowe, Sykes, Harris & Henderson, the LaSalle Street brokerage house where "Handsome Tommy" is a partner and treasurer.

Henderson, son of the late Marshall E. Henderson, a justice of the Illinois Supreme Court at the time of his death and a long-time power in Cook County's Democratic Party, was arrested at 10:15 A.M. yesterday in his office and without so much as a by-your-leave escorted immediately to the court house for arraignment.

"Handsome Tommy," who owns his own string of polo ponies [this was not true] and knows his way around the locker rooms of the Onwentsia, Saddle & Cycle, Racquet and Wheaton clubs, was forced to spend six hours in the lock-up until a $50,000 bond was posted by his father-in-law, William A. Kemper, the publisher and philanthropist. Kemper's charities include homes for the rehabilitation of unwed mothers and alcoholics, the Audubon Society, the Chicago Symphony Orchestra Association, the Opera Guild, the Boy Scouts, the Society for the Prevention of Cruelty to Animals and the American Association for Better Family Planning.

Yesterday's electrifying revelations recall the arrest on similar charges three years ago of Lake Forest's Lloyd ("Doggy") Fairchild, a sometime polo-playing teammate of "Handsome Tommy." "Doggy," you remember, fell accidentally to his death from a twelfth-floor room in the Palmer House before his case was brought to trial.

Neither "Handsome Tommy" nor his lawyer, Charles ("Chip") Norris, would comment on the case yesterday. A secretary at Henderson's office, who cannot be identified, discounted the allegations. "I'm sure it's some kind of bookkeeping error," she said. "Mr. Henderson isn't in the office often enough to get away with that kind of money."

"Handsome Tommy's" wife, the former Mary Lewis Kemper, Jr., was reported last night to have left the Orangerie, the palatial Henderson estate in Lake Forest, and gone home to Mummy and Daddy at Chantilly, the even more palatial Kemper estate just down Sheridan Road. Mary, a regular on the best-dressed lists and known for her wit, is described as "distraught" and under a doctor's care. With her are the couple's two sons, Thomas, Jr., 13, and Marshall, 9. Where "Handsome Tommy" is bunking, only "Chip" Norris knows, and "Chip" isn't telling.

Ma wrung her hands, cried a lot and, whenever I was dumb enough to pass through a room she was occupying, she'd make a lunge to comfort me, though I don't remember any emotion except excitement. Every time the telephone rang she'd yell that she certainly was not going to talk to any *more* reporters, but this finally came to seem wishful thinking. The few times I could get to the telephone first, it was never anything as interesting as a reporter, just a friend. While Tom stayed in his room whittling a model of the *Bremen*, I monitored the events downstairs with the impartial ear of a court stenographer. When Ma, Tom and I moved back to our own house a week later, it was Tom who brooded. Several nights later, Our Father came home too. Tom and I were being fed in the butler's pantry—Ma, I think, was still forcing down what food she could wolf from a tray in bed—when Our Father suddenly appeared in the doorway to say hello. Tom sort of blushed and stood up, as I did. Tom looked intently at the floor, Our Father looked from Tom to me, and I looked at Tom. Our Father appeared to be indecently well and chipper. At last he came over to me, extended his hand, and then as we shook he leaned over to give me a peck on the cheek and I could smell the booze on his breath. He went to Tom, extended his hand to him. After a second's hesitation, Tom collapsed, bursting into tears and throwing his arms around Our Father, who was first surprised, then (he wasn't completely insensitive) moved to a tiny tear. "There, there, son," Our Father said cheerfully. "Nobody's going to put me in jail. . . ." Which was Handsome Tommy missing the point again.

What was Handsome Tommy like in those days? Totally free of guile and, as Ma put it, good-looking, incredibly. These were his Original Sins. Everything about him was easy and self-assured and without arrogance. He was one of those people who never have to open their mouths and still friends will say how interesting they are. He was taller than polo players should be but he was in such harmony with his pony that one was never aware of the abrupt, jerking, reining-in movements one saw in the other players as a match became heated. His game wasn't recorded in highs and lows but in a single graceful parabola. Because he had everything an ordinary man might want, ambition was unknown to him. Fulfillment came so quickly atop desire, the two were one. As a result of his good fortune there were great blank spaces in his character. He had scarcely any curiosity about anything that wasn't in his field of vision. This may be one of the reasons he was such a good athlete. There was nothing to distract him from the business at hand. I suspect, though, from the hints that Ma has let drop like boulders, that he wasn't the most inventive lover. I suspect, too, that he had no real passion for anything. He could read, of course, but I never once saw him with a book in his hand or even a magazine. We have exchanged letters so rarely in our lives that when I do receive one I'm always surprised at the large, casual beauty of his hand. Writing is not something one would ever associate with him. Tommy was a void—a vacuum in the form of a handsome man—someone who had no appreciation of experience, no sense of history, no memory of Something Other.

He was the youngest of three sons of a federal judge of the kind that was a rarity in Chicago at the turn of the century: a white Anglo-Saxon Protestant who was also a member in good standing of Chicago's Democratic Party, then dominated by Roman Catholics who spoke with brogues and hailed Mary while organizing one of the most long-lived, efficiently corrupt political

machines this country has ever known. A widower from the birth
of my father, the Judge brought up his sons in home territory—
the South Side—but as his fortunes increased he sent the boys
north and east into social respectability that would be denied his
Roman Catholic cronies for at least two more generations.

Ma first met my father in 1916 after a polo match in Lake
Forest and it was—according to one of the dozen or so folios she
keeps on the occasion—love at first sight. The second time she
met him, three nights later at a dance at the Saddle & Cycle Club,
she asked the question directly, "Are you Catholic?" I can see and
hear her, batting her lashes in mock southern belle innocence
while asking a question of staggering rudeness. "Are you Catholic?" She would as easily have asked him if he had a black mistress, kissed Paris whores on the mouth or groped his buddies in
the shower. Boo had warned her that the Hendersons were Catholic. "They all are," he said. "They're mackerel-snappers." When
my father said he was a Lutheran, Ma was relieved but also disappointed. She had never known any Catholics and everything she
assumed they stood for intrigued her—superstition, passion, un-
mentionable vices, secret rituals, though she did think that the
holding of wakes was terribly lower class. Even if the Catholic
churches one saw in Chicago were of a garishness to make any
sensitive Christian sneer, one must remember that Catholics also
were responsible for Chartres, Notre Dame and the Sistine
Chapel. How splendid to be introduced to all this in the person of
Handsome Tommy Henderson, though, of course, if he had been
Catholic she would never have been allowed to invite him home.
As it was, Judge Henderson's prominence in the Democratic Party
—for whom, it was rumored, he acted as bagman in the business
community—was bad enough. Ma's marriage to my father was
approved by Boo only after Handsome Tommy had served in
France with the Illinois National Guard, in a cavalry outfit that
was otherwise manned exclusively by North Shore fellows of the
kind whose names were familiar as department stores, brokerage
houses, streets, hotels, museums and sausages. It was also approved
because Ma was an only child and what she wanted she got. Sooner
or later.

.   .   .

A few words about the source of Boo's loot. Boo discovered his
mother lode in the rapidly expanding American public school
system. Kemper & Company, the country's largest, most aggres-
sive publisher and distributor of textbooks, was then a privately
held company controlled by Boo, who devoted himself to American education with the kind of selflessness that God Himself rewards. Like his friend Henry Ford, Boo believed in bringing
system to progress, putting progress on an annual basis and making it pay by the expedient of producing new models every year.
Each Kemper textbook was revised annually so as to require each
schoolchild, no matter how penurious, to purchase new books
come September. The reuse of last year's books by a following
class was discouraged by Boo's salesmen on the grounds that
American schoolchildren had the patriotic right to be kept abreast
of the latest developments in knowledge. To Kemper & Company,
first-year French, spelling and woodworking were as volatile as
nuclear physics was to be some years later. There were break-
throughs constantly. Kemper salesmen bought back their own
second-hand books, but always at a fraction of the original
purchase price, and these were then recycled for a new line that
would appear three years later. Kemper & Company constructed
school books sturdily, with fine bindings, to withstand the boredom of the most destructive child. Kemper & Company designed
its books to last forever—and to be out of date in a week. The
profits that were made from all this equaled a small Klondike and
were, eventually, self-generating. Not long after Boo's death in the
thirties, Kemper & Company was acquired by an even larger New
York publishing house through a highly beneficial (to Kemper
holders) stock exchange arrangement and a sizable amount of
cash. When this firm was eventually absorbed by a radio-televi-
sion network, which was also to become heavily involved in
electronics and aerodynamics, what had once been simply a-very-
good-thing had quadrupled and quintupled into blue chips that
reproduced themselves as do living organisms.

Although he was not an alcoholic, Handsome Tommy had always
drunk a good deal; but it wasn't until After the Fall that it showed.

It was like drinking on an empty stomach. Too many drinks with good friends after polo or golf or tennis is one thing. Drinking directly from the bottle, alone in the kitchen, is something else. "What's wrong with *you*?" Handsome Tommy said when Ma caught him sucking off a fifth of Gordon's gin. "I think it's disgusting," said Ma. "Why is it disgusting?" said my father. "Here—have a drink." "I don't find that sort of drinking very convivial," said Ma, who then went upstairs to cry, leaving Tom and me and Our Father to finish getting supper any way we could.

After the Orangerie was sold with everything in it for a fraction of its worth on the depressed market, we had two months in which to make our move to the house that Ma had rented in Barrington, another Chicago suburb so perfectly ordinary that Ma chose it as her Siberia. As was her way with unhappy tasks, she put off all preparations for our exile until the last minute. One hysterical afternoon she was sorting the contents of my father's bureau where, in a top, right-hand drawer, in a mess of odd cufflinks, shirt studs, old letters, polo programs, a life insurance policy and other forgotten paraphernalia, she found their wedding license as well as my father's birth certificate. According to the birth certificate, the child was a white Caucasian male, religion—Roman Catholic.

Ma carried her bombshell around the rest of the afternoon, huffing and puffing under its weight, refusing to drop it until that evening after both she and my father had each had two martinis and we were all seated at the dinner table.

"You lied to me," said Ma, attempting to giggle as if she really thought Tommy had pulled off a good one. "I didn't lie to you," said Our Father, smiling, though he had no idea where Ma was leading him. "You certainly did," said Ma, mostly to Tom and me. "When we first met and I asked you, you said you were a Presbyterian." "A Lutheran," said Our Father. "And," said Ma, "your birth certificate says you are a Catholic." "I'm not anything," said Our Father. "I just said the first thing that came into my mind." "But you're a Roman Catholic," said Ma, getting very excited. "Your birth certificate says so." "That was just my mother," said

Our Father. "She was Catholic and the Judge let her have her way. He didn't care." "Imagine," said Ma, "I've been living with a Roman all these years and didn't know it." "What's a Roman?" I said. "A Catholic," said Ma, "what Boo calls a bog-trotter." Our Father looked puzzled. "A bog-trotter is an Irishman," he said. "Catholics are mackerel-snappers because they eat fish on Fridays." "Well," said Ma, giving Tom and me a look of sweet pain, "they're all the same to me." Tom, solemnly: "Does that mean I'm a Catholic too? I thought I was baptized and confirmed in an Episcopal church." "You were, darling," said Ma. "Your father is the only Catholic in the family—just don't tell Boo. He'd have a fit." That effectively ruined the rest of the meal. Our Father remained cheerful enough but uncertain. Ma was predictable, all right, but never in ways he could get the knack of.

Several months before Handsome Tommy's case came to trial, Boo, against the advice of my father's lawyer, reimbursed Marlowe, Sykes & Harris, which saved the firm but acknowledged Our Father's guilt, not of a crime, even though it was classified as such, but of complicity in procedures that were in those days accepted. Nobody, not even Boo, believed any of the money or stocks had gone into Tommy's pocket. As the treasurer of the firm he had regularly signed papers permitting the transfer and sale of stocks and bonds without the clients' knowledge. This was done all the time, ostensibly in the clients' interests, but it was also a way to provide the firm with a cash flow for other investments that were as often in the partners' interests as in those of any clients. When the market remained moribund, Our Father was left holding a bag that was empty. His partners and other friends up and down The Street would never forgive him such a frightful breach of etiquette. He was cast out of the only world he knew. He was found guilty on all three counts but he never went to jail. He was given a suspended sentence and one year on a parole so liberal he and Ma could have spent the winter in Palm Beach if anyone there would have had them. Instead of the pen he went into his own depression, which was not a thing he had the means to identify.

·   ·   ·

The next years were hard for all of us—harder for Our Father than anyone else—though it was Tom who finally put an end to them.

Before the Fall Tom and Our Father had been boon companions. Our Father had given Tom a miniature polo mallet when he was four, taught him how to ride when he was five and presented him with his own mount when he was six—a Shetland named Henry that Tom lost interest in after Henry bit him on the arm. Our Father took Tom with him to the North Woods to hunt and fish. On Sunday mornings in Lake Forest in the autumn they shot skeet together. Our Father treated Tom as an extension of himself. He called Tom "son" and me "sonny," which was what he also called caddies, grooms and shoeshine boys. Their intimacy infuriated me though I told myself there wasn't much they did together that I could do or wanted to do, yet I would have liked to be asked whether I wanted to participate. One time when Ma was away with Lockie and Boo—probably in Europe because Lockie said it was cheaper to live there during the Depression—Our Father promised to take Tom and me to an air show where Lindbergh was to appear IN PERSON. Tom, who was passionately interested in airplanes, thought Lindy the greatest man who had ever lived. So did I, naturally. The morning the three of us were to go to the show I awoke to find that, with the exception of the servants, I was the only person in the Orangerie. They'd sneaked off without me. I was no more than four and not the liveliest of companions, but I remained furious for a very long time. It's no wonder, I guess, that when I went to Lewis's Landing that time with Tom and Lockie, I signed my first letter home: "Love, Marshall Lewis Henderson (your son)." I was afraid that in the week or so I'd been away they would have forgotten who I was.

Under ordinary circumstances the closeness between Our Father and Tom might have evolved into something else without special incident, like a love affair that ends with the season, naturally, with fond feelings instead of the sense of terrible, unbearable loss. When we moved to Barrington, it was Handsome Tommy's turn to feel abandoned.

Tom and I were enrolled in the public school, which I loathed from the first day when a little girl named Jane-Marie Hendke, who sat at the desk directly behind me, expressed her panic with the new surroundings by vomiting all over my neck and back a mixture whose base was cream of tomato soup with flecks of egg salad sandwich and dill pickle. Being a snob at a very early age, I thought Barrington was the sticks. Tom loved it. He entered the activities of the school and the town with enthusiasm. He had the freedom to move and choose companions he would never have known in Lake Forest. The friends he made were his own, without connections to family. Never in Lake Forest could he have had a best friend by the name of Benny Popp, whose father was the local chiropractor. Tom was not a good student—each semester he scraped by—but he was a natural athlete like Our Father and his first year on the Barrington High football team, when still a substitute player, he scored three touchdowns. In his junior year he was the team's co-captain, an honor for a junior that was without precedent in Barrington.

Ma played the role of loyal wife sticking by her man as best she could. She did her own housework, which in practice meant she took responsibility for not doing it. She was bored with brooms and mops and laundry, and vacuum cleaners frightened her—something to do with the noise they made. Once a week she'd smuggle in a local wetback to do a wild cleaning job and then accept credit for it at the end of the day by being too exhausted to cook. Ma was no better as a cook than as a cleaner. She didn't have the patience for cookbooks and never read the directions on the side of anything.

Met in a roadhouse on the highway between Barrington and Des Plaines, where he had a job as the traffic manager for a small trucking company, Handsome Tommy was a most jovial drinking pal. In those bleak, dark, chilly taverns that smelled of hops, he was appreciated as a gentleman who was never high-hat. Tommy remained neat in his decline, though his expression was emptier and his collars and cuffs became frayed. The shirts were always washed but finally the only way he could hide their loose threads was by taking the scissors to them. He was cheerful in the morning when he left the house, his linen newly mown, but more and more

often maudlin when he arrived home at night. Ma didn't help.
He'd walk in the door and Ma would take one look at him and
announce, "You've been drinking." They became characters in a
two-reel comedy, Edgar Kennedy and Florence Rice. After a
while, "You've been drinking" was not an accusation but the perfunctory signal that started the night's revels. Sometimes he'd
laugh at Ma and pussyfoot around the kitchen, patting her ass,
throwing an arm around her shoulder, kissing the nape of her
neck, persuading her to join him in a quick one before dinner.
More often he'd look wounded or become sullen. Sometimes he'd
stalk out of the house saying that we needed toothpaste, which
meant that we wouldn't see him for the rest of the evening. On
special gala nights toward the end he'd cry at the dinner table and
tell us how at his office that day he'd gotten down on his knees and
prayed to God for His help. As if to certify the truth of the story
he'd slide halfway off his chair, one knee on the floor, to demonstrate the manner in which, during office hours, he approached
God. Tom, who sat on his right, would look away in anger and
embarrassment. Ma's lower lip would tremble. Me? I wept right
along with the drunken bum though I didn't believe a word he
said. When Ma finally decided she could no longer share Our
Father's bed, Tom and I were moved into their room while Ma
took Tom's and Our Father took mine. It was little more than a
matter of switching clothes from one closet to another for the rest
of us. For Tom it was an eviction.

It was a remarkably ugly room with shiny black woodwork and
old wallpaper of yellow leaves against a background of brown tree
trunks. The front windows faced the street and into a vacant lot
that became an empty country field beyond. A window at the side
overlooked our yard. The furniture included a double bed that
had once belonged to Lockie and Boo, two dressers and two upright chairs of the sort one might find in the waiting room of a
charity hospital.

When we first moved to Barrington, Tom had spent long
hours fixing his room to look like his idea of the all-American
boy's den. He mounted his .22 rifle, his shotgun and his fishing

rods on wall brackets. He built bookcases and a display case for the flies Our Father had taught him to make and which were objects of delicate beauty—small lethal hooks that, with bits of brightly colored pheasant and mallard feather, were disguised as insects of fantasy. He had a stuffed raccoon, a scale model of the *Santa Maria*, two scale models of the *Spirit of St. Louis*, his midget polo mallet, a baseball mitt, two baseball bats (one autographed by Babe Ruth), a football that he rubbed regularly with Needsfoot oil, a tennis racquet and a press, two golf clubs—a driver and a putter—a complete set of Hardy Boys books, Admiral Byrd's *To the Pole with Byrd*, two books about Lindbergh as well as a framed autographed picture, several books by Richard Halliburton, a stack of back issues of *Popular Mechanics* and *Boys Life*, a pair of semaphore flags, a shortwave radio he'd made and a directory of call letters of ham operators with whom he corresponded, a set of barbells, a Boy Scout manual, books on how to teach oneself semaphore, the Morse Code, backgammon, good manners, chess, golf, as well as several inspirational books including one titled *Make Each Day Work for You*, from which he got the idea of setting daily schedules for himself.

If we were alone—if none of his friends was around—he could be kind and generous with those possessions. At that time he would share his knowledge with me. He attempted to interest me in barbells and baseball, though I was hopelessly inattentive, and he would take me with him on hikes into the country where we would cook lunch over a campfire with an official five-piece Boy Scout cooking kit. Mostly we ate baked beans but our favorite lunch consisted entirely of bacon. A pound split two ways. Once when Tom had forgotten to bring matches and failed to strike a spark with a flint mechanism—a camper's companion purchased from Dan Beard—we attempted to eat the bacon raw. Tom said he liked raw bacon almost as much as cooked bacon, but we both gave up after one bite and a long, greasy chew. Instead of taking the uncooked bacon home, we buried it, evidence of failure in which we were allied but which also separated us. When Benny Popp or any of Tom's other classmates were at the house he ignored me, called me creep, told me to get lost and, to make sure I wouldn't disturb them, he'd lock his door. He came to lock his door more and more frequently as time went on and was the only person in the house to sleep with his door shut tight.

When Ma decided to switch our sleeping arrangements, Tom gave up on that house. He carefully dismantled his old room but he never got around to putting the things up or away in our new room. For almost two years the guns, fishing rods, books, raccoon, shortwave radio and all the other paraphernalia that once he'd cherished, and which defined his life, remained standing in corners or stacked against walls. After several nights of attempting to sleep in the double bed with me he took to sleeping in his sleeping bag on the other side of the room. Each night he'd methodically unroll it and each morning as methodically roll it up and put it away. My feelings were mixed. I was furious but fascinated.

In addition to growing up—growing very muscular as well as very tall—Tom had shot through puberty when I wasn't looking. Puberty was something I wasn't at all sure about then. I was shocked and jealous the first night we shared the double bed and, even though he'd turned off the light for modesty's sake, I could see that he'd become a reasonable facsimile of a man. At that point I hadn't begun to grow at all. A bit of tantalizing fuzz but that was all. Suddenly there was Tom, struggling to get out of his clothes and into his pajamas as quickly as possible, exposing briefly to my wonder a fully developed, obviously operable cock lolling over a pair of balls as big as the Ritz. This was not the first time we'd shared a bed. We'd done so often in the past, usually when on motor trips or when staying with Lockie and Boo. Now it had become for me a rather different experience. It was a cold night and several minutes after Tom had crawled under the covers, I, with my back turned to him, stretched out my legs looking for his feet—a way we'd slept before. I found one foot, colder than mine since he'd just gotten into bed, and bracketed it with my two warm ones. The affair was short-lived. As violently as he could he kicked me away, whispering, "Stay on your own side, creep."

A lot of things went into that fatal stew, among them the absolute end of Tom's privacy.

. . .

Our Father's drinking got worse. There was a drunk-driving arrest that in Lake Forest would have been funny and in Barrington was a disgrace. One night he brought home two new roadhouse friends who looked like Maggie and Jiggs and to whom he bragged boozily about Tom's skills on the football field in front of Tom, who told Our Father to shut up, that he was drunk. There was the disastrous summer evening when I was not yet eleven and Tom was fifteen, an evening like so many others that seemed to start out well and then to disintegrate for reasons no one could any longer control. Our Father did not appear to have been drinking when he arrived home and Ma, thus encouraged by the memory of the old Tommy, decided to dress for dinner. By the time she came downstairs, though, Our Father, having been slurping the gin from a bottle in the kitchen, was quite quickly pissed, which prompted Ma to wonder where all the gin had gone since, she said, she'd been looking forward to a martini before dinner, which, in turn, prompted Tommy to become sullen and then, rare for him, sarcastic.

To backtrack a moment: Boo had died that spring, leaving large bequests to Columbia University, the University of Illinois, Johns Hopkins, St. Luke's Hospital and the Moody Bible Institute, with smaller amounts to smaller purposes. The bulk of the estate went to Lockie who, Boo said at some length in his will, would make the proper decisions relating to his daughter and grandsons. Trust funds had already been set up for the three of us, but the interest was to go back into each fund until such moment as Lockie thought it proper to turn the funds over to us. Because Boo had gone to great pains to make sure that Our Father would not benefit, the subject of Boo was one Our Father couldn't stay away from once he was on the sauce.

We sat in edgy truce at the dinner table. Ma was looking worried and sad in a way she knew to be most becoming. Tom concentrated on his plate, picking at his food as if he suspected it had been sprinkled with ground glass. Our Father, who was drunk, looked healthy as usual but his gestures were elaborately refined in a way that had nothing to do with Tommy sober. Because Ma and Tom avoided Our Father's eye as he talked, he talked to me. The way Tom lifted weights, played football and read self-improve-ment books, I worked from an early age to meet an eye with an eye. I'm not the sort to glance away from a drunk, which would be to admit that a bleary eye can penetrate the soul, can enter to do damage to it. To others', perhaps, not to mine.

Silence.

Our Mother (to no one in particular): "I had a letter from Lockie today. She's taken a house in Florence for October."

Tom: "When's she coming home?"

Our Mother: "She hasn't made up her mind. She's with Elsie Mendl."

Me: "Who's Elsie Mendl?"

Our Father (to me): "A sponger."

Our Mother: "She's not a sponger. She's Lockie's oldest friend."

Our Father: "She's Lockie's oldest friend as long as Lockie pays the bills."

Our Mother (to me): "That's not true. Besides, your grandfather wasn't made of money."

Our Father (to me): "Of course. I forgot. I never remember how poor your grandfather was, but he worked hard and he saved his pennies so he could put a little something aside for Lockie. Lockie won't have to go on relief, not right away. . . ." (He starts to laugh) "Lockie . . . on relief . . . what a sight. . . ." (He picks up his napkin to dab at his eyes as if the image of Lockie on the dole were the funniest thing he'd ever thought of.)

Tom (to Our Mother): "What's so funny?"

Our Mother (carefully, as if she might get a belt to the jaw): "I haven't any idea."

Our Father (to me): "Your grandfather was a stingy old fart."

Our Mother (genuinely shocked): "Tommy!" Fart was not a word that had ever before been used by Our Father in my hearing.

Our Father (to Our Mother): "He *was* a stingy old fart. FART."

Our Mother's eyes fill with tears.

Tom (to Our Father): "Don't use that kind of language to my mother."

Our Father (sweetly): "I'll use any kind of language I want to your mother."

Tom: "No, you won't."

Our Father (surprised, amused): "It's my house. Your mother is my wife. I'll say anything I want. . . ." (He thinks, searching for a word guaranteed to insult the assembled crew) "Turd!"

Tom: "Shut your filthy mouth."

Our Father (still amused): "Who's going to make me?"

Tom: "I will."

Our Father: "You and who else?"

Tom (suddenly uneasy but nevertheless resolute): "I don't need any help."

Our Father (takes out his wallet and puts $5 on the table): "That says you can't."

Our Mother (to Tom): "Don't listen to him. He's drunk."

Tom (glaring at Our Father): "I don't care if he's drunk or not. He's got to be taught a lesson. . . ."

Our Mother rises from the table and beats a quick exit upstairs.

Our Father rises from the table and he seems to be smiling, listening to something that we can't hear. He folds his double damask dinner napkin with more precision than is necessary, blinks, and turns a fond eye on the furious Tom. I follow them out to the side yard and watch what happens with no more sense of involvement than I would had I witnessed the event from the window of a passing train. Our Father moves as if making his way through shoulder-high grass. First he takes off his tie, hangs it over the back of a lawn chair, then removes his jacket. He rolls up his shirtsleeves to expose white forearms that are in contrast to Tom's deep tan as he pulls his polo shirt over his head. Our Father is taller, a little heavier around the middle, than Tom, but not much. In the twilight the two could be twins, or one real figure and one mirror image. Which was which?

Our Father steps back from Tom, extends his hand as if to shake. The gesture is the starting bell. Tom explodes with movement. He slaps aside Our Father's hand and rolls into the older man like a thrashing machine. Our Father stands in focus in the center of a cartoon blur of fists as Tom dances in, out and around him in imitation of a professional boxer. Everything is an exaggeration. Tom feints from blows never initiated. Tom's attack appears to have the effect of keeping Our Father upright. Our Father's nose begins to bleed. There is a gash on his forehead. A lip is sliced. He seems so completely surprised he registers no pain or anger. Then Our Father rouses himself to give Tom one tremendous punch in the stomach. It sounds as if a pillow had been swatted. Tom sways from side to side and begins to double up. Our Father, without the supportive assaults, drops slowly to his knees. Tom tries to hit him again but he's winded. As Our Father goes down he reaches out, clutches Tom's arms and pulls Tom down on top of him. They look as if they are embracing. They alternately flail at each other and hold on, wanting more. Once on the ground Our Father finds new strength. He pounds Tom's kidneys with his fists. Lovingly. They are moaning. The stabs become shorter. The tempo increases, the pain delirious. Then, abruptly, they are spent. Tom rolls off Our Father and away from him, blood and tears smeared on his face and chest. Tom is crying. Our Father is silent. For a few moments Tom lies in a fetal position on his side. Then with decision he picks himself up, grabs his polo shirt and staggers toward the house, yelling back at Our Father between hiccups and sobs, "I hate you, you goddamn dirty drunken shiteater. One day I'll kill you."

Tom had no serious injuries. Our Father's nose and one rib were broken.

9

It's hopeless. I'm fed up with the Pittsburgh-born New York stockbroker who now says we can have Wicheley for two million. Two million! I told Jimmy to tell him to stick it up his ass. One-point-seven-five is our bid and what he was originally asking. The bastard. I'm also fed up with Jackie. She has no business being away this long. Nearly a month. She's a thoughtless, self-absorbed bitch but I suppose I shouldn't be surprised. I should have known I couldn't depend on her. She's been asking for trouble for months. To abandon a topic when both parties are in complete agreement and, instead, to fix on another, preferably related topic on which there are age-old differences—this must be one of the sèven danger signals of coming apart. It's typical of the sort of thing she's been doing recently.

The Sunday night of the Israeli raid at Entebbe, after we'd spent a dreary afternoon at a rock concert in the Village where everyone tapped his toe except me and a Vietnam veteran (who tapped his crutch), I was anxious to see how television covered the story which, to me and I know to Jackie, seemed to be the first encouraging thing that had happened in the world in years. At the end of one news report I said, "Israel's finest hour," or some such thing not in character. I found it fine, old-fashioned fiction of the most invigorating sort. In this single act the lunatic Amin, who'd been a friend and protector to Baby Pru, had suddenly been reduced to his true proportions and the Arab extremists had been shown that hijacking needn't always succeed.

Jackie (frostily): "What's this concern for Israel all of a sudden?" Me: "What's that supposed to mean?" Jackie (watching a bleach commercial as if it were Olivier in *Uncle Vanya*): "That's the first decent thing you've ever said about Israel." Long pause. We study a pretty, artificial-looking black girl solemnly describing the details of a drug bust in spic Harlem. Me: "Wait a minute. . . ." Jackie (angrily): "I really think you're an anti-Semite . . . the worst kind." Me: "Oh, shit. . . ." We've been over this ground with increasing frequency in the last several years. Me (patiently): "I'm not an anti-Semite." Then I add with a stroke of the old Marshall Lewis Henderson adolescent genius, "For Christ's sake, Higgenbotham was Jewish." Jackie (pointedly looking at the TV screen, which she obviously can't see in her rage): "Higgenbotham is hardly a very Jewish name." Me: "So are Burke, Douglas, Curtis or Reade Jewish names? Her grandfather changed it when he came to this country." Higgenbotham was no more Jewish than Marian Anderson but I figured she owed me something after all these years. Jackie: "You've always been anti-Semitic. You didn't want to go to Israel that time. . . ." As is her way Jackie has now successfully fused two entirely different subjects, bigotry and travel. Me: "I didn't want to go to Israel that time because I had no particular interest in going to what I anticipated to be a sort of serious Atlantic City, or maybe a kind of giant United States industrial fair, a place made out of samples." Jackie: "Fuck you." Me: "Your Israeli roots, darling, are about as deep as my Chinese roots, probably not as deep. Don't we all owe something to the Peking Man? You may be Jewish but you have about as much Semitic blood in you as that goddamned cat." Jackie: "Jesus, you can be a shit sometimes. . . ." Me: "What's being a shit about that? It's true." Jackie: "It's not what Israel is, it's what it stands for." Me: "What it stands for scares the hell out of me." Jackie: "Meaning exactly what?" Me: "Meaning that it's a fabricated state, created in guilt and sentimentality, and absolutely guaranteed to bring disaster to the world." Jackie: "You wouldn't mind if the Arabs overran it tomorrow." Me (masterfully controlling my impatience): "Of course I would. I'm perfectly aware that we can't let that happen now. We've gone too far. We've made too many commitments, but that still doesn't make me happy about the circumstances that led us to this position. Christ Almighty, Jackie, I don't know anybody who can be more anti-Semitic than you. All those dumb jokes about Miami Beach and mink stoles and people in the garment industry. My God." Jackie (steadily): "I've resolved those conflicts." Me: "Bullshit. You just pay that quack fifty bucks an hour to tell you it's all right. Give me the fifty bucks, I'll do the same thing. . . ."

That night as we go to sleep in our usual position, Jackie on her right side facing away from me, me, on my right side relating to her spoon-fashion, my left hand holding her left tit, her left arm pressing my arm in place, I wonder if she's right. May I be not only anti-Semitic but also anti-black, anti-Catholic, anti-Irish, anti-English, anti-French, Italian, Polish, Chinese, Indian (American and East), anti-poor, anti-deprived, anti-talented, untalented, anti-believers, unbelievers, anti-everyone, in fact, who is not me? And, as the joke goes, I'm not sure about me.

10

That fatal night in June 1935, two nights before Ma and Our Father and Tom and I were to drive to Harbor Point to spend a vacation with Lockie:

It had been an unspectacular evening, no scenes. Tom had had the use of the car to have one last date with Molly, the Barrington High cheerleader with the pendulous breasts whose brains he had been fucking out, I now suspect, for the year they'd been going steady. They were both physical culture nuts of the sort that would regard fucking as exercise, next to cleanliness and then godliness. Bores.

After supper I went upstairs about eight, lay on the bed with *A Tale of Two Cities* and read selected passages dealing with Sidney Carton's sacrifice on behalf of the happiness of Lucie Manette, something I once found extremely erotic. The vision of the heroic Sidney giving himself up to the guillotine, putting his neck in the bloody slot, thinking about the far, far better thing he was doing, excited me at that time of my life as much as did the pictures of the Watusis in a book we had about Stanley and Livingston. Though I was experimenting conscientiously every day, I hadn't yet had an orgasmic emission and, indeed, had no hints that such a thing was possible, much less on its way and no more than a few days off. Perhaps decapitation equaled circumcision, a barbaric rite whose victims included Tom and me and Our Father. It's an indication of the manner in which I was raised that in the shower room of the Barrington public school a few years earlier, when I noticed for the first time that the head of my nine-year-old tool looked different from all of the others, I attributed it to my higher social caste. There were times years later when I was to feel ignominious and deprived by the action of the knife that forever separated me from my foreskin, a practice I believe now to be just more medical quackery. Alas, where is your foreskin now, poor Marshall? Had I been spared would I have been dramatically hooded like Philo Lumberton, the St. Matthew's tattoo artist-and-model whose cock looked like a rubber sledgehammer? Would my prick, like Deke Crozier's, have ended in a long twist of skin that extended at least an inch beyond the actual head, suggesting a croissant? Or would it have been an idealized dong like the one on Michelangelo's David, the cap hanging over but not obscuring the perfectly sculptured corona? It's one of those things I will never know but I've always found it difficult to accept the unalterable, the act that cannot somehow be reversed with love or money.

After becoming aroused over Sidney Carton's bloody fate, I inventoried the books, writing materials and clothes I was to pack for the journey to northern Michigan. This also provided me the opportunity to try on the PAL jock strap (size, small) I'd bought the day before at Puhlmann's Pharmacy, feeling as guilty as someone purchasing a surgical truss, which, when I was not much younger, I assumed to be some sort of appliance necessary to the satisfactory completion of a sex act. The trying on of the jock strap was not erotic at all. It brought forth only longing. The jock strap still didn't have anything to do. I was growing tall very quickly but I was still underdeveloped in every other direction. Unless I stimulated myself, the jock strap hung off me in folds, looking uninhabited by anything except a package of Spearmint chewing gum. On the beach at Harbor Point, or at the Little Harbor Club pool, my two-year-old swimming trunks were still capable of providing all the cover and support I needed. There was no danger of my shocking old ladies with the inadvertent exposure of my privates. I knew the anguish of the 90-pound weakling, which is just that much worse for an 80-pound one.

Having turned off the light at nine I was awakened sometime later by the voices of Ma and my father yelling at each other downstairs. It was the uneven tempo and the abrupt changes in mood as much as the near out-of-control tempers that scared me. There would be a rush of overlapping words, then a sudden pause, quiet, followed by something that could either be laughter or tears. This was not unusual when they were drinking together in that terrible house, and it had been happening more and more frequently since Tom had begun his courtship of Molly. Occasionally that night I made out parts of sentences: ". . . will *not*!" ". . . will *too*!" "*You* say *I* . . ." ". . . *not* stop. . . ." Then, perhaps, a crash against furniture. My father, as far as I know, never beat Ma, though there were sometimes slaps. More often the slaps were one or the other slapping his knee or the table or throwing down a magazine to score an important point such as "You stink!" Neither of them had a vocabulary of any richness. They insulted each other in single syllables. What they were fighting about, I couldn't tell. They seemed to have forgotten the issues and were volleying random grievances and challenges.

For a few minutes I pulled the pillow over my head, but I could still hear them through the down. At times one or the other seemed to be laughing but this only magnified the bitterness of the later assaults. Again, as I often did in those days, I thought of running away. I had run away one night the preceding fall and was gone four hours, but when I returned I realized that no one had known I was gone. The argument went on downstairs. Finally I threw off the pillow and got out of bed. When Tom was not there I always left the door to the hall open so there would be light. Now I went over to close the door, at the same time closing my ears to what I then could have heard more clearly. I no longer wanted to know what they were saying. I shut the door with a caution that was unnecessary since the last thing either of them was concerned about at that moment was me or what I was up to. I walked to the open window by the bed. It was a large window, the sill only a foot from the floor so that when I stood in front of it and bowed at the waist, my forehead rested on the screen. Little by little I relaxed, my hands at my sides. I could not use my hands. No matter what happened the hands had to stay at the sides. That was the point. I allowed more and more of my weight to be brought to bear against the screen at the place where my forehead joined it. Like all the screens in that house, some of which had partially rusted away, this one was very old and smelled of metal erosion and dust. The screens of that house remained in place year-around. They'd been frozen in snow and baked in the sun, poked at in places with pencils by generations of children. The fight continued below but I had no more interest in it. I concentrated on what I was doing. I increased the pressure. There seemed to be a slight promising give. More pressure, more give. Any minute the screen would fall out and I, in turn, would go hurtling to the ground after it, landing on my head. They might not notice if I ran away but they couldn't easily ignore a body on the lawn. People would talk. Poor dear Marshall, dead at such an early age. What did we do? Where did we go wrong? Suddenly their grief so frightened me that I straightened up, scared out of my wits. I might have fallen out the goddamn window! I ran my hand around the screen's bowl-shaped section that had been created by my once- or twice-a-week games of windowsill roulette and went sheepishly back to bed. The armies below appeared to have declared a truce. In the new quiet I fell immediately to sleep.

The next time I woke it seemed very late. The combatants were now three, Our Father, Our Mother and Tom, with Our Father and Tom's voices doing most of the arguing while Our Mother provided a back-up chorus consisting of wailing strings of "No . . . no . . . no" or "Please . . . please . . . please," as Tom and Our Father had begun to spar, to push each other around, bumping into a table here, jostling a lamp there. The sound of feet moving around was a prelude to serious scuffling. It was apparent that Tom had failed to make curfew by many hours and that Our Father had pronounced a humiliating sentence that Tom was unwilling to accept without a fight. When I heard Tom use the word "shiteater" I think I knew what must happen. There was no going back, no chance for repair. Shiteater was the code word for irrevocable end.

How much do I know? How much did I see? Was I aware when the fighting stopped? I'm not sure, though I don't understand how I could have fallen back to sleep in the midst of the uproar. A riot was taking place on the first floor, a first-class family insurrection. Yet I did go back to sleep. Could I have willed myself to sleep to escape? That's conceivable, I suppose, but it had never happened before and it never happened again. I try to reconstruct that night, if not to alter the unalterable then to catch the past, to trap it, afterward to stuff it, mount it and put it away on a shelf. The truth is that even though I don't remember, I saw and heard everything. I was a major participant. This is what I see:

There is unexpected light as Tom enters the room not bothering to close the door as he usually does. He wears the pale blue polo shirt that is too small for him and pulls away from his pants at the back. His face is puffy from crying. He moves around the room decisively. He goes to the closet, fetches something from the top shelf. This is followed by the purposeful slick-slack, slick-slack sounds I still hear with a kind of thrill, not with my ears but in the pit of my stomach. He has put two shells into the barrels of the shotgun. For a long time he sits on the far side of the room in the charity hospital chair, holding the shotgun in both hands, its butt resting on the floor, the barrels pointing toward the ceiling. He stares out the open window into the darkness of the empty lot and the field beyond. He does not move. What is he thinking? Could anyone reconstruct those moments in that fragile head? Sometimes I suspect that I've put them away in my head but where I don't know. At one point, holding the gun in his left hand, he leans over and takes off his right shoe—a sneaker with knotted lacings—and right sock. He has decided to go to bed. But he straightens up and does not take off his left shoe. One shoe off, one shoe on. He sits for a very long time weeping. Then the tears stop. There are no more. Everything has dried up, run out, drained away. He never looks at me. He sees nothing in that room. Finally, with the most patient care, he slides the butt of the gun away from him, drawing the barrels toward his face and, in his only awkward gesture, an obscene one to the outsider, he attempts to put both barrels into his mouth. He closes his eyes and opens his mouth as wide as he can, maneuvering his right big toe to the triggers. He works earnestly. It's a more difficult task than one might think.

The explosions that blow brains, skull, blood and hair over the wall and part of the ceiling lift me out of bed and set me down in the hall. It's as if I'd been sprayed again with someone's vomit, but there is no sickly sweet smell this time. Only the elemental odor of gunpowder.

11

It was the night of the day of Tom's funeral in Lake Forest, in Lockie's house in the guest room she always called my room, the one with the four original Lautrec drawings (one of which I was later to give Jackie), that my fancy fiddling came to a climax in the most mysterious, most delicious of physical sensations that a man can know, accompanied by a not insubstantial emission of what, over the years, I've called variously come, cream, wad, semen, load, gizum (gisum), ejaculum, spunk, it, sperm, juice—depending on the age, nationality, sex, language, class and pleasure preferences of my partner or partners, as the case may have been. Never have I used the word "scum," which would be to debase everything. Which reminds me of the malodorous Gordon Felix, youngest son of Osgood, the dreamer who lived to make his dream come true with the help of that great tax-free charitable trust which also financed little Gordon, and made his dreams come true, and often. I might have called Gordon Felix "scum" from time to time, but only in the sense that he could be said to be among the offscourings of a rotted civilization. I don't know why I'm so negative about him. If it hadn't been for Gordon Felix I would never have pursued my illusive Gethsemane with such determination, bringing her to earth, so to speak, in the shadow of my church.

In the weeks immediately following Tom's accident, which is what everyone called it, including the Cook County coroner who found that Tom had been cleaning his gun with his right foot in the middle of the night, my mother and father and I lived together in exhausted peace. We never moved back to the death house. A week after the suicide Lockie, my mother and I, and a woman who worked as Lockie's secretary from time to time, were driven out to Barrington by Garrett, where Ma went through the house, room by room, telling the secretary what to have moved to Lake

Forest, what to put into storage and what to dump. Tom's and my room had been rewallpapered in a neutral, nonrepresentational pattern of blue and green lines, horizontals against perpendiculars, and the woodwork repainted black. When I was left alone I inspected the place where he had done it and found marks on the floor and rug that I took to be the bleached remains of brainstains. I was already beginning to have dreams about Tom's not being dead. In one of a typical type I am talking to a boy who doesn't look at all like Tom though I always know he is, which makes me furious. Why has he changed so much? Is it a disguise? Does he think it's funny? But he is distracted. He refuses to talk to me though he listens to what I say. Our parents have been sick with sorrow, I say, but everything will be all right when they see that he's alive. They won't punish him, being so relieved to have him home. There'll be no more fights. The important thing is that he return. He seems ill, as if he'd been living on Skid Row—ill and experienced in things I cannot imagine. Also sullen, bored. He turns and walks away.

That summer Lockie coped and dealt. She'd always been a good old dame but after the death of Boo she became truly grand. My father was right: Boo was a stingy old fart. Unlike Lockie he was without humor or compassion, with no gift whatsoever for acting on impulse, for being extravagant, for changing horses in midstream no matter how foolish it looked or what people might say. We spent that entire summer with Lockie at her cottage on the Point. It was—is—a piece of extraordinary architecture, a midwestern Gothic pile made out of what look to be matchsticks. Imperfectly octagonal, surrounded by open galleries with views of both Lake Michigan and Little Traverse Bay, nineteen rooms that include separate rooms for cards and billiards, eight bedrooms, sleeping porches, in each bedroom a marble-covered commode containing a pisspot.

Topping the house is an elegant gingerbread tower four stories high where I spent my afternoons masturbating successfully, measuring myself, reading long, elevating articles on Albigenses, Aristotle, Aristoxenus of Tarentum, Arithmetic, Arizona and Aviation in my new *Encyclopaedia Britannica*. The day after Tom's death Lockie had asked me what I might like to have more than anything else in the world. I told her and it was delivered a week later and, in spite of its bulk, it traveled to Harbor Point with us. It was a kind of not-going-away present, a prize for my having let it be him, not me. The gift, of course, intensified my guilt at being alive, a failed defenestrator. If I'd gone out, Tom could have stayed in.

For some time I thought that my mother and father would never get over the finality of that night. My mother cried several times a day at the least reminder of Tom. My father was withdrawn. Several times he tried to talk to me as, I suppose, he thought a father should, but the conversation always drifted into silence. We shared no common interests we could talk about at length. Many of my parents' old friends were at the Point that summer and gradually, I could see, my father was recouping his former, pre-Fall self-assurance. Tom's suicide had somehow given Our Father a clean slate. He drank normally. Every day he went sailing or fishing or played golf or tennis. Once he went over to Charlevoix to play in a polo match and though he was full of it when he came back, I doubt whether he ever again played polo. At first Lockie treated him politely, then kindly, then as if he were a possible suitor. My mother, too, appeared to be successfully navigating her sea of sorrow, dolorosa. I was too involved with sexual research and experimentation to notice that the ghost that had made a couple of passes at each of them had taken up residence in me. My first wife, the socially ambitious, money-obsessed Higgenbotham, once turned on me when, deep in a depression I couldn't shake, I cut short our six-month stay in Paris to return to New York. "My God," she said, "what's so special about a brother who committed suicide? Plenty of people have survived worse. I'm sick of you and him." She settled for a quarter of a mill. Her successor, Miss Utah, hit the jackpot, though, and the one thing that made that bearable was knowing that Higgenbotham would shit bricks when she read about it. Utah, an unsuccessful candidate at Atlantic City, might have become Miss America had they asked her to demonstrate her vaginal talents instead of allowing her to sing Verdi. What a gorgeous woman! But she had habits that eventually drove me out of my mind, like shaving her pussy, something she thought was hygenic, probably because she'd once had a bad case of crabs. It was a menace, not to say unsexy. I always wondered what would happen if she went for a month without a razor. It would be to walk through a briar patch, one's most tender membranes exposed, to reach the fountain of youth. Probably not worth it. It was when the second Mrs. Marshall Lewis Henderson asked for, and received, one million that Ma, by that time the keeper of the exchequer, put me on an allowance of sorts. We couldn't both be running around marrying our money away.

It turned out that a lot of top-level, highly sensitive diplomacy was going on that July and August though I, in my gingerbread tower, was oblivious to it until the contents of several treaties were announced by Ma at a press conference for one, held on the gallery overlooking Little Traverse Bay at eventide. I was summoned by one of Lockie's Red Indian retainers who, dressed in a French maid's uniform (black dress, white lace collars and cuffs and headpiece) resembled W. C. Fields in a revue sketch. " . . . Motha wach yuh," the savage said, and disappeared in her black brogans, clomping noisily down the hall, having lost the knack for stealth enjoyed by her foremothers. She also left the bedroom door open, which had come to irritate me greatly. It was not this maid but one of the younger ones, one of the ones who were in their late forties who, when everyone was out for the afternoon or taking naps, would sneak up to my tower and peek at me as I was reading about language families or glass-blowing, at the same time working myself up to a healthy spend. She was no Pocahontas, more like Old Nikomis, but I would have given one mill to throw a fast one to her. At the age of twelve one can find almost anything erotic. I didn't know then how to operate. I did nothing but show off and afterward she would sneak carefully back down the stairs. Nothing was ever said, nor were glances exchanged if she were serving at table. It was another interim deal.

Ma's news didn't really surprise me and at the time I thought I felt nothing. She and my father had agreed to divorce. She would be going to Reno in the fall and I would be going to St. Paul's, which was where my father had gone. She planned to take an apartment in town (Chicago) and, if we liked, we could spend our weekends in Lake Forest with Lockie when I was home on vacation. My father had decided to move to New York where a friend of Lockie's had offered him a job in a firm there, which meant, I now suspect, that Lockie was settling a sizable amount of loot on him, not to buy him off but to give Handsome Tommy a Second Chance. I think the only question I asked Ma was whether I could take my *Britannica* with me to St. Paul's. Subsequently there was some serious correspondence on this point, which was resolved (though not to my satisfaction) when we were informed that St. Paul's had its own. Ultimately I had to give in but only after being as cleverly unreasonable as I could for as long as possible. I like my books. I'm comforted by their ownership if not their contents.

My father joined us on the gallery on a wicker swing. He was wearing white ducks and a dark blue blazer and seemed confident if a bit shy in his good health, general well-being and the good looks I would never have. With my father sitting on my right and my mother on my left, we rocked slowly back and forth in reedy self-consciousness. My mother, I recognized with a shock, was no longer in mourning, which in practice had meant favoring white, though white in summer is not all that mournful. She was in a pale yellow evening dress I'd never seen before and she was wearing her engagement ring and matching clip of rubies, sapphires, emeralds and diamonds that she'd not worn in Barrington in the last year. Ma's nose is a bit long and pointy, as is mine, and her mouth close to being bee-stung even when she isn't shaping it with lipstick, but the Modigliani look suits her when she's pulled together, as she was then. In the distance I could hear my father getting off a good one like "You stink!" and Ma's answering as quick as you please, "I stink?"

I touched her engagement ring and asked why she was wearing it under the circumstances. She smiled and looked at my father. "Because it is beautiful and I like it, and because your father gave it to me and because I love him very much." She took my left hand in her left hand, which was becoming very small next to mine, though they were almost the same hand. The same make, different models. I examined the ring that had hypnotized me as a baby. She put her right arm across the back of the swing and I realized that my mother and my father were holding hands. For no reason I could explain—I was scarcely sentimental at that point in history—I put my free hand on my father's leg and, after apparent consideration, he placed his hand over it. What I felt through this joining of hands was my own grief. It was pervasive and dull and, I realized, something that I was going to be living with forever. We rocked some more. My father finally spoke of St. Paul's, using the excuse to take his hand from mine, telling me about a place where the boys had bought beer in his day, what the campus was like, about weekends I would spend with him in New York, though, in fact, when I got to St. Paul's and called him several times, he'd always made plans to spend the weekend somewhere else.

Lockie came onto the gallery looking rather more like a fairy godmother than most of the other grannies on the Point were likely to look that summer, all in white, loaded with diamonds that hadn't been allowed out of the vault when Boo was alive, her white hair spun like cotton candy on top of her head. She was a tiny woman who believed that chic was as basic as good manners, like having clean fingernails. "Well," she said, "isn't it nice to be all together?" My father started to get up but she motioned him to keep his seat while she sat opposite us in a wicker chair that was her favorite throne. She took a cigarette from her purse and lit it quickly with a silver lighter she also carried with her. She smoked in a manner unlike that of anyone else I've ever seen, puckering her lips and approaching the cigarette as if to meet it halfway. She had started to smoke in public only after Boo's death.

"Have you told Marshall?" she asked my mother. "Yes." "And what does Marshall think?" This directed to me. I shrugged. "You'll like Andover, Marshall." "St. Paul's," said my mother. "Oh, yes," said Lockie. Puff, puff. "Which reminds me, Mary, what's the name of that old beau of yours from Lewis's Landing?" "David Devereaux." Lockie: "You know, of course, he's the headmaster of St. Matthew's now. What's his wife's name?" My mother: "Odile." Lockie: "Yes, well, originally from Tallahassee, I believe." My mother: "Montgomery." Lockie: "I never liked her much . . ." (To my father) "Sort of sluttish, Tommy, if you know what I mean. . . ." (To my mother) "Did you ever think of sending Marshall to St. Matthew's?" My mother: "Not really. Tommy went to St. Paul's. I always thought both boys would go to St. Paul's some day." Lockie (puff, puff): "Might be good for Marshall to spend some time in the county . . . get to know his kin. . . ." Me: "I know Lewis's Landing, Grandmother. You took me the first time. . . ." Everyone is looking at me as if I'd farted. Lockie: "Why did you just call me 'Grandmother' then, Marshall? You've never called me 'Grandmother' before in your entire life." My mother (to me): "Lockie is your name, darling. It's the name you made up when you couldn't say 'Grandmother' or 'Granny.' " Lockie (puff, puff): "It wasn't Marshall, Mary. It was Tom . . ." (puff) "I thought Tom was going to have a speech defect." My mother: "Oh, Mother, really. . . ." I steal a quick look at Ma, whose lower jaw is exhibiting a tremor. Lockie: "I didn't say he had one, just that I was afraid he'd develop one. . . . My, he was a beautiful child. . . ." I glance at Ma again. She has tears in her eyes. She stares straight ahead, working the lower jaw ever so slightly. My father says nothing. A cabin cruiser entering the Harbor Springs marina sounds its horn and Lockie turns in her chair to look, squinting her eyes. I say nothing. Nor does Tom.

12

My first approach to Gethsemane was through humor, through jokes I made up myself. Between gulps from a bottle of lukewarm Royal Crown Cola and bites from a stale Mr. Goodbar, I ask, "Do you know why the common housefly makes such an unsatisfactory pet?" She is reading a movie magazine spread out on the counter. Behind her are shelves containing boxes of corn meal, canned goods, Fel's naptha soap. Above her head is a display of fly swatters and at her elbow stands a punch-out lottery card ("Prizes! Jokes! Discounts!") with nothing more to be punched out. The bill of her New York Yankees baseball cap, which has been obscuring the upper part of her face, rises like a curtain. Could this great ebon head have once been Sheba's? "What did you say?" "Do you know why the common housefly is no good as a pet?" "What kind of a pet?" "Like a dog or a cat." "No," she says, and the curtain descends as she goes back to the study of the movie magazine. "Because," I say, "they have a life span of no more than five days and it takes two weeks to housebreak them." She shakes her head at the hopelessness of my case, and I, for a moment, have to agree.

I've read that Baby Pru has given up his Ugandan passport and that he and his black South African wife have taken up temporary residence in Cairo, at Shepheard's, where his wife has a six-week nightclub engagement.

Unknown to Jackie I once kept a Prud'homme Shackleford scrapbook. When the boy's name began to appear in print I cut out the stories and filed them in my desk until, sometime in the mid-sixties, I had such a batch of clippings that I asked Tiffany's to send me something suitable in the way of a Morocco-bound loose-leaf scrapbook, which is now in my steamer trunk. The first stories about Pru appeared in 1960 or 1961, when he and other activists began their attacks on the Congress of Racial Equality that finally led to the formation of the Students' Non-Violent Coordinating Committee. Pru did not seek stardom. I think he genuinely tried to avoid it, but it was heaped upon him anyway. He was black and he was startlingly handsome in a way that could be accepted by both blacks and whites in that brief transitional time when blacks were trying to tell themselves that being black was beautiful and liberal whites wanted to agree. His hair was suitably nappy and his skin a rich chestnut color but the features were Semitic and the hazel eyes a gift from the devil. The eyes set him forever apart. It was impossible for Pru to blend in with the black masses. If he wasn't the leader there was no role for him to play. At the time of the 1965 march from Selma to Montgomery he was taken up by reporters covering the national scene. Both *Time* and *Newsweek* devoted long pieces to him the same week. Much was made of his uneasy truce with Dr. King, whom Pru could mimic ruthlessly. The media people felt more comfortable with Dr. King but Pru provided better short-term copy. His origins then were still obscure. *U.S. News & World Report*, I think it was, made much of the paradox that one of the most dynamic leaders of the new American black movement had his origins in the West Indies, the inference being that, with the possible exception of Dr. King, American blacks were not capable of exercising the sort of leadership that West Indian blacks could. This was an extension into politics of the rationale for the popularity in the 1950s of people like Harry Belafonte and Sidney Poitier. They were not, after all, local niggers. I'm sure Pru was aware of this, which is why he has always gone out of his way to insult and antagonize as many people as possible at any one moment. When Bobby Kennedy was assassinated, he announced that the country had been saved from A Second Screwing, not denied The Second Coming. When Dr. King was murdered he had been a bit more reserved. "May God bless Uncle Tom," he said in a telegram to Mrs. King.

The scrapbook in my steamer trunk chronicles Pru's rise as reported in *The New York Times*, in pained lead pieces from the *New Yorker*'s Talk of the Town, in other pieces from the *Atlantic*, *Harper's*, *Vogue*, *The Nation*, *The New Republic*, *Commonweal*, the *Christian Science Monitor*, *Our Sunday Visitor*, *The Village Voice*, the *Berkeley Barb* and in one article that is my favorite for sentimental reasons. It appeared on October 15, 1967, in the *East Village Organ* (a publication that went out of business not long after) under the by-line of Jacqueline Gold. Some excerpts:

> Though his aides wear multi-colored dashikis and bushy Afros and tend to be exuberantly friendly, he has the reserve that suggests Ivy League, Brooks Brothers button-down shirts, black-knit ties and gray flannel slacks. In fact he wears jeans which appear to have been borrowed from someone heavier than he is and a clean white Fruit-of-the-Loom T-shirt. He is polite but far from effusive. In conversation his voice has the soft almost feminine texture and rhythm of his native islands. The famous hazel eyes do not pierce now. They seduce. When I'm shown into the sparely furnished room he rises a little too slowly, as if the leader of a people in transition, sure in every other way, has not yet decided what amenities will be retained. . . . This tall, lean, beautiful man conducts his business under the eyes of Mao on one wall and Malcolm X on another. He is mannerly, grace-

ful. . . . How different he is from the licensed goon—white, short-haired, pig-minded—who has just delivered me to my appointment in this part of town that is warehouses, packing plants and factory buildings where unskilled labor from Haiti and Puerto Rico can make a dollar an hour as long as they remain nonunion.

The city I am in cannot be identified. I am in the Middle West but not in either Detroit or Chicago. To get to this rendezvous I've taken two planes, one bus and two taxis, evasive maneuvers made necessary by the fact that the police in Newark and New York are looking for the man. . . . It is after midnight and the room is unheated against the first evidences of approaching winter's cold. He doesn't seem to feel the chill as I do, huddled in my pea jacket and bellbottoms. I take no notes. Not allowed. I smoke. He drinks from a series of cardboard containers of coffee that he abandons without finishing. Black, no sugar. We are in a corner that has been partitioned off from the rest of the fourth-floor loft that is now the international headquarters of the Reform Panthers. It is a vacant building, condemned, he tells me, like the rest of America. With the escort who met me on the street two blocks away, I've just walked up three flights, the stairs going around the wire mesh shaft of an elevator that's permanently stuck between the second and third floors. I don't know how to begin the interview and have a suicidal urge to tell him about my parents, who are on a bagels-and-lox Caribbean cruise and could, for all I know, at this very minute be on the island of Jamaica where, 26 years ago, he was born and christened Prud'homme Shackleford, now better known in the radical underground as Baby Pru. . . .

I ask him to recall his participation in the Freedom Rides of 1961 and 1962 when he was still an undergraduate at Howard University, and the bloody 1964 voter registration drive in Virginia that erupted in violence when one of his closest advisors, Roger Lonsdale, was murdered by a local black man protesting the drive. "Is that news?" he asks. "That's not news. That's history, sad history. The history of the black man here is as much one of exploitation by his black brothers as of exploitation by the white slave masters. I was 10 years old when I first came to this country and two weeks later I was caught in the washroom of the Alfred E. Smith grammar school on East 178th Street and fucked up the ass by two older boys. They weren't white boys.

They were blacks. Brothers fucking brothers. Whitey doesn't
have to do anything except stand around and watch. . . . That's
where we are in this country. Three hundred years of taking it
up the ass. . . .

"I wouldn't give a flying-fuck-one about Vietnam if it wasn't
for the fact that most of the men fighting over there are brothers.
I couldn't care less about a bunch of flat-assed middle-class white
college boys who run around saying their civil rights are being
abused because they can't stay home and sell Pontiacs. They
make me laugh. They grow beards and march all over to-hell-
and-gone carrying signs that protest injustice to gooks and making a ruckus about draft cards when all the while they's living off
the fattest land of injustices this world has ever seen. I don't
want those jerks around me. I mean it. They smell." "Does that
mean," I ask, "that you are ruling out any further dialogue between the Reform Panthers and the members of the white radical
underground?" "I ain't ruling out anything," he says, "and I
ain't ruling anything in. . . ."

I ask him about Black Power, the phrase that's been giving
people in the Establishment a lot of sleepless nights lately. "What
about it?" he answers. "It's frightened many black people as well
as white," I say. "They think it means racial discrimination in
reverse, a Black Power authority replacing the white. They think
it means violence." "You said that, woman, not me," says Baby
Pru. "The only thing I can say, and I've said it before, is that
there is one goal, just one, and that is complete and total liberation. Not integration. . . ."

"What role does violence play in your strategy?" I ask.
"You've been accused of being largely responsible for the riots
last summer in Newark and Harlem." "Sheee-eee-it," he says,
"have you ever been to Newark or Harlem or to the South Side
of Chicago?" I say yes, that I was a Vista volunteer one year and
he says, "Don't ask silly questions then. It's Mickey Mouse time
in the Land of the Free when one uppity nigger like me can be
held responsible for that kind of reaction."

"But," I say, "people burning down their own homes, destroying their own businesses and neighborhoods." "Nobody was
burning down his own house or his own business. They were
burning down the homes and businesses of the whole fucking
military-industrial complex. Do you think those people own their
own homes—those rats nests and garbage dumps, those pimp

holes and smack parlors? If you was living up to your armpits in shit, you wouldn't feel too bad if you could destroy the shit. You'd be freeing yourself from shit, that's all. We want to get rid of the shit everywhere, for everybody. We want to start over. . . . You use the word 'violence.' Well, war is violent, and this is a war and we are arming for it in any way we can. More than that I can't say, but it's a war we mean to win. If we don't I can promise you this, that we won't hesitate to bring the whole fucking country down in flames around us. . . ."

. . . Baby Pru's aides come and go, sometimes sitting with us awhile, silently nodding in agreement, occasionally bringing in fresh cardboard containers of coffee but never, significantly, removing the half-drunk ones he has finished. . . . I see no signs of weapons anywhere. Indeed, most of the followers don't look as if they'd know how to use a gun. There's no grass either. These people are young and committed and very beautiful in their belief in Pru. The air is blue with the smoke from my cigarettes but no one thinks to open a window. The cold, I guess. According to the agreement by which Baby Pru agreed to be interviewed I am not to ask any personal questions, but when you're talking to a man whose mission is his life, where does mission end and privacy begin? . . .

Baby Pru: "I'm a black bastard and I'm proud of it. I know I got honky blood in me and I ain't proud of that, though it does give me satisfaction to deny its importance. As the down-home folks say, it don't mean shit."

. . . Toward dawn I join him in a cup of that terrible coffee. "What about black women?" I ask. "What about black women?" he counters. Then he adds, "Beautiful. There could be no black revolution without the support of black women." "That," I say, "sounds like sexism." There is a long pause by which I'm given to understand that the interview has come to an end but I don't want to leave. Something draws me to this man. What is his charisma? Charisma can't be analyzed, only identified. Kennedy had it. Jimmy Dean had it. Hitler had it. Jesus had it. Baby Pru has it. As I say goodbye to him I take his right hand in both of mine and I'm startled but not embarrassed to realize that I have tears in my eyes.

13

When she interviewed Pru, dear Jackie was very young in her career and still in her Village days, only three years out of Hunter, two years out of Vista, with one year behind her as an ambitious journalist who quickly learned how to adapt her style to the requirements of the local radical sheets that would publish material that came in over the transom. The *East Village Organ* piece was not great but the tenacity Jackie displayed in obtaining the interview brought her to the attention of *The Village Voice*, which, in turn, landed her with a respectable agent who provided her with increasingly lucrative assignments for publications like *Esquire*, *Woman's Day*, *Ladies Home Journal*, *Cosmopolitan* and *Playboy*. The day after I read the piece about Pru I wrote her a note care of the *East Village Organ*, saying how good I thought it was and asking, in passing, if she had any idea how I might find Pru's mother, whom I'd known many years before. That bit of information, perhaps coupled with the fact that my return address was then the Waldorf Towers, so piqued her curiosity that she didn't wait to answer by post, but telephoned. The young man who was then working for Utah and me as our secretary took the call and, from what Jackie told me later, was not surprisingly snotty. (Afterward I learned he was on Utah's payroll to find out who, if anybody, I was fucking, which didn't pay off because at that point in our marriage I wasn't fucking anybody.)

I reached Jackie three days later at a studio she was sharing in the East Village with a would-be photographer. A would-be artist would have better fit Jackie's picture of herself in those days but all the good would-be artists she knew were gay and, in her words, she just didn't have time for that scene. I liked the way she sounded on the telephone, very direct, not one to be easily flappable, her voice rather low and resonant but without regional accent (the result of three years with voice coaches when she thought she might present herself to the theater). On an impulse I asked if she would have a drink with me that evening at "21" and on what I thought was impulse she said she would, but it turned out not to be an impulse. She knew of me and wanted to see what sort of person I was. If I'd known that then, of course, I would never have bothered. I don't have to prove myself to dopey Hunter graduates. But we did meet and it was, for me anyway, infatuation at first sight. She was—and this is something I've never said to her, though I guess she knows it by this time—so comic, not amusing but unexpected, intense, a creature of a sort I'd never known before. Also she was so young, twenty-four to my forty-four.

Jackie has never in her life said anything that was spontaneously, good-naturedly humorous. She has no sense of humor at all, but she has wit and she has shrewdness she makes no attempt to conceal. I think I responded to her that first evening the way a patient responds to a nurse who's halfway sympathetic. There is something very nurselike about Jackie. It's not compassion, with which she's not overly loaded. It's her crispness, her efficiency, her cleanness of movement, gesture and speech. There's no nonsense about her, which then was not only tolerable but endearing because she had no idea how very much she still had to learn. It's not that she thought she knew everything but, rather, that she was completely confident that one way or the other she would learn it. Then, too, she was strikingly pretty, built long and lean, like Utah, but without the charm-school mannerisms. Infatuation, hell. It was as close to love as I'd yet gotten. She was also a window on a world I hadn't paid much attention to until then. What did she see in me? At first an incredible amount of money, more than she could conceive of and no part of which she wanted. Money of that sort, unearned, unstoppable, frightened her. She saw it as a societal disease and for me an addiction that forever separated me from ordinary folk. Jackie is not acquisitive. She doesn't dream of accumulating wealth, but she wants success and she depends on the need of earning to keep her life in order. Without that need she's convinced she'd fall apart, never get out of bed, turn to drink. It's the myth that keeps the true middle classes in their places. That I wasn't an alcoholic or someone who indulged himself in extravagant sexual pursuits, but someone whose life was, in its way, as ordered and active as hers, baffled her and, finally, intrigued her.

And, unlike anyone else who had ever loved her, I could make her laugh, relax, say to hell with things at the last moment.

She's done well with me, I think. At my insistence she cleaned up her prose. She no longer feels she must sprinkle her pieces with four-letter words that stand out like maraschino cherries on a plate of Minute Rice, but unless she's angry or impatient she seldom even uses four-letter words in conversation. At heart she's a puritan. She's beaten the compulsion to relate everything she's writing about to her split-level Dostoyevskian family life in Forest Hills. The rhetorical questions are kept to a minimum and the word "charisma" hasn't passed her lips within my hearing in eight years. Through me she's met people she hasn't hesitated to use to move her career along. Though she says she loathes the East Side she's an indefatigable hustler at East Side cocktail and dinner parties, and I'm charmed watching her operate since, among other things, she sticks close to me. Some old friends of mine—holdovers from Lake Forest and Chicago, veterans of the Higgenbotham and Utah administrations—profess to be appalled at the sight of so much naked pushiness. I call it enterprising and it fascinates me. It moves me close to tears. She's given me so much —love, concern, a way of watching the world day by day as if everything mattered, transports of joy in good, honest, resolute, uncomplicated sex, all with the same single-minded intensity she brings to her career—that I'm grateful there's something I can offer in return.

With my help she's become a facile, efficient writer, which is what she set out to be. She's as good as any popular journalist writing today, largely, I think, because her interest in the contemporary scene is free of any suspicion that it all may be fashionable trivia, scented garbage. Being a beautiful woman has not been a detriment, though she has found it wise to downplay this when one of her most useful personas in the media has been as the woman who can interpret her liberation to others still in bondage. Today the usefulness of this role is not what it used to be. It's also begun to bore her so that now she refuses to do any more pieces about working mothers, raped mothers or Lesbian mothers unless they also happen to be black *and* have a physical handicap. She's awfully good with movie actors and with political personalities who don't fit into any recognizable category, like Pru, Isabel Perón and that Brazilian fellow whose name I've forgotten, the leader of the São Paulo student radicals who, in the company of Jackie five years ago, was shot to death by the São Paulo police during a demonstration at the university. Her picture on page 1 of *The New York Times*, kneeling beside the body of "the slain student leader" (not "the slain leader of the students"), helped her achieve celebrity in pop journalism—and to make life for the two of us more difficult.

There was something so earnest, so furrowed-brow, about her that first evening at "21," I couldn't let her go. We began meeting once a week, then more and more frequently, until one weekend I swept her off her feet with an unscheduled trip to Las Vegas. We'd been sharing a bottle of champagne at the Pierre bar as she told me about a trip to Las Vegas she'd made several years earlier. Her eye for detail was hugely funny because it was so accurate and specific. We were both well on the way to being pleasantly smashed when I suggested that perhaps we could go then, that night, without luggage even, to check it out. She considered the proposition for a moment, very soberly, then said yes, that I really couldn't grasp the dimensions of the American Dream without having seen Las Vegas. It was not until I'd paid the check and we were standing to leave that she smiled—a real ear-to-ear one— and said, "This *is* fun, isn't it?"

Actually we didn't see much of Las Vegas. At Caesar's Palace, in the Pompeii suite, in a round bed with scarlet satin sheets, enclosed by walls hung in scarlet velvet, Jackie revealed herself to be a superb fuck with enormous potential for variations.

If it hadn't been for Jackie I'd have probably put up with the clean-shaven Miss Utah forever, but I fell in love with Jackie, with what she was and what I could make of her. When Utah's lawyer, with apologies, repeated her annual one mill request, I said yes. Six months later Jackie and I moved to the West Side and Margaret to her co-op on the East River. It hasn't been easy with Jackie but it hasn't been boring. My money still depresses her and makes her feel guilty, and she would never, *never* marry a goy. At first I thought that amusing. Now it makes me goddamn mad.

14

The first few months at St. Matthew's were insufferable. In addition to Proust I'd brought with me my *Britannica*, a set of Balzac's *La Comédie Humaine* (in French), an unabridged Webster (I was incapable then of traveling light), a typewriter, a record player and two dozen 78 rpm albums that had to be crated and shipped separately and a radio with which to follow the new war, which was the only thing to indicate to me that Mr. Devereaux and I might have anything in common. He was convinced, as I was, that the Phony War would lead to the disaster it did. That one shared opinion was as nothing compared to our differences. My cubicle, as might be imagined, was overstuffed with possessions. It looked like an old curiosity shop. I was forced to keep my *Britannica*, the Balzac and the Webster in my steamer trunk, which itself occupied about 60 percent of the available floor space. My first brush with the authorities came when after two nights of sleeplessness I'd gone to the attic of the dormitory and found an extra mattress for my cot. Though I explained that the bow of the springs made it impossible for me to sleep on a single mattress without risking curvature of the spine, the second mattress was disallowed on the grounds that since no other student needed two, I shouldn't need two, to which was added, "What would happen if every boy asked for two?" They could do as I did, I said, that is, go to the attic where there were dozens of discards, some less disgusting than others. No soap. The ruling was upheld on appeal to Mr. Devereaux, who was at pains to point out that St. Matthew's was not like some of the other country clubs I'd recently been attending. He didn't have to tell me that. I knew quite well what St. Matthew's was, a Church-sponsored Devil's Island for Boys, staffed by sadistic, incompetent masters. It didn't help in those weeks that I refused to play football. It made no difference that I had a perfectly valid medical excuse and, more important, that I was no good. Incompetence of any kind was ignored at St. Matthew's as a matter of principle.

I suppose too that my habits in dress and manner were against me. For a year or so I'd come to believe that I looked like Lord Byron, a resemblance I sought to emphasize by limiting my wardrobe to black suits, white shirts with collars rather more ample than was the current fashion in Tatterhummock County and wide black ties (ascots were prohibited), which, I thought, combined with my fair complexion and black hair (worn as long as the barber allowed), created the impression of a man of higher, more ascetic calling than most. To the sheep-fuckers and the rest, I simply looked odd. Being of no great intelligence they all believed that the black suit I wore every day, weekdays as well as on Sundays, was one suit, not the three that I was intimidated into exhibiting occasionally. I soon realized that I'd made a mistake on the Chesapeake & Ohio when, on my way from Chicago to Richmond, I'd given away a new, vividly raisin-colored tweed suit (bought for me by Lockie) to the Pullman porter in lieu of a cash tip. It would have provided me with a change of dress and it might have shortstopped some of the rumors about my toilet, circulated most eagerly by boys who had to be reminded by the laundry staff when to change their underwear.

During the first several weeks of the term I spent that part of every afternoon which was employed by the other students at football practice or watching football practice hidden in the branches of a fine old cherry tree overlooking the river. I attacked *Swann's Way*. I kept my diary. I wrote letters to Ma, who was due to arrive at Lewis's Landing sometime before Thanksgiving, to Lockie, to my father, who had given up on me by that time, to misfits I'd come to know at other penal colonies over the years and with whom I'd exchange what we all thought were very funny horror stories. We had a sort of grapevine for the dissemination of information about schools to be avoided at all costs and those where one might be able to endure with the least damage to the soul. My reports about the sheep-fucker prompted the most response, but I also found that not many of my correspondents could top Philo Lumberton, the son of a retired U.S. Navy commander who lived not far from the school on Queen Anne Creek.

Philo was a short, stocky student of Charles Atlas and, at fifteen, well on his way to becoming a tattooed man. Already he

had an American eagle spread across his chest, the god Neptune
holding his trident on his left shoulder blade, the United States
Navy seal on the right, and a small red rose on the right side of his
groin just above the pubic hair. When he came back from Christmas vacation that year, he was sporting a breathtaking pattern of
black, red and yellow stripes down the right side of his face, from
under the middle of his lower eyelash to his chin. The three stripes,
each about a quarter of an inch wide, undulated, looking as if
they were the tracks of symbolic tears. Philo was not someone to
meet suddenly in the dark. The back of each hand carried the
remains of Philo's first stabs at self-decoration, a pathetic, fading
blue star whose five points didn't match, on one hand, and on the
other, an uneven crescent. When I attempted to be friendly by
admiring the art, Philo explained that one day he planned to have
his own handiwork redone by a professional. When I asked him
the real question, why tattoos, he became solemn. A man's body,
he said, was one of the things by which he honored God and he,
Philo, wanted to honor God with beauty as well as with health and
clean thoughts.

In the company of creatures like Deke Crozier and Philo
Lumberton I thought my eccentricities might be ignored, but they
weren't. I found no anonymity there. Of all people I was the one
who was regarded as the school idiot.

My retreat in the cherry tree was soon noted by Mr. Boyleston, a
master from the mountains in the western part of the state, a man
whose extraordinary buckteeth I blamed on his Appalachian
accent, as if the manner in which he blew forth words ("bow-
wah" for boy) and spat out phrases ("What's-the-matter-boy-sick-
or-something?") had been responsible for pushing his upper front
teeth so dramatically far forward. Mr. Boyleston taught trig and
chemistry and thus came to distrust me very early when he learned
I had no intention of applying myself to either subject. He told
Mr. Devereaux about my hiding place and Mr. Devereaux then
suggested to me that there might be better ways for me to spend
the exercise period. "Isn't there any sport you like, boy?" "Not
really," I said, "except maybe swimming." "Well, I can't have you

down on the river swimming by yourself when everybody else is on the football field." Mr. Devereaux and I compromised with my agreeing to the hiking trips, during the course of which I murdered my coelacanth, found the clay pipes and came to know Wicheley.

When the first grades were tallied in mid-October it was found that I'd failed not only trigonometry and chemistry but also English literature, which was a surprise to me. We were studying *Quentin Durward*, going laboriously through it line by line as if it were *Hamlet*. My mind had wandered. In the month's major quiz I'd written extensively if not too coherently about *Ivanhoe*, thoroughly confusing characters, situations, time periods and bits of wisdom that Scott had placed in the two novels for the edification of boys growing up in Tatterhummock County. Again it was apparent that I hadn't been paying attention, which is when my Proust was taken from me. But there was a far worse scandal less than a week later.

One of the Ruddleston brothers—Ruddleston, W., the elder—reported the theft of a portable radio and before any of us knew what was in the wind the entire school body was released from morning classes and marched upstairs to the dorm where each of us was stationed outside his cubicle. Mr. Boyleston and Mr. Twigg, my English instructor, a slight, boyish-faced man with a delicate way of putting three fingers in front of his mouth when he burped, which he did frequently, conducted the cubicle search as if they were Interpol officers on the trail of a cocaine haul. They never found the missing Ruddleston radio but in my steamer trunk they found something much more exciting, a sensitive young man's dreamlife in the form of booty, to wit, a bottle of green crème de menthe and a bottle of Pernod, both lifted from Lockie's cellar, two silver goblets I'd bought on impulse at Peacock's several days before I left Chicago, six packages of Trojan condoms, which, with three to a package, were enough to see me through several years of womanizing at the rate I was then going and, most scandalous of all, a memorable collection of dirty comic books (*Tillie the Toiler, Winnie Winkle, The Katzenjammer Kids* and such), many long out of print, which I'd put together over the years by outright purchases and complicated barter deals. As if hooting from one mountaintop to another, Mr. Boyleston made note of each bit of contraband as it was discovered, his upper front teeth being pushed ever further forward as he whistled in surprise. I had the impression that Mr. Twigg, who didn't much enjoy the assignment as customs officer, was more amused than anything else, though he was annoyed with me for all the trouble I was about to cause him. Mr. Devereaux did not like to know that his boys led private lives. The inspection of the remaining cubicles was got through as quickly as possible so that Mr. Boyleston and Mr. Twigg could report their findings to Mr. Devereaux. During the afternoon class period I was called to Mr. Devereaux's office fully expecting expulsion—I'd been kicked out of better places than this for considerably less—but no. It was, I later came to understand, impossible to get shipped from St. Matthew's for any charge less serious than not playing the game.

Mr. Devereaux sat behind his desk, the usual portrait in gray except that the pinkness of his face was now an apoplectic red. He was furious but having the discipline of an officer and a gentleman, he showed his fury only in his complexion. Stonewall Jackson was a collapsed heap of thin fur and bones on the floor beside the desk where, arranged in a neat row, as if for military inspection, were the bottle of Mère Brissac crème de menthe, the bottle of Pernod (three-quarters full), the two silver goblets (both sticky inside since they weren't the kind of personal objects one could rinse out in the communal washroom without prompting comment), the condoms and the comic books, which someone had fanned out as if they were the cards of a bridge hand.

Mr. Devereaux studied me for a moment and then swiveled around, his back to me, to look out the window across the campus, down over Mr. Whabble's sheep pasture, to the river and, beyond it, to the flat serenity of the Northern Neck. When he finally broke the silence he sounded more sorry than angry. "Boy, you astonish me. . . ." I stood at something approximating attention, then looked at the floor, at old boards whose finish had long since been worn away. "Of all the boys in the school you are the last one I would have expected to have a collection of stuff like this. . . ." He swiveled back to face me and made a sweeping gesture over my treasures. He shook his head. "I ain't talking about the liquor . . .

or the silver cups. . . ." He coughed. "You didn't steal them, did you?" "I bought them," I said, "with my own money." "Your own money . . . that's one of the problems. But these . . ." he picked up a package of Trojans and dropped it on the desk, "this . . . this *filth*." He slapped the fan of worn, thumbed, frayed comic books. "And you're the boy who thinks he's being persecuted because we took away your Proust. How'd you ever find time to read Proust when you had all this . . . junk? No wonder you're failing. . . . What am I going to tell your mother? Well?" "I don't know," I said, and for a moment I wanted to be helpful, "the truth, I guess." He cleared his throat. "The truth?" "She's heard it before," I said. Devereaux: "What do you mean by that?" I didn't rightly know. "I mean," I said, "that I've been kicked out of other schools too." He studied me for a long time. I think he was making a real effort to see who I was. It was not as if he'd ever known. I was not a Deke Crozier whom he could read like a book. Finally: "Do you reckon that's what this is all about? Just getting shipped out of school?"

I was already calculating whether I could make the 7:30 sleeper from Richmond to Chicago, which depended on the length of the dressing down. I knew that such expulsions, being final, demanded the parents' money's worth of lecture, stern warning, humiliation, a rundown on the rules that we live by plus the obligatory note that it was hurting him more than it was me. Mr. Devereaux, being a family friend, was committed to giving me the works. Another silence, then, "I ain't going to kick you out, Marshall. That's too easy and it don't do no good anyway. That's avoiding the problem. I believe you're a good boy. I've seen changes in you already. I think we can do something for you at St. Matthew's. . . ." My heart sank. I'd been seeing myself ordering a steak dinner that evening on the C&O diner, heading back to Chicago, listening to the cheerful clickety-clack, staring out into the night and wondering what new adventures awaited me.

"I wish I'd known your brother," Mr. Devereaux said suddenly. It was my turn to be astonished. What the fuck did Tom have to do with this? He could goddamn well stay out of it. "He's dead," I said. "I know all about the accident." "It wasn't an accident. He committed suicide," I said. "Whatever," said Mr.

Devereaux, dismissing unwanted information. "I understand he
was an excellent football player, a fine young man. I would have
liked to have both of you here at St. Matthew's together." He was
heading into country I was not interested in exploring. "Good-
looking boy, too, I understand. . . ." Pause. "I guess it liked to kill
your mother. . . . Well, that's done and gone, I reckon, isn't it?"
"Yes," I said. Pause. A change of tone, not exactly friendly but
not displaying the sorrow and hurt he had earlier. "I suppose," he
said, "you will not think me completely unreasonable if I dispose
of these articles in the furnace," pointing to the condoms and
comic books; "I see no reason why you can't have the cups back
but I'll take the liquor and keep that safely. Maybe when your
mother gets down here you'll offer some to us after supper one
night. . . ." Pause. I knew there must be more. He wasn't planning
on springing me quite so easily. "I'm going to telephone your
mother now. I'm going to tell her what has happened and suggest
that you be taken off your allowance and confined to campus until
further notice. No more Friday night movies in Queen Anne. No
more off-campus hiking. You can spend your exercise period
working out in the gym or on the track. In the meantime, go up to
your cubicle and bring down your radio and all of the books that
aren't immediately connected with your courses. I mean all of
them. When your grades improve maybe we can reconsider some
of these prohibitions. . . ."

In the excitement of striking it rich in my steamer trunk, all
thoughts of thievery and the disappearance of Ruddleston, W.'s
radio were forgotten by everyone except me and, I suppose, Ruddleston, W.

I think now of the parable of the sower from the Book of Matthew, Chapter XIII:

> . . . *Because it is given unto you to know the mysteries of the*
> *kingdom of heaven, but to them it is not given.*
> *For whosoever hath, to him shall be given, and he shall have*
> *more abundance: but whosoever hath not, from him shall be*
> *taken away even that he hath.*

*Therefore speak I to them in parables: because they seeing,
see not; and hearing, they hear not, neither do they understand.*

*And in them is fulfilled the prophecy of Esaias, which saith,
By hearing ye shall hear, and shall not understand; and seeing
ye shall see, and shall not perceive:*

*For this people's heart is waxed gross, and their ears are
dull of hearing, and their eyes they have closed; lest at any time
they should see with their eyes, and hear with their ears, and
should understand with their heart, and should be converted, and
I should heal them.*

*But blessed are your eyes, for they see: and your ears, for
they hear.*

*For verily I say unto you, That many prophets and righteous
men have desired to see those things which ye see, and have not
seen them; and to hear those things which ye hear, and have not
heard them. . . .*

I recite these lines from the memory of so many evening chap-
els when Mr. Devereaux read them. I would have said then the
passage meant nothing to me, but perhaps it did. I could hear but
heard not, see but not perceive. Today I remember the fierce glare
in that handsome but not old chapel that was lit by unshaded
lightbulbs just after sunset. I recall by rote the words sung and
spoken there. "The Church's one foundation/is Jesus Christ her
Lord. . . ." Portions of the 48th Psalm: "According to thy name,
O God, so is thy praise unto the ends of the earth: thy right hand
is full of righteousness" invariably brought forth titters from the
twelve- and thirteen-year-olds who well knew that a right hand full
of righteousness was nowhere near as satisfying as a right hand
full of one's own prick. I, on the other hand, would be spurred to
fantasies by "Let Mount Zion rejoice, let the daughters of Judah
be glad. . . ." I was convinced that the daughters of Judah must be
eminently fuckable. And, "Mark ye well her bulwarks, consider
her palaces" made me see Gethsemane, a woman with a fine broad
ass (bulwarks=buttocks) and the tits that were her palaces.

I am aware that I am withholding information, not reporting
everything I now know, and not necessarily reporting what I do
report in the order in which I learned it. Instead I'm reporting it
more or less in the order that I come to understand certain oc-

currences. As I go about my task I see myself as a golden hawk who, working his wings ever so imperceptibly, is able to hang in a current of air for long periods, always over the same spot. I'm a satellite to my own life and times.

A few afternoons after the discovery of the illegal contents of my steamer trunk I was taking my customary shower in the communal shower room, having worked out by running around the track several times. I had actually enjoyed the running but it was a temporary pleasure. My having been quarantined, coupled with the cutoff of all funds, left me depressed if not despondent, and totally broke. Sou-less. I was in an institution I couldn't hope to be kicked out of, and I had no money even to buy cigarettes. I again felt abandoned, snubbed, cheated and ill-used by that God who is the giver of all good things that flow naturally and promiscuously from Him. I had been standing under my favorite shower nozzle for perhaps thirty minutes when I was joined by the execrable Gordon Felix who, smiling the smile of a loathsome Panamanian whore, took a position at the adjacent shower nozzle and fixed his gaze upon my person. I retreated to my cubicle, where I was immediately joined by Felix, his short, wet, flabby, fourteen-year-old hermaphroditic form wrapped in a threadbare brown bathrobe that was decorated with what appeared once to have been Navajo good-luck symbols. I sat on the edge of my cot drying between my toes, preparing to apply the anti-fungus powder.

"Fifty cents," said Felix. Having spent most of the last four years of my life in various all-male detention centers I wasn't naïve, but because I was something of an eccentric myself I thought it more charitable in such situations to assume an air of polite but complete disinterest. The passions of others were petty but I recognized their right to co-exist. "I'll give you a dollar," said Felix, a saucy glint appearing in his heretofore cowlike eyes. I turned my back on him and continued to work on my toes. Scarpia was not to be put off with high-minded tolerance. He squeezed between me and the steamer trunk and stood watching me with his back to the window. "One-dollar twenty-five," he said sweetly, "if you let me do something I'd like to do." As he spoke he had a way of rolling back on his heels, shifting his head in quick, darting movements like someone shadowboxing. It occurred to me that more than once he had probably had to dodge the blows of outraged boys he had similarly importuned. "Really, Felix," I said, adding a world-weary "tsk." He giggled. I suppose he was happy that I hadn't picked him up and thrown him out on his ear. "I'll also clean your cubicle every morning for a week. Please." He started to sidle to the cot. He looked at me intently, though not at my face, and said in the dopey voice of one who approaches something newborn, "Just a little white dove peeking out of a soft black nest."

"Don't sit down," I said. One had to be firm with people like that. "I know what you want and I'm not in the least interested. You're barking up the wrong tree." I looked at him with a steady eye. "It's only out of respect for such men as Alexander, Pliny the Younger, Julius Caesar, Michelangelo, Richard Coeur-de-Lion, Wilde, Proust and Jack Dempsey that I don't beat you over the head with the broom there." He was delighted. "Jack Dempsey?" he said. "Of course," I said. I admit that was pure fantasy but I thought it might deflect him from his immediate purpose. Felix laughed until the tears rolled down his cheeks. He laughed cartoon laughter, "Tee-hee, tee-hee." After every second "tee-hee" his eyebrows went up in a kind of pleased tic. "Leastwise," he said, "you ain't mad, are you?" "I don't know why I should be mad," I said, "though I am becoming bored." With grace and nonchalance I stood and put on my underwear.

I think I'm being truthful when I say that Felix aroused in me no lust whatsoever. But he may not have bored me as much as I've said. In common with most red-blooded American boys, who may not admit it, I was flattered by the physical desires I aroused in almost anything, including such fourteen-year-old hermaphrodites as Felix. The next afternoon, at the same time and place, we struck our bargain. The price was to be $2 per shot. Felix's father, via the Rockefellers, provided Felix with money enough to indulge himself three times a week, which left him just enough for the Friday night movie in Queen Anne. The contract was consummated behind the steamer trunk that blocked us from the window and the prying eyes of Jojo in Mount Vernon. I turned my face away and waited to be grabbed by a clammy fist. Imagine my surprise when he turned out to be a confident, well-practiced cannibal. "Okay, okay," I said in some panic. Then, "Take it easy, for Christ's sake. Don't bite."

It got me through the temporary financial crisis but eventually placed me in an even worse bind.

15

The heat of August invisibly consumes the city. I cannot work this morning. Jackie still hasn't telephoned. Jimmy Barnes is wherever boring people go on Cape Cod. Instead of work I measure distances to the past in light years. My thoughts are of Cousin Mary Lee, the General and their son, Little Bob, who was transformed into an appliance in Vietnam. I think too of their slim, Sun·Maid-pretty daughter who, named for George Washington's mother, now goes by the name of Merrie Ball and who was described by the editor of a porn newspaper several months ago as "the southland's greatest contribution to American politics since Dolley Madison and fuckdom's fastest rising new star." Merrie Ball, who makes dirty movies in San Francisco, traveled to New York for the opening of a new film and to tape the following interview which was illustrated with conventional snatch shots and one jokey picture of her trying to arouse the possum-playing editor.

Q: You're even prettier in person than you are on the screen.
A: Thank you.
Q: How do you feel about suddenly finding yourself a star?
A: Terrific.
Q: Has it changed your life? Sometimes people have to pay a high price . . .
A (laughing): . . . If this is the price, I'm willing to pay it. Maybe I'm an egotist but I like being recognized. It's still a thrill to me to have men and women too come up to me in the street to say how much they've enjoyed my films . . . how much I've helped them. . . .
Q: Helped them?

A: Yes . . . gotten them out of themselves, loosened them up. I don't want to sound pretentious but I think porn films are very much a part of the ongoing revolution taking place in our society. I'm proud to be a part of it. Americans, raised on all of that Judeo-Christian shit, have always been too. . . .

Q: Uptight?

A: Exactly—afraid of fucking. . . .

Q: You're for Women's Lib?

A: For everybody's lib.

Q: You want . . .

A (laughs) : . . . everyone to ball everyone else.

Q: Which reminds me. . . . I understand there was quite a flap in your hometown when your first films came out and people found out your father was the General, not *any* general but *the* General. The shit hit the fan.

A: You can say that again.

Q: What happened?

A: That's a long story.

Q: Was your family upset?

A: Upset isn't really the right word. More like insane.

Q: They even attempted to have you put away. . . .

A: What do you mean, "attempted"? I *was* put away, though only for two days. Thank heavens the court system in San Francisco isn't as fucked up and corrupt as everything else in this country.

Q: It was a bum rap?

A: Completely. I was arrested on some sort of civil complaint and on the point of being sent to the Marin County nuthouse, just because my father knew a few people.

Q: Isn't that sort of understating it?

A (laughs) : Maybe. . . .

Q: He was an Eisenhower crony. Jack Kennedy called him America's greatest soldier and he was Johnson's man in the Pentagon.

A: He was also a friend of Nixon's. At least Nixon used to kiss his ass.

Q: Did you ever meet Nixon?

A: I did when I was a little girl. Not after he became President. I was by that time—how should I put it?—estranged from my family.

Q: Because of the fuck-films?

A (laughs): No . . . long before . . . there were . . . other differences of opinion.

Q: Being brought up as the daughter of a career Army officer, a man who became the most decorated, the most publicized officer in modern American history, three times winner of the Congressional Medal of Honor, that sort of thing—a four-star general and a very colorful guy, I mean, it couldn't have been too easy.

A: I don't know. It wasn't all that difficult either. I loved my father very much. I worshipped him when I was little. My mother too, and my brother. We were really a very happy family . . . and, of course, very (laughs) very F-F-V.

Q: What's F-F-V?

A: Guess.

Q: Fist-Fucking-Virgins.

A: Close but not quite. First Families of Virginia.

Q: Where did you grow up?

A: All over. I was born in Tokyo while my father was stationed in Korea. We also lived in Honolulu for a while, Paris, Washington, but our home was always in Tatterhummock County.

Q: Tatterhummock County?

A: It's in Virginia, the Tidewater, about a hundred miles south of Washington. Both my mother's and father's families have lived there since . . .

Q: The *Mayflower*?

A: The *Mayflower* ain't Virginia, honey. We always had our house there, to go back to, no matter where we were living.

Q: Plantations . . . darkies out picking the cotton . . . mint juleps on the veranda, and Mammy saying, "Ah deeclah, Miz Scarlett."

A (laughs): Not quite like that. It's just an old farmhouse.

Q: Is that where you first started copping joints?

A: I didn't know that joints were to be copped until I was nineteen or twenty. Really, you don't seem to understand (laughs). I was very strictly brought up. I knew my mother and father shared the same bed but I didn't know they ever *did anything*. I think I was eleven and we were living in Honolulu when my brother—he's four years older than I am—told me that when our parents went to bed at night, our father would put his thing into our mother.

Q: Were you shocked?

A: Not really. It just seemed such a crazy idea I didn't believe it. Though now that I think about it I guess my brother was hoping to get me excited.

Q: Did you ever have sex with your brother?

A: No, but by the time I was thirteen I could have been persuaded. But by that time he had his own girlfriends, he didn't need me.

Q: Did you ever have sex with your father?

A (laughs): Good heavens, you seem to think we were the Snopses! I don't have anything against incest, per se. It just never came up.

Q: Where did you go to school?

A: Wherever we happened to be living, but I went back to Virginia to go to college, to Sweet Briar. Ever heard of it?

Q: I think so.

A: It's to Virginia what Vassar is to everywhere else. Quite posh, with high academic standards.

Q: Did you graduate?

A: I sure did, honey. I have a degree in political science.

Q: I didn't know that. . . .

A: It's in the bio we sent out. You didn't do your homework.

Q: You must be our brainiest fuck-film queen, as well as the prettiest.

A: Well, I'd say that I'm probably more brainy than Linda Lovelace.

Q: And can give just as good head.

A: I think so.

Q: Do you know Linda?

A: We've met. She seems very sweet . . . unspoiled, really . . . very vulnerable.

Q: She's a cunt. Do you know any of the others? Marilyn Chambers? Georgina Spelvin? Darby Lloyd Raines?

A: Marilyn and I used to see each other occasionally in San Francisco but the others, the New York stars, I just don't run into.

Q: How about the male stars? Do you have any favorites?

A: Pierce Arrow (laughs). I adore his name and I adore him. We've made six films together and I think we're starting our seventh at the end of the month.

Q: He's hung. . . .

A: Honey, is he ever. . . .

Q: And he's black. Do you prefer black guys to white guys?

A: Of course not. Color has nothing to do with it. Neither, for that matter, does size. You must be able to respond to the other person. To relate. Pierce and I always seem to be able to get it on together. When I'm balling Pierce, I really get into it. There's no need to fake it. He's said the same thing about me.

Q: Do you love him?

A: You mean, as a lover? No, but I love him as a friend. Pierce is probably the best friend I have, outside of Tony. If I needed something in a hurry, Pierce is the person I'd call first.

Q: I understand he's making gay films now too.

A: He's got so much he can spread it around. That's one of the things I admire about him. He's the least uptight man I've ever known.

Q: I've been covering porn ever since it became big business. . . .

A: . . . You're our H. L. Mencken, honey—

Q: . . . but there's still one thing I find difficult to understand, and that's how, say, after you and Pierce Arrow have been fucking and eating each other all day, how you can just stop when the director yells "cut" and go home to your boyfriends or girlfriends. . . .

A (laughs): . . . Sometimes we don't just stop. . . .

Q: What I mean is, what's your private life like?

A: Much like anyone else's, I imagine. I'm an actress before anything else. I was working with the San Francisco Mime Theater when I did my first fuck-film. When you see me up there on the big screen, in living color and stereo sound, fucking or giving head, I'm acting. I mean I like what I'm doing. I'm good at it and I'm not faking it . . . but it's not my entire life. I have other interests.

Q: Including Tony.

A: Very much including Tony. Tony's the best thing that's ever happened to me up to now.

Q: Tony Galliero is your lover . . .

A: . . . and agent and manager and father and mother and brother and sister and friend. He's everything.

Q: How long have you been together now?

A: Two years.

Q: Are you going to get married?

A: We talk about it but marriage and show biz don't mix. I know that sounds like a cliché but it's true. We both know it. We're doing well now. We'll see what happens in the future.

Q: How's your sex life with Tony?

A: Terrific.

Q: Do you fuck a lot?

A: We do everything a lot.

Q: I mean, when you're in the middle of making a film, do you go home from the studio at the end of the day, cook dinner for Tony . . .

A: I don't cook . . .

Q: . . . Well, come home from Trader Vic's or McDonald's and climb into the sack and ball all night?

A: When I'm shooting a film, Tony understands the emotional and physical demands being made on me. Sometimes we fuck but mostly I just give him a hand job, or he gives himself one, and that's that until the picture is finished. After all, Tony is my manager. He wants me to succeed as much as I do. Then, also . . .

Q: Also, what?

A (laughs): Tony is a very physical lover. He can't make love without getting carried away, which is one of the reasons I love him, but when I'm filming I can't very well show up before the cameras with Tony's teeth marks all over my ass.

Q: That reminds me of the story of how Linda Lovelace held up shooting one day because she'd been sitting on a wicker chair between takes.

A: There are very special problems in this business.

Q: I hope you'll forgive me, but there's a question I've got to ask that you probably won't like.

A: If I don't like it I won't answer it.

Q: I've heard stories that Tony is a member of the Mangione Family in Frisco. . . .

A: I've heard the same stories. . . .

Q: Is he?

A: The only family Tony is a member of is ours . . . his and mine . . . the two of us.

Q: I've also heard that some theater owners have complained that Tony and his associates have brought pressure to bear on them to get better terms for your pictures and sometimes to dump other fuck-films in favor of yours.

A: I don't know anything about the business side. I leave all that to Tony; but I have enough self-confidence to believe that my films are now so good, and that I have such a loyal public, the sort of thing you mention would hardly be necessary.

Q: Are you still active in politics?

A (laughs): I'm too busy for politics now. When you're earning five hundred dollars a day sucking on something the size of Willie Mays' bat, you don't have the time and energy to demonstrate in the streets or paint slogans on walls, not that people do much of that any more. I think I'm still doing my part for the good of the country, though.

Q: How active were you in the anti-war movement?

A: I was president of the Sweet Briar chapter of University Women Against the War. I was even busted in the Pentagon March. My father had a fit, of course. So did my brother. He was on his way to Vietnam as a second lieutenant.

Q: Was your father pro-war?

A: You're kidding! My brother is just like him—but that's something I really don't want to get into. Do you want me to teach you how to suck cock?

Q: Thanks, but that's not my thing.

A: If Hugh Heffner can go to bed with a boy in the interests of science, why can't you?

Q: I take it your family is conservative?

A: Somewhere to the right of the Sun King.

Q: Why are you any different?

A: I don't know. . . . Maybe I'm not . . . though I remember being down home, meaning Tatterhummock County, in the spring of 1964 . . . I was thirteen . . . when they were having a voter registration drive and I wanted to help. My brother almost lynched me. They did kill one of the blacks who had come down from New York. One of the local blacks did it. That was the sort of place it was . . . and is, I suppose.

Q: Have you been there recently?

A (laughs): Are you real? I thought about going to the General's funeral last year, at least to the memorial service in Washington, but in the end I didn't. It wouldn't have been fair . . . to score a point just because I was alive and he was dead.

Q: What's in the future?

A: I've three films lined up back to back, the one with Pierce I mentioned earlier and two more, all of them with fairly good stories and production values. Then some people here are interested in talking to Tony and me about putting together a nightclub act. The only problem is that I can't sing or dance.

Q: How about doing a film with Gerard Damiano?

A: You mean "the Ingmar Bergman of smut"? He's never asked me, and I think I'd rather do a film with "the Ingmar Bergman of Ingmar Bergman." I know you love Damiano's films but to me there's too much angst and too little fucking.

Q: How about straight films?

A: I'm ready if they are. We've had some talks with two different producers in Los Angeles but the offers were absurd. They just wanted to capitalize on my name and reputation. I'd rather keep on making good, honest, raunchy fuck-films as long as I can than appear in some silly Hollywood shit that would embarrass me if not anyone else.

Q: Merrie Ball, I love you.

A: Can I suck your cock?

Q: I thought you'd never ask.

16

The General was called the General long before the rank was ever bestowed on him, almost from the time he enlisted in the Army in the twenties after having flunked out of West Point. He was born Stewart Fullman Carter of good Tatterhummock stock that had been poor but proud for generations. I knew him in the fall and winter of 1939 when he was home on leave to pursue the hand of Cousin Mary Lee, an off-and-on ten-year courtship that had begun when Cousin Mary Lee was still at St. Catherine's in Richmond. By 1939 the General was a colonel and already well-known in Army circles, having won his first Congressional Medal of Honor for swimming the Yangtze or some such thing during an operation in China. He'd also been awarded a presidential citation for activities in Nicaragua and the Bronze Star for something else in Lebanon, all designed, I suspect, as part of his major campaign, which was to take and occupy, now and forever, Cousin Mary Lee Moulton. The General, like me, was one of those people who've been blessed—arbitrarily, I assume—with knowing from a very early age exactly what they want from life. The General wanted Cousin Mary Lee, but it was a long, hard slog, one that began when the obstacles were enormous, really hopeless, when he was a nice but odd-looking county boy, a sergeant in the regular Army at a time when the regular Army was understood to be the refuge for society's dregs, men who would otherwise be living in hobo jungles and riding freight cars, if not serving time in prison for crimes against women, property and nature.

What could his future have been? He was fifteen years older than Cousin Mary Lee who, as the prettiest girl in the county, was being courted by dozens of much more suitable prospects, boys who went to the University of Virginia and Washington and Lee and the Citadel and who would one day be senators, judges, bank presidents, gentlemen farmers and businessmen. At the start of the race the General had been very much a dark horse. By the time I met him his odds had improved considerably, not only because his career had been so magically successful but also because the competition had thinned out. At twenty-seven Cousin Mary Lee was still the prettiest girl in the county but it was beginning to look as if she'd already become one of those women who never make up their minds, who fasten onto the temporary dead center of belledom and then won't budge. There was good reason to suspect this. Cousin Annie Lee, her mother, was not about to let her only child go without a knockdown, drag-out struggle of wills. Every time Cousin Mary Lee seemed capable of carrying one of her engagements through to the point of marriage, Cousin Annie Lee would have a violent stomach seizure, or a mysterious heart irregularity, or an acute attack of vapors of the sort that baffled the best medical minds in Tatterhummock County. Once the ring had been got off her daughter's finger, Cousin Annie Lee would start her long painful convalescence, but cheerfully. If Cousin Mary Lee ever worried about the possibility of being a spinster she could always comfort herself knowing that her dear faithful Stewart was out there somewhere, dreaming of her, carrying her kerchief into exotic if undeclared war zones, sending back presents of bits of silver and jade and ivory from China, the Philippines, Hawaii, Egypt, the Canal Zone, writing awkwardly tender love letters that he

signed, "Your faithful Stewart," preparing to return to her periodically with some new honor, which he would carry to her in his
teeth and drop at her feet, to be accepted or rejected by the adored
mistress as she saw fit. Without recriminations, with no strings.

The General was a shy bulldog. He was no more than five foot
seven, had the barrel-chested build of a tenacious scrapper and a
face that appeared to have been pushed ever further in over the
years in a series of barroom brawls on the road to Mandalay,
eruptions of the sort where soldiers, sailors and marines shatter
tables and chairs over each others' heads in simple high spirits. As
the central portion of his face had been pressed in, flattening to
pug the already small nose, the lower jaw jutted further forward to
fix permanently a cocky challenge. He was a tough-looking cus-
tomer. He also had the unaggressive grace and charm that appear
to be unique in men of that sort. When he smiled every line,
furrow and scar participated. Around Cousins Mary Lee and
Annie Lee and Ma, he was a model of courtly concern. His manners were impeccable but just clumsy enough to identify the small
boy on his best behavior. Because he said very little he seemed
mysterious, prompting heaven knows what sort of fancies in a
mind like Ma's. She and Cousin Mary Lee and Cousin Annie Lee
knew there were things he had done and sights he had seen they
could never know about, and by respecting his privacy they effectively freed him from having to say anything at all. It was largely
because of Ma that Cousin Mary Lee finally married the General.
Ma reasoned with Cousin Mary Lee, pushed her, was stern with
her, fantasized for her, rhapsodized for her and ultimately secured
a successful match. I think that if Cousin Mary Lee hadn't said yes
then, Ma would have. The General, she told me, was the only
truly romantic man she had ever met.

If Ma was able to persuade Cousin Mary Lee to take the Big
Step it was because of the influence Ma came to have at Lewis's
Landing in the weeks following what either was referred to as "it"
or, when the old Lewis sisters and Ma were together out of Cousin
Mary Lee's earshot, was whispered of as "the attack." Those may
have been Ma's finest hours.

.   .   .

Ma arrived at Lewis's Landing the Monday of Thanksgiving week and came over to St. Matthew's the next afternoon to receive a first-hand disaster report from Mr. Devereaux. She was in a new, very sporty, black-and-cream LaSalle convertible that she drove with the confident recklessness of someone who believes that money, grooming and station in life are as important in persuading a car to function as any knowledge of driving. Odile Devereaux handled a car as if she were a distracted racing driver, Ma like someone accustomed to giving orders. She appeared always to be surprised and a little exasperated when she got behind the wheel that she could not tell the machine where she wanted to go and leave all further decisions to it. When I was with her she left the driving to me and, having no interest in driving techniques and no concept of highway safety, she was a model passenger. Though she and Mr. Devereaux agreed that since my grades had not improved, I should remain quarantined to the campus, an immediate exception to the rule was made.

I was sprung to spend the Thanksgiving weekend at Lewis's Landing with Cousins Mary Lee and Annie Lee and Miss Mary Lee, the Greek and Latin teacher who was a taller, plainer version of my Modigliani-like Ma. Miss Mary Lee has no real place in these events yet the memory of her stays vivid while that of Annie Lee is dim. Miss Mary Lee, I'm sure, had a secret life. When she wore that black evening dress, which had the long tight sleeves and was cut down to the belly button, she reminded me of Lady Macbeth. Her tits weren't great but she was capable, I thought, of murder by carving knife. Ma said it was just Miss Mary's way, that she was not as cold and calculating as she looked. I saw in her demons on the point of taking charge as I wondered, quite naturally, if she had never, in all of her fifty-five years or whatever it was, been fucked. The subject of fucking much occupied my thoughts in those days.

Miss Mary came as Lady Macbeth to our Thanksgiving dinner, which was one of the more drunken though nominally teetotaling meals I've ever survived. The only outside guest was Miss Mary's beau, Mr. Hartman, who was the president of the bank at Tatterhummock Court House and had been Miss Mary's beau for close to forty years. He was a small, portly sixty-year-old bachelor with the unlined babyface I associate with celibate priests and monks who never think of abusing themselves, the youthfully puffy look being the result of all that unspent sperm bursting to get out of their balls.

We'd first had several teaspoons of sherry in the living room, which was heated by the Franklin stove and was a pousse-café of alternating layers of hot and cold air, and then moved into the equally drafty dining room for an old-fashioned Tidewater feast served by Aunt Minnie, the faithful slave with the matchstick legs and sour disposition. Turkey with chestnut stuffing, Smithfield ham cut so thin the slices were almost transparent, beaten biscuits and homemade sweet butter, candied yams, mashed turnips, hominy grits, Brussels sprouts, homemade cranberry sauce, brandied peaches, a kind of preserve that tasted like chutney, pickled green tomatoes that I suspected had gin in them and homemade cherry wine that was as sweet as Royal Crown Cola. I outdid myself, having three helpings of everything, which reminded Cousin Annie Lee how nice it was to have a growing boy in the house again, which prompted Cousin Mary Lee to say some obligatory things about boys' appetites in general, followed by reminiscences of renowned eaters in the Lewis family past. Miss Mary never addressed any remarks to Mr. Hartman, which led me to suspect that I'd been wrong and that maybe they did engage in back-seat fucking and were too guilty to talk to each other or even look each other in the eye. On the other hand, they might only have been bored with each other, which they had every right to be.

The meal's *pièce* was expected to be a mince pie baked by Cousin Annie Lee and Miss Mary as a treat for me after Ma had let it out that mince pie was my favorite. I like mince pie but it's not my favorite. I don't think I've ever had a favorite pie, as Ma well knows. She'd gotten mixed up again. It was Tom who had favorite things and his favorite pie was pumpkin, but perhaps that would have been too painful for Ma so she had said mince instead. Though it made no difference, it was total confusion in tastes and responsibilities. By the time Aunt Minnie brought in the pie, flaming as if drenched in gasoline, the two old Lewis sisters were well on their way to being smashed on cherry wine. As the pie was put on the table, the sisters displayed the ticks of junkies anticipating their fixes. One bite told the reason. The pie was awash not in brandy but in 120-proof, locally distilled corn liquor. The Lewises, who wouldn't have served conventional cocktails in that house with a gun at their heads, got around their self-imposed Prohibition by soaking virtually everything edible in sherry, bourbon, brandy, gin or corn. I ate half my piece and began to get a hangover. Ma pushed one small bite around her plate, making little hockey-player movements with her fork while exclaiming with increasing insincerity how delicious it was and how she simply had to have the recipe. Cousin Mary Lee begged off, citing her figure, while Mr. Hartman, who'd been to this well before, ate his entire portion in silence. Each Lewis sister, too far gone to notice the lack of enthusiasm elsewhere, persuaded the other to have a second helping, using coffee as a chaser.

After a suitable cooling-off period in the living room, Mr. Hartman took his leave, Ma went to her room to write letters and the two soaks retired to their rooms to sleep it off. It was only four in the afternoon and though it would soon be dark, Cousin Mary Lee asked me if I'd like to take a walk down to the river to digest some of the food that, I was aware, made me look like a snake who'd swallowed a basketball. We both put on galoshes and worn duffle coats that were placed in the hall for use by anyone who might need them—a kind of hospitality that still moves me.

It was a dank, gray winter afternoon, the leafless forest between the house and the river looking as much like a tangle of barbed wire as trees. Tatterhummock County doesn't have a real winter. It goes from the long, radiant spring and the hot, drowsy, cloudless days of summer into four months that seem like a single, everlasting November. Seldom cold enough to snow or, if it does snow, too warm for the snow to stick. The hickories, oaks and elms lose their leaves but the loblollies stay green and, under the vines of dried honeysuckle, violets continue to bloom. They are dark days, broken occasionally by one of brilliant sunshine and unusual cold when the whitecaps on the river have the look of frost.

As we walked down the muddy road to the old ferry landing, Cousin Mary Lee put an arm around my waist and kissed my cheek, then locked arms with me. She bounced as we walked. "I declare," she said, "I don't know why but I'm so happy . . . and I didn't even taste that pie." She giggled and squeezed my arm. "Poor Cousin Marshall, you couldn't eat it, could you? When we get back to the house I'll see if I can't find something else. Maybe it's having your mother here. I'm so fond of her I can't tell you. And you, dear Marshall, my Yankee cousin, you're getting so handsome. . . ." Cousin Mary Lee, Lockie said, probably flirts in her sleep. "What fun to have you down here and living so close. I guess that's why I'm feeling so gay. It's like having a new beau," she squeezed my arm again, "but one I don't have to worry about. Then too," she laughed as if to deny the importance of the revelation she was about to give the world, "my dear faithful Stewart will be coming home soon. He's going to be a full colonel. Imagine. I told him last year that I didn't want to see him until he was a full colonel. I was just joking, but I think he's going to be promoted when he gets to Washington. . . . Oh, Marshall, darling, you're going to love Stewart, I know. All his men are crazy about him. One of his captains—a boy from Roanoke?—stopped by here last summer . . . on leave? He said Stewart was probably the most popular officer in the entire United States Army. Isn't that something?" She sighed and went silent.

"What's wrong?" I said. She looked very serious and worried. "I don't think it's wrong to be so happy, do you?" I smiled at her. She was not joking. Her spirits revived. She was resolute. "Because I am happy . . . dear Marshall, Stewart wants me to marry him. He's serious this time and I shouldn't tell you this, but so am I. After all these years I really believe he's the one . . . the only one. He says that if I don't say yes this time, he won't be back . . . not that he won't still love me, but because it's too painful for him . . . and I believe him." "Do you love him?" "I do! I do!" "Then what's the problem?" "He's going to be sent back to the Philippines and I'd have to go with him, of course. I don't know what that will do to Mother. I can't leave her here all by herself and I can't very well take her with me. . . ." Pause. "Well, that's enough about me, but I'm still so happy I like to explode!"

We slid and slipped along the muddy spine of the road, finally emerging from the forest onto a broad clearing paved with the crushed fragments of oyster shells I hated as a little boy. I felt as if we were walking below the level of the river that stretched, gun-metal gray, almost four miles across to the Northern Neck. It was as if we were in a trough, the effect, I guess, of my then being used to the river at St. Matthew's and Wicheley Hall where I was al-ways looking down on the river from a bluff above. A pier of weathered gray pilings and planks reached into the stream amidst rotting, barnacled mooring posts. A small, scruffy oyster boat was anchored several hundred feet offshore. The air was fresh. Even the riverbank smell of decomposing kelp was bracing. We walked onto the pier and out to the end where, for the convenience of fishermen, a crude wooden bench had been built. As we sat on it facing the river, Cousin Mary Lee put her head on my shoulder while I slipped my arm around what waist I could feel through her duffle coat.

"Are you happy, Marshall?"

"I don't know."

"You always seem to be pretending to be somebody else."

I didn't say anything, not knowing how to reply. As if in panic she took her head from my shoulder and glanced at me.

"I didn't mean anything nasty by that," she said. "You do know that, don't you?" She put her head back on my shoulder. "I like the way you look and the way you talk. I think you dress rather oddly for a boy your age but I like your gumption. If I was ten years younger I might have fallen in love with you myself, even if we are cousins, but only second cousins twice removed. That's not so bad, I guess. . . ." Another pause. "What I meant about your pretending to be someone else . . . I'm not exactly sure but . . . you know I worked in the office at St. Matthew's for two years—before Mother had her heart attack, when I decided to stay home?—and, well, I felt so sorry for all those little boys, even the dirtiest, messiest, ugliest ones, away from home, trying not to be homesick. They broke my heart, some of them. Every night I wanted to take them home with me, give them a good meal, a scrub in a hot tub and put them to bed for a decent night's sleep. One time last year Mr. Hartman was driving Mother and me home from a dinner party in Queen Anne . . . it was late, about mid-night, I reckon, and we recognized three St. Matthew's boys walk-ing along the road to Four Corners. I know they buy beer there and get drunk and heaven knows what all. I can't imagine what David Devereaux is thinking of. He must realize what goes on. I know you've been in some trouble already, so . . ." She lifted her head to give me her widest, most girlish grin. "Now you must promise me you're not going to get into any *more* mischief. Promise?"

I promised and the head went back onto my shoulder. The scent of Ivory soap and underclothes kept in bureaus made sweet by homemade sachets exchanged at Christmas. A very long pause. "Do you think about Tom much? I do. I remember the first time your mother brought him down here when he was about four or five. You were still a baby so you couldn't come that time. You stayed home with your mammy. . . ." Mammy! I'd never thought of Mo as my mammy! Good Christ. ". . . I had the best time with that child. I was twelve and it was like having a new brother, except that he had the wickedest temper. I've never seen a child have tantrums like that when he didn't get his way. But he was so sturdy and so proud. I taught him how to swim, right down here, in one day, and after that he wouldn't let anyone touch him when he was in the water. He was so . . . independent. . . ." Long pause. She didn't move her head. "I understand that it really wasn't an accident . . . that the wound was self-inflicted? Is that true?" I said it was. "But why in the world. . .?" I said I thought it was another tantrum.

When she didn't answer me I could tell she thought I was being frivolous, but she didn't scold. "I wonder what he would be like today," she said. "I don't know," I said, but I did know or at least I suspected I did: still living in Barrington, probably married to Molly the Milk Cow and the father of six kids, running a dairy, living in a house as small and dreary as the one we'd inhabited, never spending any of Lockie and Boo's money not because he was frugal but because he had no particular interest in anything. "Do you miss him?" said Cousin Mary Lee. I said that I guess I did. "I do . . . but now we have *you*!" She turned to kiss me, then stood up. "We'd best start home. It's going to be dark walking up the hill and I don't want you breaking a leg." When we were back in the house and had taken off our coats and galoshes, Cousin Mary Lee kissed me again. "What a nice visit that was!" She sent me up to my room with a little tap on my shoulder, using her hand as if it were a dance card.

It was Jackie who first made me say what I felt about Tom. I said it out loud. Decisively. There was no way I could explain it as some sort of tongue's slip. We'd dined at a restaurant on the East Side and I'd drunk more booze and wine with dinner than was my custom. For reasons I've now forgotten I'd pursued the subject of Tom, telling her at one point the story of Tom and me and the raw bacon, but getting sideswiped by the memory of the humiliation about Lindy. Afterward as we were swinging up Park, past the Ritz Towers, Jackie suddenly said in her most self-assured, nurse-like, irritating manner, "You must have disliked him a great deal." "I loathed him," I said, and as I heard myself say it I stopped and looked at Jackie. And just like that, with no warning whatsoever, adjacent to all that expensive real estate, I burst into the tears of childhood. Jackie, who was not entirely sober herself, put her arms around my waist and hugged me. "Oh my God," I said, "what am I doing?" "You're crying," said Jackie, "and it's good for you. . . ." She pressed against me. Indecently quickly, even before the tears had stopped rolling, I said, "Let's go home and fuck," which we did.

17

On the Friday of that Thanksgiving weekend Ma and I decided to drive to Williamsburg for lunch. When we left at eleven, the Lewis sisters were making lists, which is what they liked to do almost as much as drink pie, and Cousin Mary Lee was on her way to Tatterhummock Court House to do chores. The weather, which had been rainy, cleared, and in the afternoon, on the drive back to Lewis's Landing, Ma and I made several detours looking for houses Ma remembered visiting as a child. Once, just for the hell of it, we followed a small, homemade road sign shaped like an arrow that pointed us toward CONTENT. As soon as we turned off

the macadam of the Tatterhummock Trail the road became a
sandy path running through thick scrub-pine woods. We drove for
a mile and then came upon a small clearing in the center of which
was an unpainted frame shack, newly built of raw wood, neat and
tidy, but no one apparently at home. It could have been a Tatterhummock witch's house. In Tatterhummock County no witch
would be able to afford such fairytale frills as gingerbread walls,
iced roofing and bon-bon chimneys. I turned the car around
briskly, quite aware I was playing Hansel to Ma's Gretel. When
we drove through Tatterhummock Court House we found a popu-
lace in uproar, the courthouse seeming to be under seige. Cars,
pickup trucks, even one tractor, had been driven onto the courthouse lawn and abandoned by owners who were gathered around
the building's front door. I saw the county sheriff's car as well as
the police car from Queen Anne. There were probably no more
than thirty or forty men milling about but in Tatterhummock
Court House they made a multitude. Ma told me to stop near a
young man not much older than I was, dressed in overalls. In her
best cornpone accent Ma asked the fellow what was going on. He
grinned and popped his eyes with excitement. "That's where they
got the nigger," he said. Ma, sweetly: "What nigger?" "The one
that raped Mary Lee Moulton this morning," he laughed, "just as
she was coming out of the post office!"

By the time Ma and I arrived at Lewis's Landing the rape was
four and three-quarter hours old. As we came up the driveway it
would have been difficult to tell whether the guests had assembled
for a wedding, a picnic or a funeral. Friends from all over the
county, as well as from Middlesex and Gloucester, had rallied,
most of them men. Those wives who had been allowed to come
had brought with them the substantial remains of a half dozen
Thanksgiving dinners. One of the most vivid details I remember of
that afternoon and evening is that people were always talking with
their mouths full. Though the men talked among themselves
gravely, often chewing on something too, and though they bore
their importance consciously, aware that fateful decisions were to
be made, the air was festive, at least in the first-floor rooms of that
plain old house. When Ma and I walked in, the men, most of them
in informal Saturday clothes, were standing in clusters, whispering

SCENERY   I 2 I

genteelly, sometimes laughing, but quietly so as not to disturb the people on the second floor. Some were eating cake, daintily with forks. Others were drinking coffee that often turned out to be booze served in coffee cups. Commander Lumberton, Philo's father, was there, a huge, much heavier version of Philo but without, I supposed, Philo's distinctive decor. The Commander had one eyeball that kept slipping up and away from the good eye with which he did his serious viewing. He had the short attention span and the easily distracted manner of someone definitely crazy, though none of the other men ever gave indication that anything he said or did was unreasonable. That's how friends are. Miss Mary's beau, Mr. Hartman, was there wearing his Thanksgiving suit and vest of celibate gray flannel. I recognized several other men as leading citizens of Queen Anne and Tatterhummock Court House. Cousin Mary Lee Moulton and the Lewis sisters inspired their special concern. They lived on the place without any men, not even a niggra. They were maidens unprotected in a landscape that had once again revealed itself to be alien.

Until the arrival of Ma and me, Miss Mary had been acting as a sort of hostess, wearing something she apparently thought to be most suitable for post-rape receptions—the plain black Lady Macbeth evening dress with some Belgian lace stuffed into the bottom of the V. It wouldn't do to have a tit, even one of fifty-five years, go popping out to distract the boys from their business. When she came out of the kitchen to see Ma standing there, the whole Lady Macbeth image—the air of resolute composure, cool cunning and potential for positive action—collapsed in virginal tears. She was taller and larger than Ma so when she more or less crumbled on top of Ma, weeping, gasping, making those little fore-fainting signs, she almost knocked Ma to the floor. For several seconds they tottered together as the gents looked politely away. Lady Macbeth pulled herself together bit by bit, saying, "Oh, Mary . . . I can't bear to think about it. . . ."

"Do you want me to take care of things down here?" Ma said. Miss Mary sobbed her affirmative response. Ma turned to me and saw the scene she was playing. I followed Ma as she helped Miss Mary up the stairs, Lady Macbeth whispering what I knew must be the sordid details. "How is Cousin Mary Lee?" I asked, since no one had yet mentioned her name. "She's all right," Lady Macbeth said through her tears. "She's going to be all right. It's your Cousin Annie Lee I'm worried about." At the top of the stairs Ma was firm with me. "Go to your room and I'll call you if I need you." As she walked Miss Mary down the hall to her room I wondered if Lady Macbeth had been at the corn to steady her nerves, if that was why she was so grandly limp.

To be ready for any emergency I didn't take off my shoes when I lay down on my bed, a fourposter with a feather mattress and, on top, the fancy, omnipresent-in-that-house, crocheted string bedspread. I still didn't know what had happened. From all of the activity I could hear—the sounds of doors being opened and closed quickly as if to contain pestilence, of footsteps coming and going on the stairs and in the hall and adjacent bedrooms—I realized that with the exception of Ma and me, and of Aunt Minnie, the entire household had taken to its bed to be waited on and protected by others, and Ma and I didn't count, being outsiders. I assumed Miss Mary was telling the truth and that Cousin Mary Lee was all right. I told myself that if she hadn't been all right she would have been taken to the hospital in Richmond, though Tatterhummock ladies like the Lewises always had their babies at home. They might also elect to die at home. Maybe Cousin Mary Lee wasn't all right. I heard a long sorrowful moan and went to my door to peep out. Ma was just closing the door to Miss Mary's room—whence the long sorrowful moan—and tiptoed down the hall to me. "Is Cousin Mary Lee all right or not?" I said. "Yes," said Ma, "she's sleeping now. That was Miss Mary. Dr. Perry just gave her a shot of something to calm her down. . . . She's afraid of needles. It's Cousin Annie Lee we're all worried about. We're afraid of her heart." "Where is she?" "In her room, sleeping. The doctor gave her a shot too. Mrs. Lumberton is with her. She seems to be breathing properly now." "What the hell happened? And what are all of those people doing downstairs, including the crazy Commander?" "That's just the way county people are," said Ma. She reached up to kiss my cheek in a maternal gesture that was just slightly less foreign to her nature than her Tatterhummock County accent. Ma didn't sound this way or kiss like that anywhere else in the world. "People take care of each other down here," she said. "It's the Old Manners." "I'd like to find out what's going on," I said. "I'll inquire," said Ma. "I'll let you know as soon as I can. Now go back in there and stay out of the way." Ma was as excited as the men.

It turned out that Cousin Mary Lee hadn't been raped at all, not in any medical sense of the word. She'd been "attacked," which in those days was also a euphemism for rape, contributing to the confusion about the real story. People went around saying how awful it was that Mary Lee Moulton had been "attacked," which everyone then understood as meaning how awful it was that Mary Lee Moulton had been raped. She hadn't been violated in that way, though what happened was bad enough for someone as tenaciously innocent as Cousin Mary Lee.

She had taken the Moulton Chevy into Tatterhummock Court House at 11:30 that morning, made some purchases at the Ideal Dry Goods Store and then had gone to the post office. She came out of the post office and was placing her bundles on the back seat of the Chevy, parked in front of the post office, when a black man, whose age no one seems to have known, called to her by name from the sidewalk 15 feet away. He was carrying a large bunch of bittersweet. Though Cousin Mary Lee didn't recognize the man, she assumed he must work for one of her friends who was sending her a Thanksgiving gift. She closed the back door of the car and turned to receive the tribute, putting on her most gracious-to-the-darkies smile. Darkies, she knew, liked her, as she liked them. She'd grown up in Tatterhummock County and it didn't surprise her that sometimes darkies she didn't recognize recognized her, greeted her, asked about her mother and Miss Mary, sometimes recalling incidents from Cousin Mary Lee's childhood that would fix that particular darkie in a specific time frame and, perhaps, dredge up a lost name. Cousin Mary Lee had been the prettiest girl in the county for as long as she could remember. She was known to people she did not know, and she took being gracious to the less fortunate as a serious social responsibility.

She smiled with serene kindliness at the black man as he stepped down from the sidewalk to approach the car where she stood. As he approached her he shifted the bittersweet, neatly wrapped in newspaper, from his right hand to his left. When he was several yards from her he took his newly unengaged right hand and, with a lightning stroke, undid his fly to whip forth that precious instrument that has so long united the fantasies of the white and black south. Cousin Mary Lee screamed. It was said at Lewis's Landing that afternoon that the scream was heard by everyone in Jones's Barber Shop on the far side of the courthouse green. Though she was able to scream, Cousin Mary Lee was unable to move as the man dropped the bittersweet to grab her. Rape may well have been the man's intention but he hadn't seriously thought things out. Even in a community as tiny and lethargic as Tatterhummock Court House the chances of scoring a successful rape at noon, on Saturday, on the main street, were slim. Someone was bound to interfere. Within seconds a lot of people did. In that short space of time, though, the man knocked Cousin Mary Lee to the pavement, tore her sweater down the front, dislodged the fully stuffed bra, ripped off one stocking and shoe, and attempted an unsuccessful slide toward homeplate with fingers whose nails left the inside of her thighs bleeding. It may have been this blood and its positioning that convinced many people that the black man, a known loon who'd once worked briefly at the Lewis place years before, had penetrated Cousin Mary Lee with a frightened dong whose balls were subsequently crushed by the kicks of the crowd that came to the rescue.

Cousin Mary Lee was badly battered, bruised and scratched, but nothing was broken. Her maidenhood remained intact. The only thing permanently damaged was her peace of mind, her confidence that God, who had always been good to her, would be good to her in the future. She stayed in bed for seven days, in seclusion for another five, and emerged ten days before Christmas, looking pale and becomingly thin, to attend Sunday morning services at St. Matthew's parish church on the arm of the General, who'd just been made a full colonel. After that Cousin Mary Lee Moulton was as beautiful, gracious, kind and ebullient as she had ever been, but now it took more effort.

· · ·

All through the evening of the day of the attack I could hear automobiles arriving and departing. At one point Dr. Perry, an old, easily befuddled general practitioner, opened my door, stared at me and said, "Oh, my," and turned on his heels saying, "I was looking for your sister." At seven o'clock Ma brought in a tray of food and sat with me while I ate, filling me in on the details she'd learned. The sheriff had just come and gone. He was looking for the cockeyed Commander who, the sheriff told Ma, had been raving on to some locals about taking care of that nigger. The sheriff, said Ma, was afraid that things might get nasty and he didn't think he and his deputy would be able to handle it. With two friends the Commander had left the house earlier, reassuring Ma that he knew what he was doing, just before he smashed into Dr. Perry's station wagon as he was turning his own car around. "My God," I said, "you know he's nuts, and he's got a son who's as nuts as he is. What's Mr. Hartman say?" "He says that everything's going to be all right and looks more worried than ever. He's not a very interesting man, do you think? I don't. But he is the president of the bank. . . ." "The Tatterhummock Bank," I said, "has a hole in the roof to drop pennies through."

There were six or eight men still downstairs, Ma said, and they'd been on the verge of leaving until the sheriff arrived, when they decided to have one more drink as they considered courses of action. "Courses of action?" I said. "Why don't we go back to Chicago?" The men clearly didn't trust the sheriff who, they told Ma, was inclined to pussyfoot in crises of this magnitude. Ma was silent for a few minutes, puffing on one of the cigarettes the Lewis sisters didn't approve of. Finally, guiltily, not looking me in the face: "I didn't tell you . . . but I think they have guns. I saw one of the men . . . I don't know his name . . . take one of the others out to his car to show him something in the back seat. It looked to me as if they were rifles or shotguns. . . ." "Did you tell the sheriff?" "I didn't get a chance to. Actually I didn't think of it." Ma was so involved in the crisis she didn't bother to comment when I lit a cigarette for myself. "You know," she said, "the men down here go a little haywire sometimes, in a situation like this. I wish your father or Tom were here," she caught herself, "but you're here.

I'm glad for that." Fuck you, Ma. "I don't think either you or I," I said, "is going to be able to stop those idiots if they're planning to hold a necktie party, or do the Old Manners favor tar and feathers?" She turned on me. "This is not a joke. You don't seem to realize that. Cousin Mary Lee was badly beaten. They almost killed the man who did it before the sheriff got there. The sheriff told me the man won't be able to do *that* again. . . ." "What did they do? Cut his pecker off?" "Oh, darling." "Well, what?" "I don't know . . . they gave him a bad thrashing, I guess."

Sometime around 7:30 Ma and I watched two cars come up the driveway and slow to the lazy stop of drunk drivers. I could see four men getting out of one car and six out of the other. Three of the men walked toward the house carrying guns. The Commander had returned with reinforcements. At the sight of the guns now openly displayed, Ma was stirred to action. She hurriedly left the room, telling me to stay where I was. I lay back on the bed and waited, smoking and dropping ashes all over the crocheted bedspread. The smell of burning string finally forced me to sit up to find the pin dish Ma had been using as an ash tray. Next to it on the bureau was a miniature of Meriwether Lewis as a boy. The tiny, pretty face expressed nothing. From the first floor I heard loud voices. At first I thought some sort of argument had broken out, but then I heard laughter. They don't call them necktie parties for nothing. At any moment I expected someone to wind up the Moultons' old Victrola and start the music. Ma came back panting for breath and all aglow about the forehead. "Come downstairs right away," she said, whispering, though there appeared to be no reason to, "but don't go through the living room and library. Go down and wait for me in the kitchen." "What are you going to do?" "Wake up Miss Mary. She has to help too."

I walked down the stairs as casually as I could, through the dining room, past the Commander who was now wearing a red-and-black checkered Hudson Bay hunting jacket and a duck hunter's red cap, as well as the kind of high wading boots used for swamp shoots. Lynch gear? In the kitchen Aunt Minnie sat in the corner almost hidden by the big wood stove. She was wearing her hat and coat, apparently waiting to be told she could go home. She looked peaked, her matchstick legs shoved out in front of her to make a figure of hopeless impotency, a forgotten marionette. She stole glances at me but said nothing for a long while. I realized that she must be younger than I'd suspected, that she was the sort of person who'd been born looking frail and old but who would, as Cousin Mary Lee said more than once, outlive us all.

When she finally spoke to me, though, she didn't sound abject. "That man who done it," she said, "he's crazy. That's all. They already sent him away twice but they keep letting him out. Now they's just going to kill him." She shook her head. Ma joined us, followed by a dazed but docile Miss Mary. Ma was full of purpose. "Aunt Minnie," she said, "why do you have your hat and coat on? We have work to do. Miss Mary's entertaining friends and they're hungry and thirsty." Miss Mary: "What are we going to give them?" "First of all," said Ma, "take all the liquor in there and put it on the dining room table so they can make their own drinks, and give them glasses, not coffee cups. Is there any ice? Tell them Aunt Minnie is fixing supper for everybody, and keep them busy, hear?" Miss Mary, wanly: "I think so." "Above all," said Ma, "keep them in the house. Minnie, lend me your coat for a while. You ain't going home right now." Aunt Minnie was as cowed by Ma's authoritative manner as Miss Mary. She stood up, gave Ma her coat, held it for her to slip on, then offered Ma her hat, a small, worn, wilted Dolly Varden. Ma said, thank you, but that she'd get along just fine with the coat. She looked at me. "You should have a coat too but we don't have time."

Ma and I went out the back door, walked around the side of the house away from the living room and dining room, to the driveway and the Commander's automobile, a once elegant, open touring car that was now mud-caked, its fenders misshapen, its canvas top patched like a quilt. On the floor of the luggage trunk were three boxes of dynamite sticks packed in heavy wooden crates stamped with the name of the manufacturer in Portland, Maine, and two boxes of dynamite caps. There were also a half dozen boxes of shotgun shells on the back seat of the car.

"What are we going to do?" I asked Ma.

"Hide it," said Ma. "Let's start with the dynamite."

"Where?"

"Anywhere. Just get it out and away from the car."

Dynamite in that quantity is heavy. I'd get a crate out of the trunk and onto the ground, then Ma and I would take hold of it, one on each side, and waddle our way toward the barn. Because we had to rest every six or seven steps it took us a half hour to defuse the car. We hid the dynamite sticks in the back of the barn on the east side, and the caps in the back of the barn on the west side. Neither of us knew anything about dynamite or how it was detonated, but we did know the stick was no good without the cap, or so I'd read in comic books. We placed the shotgun shells inside the barn in the corner of an empty stall, and then wondered about the guns. There were six in the rack outside the front door and as many more in the other cars in the driveway. Ma and I debated hiding the guns too. I suggested I could take them out to the pasture and leave them there. Ma thought that their disappearance might cause an ugly scene and then we'd never neutralize the lynchers. "They'd know right away we'd been up to something. Heaven knows what they'd do." I was now full of enthusiasm for our mission and suggested that the least I could do would be to make sure that all of the guns were unloaded.

"Let's go in," said Ma. "I don't want you touching any guns."

The great adventure petered out. The Commander and the others rolled off about ten o'clock, at which point Miss Mary called the sheriff to tell him about the dynamite haul and that the vigilantes were heading his way. They were too late, the sheriff said. His deputy and the policeman from Queen Anne had left for Richmond with the prisoner two hours earlier. The vigilantes, he said, were welcome to inspect the jail or do whatever they liked. In actual fact the vigilantes never got to the jail. They were tired. They drove home and went to bed.

The next morning the sheriff came by to pick up the explosives and shotgun shells. He patted Ma on the back and shook his head in wonder at her quick-wittedness and bravery. Ma was terribly gracious and offered him a glass of sherry and later said he had stayed too long. The doctor came and after examining both Cousins Mary Lee and Annie Lee told us that they would recover with absolute rest.

The last two days of the weekend were less than gay. Before returning to St. Matthew's on Sunday afternoon I knocked on

Cousin Mary Lee's door. When I entered I wasn't prepared for the obscured eye and the other swellings, the black-and-blue bruises. She was sitting up in bed wearing a pink bedjacket, her long brown hair hanging loosely about her shoulders. The physical damages embarrassed me. "I've got to go back to school now," I said. "I wanted to say goodbye." "Come in, Marshall." She smiled in the way of someone just widowed, then made a place for me to sit on the side of the bed. I was mortified by her appearance and didn't want to look at her. She took my hand, squeezed it. Her eyes filled suddenly with tears of spontaneous gratitude. She attempted to smile. "I'm afraid it wasn't a very happy weekend for you," she said. "The next time we'll have a real good time, you'll see." She dabbed at her undamaged eye with a minute handkerchief. "We did have a nice visit on Thanksgiving, though, didn't we?" Pause. What does one say to a would-be rapee? I said, "I love you, Cousin Mary Lee. . . ."

"Oh, Marshall, darling, that's the dearest thing you've ever said to me . . . and I look such a fright, too. Thank you, thank you. . . ." Another squeeze of the hand, a ferociously strong one. I said that I had to be going but she didn't seem to hear. She was looking away, weeping, rolling her handkerchief into a ball, dabbing again at her eye. I was on the verge of weeping with her. What was going on in that belle's brain of hers? "Oh, Marshall, darling. . . ." "What is it?" "Oh . . . I am so *ashamed*. . . ."

18

In the Caribbean there is a phenomenon called God's Light when, thirty-six hours before the arrival of a hurricane, the air purifies itself, becomes so cleansed and suddenly clear one can see for miles beyond the familiar world. The horizon rolls back to reveal islands usually hidden by tiny particles of moisture. Clarity of such intensity makes truth a distortion of nature. By God's Light one is given a last opportunity to take one's bearings before Armageddon, though by that time one needs more than bearings. There are no days quite so beautiful—hot, windless, magically transparent—nor quite so fearsome. One has to pay attention.

Such a time for me was that rainy Thanksgiving weekend at Lewis's Landing with its unfulfilled penny melodrama. Ma had slipped me $5 when she took me back to St. Matthew's but at least until Christmas I was still on-bounds, except when Ma might make a special request to take me away, and I was still cut off from my regular weekly allowance. Since my grades were not improving it seemed the proscriptions would be continued forever. More or less of my own volition I became the Man in the Iron Mask, a prisoner inside what I thought to be a totally impassive exterior, one that I wasn't going to allow anyone to penetrate. I would survive this ordeal without change, untouched.

That promise to myself did not take into consideration my own lust and greed. I regularly saw Ma at Sunday morning services at St. Matthew's Church, a half mile down the road from the school, and I was allowed to go to Lewis's Landing for luncheon the Sunday that Cousin Mary Lee made her comeback appearance at the church with the General. But I was still technically treed and I was quickly flat broke again. I didn't even have a friend close enough from whom I could borrow funds. I'd written Lockie but Ma had had the foresight—or maybe it was only her natural gabbiness—to shut off that potential source of supply. Thus like the poor farm boy down and out in the big city I was forced (I told myself) into male harlotry, into carrying out my contract with Gordon Felix. I know now, of course, that I wasn't forced and that as Felix, with his round heels and hairless skin that had the texture of doll-rubber, fed his soul on me, I was feeding my soul on the positions, on the choreography, of our relationship. At any moment, had I wanted to, I could have bashed his brains out.

So it came to pass that I allowed the cannibal to have his way in my cubicle, in the shower room and once, when I was being unnaturally reckless and had decided to walk boldly off the campus, in a bower of loblollies and dead honeysuckle, between and behind the school tennis court and St. Matthew's Church, a few feet off a path that was the shortcut between the campus and Shackleford's Store. As I lay back on the cannibal's windbreaker, looking up into the pines, listening to ten-year-old Ruddleston, A.

and Dale Warfield attempting to play tennis, congratulating each other repeatedly on a good shot (which only indicated that one or the other of them had successfully hit the ball over the net), I let Felix proceed with what he liked to do in the position of supplicant. That bower was later to become sacred. Then it was no more than a dark doorway. Felix was insatiable, and he was a big spender.

A week before Christmas vacation, on a Thursday afternoon, I think, because Felix had already gone for a weekly record of $8 and was about to make it an even ten, using the extra money that a maiden aunt in Newport News had sent him to buy presents for his family, we were in the communal shower room preparing for a go. The shower room was no longer as safe as it had been during football season but it was still little used, the football team now being the basketball team wearing flimsier uniforms. Mr. Devereaux had once tried to persuade me to go out for basketball—because of my height, he said, I would make a right fine center—but I begged off pleading possible upset to my chronically ill-tempered appendix, and because I received no indication that if I did go out for basketball the blockade against me would be lifted. Quid pro quo. I had no interest in making a fool of myself for nothing in a sport for a season that promised to be as disastrous as had been the football team's. Standing comfortably under my shower nozzle, lost in thoughts that effectively removed me from the business at knee, lulled into a feeling of exact isolation and security by the vapors of steam and the drone of the water, I didn't hear the door open and the entrance of three members of the basketball squad. There was no hot water in the gym that day.

They thought it a pricelessly funny scene. Even worse for me, they thought it ridiculous. I had been on the point of satisfying the humble Felix when one of the intruders guffawed and charged cheerfully into the enclosure to secure a shower that worked, followed by other members of the team. There is no humiliation quite as complete as being apprehended in an illicit act of so little joy. I grabbed my towel and fled, accompanied by the laughter of the basketball players and, even more maddening to me, by the tee-

hees of Felix, who was not in the least embarrassed. If anything, the discovery set up a couple of the voyeurs to be easy
marks for Felix in the future when he told them what the going
rate was.

In the meantime, though, I was undone. Henceforth, I knew, I
would be irrevocably linked to the smarmy, fourteen-year-old
cannibal who was, I was convinced, certifiably retarded. The word
got around fast. In the classroom, at meals, in study hall, even in
the sanctity of the chapel at evening prayers, I'd be subjected to
jokes, innuendos, gestures, outright libels, of which, "Hey, Henderson, how about doing me?" was one of the less obscene. The
masters got wind that something had happened but I don't think
they ever knew what it was. Mr. Twigg, the genteelly burping, least
offensive member of the faculty, may have suspected. He was not
stupid and he wasn't so old that he couldn't remember to what
degradation boys could be brought. He appeared to be worried
and slightly uneasy around me, as if there were things that would
only be made worse if he were forced to take notice of them in
public.

Mr. Boyleston of the buckteeth relied on his mountainman's
intuition, which, as it frequently did, told him the opposite
to what the truth was. With complete sincerity he congratulated
me on having established a friendship with Felix. The afternoon
we were leaving on Christmas vacation he stopped me after class
to say that he'd noticed Gordon Felix and I were chums. Just how,
I've no idea. Since the afternoon of the discovery I'd been most
careful not to acknowledge Felix, even when we were forced to
share a table in the dining hall. "A boy needs a chum," said
Boyleston, who would have appreciated positive thinking. "A boy
can't go through life all alone." To which I might have replied, if I
hadn't been so chagrined, that I didn't intend to go through life as
a boy. But what was the use? Like one of the Northern Neck
bumpkins I smiled, kicked an invisible turd with my shoe and
thanked him. He put out his hand for me to shake. It was a mitt,
really, a hand so big that it could lift a basketball by grasping it
from the top. He smashed my hand in his coal miner's grip. "And
have a Merry Christmas. I reckon I won't be seeing you until next
year," which was the beginning, middle and end of his comedy

repertoire. As I was going out the door he called after me, "Even your grades are getting better." I knew they'd gotten better. In my anxiety I'd begun to do my homework.

Ma and I stayed at Lewis's Landing through Christmas and then flew to Sun Valley to spend New Year's with Lockie and some people from Lake Forest, including a middle-aged, married man who, I learned, was in the process of making a pitch for Ma. He ruined his chances, though, when he got into a fist fight one night with Walter Wanger, the movie producer, an old acquaintance of Ma's. Ma, newly arrived from Tatterhummock County with a satchel full of Old Manners that didn't leave much room for humor, said the Lake Forest fellow, who was drunk, had started the fight and the one thing she couldn't stand was a man who tried to show off by starting a fight (and then getting beaten). Even Lockie was startled by Ma's new Old Manners, which, after a week of close company, frayed the nerves. It would have been a beautiful week for me if I hadn't been haunted by the dread of having to return to St. Matthew's at the end of it, but the first few days were fine. Without members of my family or of—in Jackie's jargon—my peer group to spy on me, I applied myself to learning how to ski and found to my surprise that I did it well. After spending all day on the mountain in the sun and air, I spent most of the night in the twilight and smoke of a bar down the highway from the Ketchum Lodge, in a place without antlers and where Lake Forest types were unlikely to venture and where, more important, I scored my first free fuck. She was a pretty, muscular, clean older woman of about thirty-five, a divorcée from Rochester, New York, who worked as a waitress in the bar at night so she could afford to ski all day. She must have been nuts but she liked me. Risking everything I took her back to the lodge at 2:00 A.M., had her follow me upstairs and found heaven in a room that shared a bath via unlocked doors with Ma's room. After having spent my youth paying—or getting paid—for sex, this frantic, ten-minute one-night stand was a revelation. Though there was about it a great deal of clandestine excitement I really don't need, I experienced for the first time what fucking can be like without coercion. I resolved then and there that I never again would pay, or be paid. Some resolution.

We flew back to Richmond early in the week, which gave me four days at Lewis's Landing before the end of the holiday. They were not unpleasant days though they were so busy I never found an opportunity to execute a plan to activate my appendix, thus to delay my return to St. Matthew's, perhaps permanently. Cousin Mary Lee had bloomed again in the company of the General, her dear faithful Stewart who, whenever Cousin Mary Lee called him that, sort of wagged all over and came very near to pawing her shoe. He never said very much. Mostly he beamed with happiness. He hadn't paid attention to me in the week before we went to Idaho but he was full of daily plans involving Ma and me when we returned, principally, I guess, because we were excuses for him to get Cousin Mary Lee out of the house and away from Cousin Annie Lee's unreliable heart. One day the General drove Ma, me and Cousin Mary Lee through November-in-January rain for luncheon at Old Point Comfort. Another day we went through all the major buildings at Williamsburg. When the General was not courting Cousin Mary Lee, Ma was doing it for him, saying, when he was parking the car or paying the check or being recognized by an old friend, "Mary Lee, he's the most attractive man I've ever met," or, "What a sense of humor! That story he told about the corporal in Cuba!" or, finally, "Mary Lee, if you don't, I will," which Ma could have meant with anyone except Cousin Mary Lee.

The night before my return to the school Mr. and Mrs. Devereaux invited Ma and me for supper at Mount Vernon-on-the-Tatterhummock. It was not an evening that I anticipated with much joy but Ma was all aglitter, inside and out, wearing an evening dress that would have been right for the Bal des Petits Lits Blancs, with diamonds dangling from her ears, around her neck and on five out of ten knuckles. She was overdoing it and was, of course, quite aware of the fact. She was so gay and kittenish, I told her in the car, that I suspected she'd been at the keg of corn in the kitchen. "Oh, darling, what a thing to say, I declare. . . . I'm just looking forward to seeing old friends, that's all. You forget, David might have been your father," I groaned as I knew I was supposed to do, "I certainly hope Odile is all right, though," which was the last thing in the world she hoped at that minute. She was hoping that Odile would meet us with a bottle of whiskey in one fist and a beer in the other.

The campus buildings looked more ugly, barren and forbidding than ever with their windows dark and no midget silhouettes in view. I parked the car in the driveway behind the remains of Odile's Buick and Mr. Devereaux's Ford coupe. When we walked around to the front terrace that overlooked the river, Odile Devereaux was waiting for us, slouched, round-shouldered and disheveled as always, but unmistakably sober. She could have been a pretty, sweet-looking woman and I guess she was when Mr. Devereaux married her but, as Ma later told Cousins Annie Lee and Mary Lee, "She's let herself go. Poor Odile. She ought to wear a girdle." To which Cousin Annie Lee said, "I think she does."

Ma and Odile kissed each other and admired each other's clothes, Odile saying something that indicated she thought Ma had overdone it and not played fair. Ma was almost weeping with delight at the pink sack Odile was wearing with soup stains on the skirt. Her only jewelry was a dangerously long string of fake pearls that looked as if they'd been restrung at the Lighthouse for the Blind. Behind Odile, Jojo was jumping up and down in last year's party dress, white anklets and black patent leather dancing shoes with taps on the heels and toes. Around her tortured corkscrew curls was a white ribbon tied in a bow big enough for a circus horse. It gave her a top-heavy, mongoloid aspect. Mr. Devereaux, the same old portrait in gray, emerged from his library to greet us, laughing with what I took to be shy pleasure at Ma's remarks about how handsome he was with his gray hair. Later on I decided this was his way of hiding complete boredom.

We had drinks in the living room, a comfortable, characterless room inhabited by transients, sitting in front of the fireplace that had been so positioned that the magnificent view of the river was completely obscured. The adults had whopping old-fashioneds, Jojo orange juice, while I sipped at some terrible sherry. The old-fashioneds prompted Ma to report very funnily and cattily about the Thanksgiving mince pie afloat in corn, and Odile to say with interest that she didn't know the Lewis sisters drank, which Ma had to clear up, but maybe not quite. Mr. Devereaux asked about the week in Sun Valley and Ma went on about what a good skier I'd become, which made Mr. Devereaux perk up and look at me with curiosity. Or maybe it was the liquor and boredom. Ma told about the fight in the nightclub with Walter Wanger and how embarrassing it had been, what with the newspapers making such a thing of it and all, but that didn't impress the Devereauxs, who had no idea who Walter Wanger was.

Mr. Devereaux pressed for details about my skiing. "After the fourth day he went all the way down Rustler's Glen," said Ma. "That's an intermediate slope but one that a lot of people who go to Sun Valley every year don't try." Mr. Devereaux, laughing: "Well, I'll be dogged." Me: "That's not quite true, Ma. I didn't go all the way down, just the bottom third." Ma: "But he didn't even fall." Me: "I fell four times. You weren't there." Ma: "But you told me about it." Me: "I told you I fell four times but you weren't listening." Ma (to Odile): "I was listening." Mr. Devereaux (to me): "Marshall, that's fine. I know you could be a good athlete if you'd just try. Your father was. Your brother was. . . ." (to Ma) "Mary, this boy's going to surprise us all one day. You wait." Ma (a tiny bit worried): "Oh dear. . . ." Mr. Devereaux (laughing): "He has good stuff in him. You'll see."

I didn't recognize her at first when she served the soup. Gethsemane was out of her pants, shirt and construction worker's boots and New York Yankees baseball cap and, instead, wearing conventional black pumps and a royal blue Sunday church dress. The dress was without particular distinction but the creature in it was splendid—tall, graceful, robustly proportioned. She was a priestess in her reserve as she moved around the table, taking her time, performing her duties as if they were religious mysteries. She looked at no one and no one looked at her but me, then Ma appeared to notice her. When at last she had placed a bowl of soup in front of each of us and returned to the kitchen, Ma lowered her voice and asked Odile who the girl was. Jojo (bored): "My second nurse." Odile (picking up a spoon, her left hand clutching her pearls in an unsuccessful attempt to keep them out of the consommé): "She helps sometimes when Jojo's nurse is off, or when we entertain here." Jojo: "She's mean and I don't like her. She never laughs." Mr. Devereaux: "Maybe she does when you're not around." Ma: "She could be the Queen of Sheba. She's beautiful." Jojo: "She's my second nurse and I think she's ugly. She's got kinky hair. I despise her worse'n poison." Odile (to Jojo): "Now, Jojo. . . ." (to Ma): "She's a very strange girl. She's the daughter of Reverend Shackleford. You must remember him, the minister of the colored church on the way to Walden's Point? If he wasn't the minister when you were down here, then his father was. The Shacklefords have been running that church for years." Which reminded Ma to ask Mr. Devereaux about his father, the Old Doctor. Mr. Devereaux: "He retired from his parish last year but he's still going strong at eighty-nine. He still drives his own car. . . ." Odile: "Not too fast, thank God. He can't see. Blind as a bat. . . ." Mr. Devereaux: "He has a little house over in Middlesex." Ma: "Does he live alone?" Mr. Devereaux: "Yes, but he has a colored lady who comes in to look after things every day." Ma: "He isn't thinking of getting married again, is he?" Mr. Devereaux (laughs, shakes his head): "I don't think so. . . ." Odile (fiercely): "Over my dead body. . . ." Jojo: "Why over your dead body? Why not your live body?" Mr. Devereaux: "Hush, Jojo." Odile: "Shut your mouth, Jojo, or I'll give you a smack." Ma may have been disappointed that Odile had not displayed any symptoms of advanced alcoholism but that last remark made the entire evening worthwhile. She could feel sorry for poor David.

The lights were on in the library when we returned to Lewis's Landing shortly before midnight. Cousin Mary Lee and the General were waiting to tell us the news: Mary Lee had said yes. After ten years, two months and five days, the castle had surrendered unconditionally. There were no more secret agreements. Cousin Mary Lee's ring was a tiny square diamond that appeared to have been purchased at a Post Exchange some years before. Everyone admired it. Everyone kissed. "What about your mother?" Ma said. "She's accepted the idea, I think," said Cousin Mary Lee. "My dear faithful Stewart knows about a sweet little house right in Tatterhummock Court House he thinks would be just right for Mother and Miss Mary when she's home from school, and we'll get Aunt Minnie to live in." "You won't give up this place?" said Ma. "No," said the General, "It's Mary Lee's and I want our children to grow up here like she did." "Oh, dear, dear Stewart," said Cousin Mary Lee, kissing him, "now I can kiss you any time I want and people can go ahead and gossip as much as they like because I don't care!" Another kiss. The General asked to kiss Ma again since we were now all family, or about to be, and without Ma, he said, he wasn't sure he could have made it. "I declare, Stewart," said Ma, "there never was any doubt. It was just a question of time." The General kissed her on the cheek, beamed some more, his chest swelling as if being pumped full of helium. We toasted the couple in sherry, Ma saying, but not casually, "You're going to be the happiest two people I know," which they were for most of the rest of their lives.

19

Couples. Two by two. Why do a few survive while so many do not?

The General and Cousin Mary Lee were married in August of 1941 at St. Matthew's parish church, the delay of more than a year having become obligatory when Cousin Annie Lee suffered a minor heart attack. It was the last heart attack that Cousin Annie Lee ever had until the one that carried her off seventeen years later. On December 7, Cousin Mary Lee was en route to join the General in the Philippines. She was somewhere at sea between Honolulu and Manila, accompanied by a cargo of Lewis furniture, Lewis portraits, Lewis silverware, when she was forced to make a U-turn in mid-Pacific. They didn't see much of each other during that war in which the General won his second Congressional Medal of Honor, in Guadalcanal, I think for swimming again, but from all reports they became the perfect couple. Ma kept up with them and when the war was over she visited them whenever they were stationed in a place she thought was interesting. In the fifties she spent six weeks with them in Paris where the General was assigned to NATO and, according to Ma, Cousin Mary Lee was the most popular American hostess in France.

The General attended Cousin Mary Lee with love. He continued his courtship into their honeymoon and beyond. He never ceased to be amazed at his success even though he'd been remarkably successful in all of his other endeavors throughout his life. Not only was he a fellow who got what he wanted, he was a fellow who did not tire of what he got. In her turn Cousin Mary Lee opened up with him, grew up with his love, not too much (he hadn't been courting Clare Booth Luce all that while) but enough to stay abreast of him. Though she never stopped being the prettiest girl in the county, she also became womanly in a way that matched her age and that, Ma said, was even chic, in a casual Tatterhummock fashion. Ma introduced Cousin Mary Lee to haute couture in Paris, which Cousin Mary Lee thought of as a great convenience since she was so far from home and couldn't easily ring up Mrs. Whatshername who made all of her clothes in Tatterhummock County.

Perhaps because Cousin Mary Lee had grown up knowing that she was the center of the universe, the world outside did not intimidate her. A boring Norwegian ambassador was Mr. Hartman with a foreign accent. She accepted it all as an extension of Tatterhummock County. At the heart of the marriage, I suspect, was a miraculously enduring sexual love. The General sought and won a pretty, romantic, twenty-nine-year-old virgin. Cousin Mary Lee, after years and years of reassurances, had entrusted her deflowering to a man who worshipped her enough to be patient and gentle and, later, always on call for—as I imagine it—they were one of those couples who, year in and year out, through sickness and in health, make love every night, who feed upon it as much as food but who are never perfunctory about it and whose pleasure increases, piles up, fuck-by-fuck, in the awareness that each is a being of continued undiscovered mystery to the other. I'm sure the General was a man who'd had two of everything between Tatterhummock Court House and Hong Kong, but once he and Cousin Mary Lee were married, he would have been as faithful sexually as he had been faithful emotionally for all that time before they were married. A man of experience, he could instruct Cousin Mary Lee. He could explain and demonstrate the ecstasy of orgasm as one of God's most loving gifts, which, in not having a name that Cousin Mary Lee could bring herself to say, made more profound her awe. He whose name they dare not speak had presented them with a joy they did not talk about. The General and Cousin Mary Lee were rare lovers throughout their marriage. Each change or modification of habit or interest or physical need in one was met by a corresponding change in the other. They expanded, contracted, grew old. But though their marriage was ideal they produced one child whose rage has taken the form of a competitive, virtually suicidal stoicism, and another who noisily blasphemes God and His Gift by making fuck-films entitled *The Great Bandersnatch Raid* and *Come On Me, My Faithful.*

Couples. I think of my mother and my father. I believe they loved each other as well as most and I know each carries around an empty pocket that is all that remains of the space once occupied by the other. I remember a Sunday night when I was probably no more than three and we were still living at the Orangerie in Lake Forest. Sunday nights were a time for informal dining with just the four of us—Tommy, Ma, Tom and me, when we would have something like Welsh rarebit or beef fondu, specialties that could be prepared over a fire in the living room fireplace. These were particular occasions for me since I wasn't yet allowed to join the others at any dining room meals except breakfast. On the Sunday night I remember my father and mother had dressed to go to a dinner party, but they supported the family ritual to the extent of staying with Tom and me while we had our supper before the living room fire. They had had one or two drinks and, as I reconstruct it, began to feel libidinous. My father asked me if I would mind if they didn't go out for dinner after all, if I'd share some of my food with them. I was ecstatic. Ma wondered how they could cancel a formal dinner party at such a late hour. My father said that was easy. He would do it. He went to the hall, followed by Ma, who was followed by me. My father explained over the telephone that he was terribly sorry to have to do this at the last minute but the fact was that he and Mary would not be able to dine. Something had come up, he said. Well, he said, well, to be perfectly honest, the problem was Marshall. Marshall didn't want them to go out. Yes, he was spoiled and when he'd heard they were going out he began RAISING THE ROOF. That was the phrase—RAISING THE ROOF. As my father talked he put an arm around Ma's waist and gave her a fast kiss on the cheek. Ma was giggly and as my father said again MARSHALL IS RAISING THE ROOF my mother looked down on me and winked. I was so carried away by the picture of myself RAISING THE ROOF, holding it up like some kid-Atlas, I suppose, and so flattered to be part of this deception, so moved by their love for each other, that I put my arms around their legs and laughed and laughed, and buried my face in their extremities. Of course, while I was RAISING THE ROOF, my father was RAISING HIS COCK.

Where did their love go? I suppose there wasn't enough to start with, or that what was there wasn't deep enough to survive social humiliation, economic distress and, in particular, the death of a son who, instead of putting that gun to his own head, could as easily have chosen to murder the rest of us in our beds. In retrospect I guess each of us was furious to be in eternal debt to Tom for having blown out his own brains instead of ours. The prick. My mother and my father moved apart and on. Not enough there. Nothing left to explore that wasn't dangerous territory.

The fall that Ma went to Reno to establish residence for her divorce from my father she went into what Lockie called a tailspin. Toward the end of her six-week stay she met a man named Pollock who described himself to Ma as a detective with the Los Angeles Police Department. He had come to Reno, he said, for a holiday. He liked to ride. In the subsequent newspaper pictures, Pollock looked like a classic New York City flatfoot so I suspect he must have been a good lay or Ma wouldn't have become so nuttily involved. On the day her divorce was granted, Ma married Pollock in a simple little ceremony at the J.P.'s office and retired to the New Life Honeymoon Court to celebrate. It was there that the first and only legitimate Mrs. Pollock and her witnesses discovered the happy couple about to consummate their marriage. Ma screamed and sought sanctuary in the bathroom. Pollock slugged the private eye so hard it shattered his private jaw, which landed Pollock in the Reno slammer. It was a fine mess all round. Pollock lost his position as a traffic patrolman in Denver and Ma was named co-respondent when the real Mrs. Pollock brought her suit for divorce. There was also some nonsense about an alienation of affections suit, which suggested to Ma's lawyers that the whole thing may have started as a con game. Whatever it was, Ma had to pay a pretty sum to get sprung from the jurisdiction of the Nevada courts.

A year later Ma married Billy Summers, who'd been a friend of both my parents in Lake Forest, after Billy's wife of twenty-one years divorced him to marry someone else. Billy was harmless and good-looking except for skin that was pitted like the rind of a navel orange, and he fitted in with the new house that Ma had bought in Lake Forest. When Ma later decided she wanted to get out of that rut, she sold the house and got rid of Billy, who married another friend of my mother's and carted his clothes and golf clubs across the street. Divorces in Lake Forest are less complicated as legal proceedings than as real estate maneuvers that demand the services of the town's limited number of movers and haulers. June and September are the busiest months. Ma remained single if not celibate for twelve years, liking her freedom and, following the death of Lockie, having the means to do exactly as she pleased, which included a Swiss ski instructor at Sun Valley, an American who made paintings in Cuernavaca—he couldn't be called an artist—and an English architect who designed houses in Barbados and was so happily married he had no intention of leaving his wife.

When she became involved with a second-rate New York actor she'd met in Palm Beach, a fellow who dyed his hair and whose first preference was young men, probably ones he had to pay to punish him for being so beautiful, I thought Ma was well along the path toward that bourn from which no woman returns without skin tanned to leather. Not so. She met Paul Plyant, a nice, tall, stammering, stoop-shouldered Englishman, a business-man semi-retired at fifty-eight, a widower without children (who might have screwed things up for me), a club man with a fondness for limericks, Latin puns and medieval history, and a passion re-born by Ma. She married him after having known him only three months. I thought it wouldn't endure a year but last April they celebrated their twenty-third anniversary, which is six years longer than Ma and my father were together. At eighty-one Sir Paul is fit and kind, so solicitous of Ma that I wouldn't believe it if I hadn't seen it, and Ma, at seventy-five, looks late fifty-ish and is, at last, at some approximation of peace. Neither Ma nor Sir Paul asks for more than the other can give. Years ago I would have said they had struck a bargain, compromising things that one shouldn't compromise, but I would have been wrong. They have found a balance, which is much more difficult. They are good friends, generous to each other, capable of surprise, mindful of the other's privacy. From her settled state Ma now gazes down upon me with controlled sadness, as if I were an eccentric younger brother doomed always to fail, always in need for her to come bail me out. She no longer remembers the events in Reno and having said to me, "I will never get another divorce in *Nevada!*"

They give me hope.

Last night I dreamed of Higgenbotham, the cool Christaphine, who used to come on as if she'd just graduated from a finishing school that taught snobbery to the nouveau riche. She was—is—a terrible climber but not, unfortunately, interesting or even rich enough (on her own) to make it except on the fringes of the worlds of arts and letters and theater that dazzle her. She can cut it in Lake Forest and Chicago but she's just one of the gang in New York. She even bored Wallis at that crucial period in Ma's life when Ma and their R.H.s were becoming bosomy in spite of the fact that Ma had known Wallis back in the days when she was plain Mrs. Spencer. To bore Wallis was not easy if you were as pretty as Higgenbotham, dressed well and had access to the money she had then.

Higgenbotham and I were a match made on earth by proximity, friends, parents and a desire to put down roots in New York, where I was planning to do some research at the Metropolitan on a project associated with the Albigenses. Since we didn't fuck until our wedding night, it wasn't until then that I realized I didn't like her at all. It had nothing to do with the fucking. There would come a point one-third of the way into any screw when screwing took over and she'd forget herself long enough to reach a few glorious climaxes, which had the effect more or less of catapulting me over the top. Once done, though, she'd race to the bathroom to douche and then spray herself from head to foot with cologne. Five minutes after I'd come you wouldn't have known that that beautiful body, enveloped in scent, had ever been in the same continent with a lost spermatozoon. Still, fucking was not her weak point. It was greed, not about money as much as friends, position, intelligence, reputation and interests. Toward the end she couldn't even tolerate the sight of my reading junk mail. She wanted everything for herself, including my attention in those increasingly rare moments when there were no other people around. It wasn't until our wedding night, after having a fine, bouncy, champagne-high fuck in the lower berth of a drawing room taking us to Palm Beach, that I understood she had nothing to talk about unless it could be immediately connected back to her. She was so adept at this that I'd been fooled for over a year. She wasn't dumb. She could grasp the moral issues raised at Nuremberg by, say, noting first that she had an uncle who had been married to a woman whose brother had been on the staff that prepared the dossiers for the Allied prosecutors. The world had to relate to her. She didn't want children, at least not by me. I think she was afraid they'd be crippled in some way that would reflect on her. In last night's dream I saw her walking along a sidewalk and caught up with her. Her hair, which had been dark brown shoulder-length and worn loose when we were married, had been cut short in sort of shingles and dyed an unconvincing gold-blonde, already dark at the roots. When I drew abreast of her I said, "You've had your hair dyed and it looks terrible." She was so surprised and hurt she didn't reply, which made me sorry that I'd sounded so rudely triumphant. In mortification I awoke. It's one thing to decide you don't like someone and then split with as much calm as possible. Even good will. It's quite another to dream of an attack like that one. Christaphine Higgenbotham and I were never a couple.

Neither were Miss Utah and I. Utah has a first name, Maryjane, which I declined to use on the reasonable grounds that the Mary quota in our family had been filled ever since Bethlehem. I didn't care what other people called her but she'd always be Utah to me. Besides, one of the reasons I thought I really loved her was that fake, studied runway walk she'd worked so diligently to perfect and used even when coming out of the bathroom at 7:30 A.M., starkers, having had a most satisfying and noisy shit. I'm a great fan of beauty contests on television. They are funny, crass, sad and very, very sexy. I always wonder which one is wearing the

Tampax. For years I'd wanted a woman who walked that way and when I saw Utah at Cap d'Antibes I moved in, deaf to any sense of caution, to separate Utah and her traveling companion, a youngish, well-to-do dress manufacturer from New York.

Why didn't I listen? Not to myself but to Utah. I first noticed her by the Eden Roc pool, very tall, serenely, healthily beautiful in a slightly ordinary California way, wearing a tiny white bikini and walking around the pool in that shoulders-back, chest-out, tight-assed way that so fascinates me in the Miss America, Miss World, Miss Universe events. When she and the dress manufacturer came up to the terrace for lunch, I arranged to have the table next to them. How innocent and faultlessly suited they were. Even their tans matched.

Having been moving through Egypt alone for the last six weeks I took in their conversation less critically than I might have at another time. She: "That's good what you said about fantasies. I don't think I entertain fantasies. . . ." He: "You should. Everybody needs fantasies." She chews on a thin hard slice of Italian salami whose skin, as indestructible as nylon, she tries to untangle with her perfect teeth while nodding a vigorous agreement. A little later he says with authority, "It's very boor-gee-wah, in the worst sense. You know what I mean? It's a strata within a strata. It's boor-gee-wah." Again the nods of approval so hopelessly sincere that they deny the charm-school mannerisms. I realize the conversation is muddled but he, clearly, is the idiot, not that gorgeous clenched ass. He: "I make moves and every move has a countermove . . . by destiny's sake." Over dessert, when he is telling her about his self-aborted career in the theater (whether as an actor, producer or angel, I can't make out), he says for her continuing adoration, "I noticed I was too much the artist. I needed stability in the business sense. I didn't need the . . . the . . . the ambiguity of the theater."

The dress manufacturer was well-to-do but I was loaded. I was also sly. One afternoon while Seventh Avenue was off playing a game with the tennis pro and Utah was studying the postcards at the *caissier*'s desk, I dropped a crutch. One thing led to another and I insisted on buying her a drink at the Hôtel du Cap bar, though she didn't ordinarily drink between meals. When they went up to Paris for a week before flying home, I ran into them again at the Georges Cinq, accidentally with Utah's help. She was becoming bored and she enjoyed the intrigue. Also, he was married. Once back in New York, Seventh Avenue had to go to work again, leaving the field to me during the daylight hours.

Utah was, I'm afraid, truly dumb though shrewd. Her grounds for setting a new alimony record after eight years of marriage were based on the debatable premise that I had, by the jealous and selfish restrictions I imposed, deprived her of the artistic satisfaction of pursuing her career, of doing toothpaste commercials for Gleem and of auditioning for the Jackie Gleason Show where, had she been lucky, she'd have had the pleasure of letting Gleason pinch her tail just as she squealed ". . . and away we go!"

There have been bad times but Jackie and I are surviving, not without pain occasionally. I've had to be firm, which isn't easy for her or me. If she'd continued in the direction she was going when we first met, she'd now be ghostwriting dreadful memoirs for has-been movie actresses or surveying the market quality of false eyelashes for some slick magazine devoted to teenage survival and sensuality, living with a series of men not as bright or talented as she is, hating herself for it, and taking dance lessons at night to work off the aggressions built up during the day. She's still on the mailing list of half a dozen thieving institutions that prey on such women through what are generally called Continuing Education programs. This morning she received the fall catalog from a particularly ridiculous school, and since it was obviously a catalog I felt free to open it. In addition to offering Karate for Little People (ages 5–7), the school lists such courses as Basic Sewing, Quilt-making, Clowning (". . . emphasis is on the communication achieved between one's personal clown, other clowns, and the audience"), and Brunch ("designed to teach interesting techniques for cooking and presentation of brunch-time foods"). Early on I persuaded her to study French at the Alliance, which may be one of the best things I ever did for her. Left to her own decisions she would have devoted herself to contemporary Yiddish poetry. Several years later when we took an apartment in Paris for a winter that stretched into eighteen months, she enrolled at the Sorbonne to be able to study with Jean-Marie Prédie, a Fanon disciple and interpreter who ultimately turned out to be anti-Semitic in a serious way. Her accent is atrocious but she is now virtually bilingual, though unlike me she has never been able to do crossword puzzles in French. Her mind can retain no more than one synonym for any word.

I'd say we have a settled, rewarding life. I wasn't keen on moving to the West Side but now I'm used to it, even to Zabar's, whose delights are, to me, overrated. After spending much more time than was necessary, and vast amounts of money I never told Jackie about, our cavernous apartment (which we only rent) is most comfortable and livable even though it gives Ma the willies; but Ma confuses the apartment with the neighborhood and when she can hear transistor radios being played in the street she's sure revolution is at hand. Jackie and I each have our own library and workroom and each has his own bathroom, which is, I think, one of the secrets of our success. Jackie is, in her words of a few years back, compulsively anal about her bathroom. I'm a slob. By having separate bathrooms we've eliminated one of the early causes of friction between us. We have a single oversized bed, built to my design, and two telephone lines, though I can cut in on hers if I want to listen to her conversations. She used to be touchy about this. She had no conception of what sharing meant. She now accepts our singleness, our couplehood. In matters involving her career she can still be unbearably positive but in our relations she has become marvelously, surprisingly flexible, capable of seizing the moment when the moment is right, telling all outsiders (except an analyst) that we—she and I—come first. She's frugal about money, which is certainly not a problem, but she's not frugal about affection, feeling, companionship, honesty. I love her. I've said that before on more than one occasion but I think now I've some understanding of what it means.

Jackie? I'm not sure. It's asking a lot of someone to care for a doggedly raging ego who has a backyard full of buried bones. Yet I think she loves me more than she ever thought possible. It's that which frightens her—why she has fled—but she'll come to her senses. She hasn't been in analysis all these years simply to interpret dreams. She'll be able to acknowledge what we have.

20

When I arrived back at school after Christmas vacation Mr. Devereaux announced that my name was on the New Year's amnesty list but that, naturally, I'd be on parole. To keep out of the thoughts of Bucktooth Boyleston and the others I studied enough to get average grades, which, in that non-think tank, was not difficult to do. To please Mr. Devereaux I "worked out" in the gym every afternoon, meaning that I ran a few laps around the basketball court or tried to lift the school's single barbell when Philo Lumberton wasn't grunting and groaning under it, making his muscles apelike while the eagle on his chest broke into a sweat. The red, black and yellow stripes that connected his right eye to his chin, the surprise he'd acquired during Christmas vacation, had the effect at last of winning for him the awe of and isolation from the rest of the students I'd failed so totally in achieving. Nobody knew what to make of him. Philo was not an unfriendly boy. He was not antisocial in the way I was at heart. He was always around. He participated, but in a manner that never left any doubt that he was, in fact, removed. He was polite even to me. He had declared an independence that could only be taken away from him by surgery: "There once was an old kangaroo/Who painted his children light blue/When his wife said, 'My dear/Don't you think they look queer?'/He said, 'I don't care if they do.' " His temple, that body, was not uninhabited, but what inhabited it I could not know. Philo would never have laid back for a two-buck blow job.

Money was no longer a problem but I was still pursued by the reputation of being Gordon Felix's chum, pal, buddy and, worst of all, lover. It was reasoned, correctly, I think, that anyone who'd tolerate Gordon Felix, excepting a mother, had to be subhuman. It made no difference how much I worked out in the gym, how wildly I applauded for the Saints at our unfortunate basketball games, how friendly I was at meals, how willingly I helped the slow-witted sons of oystermen do their homework, how loudly I joined in on the choruses of "Clementine" on the old school bus, driven by Gethsemane in her baseball cap, which transported us to and from Queen Anne for the Friday night movie. I would think the affair forgotten when some twerp, who happened to be sitting next to me at evening prayers, would whisper during "Now the Day Is Over" or "Bringing in the Sheaves" (which never prompted insults to Deke Crozier even though most of the boys, being witty, sang "sheeps" for "sheaves"), "Hey, Henderson, I got something here" (patting his crotch) "I'd like you to take care of." They were too lazy or dumb ever to have analyzed properly the differences in the roles being played that unlucky afternoon Felix and I were observed in the shower. Perhaps to them there wasn't any difference. Since the discovery, for the first time in years, I was doing everything right. I was actually trying. When Mr. Devereaux announced in January that the long-defunct St. Matthew's Dramatic Society was to be reactivated to put on a production of *Journey's End*, I was the first to volunteer help. The next Saturday afternoon Mr. Devereaux asked for boys to begin to dismantle the school's ancient pier on the river. I joined the wrecking party. Still there would be someone to write on the top of a classroom desk, "Henderson jerks Felix of" (sic).

Thus it began as braggadocio whose origins I've already described. I was in my cubicle one evening dressing for chapel when Deke Crozier stopped by, looking offensively self-assured although he was wearing green slacks that were too big, an orange sports jacket that was too small, while his red hair stood straight up in an uneven homemade crewcut. "How's Felix's ass?" said Deke in a manner that I realized too late was meant to be friendly. "I don't know," I said, "how's yours?" "I don't go for that myself," said the sheep-fucker. In my wallet, lying on the shelf of my locker, was a package of condoms left over from Sun Valley. I pretended to be looking for something in my wallet so that the condoms dropped to the floor at Deke's feet. His face lit up in a dumb sort of conspiratorial way. He picked them up and handed them to me. Broad grin. "What do you use these on?" Note the preposition. "I got a girl," I said. "I don't never use cundums," said Deke, "cuts down on the feel. When I was a kid I did, but I didn't know better. Then, too, my mother was always finding them. She had a nose for finding cundums. I don't care where they was hid, she'd find them," he laughed, "and then would I get a licking! My daddy uses a belt. He'd tan my hide, I promise you. I'll never forget the time he caught me jerking off. Wowee! I was five or six, I guess, and there I was, in the back of the barn, you know? Looking at pictures in the *Saturday Evening Post* and pulling my pecker so hard I liked to pull it off. Well, when he caught me he put the fear of God in me, did that man! He told me about the sins of Onan and spilling my seeds on the ground and all that stuff . . . and do you know? I hardly never pulled my pecker again. He taught me a lesson, my daddy did." Pause. Note also the time elapsed for his take. "You got a girl to fuck? I don't believe it." "I haven't yet," I said, "but she wants it, I know." "Who is it? Shit." "I'd rather not say. . . ." "You'd rather not say because you ain't got a girl, that's why." He laughs. "Shit, Henderson, you'd be lucky to lay Stonewall Jackson and he can't run." I lost control for a moment. "You fuck sheep," I said. I thought he'd slug me. I'd never heard anyone bring up the subject of sheep-fucking in Deke's presence. There was a half-beat pause, then another broad grin. "Shit, Henderson, I like to fuck. I'll fuck anything, except maybe Gordon Felix. That's something I don't think I could ever do. . . . But they's nothing wrong with a nice wooly sheep's cunt." "Cunt?" I said. "You aren't fucking cunt. You're fucking ass." Deke was patient. "Same thing, boy, at least to a stiff pecker. You got a lot of things to learn, Henderson, but you ain't a bad guy. Just strange. Who's the girl?" I said I didn't want to say. "Come on, boy, you don't tell me I know you full of bullshit." "I promise you," I said. Finally, after four and a half months, I allowed myself to slip into Tatterhummock Elizabethan. "I ain't fooling," I said.

For some reason I'd impressed him. He put back his head and yelled so that the entire dormitory of cubicles could hear. "Henderson is going to fuck a real pussy! Hot shit!" In the distance someone responded, "Bullshit." Deke lowered his voice. "Come on, Marshall, you can tell me. I'm your buddy. Maybe we can handle this thing together." "Gethsemane Shackleford," I said. It just popped out. I hadn't been thinking of Gethsemane especially, but some inner protective mechanism had been at work. If

I'd mentioned the name of any local Queen Anne or Tatterhum-mock Court House girls, whom we saw at church, who came to our football and basketball games and who the boys sometimes sat with at the Friday night movies, I would have been too easily exposed as a fraud. There wasn't likely to be anyone to contradict anything I might say about Gethsemane, who maintained absolute silence and apparent indifference to us when she drove the bus on Friday nights and when she was on duty in the afternoons at Shackleford's Store.

At this point we were joined by Ruddleston, W., Deke's clos-est friend in spite of the fact that Ruddleston, W. was from civili-zation (Washington, D.C.), wore clothes that fit and didn't, as far as I knew, fuck sheep. We were all approximately the same age, though I felt infinitely older and wiser than these two who, in reality, had nothing more in common than a minor talent for football. "What's up?" said Ruddleston, W., bored, looking past me to Deke Crozier. "Henderson says he's going to fuck Gethse-mane Shackleford." Ruddleston, W. (to me): "That nigger girl?" "They's nothing wrong with nigger girls," said Deke, slapping me on the back, the first time anyone had slapped me on the back in a comradely way the entire time I'd been at St. Matthew's, "that's just poontang." Deke (voice lowered): "The thing is, Marshall, you don't pay for it. If I have to pay for it, I don't want it." "I ain't going to pay for it," I said, adopting a brand-new character. "I don't have to. She's got the hots for me." Deke: "No kidding. How do you know?" "I can tell," I said, "from the way she looks at me when I'm down at the store." Ruddleston, W.: "Did you show her a hard-on?" Me: "I didn't show it to her exactly, but when she came around the counter the other afternoon to put some more soda in the icebox, I just leaned back in the chair and let it jump up and down a little as I was reading a magazine." Ruddleston, W.: "What'd she do?" Me: "Knocked against me as she opened the icebox door." Ruddleston, W.: "No shit. . . ." Sixteen- and seven-teen-year-old boys in those days, as, I suppose, now, could be convinced of the truth of the most overwrought lies if, in some fashion, those lies conformed to their own fantasies. Even in her construction worker's gear Gethsemane Shackleford had probably at one time or another been the masturbation picture for every boy at St. Matthew's over the age of ten. "I don't know," said Ruddleston, W., "I don't want to fuck something black if I can get something white." "What's wrong?" said the sheep-fucker. "The color don't rub off . . . but they do smell different."

I couldn't have picked a better agent to effect the change in my image than Deke Crozier, football star, basketball star, hero to small boys, Devereaux ideal, sheep-fucker. If he accepted me, if he took my eccentricities (and lies) seriously, the others would follow, as, indeed, they did. I was not the sort of fellow ever to become a big man on any campus, but at least I needn't be ridiculed and shunned. The next Friday night when the old yellow school bus pulled up to the campus to load its live cargo for the trip into Queen Anne, the other students, prodded by Deke, who winked at me grotesquely, left vacant the seat directly across the aisle from the driver's seat. When we got out in Queen Anne and were making purchases of candy and cigarettes at the drugstore before going to the movie theater, Deke whispered to me, "Did you get a chance to show her a hard-on?" I said yes. He clapped me on the back and headed for the movie with Ruddleston, W. The next night, a few minutes after lights-out, I was aware of someone's tip-toeing into my cubicle. It was Deke. "Hey, Henderson, you awake?" I said I was. "Me and Ruddleston and a couple of other guys are going up to Four Corners for a few beers. Maybe find something to fuck. Want to come?" I said no thanks. "Take care of yourself, boy," Deke whispered, and slipped out. The Gordon Felix scandal was being put to pasture. "What's he say?" someone waiting outside the cubicle asked. Said Deke, "He's saving on it."

21

The heat wave continues, the Pittsburgh-born stockbroker dawdles and still no telephone call from Jackie, though she's been gone for more than a month. Even if she's in Teheran or São Paulo or Hollywood she finds time to call me at least twice a week. She knows it bothers me when we don't talk. If she were any place but

Fort Lauderdale I'd call her, but it just contributes to a scene if her mother happens to pick up the telephone. Why isn't she married? How can she live with a man old enough to be her father (which is not strictly true since her father is in his mid-sixties)? It's not right. Mark her words, and on and on and on, carefully avoiding the key issue of my not being Jewish, which Mom believes makes her a liberated woman. Jackie and I have been together nine years, which is longer than either of my marriages, and we have among other shared pleasures a self-possessed, talkative, neutered black Burmese male cat I gave her on her birthday five years ago. I'm fond of the cat and, unlike Jackie, I don't care how many sofas and chairs it rips apart sharpening its claws, but I don't enjoy picking up the telephone and asking Fraser-Morris to deliver a box of chlorophyled Kitty Litter and two bags of Meow Mix, only to be told they don't carry such things. They'll have to send out for it. Don't limey cats ever shit? In five years I've never before had to deal with such problems. Jackie's always done it, or Margaret, and Margaret is off on that goddamned cruise finding romance under the Midnight Sun. If for no other reason Jackie has to come home to start emptying the litter box. I can do it and have done it, but I'm getting fed up with it. I refuse to empty it once more. The cat has been shitting in the same pile of shavings for three days and when it gets too much for his sensitive spirit, he starts using the tub in my bathroom. There are, of course, all sorts of special agencies I might call to come clean things but I don't like to have strangers poking about, probably casing the joint for some future heist. The cat also gets upset. It doesn't mind strangers who are guests but it takes immediate exception to unfamiliar servants—a high-toned cat. I worry that if Jackie ever does leave me she'll take the cat with her. He's hers, technically, but he's also us. We can't cut him in half, or can we?

I inventory future defeats. Why the fuck doesn't she call? I'd like to tell her of a decision taken in her absence. I no longer am going to call her Jackie. Her name is Jacqueline, a fine, bold, beautiful name that perfectly describes her. Jackie, to me, is something borrowed. There is the obvious association to the figure of headline and gossip column. There is also a boy I went to kindergarten with in Lake Forest. He was a Jackie too, a pale, undersized creature who cried easily and whose eyes in summer were always red-rimmed from the chlorine in the Onwentsia swimming pool if not from some emotional disturbance. The nickname Jackie has nothing to do with the woman I'm living with. Henceforth she is Jacqueline. It's a big step, I know, changing the name of someone you know and love, a step that Jacqueline will want to analyze at length. I wouldn't even mind that if she'd just come home. We might do it over dinner at the Madrigal (the Côte Basque is closed for the month). I also want to apologize for not asking her to come with me when I took the trip to Tatterhummock County this spring. I don't think she would have come anyway, but at least I could have given her the option to decide for herself. She wouldn't have fit in, though.

When I telephoned Cousin Mary Lee from the Walden's Point motor court she sounded unchanged in the thirty-six years since I'd last seen her, and when I met her the next afternoon for lunch at her house on Queen Anne Creek she hadn't changed in any usual way. It was as if the twenty-seven-year-old woman I'd known had existed as a color photograph, and the woman who greeted me on the screened porch was the same photograph that over the years had faded to black and white. Her figure is much the same. The eyes are large and luminous and still ready to reflect the slightest variation in feeling, but all the color has gone. The hair, as full and soft as ever, is now gray. The features remain fine, youthful. Though the skin doesn't sag, it's now decorated with small liver spots on the face and the backs of her hands. At sixty-three she's still the prettiest girl in the county. She'd given me long, complicated, contradictory, Cousin Mary Lee directions to find her road ("You take a left by the old Bristow place. . . . You remember little Sally Bristow? She married the boy who played the harp? Was that before your time or after your time? I declare, Marshall, I'm getting old. The General always said. . . ."), so after spending all morning at Wicheley I was an hour late. She could have told me her house—a cheerful, rambling wooden construction, set deep in a forest of elms, oaks and loblollies—was the old Lumberton place, which it had been in my time. It was also just a mile or so down Queen Anne Creek from the dark pool where I found my coelacanth.

In my self-absorption I'd worried how the changes in her would affect me. Would I be saddened by the loss of beauty and innocence? I hadn't thought what effect I might have on her. When the chauffeur stopped the car, got out and ran around to my side to hand me my crutches, it suddenly occurred to me that she'd be the first person I'd met in years who'd known me when I could walk normally. I swung myself up on the crutches and proceeded over the gravel of the driveway to the screened door of the porch. I can walk as fast as anyone but it involves a good deal of sharp swinging of each calf and foot by a jerk of the upper thigh muscles. I don't have to wear braces any more, though I do wear them when I know I'm going to be doing a lot of walking and standing, but even the most expensive braces clank. I don't enjoy that. I forget—I make myself unaware of—the commotion that the spectacle of my walking can prompt in others. I can't stand children who stare, adults who look away in embarrassment, and I don't like giving others pain, which is what I was giving Cousin Mary Lee, or so I thought. But the tears in her eyes were not so easily explained. She held the door open and I leaned on the crutches, shifted my feet so I could stand without the crutches if I had to, and held Cousin Mary Lee as she held me.

"Come around to the back," she said finally, leading the way along the porch to the open gallery at the rear overlooking Queen Anne Creek. "We have time for a drink. . . . I know you'd probably love to have a drink before lunch? . . . Your mother would. Little Bob and Melanie . . . that's my daughter-in-law . . . are driving down from Washington and won't be here for another half hour at least. There . . . sit in that chair. It's a little higher than the others, and it's easier to get in and out of. That's what Little Bob says, anyway. You do know about Little Bob? Oh, Marshall, darling. . . ." Her eyes fill with tears, but stop immediately. "Now what are you going to have to drink?" She laughs. "I have everything but your favorite Tatterhummock County homemade corn! Will you ever forget? I've told that story for years and I still laugh all over again. You were so sweet! If you could have seen the expression on your face! That was so long ago. . . . Now what will you have? I can make a very good martini, or a Bloody Mary or a bullshot? I think I'll have some sherry. I've got to drive over to Middlesex for a meeting this afternoon. Can't you drive? Little Bob does and . . . you know. . . ."

I say that I can and do drive when I have a car that's properly equipped, but that this time it seemed easier to fly to Richmond and pick up a car with a driver there. "Of course," she says, going to the portable bar that would never have found its way into the house at Lewis's Landing, which reminds me to ask what's happened to the old place. "I gave it to Little Bob and Melanie when the General died. I couldn't stand to live there alone, and Little Bob loves it so. They don't get a chance to use it often. . . . Little Bob's a lawyer, you know, in Georgetown? so they're. . . . Isn't it remarkable, Marshall? After he got out of the hospital he went back to the University and went to law school, just as if nothing had happened?" She considers three different sizes of glass before settling on the claret glass. "This is a beautiful spot," I say, "the old Lumberton place, isn't it?" "Of course! You went to school with Philo, didn't you?" She hands me my drink, sherry, as is hers, since she hadn't gotten around to letting me answer her original question. Me: "Whatever happened to Philo?" Her face clouds. "Oh, Marshall, he finally became so strange they just sort of put him away." "In an institution?" "I don't know exactly what it is. It's in Oregon or Arizona, some place out west, where he isn't so . . . apparent. By the time he was twenty-five his entire face was tattooed . . . there were some other things too, like a totem pole or something." I say, "I always thought he was peculiar but not necessarily crazy." "Like the Commander," she says. I raise my glass to her. "You're still the prettiest girl in the county." "And you're still giving the girls your line." "I don't have a line. I never had a line. I used to be tongue-tied with girls my age." "Oh, Marshall," she winks, "you and your rich society girls and glamorous actresses, come on. I keep tabs on you. Tell me about your mother. Isn't she grand now? I'm always reading about her, traveling around, opening up houses here, closing houses there. Is she happy? I love her so. She wrote the dearest letter about Little Bob. Even the General cried when he read it. And it took something to get that man to cry, let me tell you, and then when the General died last year . . . she was so kind. I still say that if it hadn't been for your mother I probably never would have married him. She was so sweet. When the General died she telephoned to ask me to come to London with them. . . . I don't reckon I'll get there now. I think I'm back in the county for good this time."

Cousin Mary Lee is one of the few women I like being around who talks in such a nonstop, non-listening way. The original story, the point of departure, is inevitably forgotten as she leads herself further and further into an interior where everything is accommodated, as in nature.

While she hurtles verbally on, I remember that before Lockie died she had, for several years, been doing and saying things that doctors said were symptoms of senility—hiding things such as bank statements and checks, accusing Ma of not having carried out a task that had never been commissioned, confusing Ma with Lockie's younger sister who had died of polio at Lewis's Landing at the age of eleven. I stayed with Lockie the last two months of her life at the big, fully staffed Lake Forest house, Chantilly, where everything was kept up—gardens, pool, tennis court—as if she would come home at any minute, so that she could die in her own bed, hearing familiar sounds, if only those of the power mower. If she had cared to listen she would have been reassured that life was continuing, that the grass was being cut. Ma came and went by the day. The disintegration was too painful for her to deal with. Much earlier I'd thought I'd experienced every humiliation but I hadn't reckoned on the surpassing insult to the human spirit in the twentieth century: advanced old age. I watched life sneak off from Lockie like an unfaithful servant, leaving organs untended to clog and malfunction. They said early in Lockie's final illness that her mind was going. It was true that she had become more and more forgetful of names and details and increasingly ignored the present, but her mind hadn't gone anywhere. Her eyes were alive and so was her reason. She was only tired and slowly, methodically, going through the closets of her head discarding the superfluous. It's no wonder that items recently acquired, associated with the fearful present, were the first to go, while she clung to things she'd guarded from childhood. I watched her die, full of love and sorrow until one unexpected moment when I was saying again, It's you, not I.

Instead of finishing the sherry I got up, went to the bar and mixed myself a scotch. Cousin Mary Lee watched me without sentimentality. She had an experienced eye in such matters. "You know, Marshall, you're *very, very good*. . . ." as if I'd just executed a full gainer. "When Little Bob was in the hospital I saw so many boys who just gave up, who wouldn't try. I was afraid Little Bob was going to be like that. Oh, darling Marshall, I nearly died when we walked into that hospital room and saw him there. I just burst into tears and ran back into the hall. I couldn't look at what they'd done to my baby, and while I was outside the door I heard the General say . . . you know, making a joke of it . . . 'Your mother's taking this real bad, son, so we have to watch out for *her*. We're *soldiers*.' Imagine that man—and they did! They took care of me! But that wasn't the worst thing. . . . Everything that happened to Little Bob had a purpose. There was some point. I could understand. But with Mimi, that's something else. You are . . . aware of Mimi? You know, Marshall, as far as I'm concerned, that child is dead? Isn't that a terrible thing to say? But for me she no longer exists. That woman, doing and saying all those filthy things, has no relation to the child I brought up. None. Maybe it's not as if she's dead exactly, it's as if she'd disappeared. She liked to kill the General ten times over. It was bad enough when she got involved with all those radicals and Communists at Sweet Briar. Sweet Briar! If you can't send your daughter to Sweet Briar, what's the world come to? Our world was bad enough, Marshall, but this one is beyond my comprehension . . . so I keep busy and try not to think about it.

"Now tell me about you, Marshall. You were married twice? Nice girls? Well, I suppose if you had to divorce them . . . but I mean, did you *love* them? Like the General and I loved each other? Oh, Marshall, there are times at night I wake up and I forget he's gone and I reach over . . . and he's not there and then I think of that child, Mary Ball. She's the thing that killed the General, Marshall, not what happened to Little Bob. Do you know she never once wrote Little Bob when he was in the hospital? Not that

he wanted to hear from her by that time. I can't tell you the names
he called her. Isn't it strange the ways in which the Lord works?
All the time they were growing up it was Little Bob I worried
about . . . I mean, when I was worried about the children at all.
What happened? They were such happy children. We were, I
thought, a blessedly happy family. Sometimes I'd worry about Little Bob. I mean, growing up with the General as a father, feeling
he had to do things just because the General had done them, or
because the General wanted him to. The General was a pretty
overwhelming man and sometimes I was afraid Little Bob resented him. I once made the General tell him, when Little Bob
was fourteen or fifteen, 'Little Bob, I want you to make up your
own mind. Just because I'm a soldier doesn't mean you have to be
one and go to West Point and all that.' I think Little Bob appreciated that, coming from the General that way. For a while he
thought he wanted to be a writer or a teacher . . . he went to the
University, you know? Then when Vietnam came along, and he
saw his father fighting again, wild horses couldn't keep him from
signing up, being an Army man like his father? And he was a
good one. He was given a presidential citation for that action
when he was wounded. President Nixon himself went to the hospital, and not just because Little Bob was the General's son, but
because if it hadn't been for Little Bob's platoon, the whole north
perimeter would have collapsed. Can you imagine? I don't believe
all those things they say about Nixon now. The General never had
much use for him but that had nothing to do with politics. He
didn't like his personality. But we loved Pat . . . Mrs. Nixon? She's
so charming and sweet, just like everybody else. . . . I do go on,
don't I? And I haven't even touched my sherry! The General used
to say I was the cheapest date in the entire Army. When we'd go
out he'd buy me one drink and I wouldn't touch it but I'd get high
anyway, just being out with my dear faithful Stewart. . . ."

Cousin Mary Lee sighs. We both look down into the waters of
the creek 30 feet below. I can hear tree toads. No sign of another
habitation for miles. "It's peaceful, isn't it?" says Cousin Mary
Lee, which is the cue for a crash of silverware in the kitchen. We
both laugh. "You know who's fixing lunch?" I say no. "You'll
never guess. . . . It's Aunt Minnie. Aunt Minnie! Ninety-three

years old, skinnier and crankier than ever, but stronger and tougher than you or me. Thank the Lord for Aunt Minnie! The morning the General died, Aunt Minnie's the one who took care of things. She'll bury us all. She's becoming absent-minded though, forgetful. When I told her you were coming to lunch she didn't remember you at first. Then I reminded her of your mother and she recalled—Lord, it's something I'd put out of my mind— that awful . . . you know . . . *attack* and you and your mother hiding the Commander's dynamite? She thinks your mother is a real Betsy Ross, or maybe Virginia Dare? The one who fought the Indians? I don't know as I ever really believed that story. Did you? Oh lord, Marshall, there are times when I miss the General so I don't know what I'm going to do, and then I think of Mimi and wonder what went wrong. What could we possibly have done when all we did was love each other? That can't be a sin, can it? You should have seen her as a little girl, Marshall. She looked just like me, except thinner? She never had the weight problem I did. She was so pretty, and she worshipped the General as I did . . . and to think, when I was a girl, you were considered fast if you so much as kissed a boy goodnight on the first date. It's beyond me. I don't think of it any more. But I'm doing all the talking. Tell me . . . do you have a new girl?" I say I have and she says that I should have brought her with me. "I have two guest rooms and they're always empty. . . ."

Melanie, Little Bob's wife, was a Dixie Cup blonde from Texas, a young woman with the determined sunniness of a counselor at a Girl Scout camp. Because she and Little Bob had been married for a year before he went overseas I wondered if this quite terrifying enthusiasm, expressed to the same degree for a cold soup and for her own pregnancy (just three months old), was something she'd adopted as her contribution to Little Bob's rehabilitation.

Approximately one-third of him appears to be missing. To see Little Bob function—climb out of his car, get in and out of a wheelchair, drink soup with a spoon held in a metal claw, brush back a lock of hair or mop his brow—is to see an extraordinary machine in which has been planted a human torso and a head. The land mine he stepped on ripped off both legs just above the knee, one arm at the shoulder and the other below the elbow. His face and head seem not to have been damaged, which makes the total impression that much more weird. He's a living, breathing, talking electric can opener. Sometimes he's a collection of dentist's tools. Then a mobile sculpture, a battery-powered construction composed of systems of weights, pulleys and lifts, in the center of which a portion of a recognizable man has been glued. The effect at lunch varied with the endeavor.

He's also a most arrogant, opinionated, unpleasant young man. Perhaps that's not fair since so much of him has been removed. He was even more gung-ho than I might have expected of the General's son, and as he talked (the only man, including his father, to whom his mother would listen quietly), I tried to hear some echoes of the boy who wanted to be a writer or a teacher. Nothing. His facial features are the General's—the jutting jaw, the flattened nose, the pale blue eyes—though they lack the age and authority to give them their own identity. Most curiously, although he looks like the General, he gives the impression of being soft, very nearly pretty. As we were served by Aunt Minnie's shaky hand, Little Bob talked without letup, but without his mother's humor and candid self-interest, mostly about politics, which, for him, means finding a way to stop the clock, to turn back the tide, to reaffirm our moral and spiritual values. I wasn't particularly surprised, therefore, when after he and his goonily grinning wife had left to drive over to Lewis's Landing, Cousin Mary Lee told me that Little Bob was going to run for Congress in the November elections. I didn't think to ask which party.

After lunch, Carroll, my chauffeur, drove me to St. Matthew's. The campus was considerably changed and looked almost posh. The grounds seemed smaller, more constricted, of course, but the oak trees and elms were tremendous. There were three handsome new buildings, modern glass-and-brick variations on the original buildings that were now painted a pleasant white. There were also a new athletic field and a new field house, as well as a swimming pool. The small chapel was exactly as I remembered it, the lines now softened by the growth of shrubbery surrounding it. It was apparent that the boys must be on their spring vacation so, after driving around for a few minutes, I asked Carroll to park behind Mount Vernon while I got out to walk. It was a fine, clear Tidewater afternoon, very warm without being hot. I walked up the brick path next to a square of lawn that, thirty-six years ago, had been the untended garden where I first set eyes on Gethsemane, around to the front terrace that faces the broad gentle river. A pleasant-looking young man, wearing khaki pants and a white T-shirt, was putting up screens. He glanced at me in my city suit, hanging on my crutches, as if I were the most ordinary sight in the world. "Hello," he said, putting down the screen he was fitting, "can I help you?" I said no, that I didn't want to disturb anyone, that I simply wanted to look around. "I went to school here many years ago," I said, "and I haven't been back since." He walked over to me, wiping his palms on his pants before offering to shake hands. "I'm Gardner Purdy," he said. "I'm the headmaster." I had thought he might be one of the older boys. We shook hands and I introduced myself. "Henderson, Henderson," he said. "The name is familiar but I don't remember seeing it on any of our alumni rolls." "It's probably not there," I said. "I didn't graduate. I left under something of a cloud." I hadn't left under something of a cloud. I had vanished overnight. I simply disappeared. I was hauled away in a van during the height of the hurricane. "When was that? What year?" "The spring of 1940." He said, "Oh," but I couldn't tell whether he knew something. The events were so old they no longer qualified as scandal.

He offered to show me around but I said I didn't want to interrupt him. No interruption, said Purdy. His wife and children were in Richmond for the day and he was taking the opportunity to do some physical labor. Did I want to sit down? I said no, that I just wanted to refresh my memory of place. He told me the school now has 206 students, including 25 women and 14 black students, most of whom are county children. "How can they afford it?" "We have a fairly liberal scholarship program," he said. "They also had when I was here," I said, "but the school was broke. . . ." He laughed. "That must have been when Devereaux was headmaster." I said it was. "I remember hearing about that. . . . Didn't he run off with some black girl and take all the school's money

with him?" "I don't think there was much to take," I said. "I
understand he had something of a problem," said Purdy. "A problem?" How curious to remember Devereaux as having had something of a problem. Don't we all? "Yes," I said, "I suppose he
did." "The Bishop once called him a pervert," said Purdy, and
laughed. "The feelings he had," I said, "were not especially common, but I don't think they could be called unnatural." The idea
of describing Mr. Devereaux as a pervert seemed so comic that I
smiled. Purdy smiled. "He was an eccentric," I said. There was
some more small talk and I said I'd leave him to his chores while I
poked around a bit. "Help yourself," said Purdy. "All the buildings
are open. The boys come back on Monday." I looked up to what I
judged to have been the window of my cubicle, from which I'd
first spied Gethsemane trampling the stalks of dead hollyhocks. "I
hope the cubicles are more comfortable now than they were in my
day." "Cubicles?" said Purdy. "No more cubicles. We wouldn't
have five students if they had to live in cubicles. That entire building is now a dormitory but the students have rooms, three students
to a room. The seniors even have private bathrooms. . . ."

I had no interest in the new classroom complex and the science building. Instead I made my way across the campus, along
the edge of the bluff, over the spot where my old, sterile cherry
tree had once grown, now gone without even a root-trace, to the
chapel. Inside the chapel time was stilled, with decency. Walking
on the wooden floor created a hollow sound so that students, filing
in for their devotionals, gave the impression of a stampede even
when they weren't horsing around. Nothing had changed. The
altar remained unadorned except by the small, highly polished
brass cross, framed by the three tall, arched windows that saw
only blue sky. The last hymns to be sung there, according to the
board by the lectern, were numbers 107, 232 and 58. I sat down
in a pew to look them up in a hymnal that, in my day, would have
been a black, clothbound book but today was a shiny white paper-
back with, inside the back cover, a list of other titles available
from the same publisher. As I reached to replace the hymnal I
read on the back of the pew in front of me a message recently
scratched with, I assumed, the sharp end of a geometry compass:
LINDGREN SUCKS AND SO DOES THIS SCHOOL.

When I went back to the car, Purdy came over to ask me if I would come in for a drink. I told him that I must be going and he asked that, in any case, could he have my address so he could give it to Gordon Felix, the president of the Alumni Association, who would see that I was put on the mailing lists. "Gordon Felix?" "Yes. . . . Were you here with Gordon?" I said that I thought I was but I wasn't sure. "Gordon's the best fundraiser we've ever had. His youngest boy is graduating this year. . . ." I couldn't gracefully say no to Purdy and gave him my address, well knowing that it would be the start of a new relationship that would cost me a building or a scholarship. The cannibal knew his Ecclesiastes.

Carroll next drove me to the church. I also descended there to walk around the peaceful, immaculately tended graveyard where a tree had split an anonymous sarcophagus. A large new obelisk of pink Aswan granite marks the grave of the General, in death once again simply "Stewart Fullman Carter," his dates and, in smaller letters, "General, United States Army, Three Times Recipient of the Medal of Honor." The grave, in the rear of the churchyard, is next to the low Georgian brick wall that for 300 years has kept out the forest. The wall runs along the crest of the ravine where, 100 yards further on, I was once had by the abominable Felix and then I had my Gethsemane. To set matters straight. It's beautiful, verdant forest still, untouched by the civilization creeping into the rest of the county.

The drive back to Walden's Point on the Tatterhummock Trail—this section of which had been renamed the Stewart Fullman Carter Highway—took us first by the All-Saints Christian Brotherhood Baptist Church, a big, substantial wooden box of a building newly painted white, set back from the highway on a broad, grassy green and surrounded by elms, and, just a few yards beyond, the other side of a field planted with chickpeas, a new building that a sign announced to be the Shackleford Shopping Center Grand Opening. The one-story building, L-shaped and constructed of cement blocks painted light blue, looked as yet uninhabited, as was the parking lot that fronted on the highway. To the side of the Shackleford Shopping Center Grand Opening the old store still stands on its small knoll, abandoned, leaning a bit to the left, its gas pumps gone but a Nehi sign still tacked to the front door. The store—the facade of unpainted wood now weathered to a rich gray—seems as frail as Aunt Minnie and as old. I was also struck by its shape, about 25 feet wide across the front but no more than 10 feet deep. It looks like the dollhouse of a deprived child. Somehow I'd always assumed that the door behind the counter, through which Gethsemane made her exits to fetch new cases of soda pop, led to another room. It must have led directly to the open air. Why didn't I know that or, if I did know it, why had I forgotten? The building is so small and narrow it hardly seems possible that it once could have contained such passion. I was clumsy, of course, but then I was also quick.

22

"Oh," says Mrs. Gold on the other end of the line in her retirement community. "Oh, oh, oh." Then: "Is this Mr. Henderson?" I say yes and there are more "oh-oh-ohs." "I would like to speak to Jacqueline." Pause. I think I hear a cricket's cry or is it a Barcalounger? And it's only a little after eight o'clock in the morning. Do they rise at six, have their prunes and then immediately take up their missionary positions in front of the television set? "It's that man," I can hear Mrs. Gold saying to Mr. Gold. She hasn't planted her palm as firmly over the mouthpiece as she should. "He wants to speak to Jackie. What should I tell him?" There's some fumbling with the phone. I've probably cut into the Today Show and an in-depth interview with President Tito. Mrs. Gold returns and frees me from the cave formed by her hand. "Jackie's not here." "When do you expect her back?" Pause. "For Passover." Passover! I've stumbled into a nightclub act. "Isn't she there, staying with you?" "She was here but she left." "When?" I would never have expected Jackie to enter into an agreement of intent with her mother. Most of the time they don't even speak. "Two weeks ago," says Mrs. Gold. "But where did she go?" "Back to New York," Mrs. Gold says. Knowing she's walking on troubled waters, she adds, "I think," but without conviction. "I'm in New York," I say, "and she's not here." "Yes," says Mrs. Gold, "she took the Whisperjet to New York two weeks ago Thursday morning. We saw her off." I'm aware of the first faint stirrings of one of Jackie's anxiety attacks, but within me. "And I talked to her last night." "Why the hell hasn't she come home?" Pause. Mrs. Gold is gathering together her collection of two attitudes, hurt and self-righteous. Then, so weakly that I can hardly hear her, "Maybe it isn't home, *for her*." "Oh shit," I say. "Mr. Henderson, I can't talk to you if you're going to use that kind of language. I will not be abused." Hand over the receiver again. She's telling Dad that I said shit. More fumbling. The telephone changes hands and Mr. Gold comes on, reluctantly, to protect Mom's dignity. He's not talking to me. He's talking for Mom's benefit while trying not to miss anything that Barbara Walters is telling President Tito about Soviet foreign policy in eastern Europe. "Mr. Henderson, we have nothing to say to you. Jackie's in New York and I'm sure if she wanted to see you, she'd contact you. That's all." "That's not all, Mr. Gold," I say, "because she can't run out on me. Her clothes and books and electric typewriter are here. Her manuscripts. Her filing cabinets. Her records. Her diaphragm. An original Lautrec drawing I gave her and her cat. To say nothing of all those letters you and your wife have written her about your lawsuit and which she's never even opened. . . ." "What's that?" I hear Mrs. Gold scream. "That's not true!" She'd been sharing the earpiece with Dad. "If you want," I say, "I can send them all back to you, in the pristine state in which they were mailed." Mr. Gold, now interested, to Mrs. Gold, who has taken over the telephone: "What's he say?" "He says Jackie doesn't read our letters. You are a bad man, Mr. Henderson. I can understand why Jackie had to leave you, even if you are a cripple." "Fuck you, Molly Goldberg, and Sam Levene too!" I slam down the receiver and crab-walk to the kitchen to pour myself a drink.

An hour later I've gathered my wits sufficiently to realize that I probably shouldn't have told Mr. and Mrs. Gold to go fuck themselves. It's not the sort of thing one says to potential allies. I pick up the telephone and dial Fort Lauderdale. By this time they are probably watching a rerun of "You Bet Your Life." Mrs. Gold answers. "Please, Mrs. Gold, don't hang up," I say in a panic. "I apologize. I'm sorry. I was rude and obscene and I didn't mean it.

It's my temper and the idea that Jacqueline might be in New York and hasn't come home. . . ." "It's no *might*, Mr. Henderson," Mrs. Gold says in complete possession of herself. "She *is* in New York." "Now please don't hang up, Mrs. Gold. . . ." "I don't hang up telephones," says Mrs. Gold. "I've never hung up a telephone in my life, have I, Dad? Except when the other party and I have concluded our conversation amicably." "The thing is," I say, "I love Jacqueline. . . ." "What's this 'Jacqueline'?" says Mrs. Gold. "Who calls Jackie 'Jacqueline'? Have you been drinking, Mr. Henderson?" I hold my tongue and I can hear Mrs. Gold say to her husband, who sits in his Barcalounger not wanting to miss Groucho's upcoming punchline, "He's been drinking . . . at this hour," to which I know Mr. Gold only nods, refusing to look away from the TV screen.

"I'm sorry, Mr. Henderson," says Mrs. Gold, and I want so much to believe she really is sorry. I think she is. "When I talk to Jackie I'll tell her you were asking for her." "You won't tell me where she is?" I say. "Or give me her telephone number?" "No, I couldn't do that, Mr. Henderson." "I don't want to abuse her. I love her. We've been together nine years, Mrs. Gold, and sometime I'd like to meet you and Mr. Gold. . . ." "We don't come to New York very often any more, you know, since Dad had his . . ." "I know, I know," I say, "but sometime you might, or sometime Jacqueline and I might come down there together. . . ." "Yes," says Mrs. Gold, "I'll let Jackie know you telephoned and I'm sure she'll contact you real soon. . . ." "But real soon isn't soon enough. I want to speak to her now, THIS MINUTE." "Now, Mr. Henderson, don't get yourself excited again. That's the best I can do. I can't do any more than that." I calm down but I'm skidding across thin ice. It seems as if I always have been. "I know that, Mrs. Gold, and I appreciate it. I really do. . . ." Pause. I say, "I've been good to Jackie. I've never wanted to hurt her or make her unhappy. . . ." "I'm sure that's true, Mr. Henderson. Now this call is costing you a lot of money. It's not the cheap rate any more, so why don't we say goodbye and when Jackie telephones me I'll give her your message. . . . Mr. Henderson . . . Mr. Henderson . . ." My mind is wandering. "Yes," I say, "and thank you . . . I . . . I . . ." "What's that?" "Are you watching 'You Bet Your Life'? I am." "No," says

Mrs. Gold. Pause while she looks at the set 6 feet from her. "It's 'What's My Line,' I think, when Dorothy Kilgallen was still alive. Now, goodbye, Mr. Henderson. It was nice talking to you. Goodbye." I say goodbye and she's banged down the receiver before I can reach the second syllable.

Now I'm in the mood for telephones. I next dial Ma at Harbor Point. Ma picks up the phone on the second ring. "Ma," I say. "Darling," says Ma, "how sweet of you to ring. You're an angel. Where are you?" "In New York." "What time is it?" "Nine-thirty here, eight-thirty there, I guess. Don't you have a clock?" "I haven't even gotten out of bed yet. Isn't that terrible? John was up at six to sail over to Charlevoix with Teddy and some other people. Teddy's been so sweet to us. . . ." "Who the hell is Teddy?" "Teddy Lowry, Christaphine's stepson. . . ." "Christ." "They're in the Caffrey house for the summer. Are you all right?" "Of course, I'm all right. Why shouldn't I be?" "We were talking about you last night, wondering why you stay there alone in that steaming city in August when you could be up here. Could I possibly persuade you to come up? Why don't you get on a plane this morning and just come? Please." "I'm not all alone," I say. Pause. "I received a letter from Jackie yesterday," says Ma. My blood runs cold again. It's the thin ice. "She told me she was leaving you . . . that she'd left." "She's in Florida," I say, "with those sitcom parents of hers." "This letter was mailed from New York three days ago." "Well, I haven't talked to her," I say. "She seems to be blabbing to everybody except me." "She sounds very unhappy," says Ma, "and very worried about you. . . ." "Worried about me? She's so worried about me she hasn't written or telephoned in over a month. . . ." "I know that, darling. . . ." "She's full of shit," I say, "just like all the rest. She's out to get all she can and then she takes off. She's a goddamn calculating, untalented Jewish princess bitch." "Darling, darling," says Ma, "that's not true." "What do you mean?" I say. "You don't even like her. You never have." "I don't *dislike* her," says Ma prissily. "She's one of those people I don't understand and never will. That's all. But I certainly don't dislike her. I admire her and am grateful to her because she's been so good to you." "Good to me! Do you call taking off like that without one goddamned bloody word being good to me? Jesus, Ma. . . ." "Now, darling"

(a winning laugh) "I know you can be difficult to live with sometimes. . . ." "I may be difficult," I say, "but I'm not impossible.
There's a difference." More giggles from Ma. "Oh, darling, I think
I love you even more now than when you were a little boy. Isn't
that strange?" I let that bombshell go without attempting to return
one of my own.

"She hasn't telephoned me," I say, "and her mother refuses to
tell me where she is. Was there an address on your letter?" "No,"
says Ma. "I'll call her agent's office," I say. "If I don't get it from
him I'll hire some private detectives. It shouldn't be difficult. We'll
just stake out the five psychiatrists in the city who aren't on vacation in August. She won't be taking a step like this without at least
forty hours of consultations." "Darling, don't do anything. When
she's ready, she'll contact you." " 'Contact' me! 'Contact' me!
Why does everybody say 'contact' me? I'm not someone applying
for a job. I'm not a government bureau. I don't want to be con-
tacted. I want to see her. For all I know she may be sick or in
trouble." "She's not," says Ma, "so that's not why you're so
mad. . . ." "I'm not mad, I'm just worried." Pause. "Darling, please
fly up here for a few days. You could be here this evening. The
weather is lovely, clear and hot during the day and down in the
fifties at night. I'd love to see you, and John is so fond of you. . . .
Darling? Are you there?" "I want to find Jackie," I say, "and I don't
like to travel any more unless I have to. You know that. It's too
much trouble." "Would you like for me to come there? I will, if that
will cheer things up." "No, for Christ's sake. I don't want you mop-
ing around this apartment, moving all the furniture about. . . ."
"Oh, darling. . . ." "No," I say, "I'll wait this out myself, and when
I see her, she'd better have a goddamn good explanation." "I think
she does," says Ma. "She doesn't love you any more."

I refuse to be capsized by this sort of petulant, capricious, cow-
ardly behavior. I take measures. I follow routines. Up at 6:30,
read until 8:30, breakfast, then correspondence with Louise, daily
telephone conferences with Jimmy Barnes on the progress of our
negotiations for Wicheley. The car comes at twelve to take me to
the club. I swim, am massaged and then lunch at 1:15, most of the

time with someone who doesn't know Jackie, someone who is sure his wife is having an affair in a Hampton, or who himself is having an affair in the city, or sometimes both. Not very stimulating, perhaps, but being boring is no sin. At 2:45 the car brings me back to my desk and to the Albigenses. I plow on, sentence by sentence. If I'm lucky I'm sidetracked by an obscure construction or an unrecognized verb form. This necessitates telephone calls to pedants who are not always flattered to be hunted down in the Thousand Islands or Turkey or even a dingy New York flat. I'm very good at finding such people and rather enjoy it. Though I have little patience with chat on the telephone I receive satisfaction in employing it in the cause of learning, in smoking people out of their hiding places. Our long-distance bills have always been staggering. In the evening I dine alone out of the fridge and allow myself the pleasure of a certain amount of booze. I've finally stirred myself to the extent of having a domestic employment force in for one day to clean out some of the detritus of my grief. Three worried-looking, elderly Haitian women who in six hours accomplished less than one-quarter of what Margaret can do in two. When they'd completed their tasks I broke out the rum and amused them greatly by playing tapes I'd recorded years ago in Provence. They didn't understand one word, of course, but I think they did appreciate the gesture. Even though the air-conditioning system's been fixed and heat is no immediate problem, I wake at odd hours. Since I don't like being in bed alone I get up and sit in the living room windowseat from which, I find, I can sometimes observe the most bizarre adventures. The other morning, about four, I watched an armed (as opposed to *un*armed?) robbery of the all-night hamburger place on the corner of Broadway and 86th, two blocks south. The next morning the doorman told me it hadn't been a robbery at all, but the arrest of a narcotics pedlar by plainclothesmen. Thus I've had two melodramas for the price of one. I may buy myself a telescope.

I no longer listen to the Mozart operas that once were able to get me through hard times. They're too closely associated with Jackie, not because she ever shared my joy and wonder in them but because I had to work so long to teach her how to listen to them. Now I hear them through tin ears. The bitch. Yesterday I had all the locks changed and today I deposited $40,000 in her savings account, which is not enough, I know, and which is why I keep on. No matter what.

23

I can't believe that Jackie is still upset about that matter with the lobster salad. That was months ago. Jackie's not mentioned it to me recently, though she's probably still picking at the carrion with her analyst, searching for some previously overlooked, juicily putrefying morsel for a joyous, fifty-minute chew. For Christ's sake, I'm the one who should be paid. Without me she'd have nothing to tell that quack except her boring dreams and her guilt feelings about her awful parents. The business with the lobster salad wasn't pleasant and I'm not proud of it, but it wasn't all that major a deal. I did apologize at length and even after I refused to apologize any more, the goddamn oil stains from the mayonnaise continued to reproach me for months going on years. Not just on the suede couch near the bed, which I had re-covered immediately, but on the walls behind the bed, on the back of the door to my bathroom, even on the ceiling. When we went to Paris last year I had the entire room repainted for a second time, but I'm still discovering new oil spots that have fought their way to the light, making their way through the tightest molecular structures devised by man. Lying in bed last night I saw several new ones, on the ceiling over the door to her bathroom. On the other side of the room! There's something grand about being haunted by apparitions, like the unfortunate Macbeths, but another thing entirely to be pursued by spots on walls. After all, it was just a plate of goddamn lobster salad, and she asked for it. I can be patient for only so long. What surprises me is that it seems to have splattered so far and wide, although I'm sure I didn't fling it at her. At the time I thought I'd just smeared it over her face and hair and into one ear. Understandably, she was screaming and crying, but in anger and humiliation, not because she was in physical pain. I didn't hurt her. I had no intention of hurting her, even though I'd lost control of myself. I never had before or since. That night after we'd cleaned things up—changed the bedspread and the sheets and gotten rid of the most obvious bits of mess that would have required some explanation to Margaret the next day—we went to sleep in our usual spoon fashion. I'd have liked a goodnight fuck but Jackie was still shaky. I suppose she was even scared. I dropped into a deep, untroubled sleep almost instantly. But it was her fault.

That happened on a Sunday. The time of year isn't important—in any case, I don't remember. Some events, by their character, are linked to season, but this was one of those spasms that can occur any time, an indoor freak of nature like a hurricane, an Act of God. I've no memory of what was going on outside. All that is lost. What isn't forgotten is that I'd caught her fucking around, in a lie so bald I couldn't believe she hadn't set it up in such a way that I'd have to confront her with it. She'd been in California for ten days doing what she always says she hates while loving every minute of it: living it up at the dreadful Beverly Hills Hotel where, unless you have a doctor's certificate, you aren't allowed to swim in the pool without a five-week tan, hobnobbing with the ephemerally famous, gathering material for a big article she was doing on "The New Hollywood." I was always somewhat circumspect about what I said when she had to go on these trips. They were what she wanted to do. They were necessary, but I missed her terrifically and, I told myself, she missed me. She'd call every night when she was away. I seldom went out by myself, which, I suppose, is something else I came to resent. Time had been when I couldn't wait for Utah to take off somewhere—a garden club tour of Charleston (when she was briefly aspiring to upper-middle-class gentility), to Salt Lake City to visit her widowed, non-Mormon mother, a teacher of voice (who failed spectacularly with Utah's middle and upper registers), any place. Utah's absences were things I encouraged. They gave me time to explore the secretaries of friends, unhappy wives, hookers who hang out in the lobbies and bars of our better hotels, call girls who cost a fortune and are seldom worth it.

Jackie's absences left me bereft, as much for the lack of her presence as for the suspicions I could never hide from myself that while she was out of my sight, she was being laid by every man she met. I was, I thought, quite mature on this matter. Also a realist. Jackie was—is—an extremely good-looking, sexy, beautiful, intelligent young woman. Intelligence, especially, would appeal to the sort of men she met in California, fellows who'd recognize that she'd read the front page of that morning's air-mail edition of *The New York Times* and who'd appreciate her disinclination to giggle. It would be strange, indeed, if she weren't propositioned occasionally, and I suppose I realized that at least some of those phony, machine-tooled creeps would, in the ordinary course of events, have appealed to her. Early on in our relationship I told myself that what happened when she was away was no business of mine. I trusted her. I was confident that she could never find another man like me. I turned my thoughts in other directions. Never once before did I have any reason to mistrust her.

What happened is not difficult to reconstruct. She had been scheduled to fly back from California on a flight due at Kennedy at 5:00 P.M. and, as I always did, I sent a car out to meet her. The chauffeur called me at six to report the flight had landed a half hour late but that Jackie was not on it. She wasn't even on the passenger list. At that point the salad had been made, the lobster's carcass neatly disposed of, the table set and the champagne (which Jackie loves and gives me indigestion) cooling. I was on my second martini in anticipation of the arrival of an elated Jackie—she was always exhausted after such trips, but also pleased with herself and invigorated with whatever the project was. Margaret was in the kitchen listening to Oral Roberts or Norman Vincent Peale or the Evangelical Crusade for the Blind or some such, but still tsking loudly enough for me to hear every time I went into the butler's pantry for a refill. I'd asked Margaret to stay over to serve supper since I knew Jackie would be tired and in no mood for domestic duties. It wasn't this delay that Margaret minded. It was sitting around with nothing to slave at. Margaret is a compulsive worker of the most driven sort. When she's idle she has the manner of someone whose soul is double-parked outside heaven.

After hearing from the chauffeur I immediately called the Beverly Hills Hotel where I was told Jackie had checked out the night before, which was decidedly odd since we'd talked Saturday morning when she'd given me the number of the Sunday flight. She was going to a showing of a new movie that night and to a fancy party afterwards. She'd sounded very up and genuinely eager to come home.

More furious than worried—Jackie is capable of taking care of herself in any circumstance from revolution to rape—I went out to the kitchen to find that Margaret had begun to shine a silver tea set, a Lockie heirloom, which was usually kept in the back of the silver closet and, to my knowledge, hadn't been used since Utah's reign. Me: "What *are* you doing?" Margaret (grumpily): "I noticed the finish looked a little dull." Me: "Don't be absurd. You couldn't *notice* it. You went *looking* for it. You polished it two weeks ago. Now stop it." Margaret: "It's only because I don't like to waste *my* time and *your* money. . . ." "Don't worry about my money. It's not as if you were paid by the hour, for Christ's sake. Now stop it!" "I'm just trying to be useful," says Margaret, putting the stuff away, "until the miss arrives." I was pouring myself a slug of straight vodka in the butler's pantry. "Well," I say, "the miss may not be arriving." "Oh," says Margaret a little wickedly, "has her flight been delayed?" "No," I say, "and you might as well go home. I don't know when she'll be getting in."

Margaret disappears into the maid's room next to the kitchen and cheerily continues our conversation through a discreetly closed door, behind which she's changing out of her uniform into her Hungarian peasant's costume. "You just can't trust airplanes, can you?" says Margaret. "I told you about my baby sister, didn't I? Last year when she was flying to New Orleans from Richmond and had to spend the night in Atlanta? Didn't know a soul in Atlanta, though we used to have an uncle who lived there, and they put her up at that hotel . . . you know the one . . . the one that . . ." And on and on.

Around 8:30 Jackie floated in, stoned, drunk and, I assumed, fucked out of her skull. She knew it wasn't going to be easy and was accompanied up by a slight, dapper, deeply tanned young man, so pretty he seemed unreal in a New York apartment. Unlike Jackie he was completely sober, self-assured and in charge. His polo coat was out of *Gatsby* but the man was from *The Last Tycoon.* There were confused introductions at the door. Jackie wanted him to come in for a drink. He admired a small, not very good Kandinsky in the hall and said he had to run, the car was waiting downstairs. Jackie (all giggles): "Tell him about the party." Man (to me, laughing, as Jackie begins to laugh): "The party last night was in Dallas. That's where we had our 'sneak.' " Jackie (almost hysterical with giggles): ". . . That's . . . why . . . I'm late. I thought it was going to be in Hollywood. . . ." Man (sensing that I'm not finding the scene funny at all): "Well, love . . ." (kisses her on both cheeks) ". . . I must run. . . . We'll do it again sometime." He shakes hands with me. Jackie (helpless with laughter): "Dallas!"

Fifteen minutes later when I pushed the serving cart into the bedroom, Jackie was lying on the bed, fully clothed, a stoned heap.

"What's that?" she said without interest.

"It's our dinner."

"I just want to go to sleep," she said. "I'm not hungry."

"I asked Margaret to fix this for us," I said. "You always say the one thing you miss in California is real lobster salad. This is fresh Maine lobster. . . ."

"I couldn't eat it now. I've lost my appetite."

"Do you know how difficult it is to find a live fucking Maine lobster in New York on a Sunday? I had to go all over the city."

"Don't be silly. Margaret got it."

"She did not. I went. I wanted to do something special for you."

"I suppose you made the mayonnaise too." Laugh.

"No, but I went out and found the bloody thing. I persuaded somebody at the Plaza to sell me one. It's against the Plaza's rules."

"Oh, Marshall, don't be so old-womanish. . . ."

"Old womanish? Is that what you call 'old womanish'? You come in drunk and stoned and fucked out of your mind, hours late, having flown all over the goddamn country with some Technicolored creep . . . and you call my behavior 'old womanish' . . . ?"

Which sent her into another fit of alien giggles.

"But you're the one who's drunk," she said, weeping at the hilarity of it all, "and, after all, it's just lobster salad."

I sat on the side of the bed, staring at her. Her eyes blinked drowsily. I reached over to the serving cart, scooped up a handful of salad and, instead of throwing it at her, threw it at the floor as hard as I could.

Jackie (instantly sober): "What *are* you doing?"

Me: "It's just lobster salad."

"What's wrong with you?" she said.

"I don't like you like this," I said.

She attempted to laugh again but she's not at her best trying to fake spontaneity. I scooped up another handful of salad, grabbed her by the nape of the neck and smeared it over her face. "Eat it," I said. "Goddamn you, eat it!" She struggled but I am still stronger than she is. I rubbed it into her eyes, her hair, her ear, at the same time getting it all over the bedspread and much of the wall and floor. She began to fight furiously, looking as desperately frightened as I've ever seen anybody. She looked like a cornered cat. I was so amazed that I stopped to take in the sight, which gave her the opportunity to roll away and dash for her bathroom. I tossed another scoop of salad after her, waited a few minutes, then got up and followed her to the bathroom. I swung open the door, expecting to find her cleaning her face. Instead she was squatting for a piss, her skirt pulled up around her, leaning forward at a dangerous angle. "Oh," I said with automatic politeness. One of the things each of us has always granted the other is the privacy for toilet functions.

She was a wreck of smeared food and tears. "You bastard," she said, sobbing. "Get out of here. You don't know anything. . . ." by which time she was crying fully in a way I'd never seen before, and so was I.

As best I could, I swung myself out of the bedroom, down the hall to my study, slammed the door and felt—in a sudden explosion of guilt—caved in.

24

Who loves whom for how long, and why? Ma and Handsome Tommy? Ma and the Denver flatfoot? Ma and Sir Paul Plyant? Ma's had a string of them. Cousin Mary Lee and the General? Merrie Ball and Pierce Arrow, whom she balls, and Tony Whatsisname, whom she lives with? My father and the grandmotherly Claire? Jackie and I? We are a permanent floating crap game.

I made no play for Gethsemane but I made a point of hanging around Shackleford's Store at every opportunity, first to convince Deke and the others I was serious in my campaign, and then because she began to take shape in my consciousness as someone who represented the perfect challenge, impregnable, unobtainable, the inhabitant of a country I could never visit, someone met in passing who might provide me with a victory but could never defeat me. One afternoon in late January, when it was raining so hard that even the turkey buzzards weren't flying, between my gym period and evening chapel, I slogged down to the store to buy cigarettes and to whet my appetite for supper by having three Mr. Goodbars and a Royal Crown Cola.

When I entered there were no other students around. Gethsemane was leaning on the counter reading an old copy of *Peek* in which someone had penciled in all the nipples we would not otherwise have known to be there. She reluctantly withdrew her attention from the magazine to accept my change and ring up the purchase on the cash register. In her automatic operation of the cash register she looked at me for the first time. "Boy," she said with no interest whatsoever, "you're soaking wet." "I guess I am," I said. "Take off your jacket and hang it over the back of the chair by the stove." As I did, I noticed the stove was far from hot. "I think the fire's gone out," I said. "Shit," said Gethsemane. She put down her magazine, came around the counter and touched the stove to verify my report. Did she think I'd lie about a goddamn stove? She disappeared through the door behind the counter to bring in some logs. I sat down in the chair by the window that faced the gas pumps and the highway, munching my Mr. Good-bars and swigging my Royal Crown. I watched her fetch two armfuls of wood and then asked her if I could help. "Thank you," she said, "but you're too late." "I'm sorry," I said. She stuffed some rumpled newspapers and logs into the stove, relit the fire and stood for a few moments staring into the grate to see if the logs caught. Even in her construction worker's gear I could see the line of her tits and, in the way the pants hung on her ass, I imagined I could make out the dimple in one buttock. I said, "Why don't you ever wear that blue dress?" Not looking at me, still staring into the fire: "What blue dress?" "The blue dress you were wearing the night my mother and I had dinner with the Devereauxs. . . . My mother said you were beautiful." She turned to me with an expression that was part-smile, part-sneer. "Boy," she said, "you're as full of shit as a Christmas goose." "It's true," I said, "and my name isn't boy. It's Marshall Lewis Henderson." "I know what your name is, boy," she said cheerfully, "and you're still full of shit." She returned to her *Peek*. I finished my hors d'oeuvre and left, wearing a jacket that was hot but very, very moist.

Several afternoons later I was alone with her again. She was reading a *Reader's Digest*. As I paid for my purchases I said as casually as I could, "How are you, Gethsemane?" "Why I'm right fine, thank you. How are you, Marshall Lewis Henderson?" "My friends call me Marshall." "Why I'm right fine, thank you. How are you, Marshall Lewis Henderson?" "Come on . . ." I said. "I'm okay," she said, and returned to her *Reader's Digest*. I tilted back in the chair, ate my candy, drank my Royal Crown Cola and lit a cigarette. As I smoked serenely and watched the traffic on the highway, an occasional truck or a flivver, I was aware of the not uncommon but always pleasant sensation of getting a hard-on, which begins as a slight tingling in the back of the balls and grows upward into the longed-for thrust of satisfaction. Should I or shouldn't I, I wondered. I continued to look out at the highway, unable to be sure whether or not Gethsemane was watching me. What the hell, I said to myself. Having unrestricted play in the kind of fully cut pants and boxer shorts one wore in those days, my cock, given a couple of thousand volts, bounced spectacularly.

I held still for a moment, not daring to check whether I'd performed for a live audience. She was probably deeply involved with the most unforgettable character ever met by Frances Perkins. An unread, rolled-up Richmond *Times-Dispatch* suddenly connected with my head so that I almost lost balance on the chair. I sat up. Before I could say anything, she said, "You better go back to school now. I got to close and go up to the house to fix dinner."

She had seen it! I had shown her a hard-on! I was almost coming with triumph. I didn't dare say anything as I walked to the door, followed by Gethsemane. I could only nod but given one more second I might also have thanked her for the relationship. She said, and I remember it exactly because I eventually gave it more interpretations than have been given the Declaration of Independence, "Take it easy, boy." She didn't want me to sprain anything by giving such exhibitions. She was telling me not to jerk off. Be kind to one's pecker. Fondle it, don't beat it. I was halfway back to school, traveling the shortcut through the ravine behind the church and the tennis courts, when I realized that all the hurled Richmond *Times-Dispatch* could have meant was that she did have to go home to cook for her family. In any case I'd finally allowed myself the courage to become erect in her presence. The next story I'd tell Deke Crozier and Ruddleston, W. need not be a fabrication but a legitimate report from the front.

I was so busy at school and sneaking visits to Shackleford's Store in the next few weeks that I had little chance to see Ma except at church and, afterwards, at Sunday dinner at Lewis's Landing. Toward the middle of February Ma was itching to get on with things. The charm of the Old Manners and of the county had begun to dim. She took off to visit Lockie in Palm Beach for several weeks, which, with one thing and another, were successfully extended almost until the end of the term. I wasn't sorry to see her go. What was happening to me, and what I was doing, didn't have much to do with the son she knew, and the time spent together every Sunday had the effect of throwing me off my stride, making me feel prepubescent again. When I dreamt of Tom it was always on Sunday nights. One of the last things Ma said before leaving was, "I'm just in the way," which she was. I was studying with some regularity to keep ahead of the masters. I was helping

Mr. Devereaux prepare for the production of *Journey's End* he was so keen on doing though, after reading it, I didn't know how we were going to lick the casting problems or the sound effects. Mr. Devereaux didn't recognize these as impediments since, I'm sure, in his mind he was already enjoying the finished production.

The casting problems were quite simply licked. I was assigned the leading role of Stanhope, the gallant, battle-weary, boozing officer who's so noble it hurts. I agreed to do it because I was really the only suitable choice and because we weren't scheduled to put on the play until May and anything might happen before then. The other major roles were filled by Ruddleston, W., who also spoke recognizable English, as Osborne, Stanhope's avuncular, pipe-smoking second-in-command, who is killed offstage, and by Deke Crozier, who spoke undiluted Northern Neck, as Raleigh, the hero-worshipping younger brother of the girl Stanhope left on the playing fields of home, who dies onstage. It's Raleigh who must say to Osborne at one point, "I say, how topping—to have played for England!"

My time was neatly divided by my responsibilities: classes, gym, study hall during the week; and on the weekend by the first rehearsals for *Journey's End* and, every Saturday morning, by several hours of duty on the riverfront, where we were tearing down the old pier and unloading material for the new pier that was to be built as soon as the water was warm enough for us to work in it. Nevertheless I'd find time every weekday afternoon to visit Shackleford's Store. Sometimes Deke Crozier and Ruddleston, W. would accompany me but if they did they'd usually excuse themselves as soon as they decently could. If there were other students around they'd see what they could do about getting them to leave too. I would have liked to join the after-lights trips to Four Corners to drink beer and, maybe, find something to fuck, but I was too tired. Deke, short, bullet-shaped and strong, possessed reserves of energy he never even touched. Once out he'd stay out most of the night. I'd joined one such Crozier-led expedition early in the fall term, long before any of us knew one another, when five of us went down to the river hoping to find a boat to borrow to sail around to the roller-skating rink at Queen Anne. But there was no boat and we spent most of the night on the pier, drinking from a quart of orange-flavored gin, getting very sick and then watching solemnly as Deke Crozier fucked one of Mr. Whabble's sheep in slow motion. Deke had the Old Manners. He always included me in his late-night excursions but he also understood that when I didn't go it simply indicated that I was saving on it.

I was then as committed to the herd as I've ever been. I was showing Gethsemane my hard-ons two and three times a week, a dizzy, mad pace that startled even me though the physical toll was not great.

Late one afternoon in early March after a day of radiant Tatterhummock spring, I was tilted back in my favorite chair, drinking a Royal Crown with one hand, holding a *Police Gazette* in the other, bouncing the magazine lazily up and down without benefit of hand, a spectacle designed to amuse anyone who might be watching without distinction of race, color, creed or sex, when Gethsemane left the book she was reading on the counter. She walked to the front door, turned the OPEN sign to CLOSED, locked the door, and went back to the counter where she switched off the lightbulb by the icebox. I couldn't move enough to look at her. My hard-on disappeared. I wondered how to get out of there. Finally she said, "Marshall Lewis Henderson, have you been joking me all this time?" I stood up, breathless, petrified. "Come here," she said gently. She smiled in a lazy, dreamy way that, of course, I didn't recognize. "I haven't been joking you," I said. "I know that, baby. Come to mama. . . ."

Everything took care of itself, and so quickly that I didn't have a chance to put on one of the condoms I'd been carrying around in my wallet. We stood behind that familiar counter, trousers and underpants down around the ankles, shirts pulled up, exposing for my immediate, unbelieving surprise those fine, firm, large-nippled black tits I'd been dreaming of most of my life. If she hadn't been almost as tall as I was, and as strong, I would have broken my back. But we were a perfect fit. A slight bend of my knees, followed by an arc-described thrust out and up, and we were joined. She moaned and laughed and pulled first a little to one side, then a little to the other. Suddenly I held still. "Maybe we shouldn't be doing this," I said. "Why not?" said Gethsemane. "Why the fuck not!" I said, and laughed and tried to bend over to suck the left nipple into my mouth. Lapping, fucking away. I was also panting by this time. Sweat was pouring off both of us, pasting us together, creating a suction that sounded a sort of PLOP every time it was broken. "Have you ever done this with any of the other guys?" She froze. Her beautifully responsive cunt grabbed me in the cunt's equivalent to the hammerlock. "What do you mean?" "With any of the other guys at school?" The cunt relaxed without letting go. She laughed and I opened my eyes to look directly into hers for the first time of our conjunction. "Honey, I don't know you well enough to answer that. . . . Oh, daddy. . . ."

We moved toward the top. She said carefully, each syllable accompanied by a motion, "Not . . . yet . . . not . . . yet . . . not . . . now, oh now!" And now was then for me too. There was a long pause. We were still together. "Oh, my God," I said, "it's never been like that before. I swear it hasn't. . . ." "Aw, honey." She kissed my neck, tasted my sweat, ran a hand around the back of my neck and then we realized simultaneously, as if it were a part of a rite we should observe, that we hadn't kissed on the lips. We put our mouths together but I was uneasy. We didn't know each other that well. "I love you," I said, to make up for the non-kiss. "Now what kind of talk is that?" she said. "I don't know," I said, "it's my talk." We separated. "Gawd," she said, pointing at me, "that thing ain't never going to get enough." She patted it. "Now put it away and pull your pants up because I got to get on home."

I was out on the highway, headed for the shortcut, when I looked at my watch. To the best of my calculations the whole thing—from my getting up from the chair until she locked the door behind me—took less than three minutes.

Those months in the spring of 1940 were a happy period, the last time in my life when I was complete, whole, or as complete and whole as I was ever to be. I didn't once dream of Tom's return. I didn't think of him at all. The seas were stilled, mirror-flat, another period of God's Light.

I couldn't wait to get to Shackleford's Store the next day, being afraid that I might somehow have misremembered the events or, worse, that I had hallucinated. I sometimes do if cornered. When I arrived Gethsemane was in her usual position, bent over a magazine on the counter. This time, however, when her eye caught mine there was just the slightest suggestion of a smile that, being indolent, was hugely, dangerously erotic. Nothing happened though. A half dozen of the younger boys were there and refused to leave until Gethsemane kicked us all out together at 5:15. As she closed the door she said as if talking to someone behind me, "Don't look so worried. It'll still be there tomorrow. It's something I always carry with me." She laughed and turned the OPEN sign back to front. The next day I couldn't make it because of a meeting of the cast and director of *Journey's End*. The day after it was BINGO again, fast and furious and standing up. When, before returning to the campus, I whispered that it might be a novelty, nice even, if we could try it lying down like other people, she dismissed it as a lunatic proposition. "Baby, that's the way a girl can get herself knocked up." "I can use a rubber," I said. "I don't trust no cundums," she said. "Plenty of girls have trusted cundums and where are they today?" I shrugged. "That's right," said Gethsemane, "and worse." What, I wondered, could "worse" mean? But I said nothing, not wanting to rock the boat so early in the voyage.

Afternoon after afternoon. It became a prize for a day well spent at work. We talked hardly at all, before, during, or after. One of the revelations to me—and an unsettling one too, I guess —was my awareness that Gethsemane was quite as eager as I was, that she was looking forward to it with the same impatience I was when the untidy, meatbeating younger boys stayed too long at the store over their bubble gum. I never described the details of the encounters to Deke Crozier and Ruddleston, W. I wasn't the sort of cad who bragged about his conquests over brandy and cigars in the smoking room. This was a matter of honor and trust. It was a choice I made. Yet I couldn't hide my new sense of self-satisfaction and well-being. If I wasn't acting lordly, being kind to peasants, I was euphoric. It was the real me.

Deke Crozier and Ruddleston, W., I assume, divined very early what was going on, and they were gentlemen enough not to enquire of the particulars unless I wanted to volunteer the information. The foreplay had ended and the serious fucking had begun, they knew, when one Friday night I declined to take the seat in the bus across the aisle from Gethsemane. They understood when discretion was required. It didn't pay to cause tongues to wag when real fucking was involved. Deke was especially protective of my privacy. After all, he didn't expect anyone to ask after the last sheep he had fucked. As if he were a younger brother he treated me with deference and a sometimes uncomfortable awe, of which, I'm sure, he was totally unaware. He wanted *me* to like *him*. How sad. In one of the books I'd read on the conduct of a sane sex life I'd once come across a paragraph that warned of the terrible problems that could arise when an adolescent boy failed to clear successfully "the homosexual hurdle." What would one have called the hurdle that Deke had yet to clear? A stile? Once when we were showering together in the dormitory Ruddleston, W. forgot himself long enough to comment on the intense rosiness of my cock, which, that afternoon, had scored two home runs back to back in the same inning. Deke was appalled by Ruddleston, W.'s gaffe. To appease Deke and to mislead two of the lower-form boys who were in the shower, Ruddleston, W. suggested that I must have a knothole somewhere I was fucking. Knowing the literalness with which small boys take in such information I'm sure they spent weeks looking for that knothole or ones of their own. I hope no one injured himself.

At this time we began rehearsing *Journey's End* regularly if not seriously three times a week in the hour between the end of supper and the start of evening study hall, with an additional two-hour period every Saturday evening, at which point I came to realize that Deke was acting out in real life the relationship between Stanhope and Raleigh within the play. The only acting he ever mastered was unconscious.

It was about this time that I started to call Deke by his full Christian name, DeKoven. DeKoven Crozier was—is—an impressive Tidewater name. There were DeKovens and Croziers in the House of Burgesses before Patrick Henry was born. I gave DeKoven his name back to him, bestowing it upon him as if it were a knighthood. Other fellows took it up, even Ruddleston, W., and though the other fellows paid no attention to the source of the honor—on the campus I was still a character of some strangeness and Deke was Mr. Big—he recognized the shift in power in all of our bilateral relations. To the other fellows DeKoven was just another nickname, which, by chance, was Deke's full Christian name. Between Deke and me it was acknowledged to be a small estate from which, from time to time, he might be asked to pay dues to his prince.

25

I'm growing lazy in ways that make even me impatient. I live in an isolation I haven't known since childhood and, being unobserved, I seem to find flushing the loo after taking a piss too much trouble. In years past I welcomed the challenge of the maneuver, the bending over, the flick of a handle sometimes with a crutch. Now I couldn't care less, though I'm no more fond of walking into the bathroom and coming upon a bowl of my own urine than I am of finding cat turds that have been kicked out of the box. No, I'm not trying to save it. I just don't give a goddamn about flushing toilet bowls after a quick piss. Toward the end of Utah and before Jackie I was attracted to a young woman who has since made a success as a novelist. She is skinny, frail, incomparably beautiful in the way of someone who hasn't long to live, and she can lift a freight car when she puts her mind to it. When I was introduced to her she was busy searching for SuperPill, the pill that would raise her spirits in the morning, calm her at night, give her an appetite but keep her thin and continue to work for thirty-six hours like a cold capsule. After frightening experiences with speed disguised as vitamins and with Valium, Seconal and booze, she became re-signed to the torment of being herself. The trouble, she would say, gently fluttering her delicate hands, was that she couldn't concen-trate. "What kind of a day has it been?" I'd say on the telephone. "Oh, Marshall, I may commit suicide. I don't know what I'm going to do. I think this time I really am losing my grip. It's not a joke." "Why?" "Today I didn't get out of bed at all. I started with 'The Price Is Right' this morning and went on until 'The Edge of

Night.' Am I crazy? Tell me that I am and I'll feel better." Later in the evening I'd find that she'd completed a short story and had re-typed all 8,000 words of it twice to get the margins aligned prop-erly. She never flushed the loo either. "Oh, dear," she'd say when I headed for the bathroom. "I'm afraid I forgot to flush again," and I'd say it didn't matter, but it did. "You're used to living alone," I'd say. "Is that it?" she'd say. "Do you really think that's it? You're probably right. Marshall, I think you've hit the nail on the head."

Finally I tired of flushing after her. I thought she'd walk into the sea at Tinos and never emerge. Instead she was elected to the American Academy and Institute of Arts and Letters. I wonder where Jackie is. It's six weeks now. Last night a woman called the host of a radio phone-in show to complain about the nasty re-marks he'd made about the mayor. "You can't put yourself in some-one else's shoes," said the woman, "in any way, shape or form."

Notes from the steamer trunk:

July 10, 1940. It is 2:30 P.M. The temperature is 87°, humid-ity is 87, the barometer is steady at 29.9 and the wind velocity is zero. Tom's revenge: I am in a room on the fourth floor of Grace Hospital, Richmond, Virginia. If I were lying on something I would be lying on my stomach but instead I seem to be sus-pended in air, pulled by a benign rack. Two hours facing down, two hours facing up, my head and shoulders resting on hospital linen that turns on the spit with me. The bed is a scientific won-der, the only one of its kind in the state of Virginia outside the military hospital in Norfolk. It is a definition of the term "hos-pital bed." At times it even feeds me. It accepts my waste matter. I am paralyzed from the waist down. My spine is broken in two places and may never heal properly. This meantime I'm now in is devoted to what everyone except me gaily calls waiting-and-seeing. I write these words as if the movement of my right hand on this paper could coax responses from my toes, which, when I twist the mirror by my pillow, I can see are still there, by the dawn's early light, so to speak and write.

It's a curious sensation when the pain subsides, for I can feel the inside workings of myself with a newly discovered sensitivity, and not just when I'm being given an enema or when the urethral hose is being inserted. I feel arteries, veins, subcutaneous regions that nerves don't ordinarily service. Muscles have independent lives, I have learned, and nobody listens to me. I can feel my legs and feet down there, at such great distance. They are in working order, I perceive. Sometimes it's rather as if I did not want to move them, the way one feels when one is dropping off to sleep and knows there is a more comfortable position but somehow can't move, even a hair's breadth. It's as if it were too much trouble. I'm an amputee unamputated, even to the cramps I have and the sudden bolts of exquisite pain that go ricocheting through the pelvic region that at all other times belongs to someone else. But to see me is to see someone who is whole, undivided. I am able to take my own pulse simply by focusing my attention. The other afternoon I awoke and thought I was alone. I was facing down. Miraculously I was able to release a long, loud, deliciously satisfactory series of small, presumably dry, popping farts, when I heard a polite cough at the other end of the bed. I turned the mirror and saw Lockie. She had pulled up a chair and was sitting there, her cheek pressed against the sole of my left foot. I've since given instructions that I don't want anyone slipping into the room when I'm asleep and sitting where I can't see them the first thing when I awake. I have few pleasures. I'd like to be able to fart without embarrassment. That was the afternoon that Lockie and I experienced Darshan, One Man's Family-style.

July 11, 1940. It is 4:00 P.M., temp. 88°, humidity 81, barometer 29.9 and steady, wind velocity nil. I am unclean. I'm aware of dust and other forms of sediment accumulating on my legs and feet. I feel as if I breathe the fumes of a cesspool, inhaling corruption that, as it erodes the walls of the ventricles and slowly suffocates the minute, comma-shaped corpuscles that transport oxygen, has made me a bit light in the head. I long for the morphine they gave me early on, but no such luck. Nurse Match reads from the *News-Leader*: " 'Whooping Cranes Thrive in Canada!' Did you know that, Marshall? I thought they were all dead already, imagine that . . . oh, you're writing again, aren't you? If you don't want me to read to you, I won't. Do you want me to read? After all, you can write almost any time and it isn't often that I get a chance to come in like this." Miss Match, for all her pretenses at working hard and being efficient, is a lazy lob who goofs off at every opportunity. The only reason she hangs around all the time is to enjoy the occasional spectacle of one of my involuntary erections. Poor old biddy. "Well, I dee-clare! There are more cigarette butts under your bed. You keep bribing the orderlies . . . that's not fair. A boy your age shouldn't be smoking at all. . . ." I write and do not answer. I make myself breathe deeply when I feel the air stirring, making believe those wan gusts of hot city air are northeast gales. I bury my face in hospital linen and at night I'm wretched because no matter how I turn my head I can smell the putrescence with which, during the day, I've soiled the pillow. I now have the pillowcase changed three times a day. Last week my gums became sore and would bleed on the application of the least pressure of my tongue. I was sure that in some manner I had contracted trench mouth in this antiseptic limbo. Probably from Miss Match, I thought. All her nervous breathing over me through those choppers that have the color and texture of bull antlers. I was stricken with the fear that I was about to lose all my teeth (castration, I know) but the pain immediately subsided when the doctor reduced my doses of mineral oil and gave me Horlick's malted milk tablets to chew.

In the time I was under sedation after the accident the Germans moved against the Lowlands and swept into France, occupying Paris with no opposition. When I came to, the first thing Ma said was "Thank God, Elsie Mendl is safe."

—End of Marshall Lewis Henderson's Hospital Journals

In the autumn of 1969 Baby Pru was leaving a party at the apartment of friends on Chicago's Near North Side. It was 2:00 A.M. As he was unlocking the door of his car, a black Toyota, one man, who reportedly was standing in a nearby doorway, shot at Pru five times, putting slugs into his chest, arm and leg. A spokesman for the Reform Panthers accused the FBI of the assassination attempt. The FBI accused the Black Panthers. The Black Panthers accused a splinter group of rejected Reform Panthers. The splinter group accused Pru who, they said, had set himself up in an attempt to discredit other black groups and to gain publicity for a book he had recently completed, *A Race with Time: The Successes and Failures of the Black Power Movement.*

The newspaper pictures of Pru leaving St. Luke's Hospital two months later showed a tall, gaunt young man, as beautiful as ever and even more aloof. His only statement when asked about the still-unsolved shooting: "Ask Daley's pigs." Until the assassination attempt it had never occurred to me that people like Pru went to the fuss of owning automobiles. I was aware they didn't always steal them. Perhaps I assumed they rented from Avis. I don't know. It does seem that a revolutionary who has successfully dealt with a Department of Motor Vehicles, who has passed a vehicle operator's test—written and road—who has negotiated a new car loan and then dickered with some automobile salesman about such extras as a radio, white walls and air conditioning, must be less menacing than a revolutionary who has not.

Not long before the assassination attempt I had come upon him by accident:

Baby Pru sitting in one of those contoured swivel chairs favored by set decorators for television talk shows. He faced the fair-haired, even-featured Ivy League interviewer who also sat in a contoured swivel chair and held a clipboard with his notes. I was in bed alone, Jackie being in California to do a hatchet job on a rock singer whose vanity was greater than his instinct for self-preservation. Clicking from one channel to another I suddenly saw a close-up of Baby Pru's fine, chestnut-colored head with those hazel eyes that always suggest he may be inhabited by someone quite other than the man we see. They are, I suspect, as much responsible for making him a leader as anything he has ever said or written. He'd never before consented to appear on national television in a full-fledged, formal interview, and the interviewer was clearly uneasy, sending out periodic smiles that had no relation to what was being said, coughing importantly before saying something unimportant. Pru, on the other hand, possessed the ease of a star, well aware, I'm sure, of that beauty that's composed of equal parts of the saintly and demonic, always an irresistible combination to audiences that brush twice daily to avoid tooth decay while consuming gallons of soft drinks to hasten complete body rot. I was not prepared for the style, the professional charm. It's no accident that the woman he married is a performer. Revolution is show biz too.

Some of his statements: "Hatred is very much an element of the struggle. It transforms the black man into an effective, violent, cold killing machine. . . ." "We are organizing urban guerrillas for a fight to the death. . . ." "Liberalism is just an extension of paternalism. When the honky asks what he can do for me, I say he can give me some guns. . . ."

He wore gray pants, neatly pressed, and a dashiki of abstract designs in black, brown and white. His Afro was so modified he looked less radical than a Madison Avenue copywriter, though the manner was calmly fierce, arrogant. He's one of those men who knows he doesn't have to smile to win friends, so that when he does smile, it's usually a sneer, on rare occasions a blessing.

". . . White people cannot relate to the black experience. They don't know what the word 'black' means. They cannot relate to the experiences that brought such a word into being. They don't know the taste of chitterlings, hog's head cheese, pig's feet and ham hocks. They don't know their (bleep) from their elbow about the black church, unless the church has taken on white manifestations. . . ."

I'd never heard such nonsense in my life. He also took the opportunity to tell us again about the attack on his ten-year-old person in the washroom of the Alfred E. Smith grammar school in the Bronx.

All along I'd had suspicions but suddenly there was no doubt: I was watching myself in Lenten ash.

26

The first time I met my stepmother, Claire, at the bar at the Yale Club, I thought she might well have been chosen by Ma. She was not the sort of person Ma would worry about. She was gray-haired, on the plump side, short, plain-featured but in such robust good health that this passed for a kind of beauty, college-educated, incapable of sarcasm, given to tweed suits that were expensive but without style and shoes that looked sensible even when the heels were high. She was the sort of woman who had looked middle-aged at twenty-nine and would look that way forever. She was the mother of four and the grandmother of seven. Hers was a family of close, uncomplicated attachments which, when Claire married my father, came to include him. In his middle years my father became the active head of a large loving clan of a sort he'd always needed and that seemed to me as alien as a tribe of Hairy Ainus.

It was when I saw him and Claire together for the first time that I understood that everything that had happened to us, to him and Ma and Tom and me, together, had become for him as well as for Ma only a minor chapter in an ongoing life. Ma, who had met my father and Claire shortly after they were married, could barely contain her pleasure as she described "the woman your father has married." Said Ma, "She's Catholic, of course. Wouldn't you know? Your father was always a Catholic at heart. I told you . . . she's at least ten years older than he is" (which was untrue) "and a widow, very sweet in a placid sort of way that I don't find terribly interesting. She didn't say a word the night we had dinner together. I had to do all the talking. We dined in the Oak Room at seven. I'd had luncheon with Lockie and we hadn't left the Colony until four, so I was hardly famished. But I suppose they get up early, you know, on the farm. Well . . ." (sigh) "I certainly hope your father's happy."

He was very happy. They moved permanently to Claire's farm, Clusters, on the eastern shore where they raise Morgan horses and Aberdeen cattle and supervise an extensive experimental agricultural program designed to produce vegetables that will tolerate the four-month November that the eastern shore shares with Tatterhummock County on the other side of the Chesapeake Bay. After seeing my father with Claire I often wondered how he had put up with Ma for as long as he did. They hunt and fish together and Claire, my father told me with pleasure, is almost as good a shot as he is and even better at running outboard motors and fixing them when they break down.

"The farm," as it's called, is almost as big as all of Tatterhummock County and far more civilized. The centerpiece is a handsome, modern, fourteen-room house of brick and wood that makes no attempt to disguise place or time. The outbuildings include two cottages for Claire's children and grandchildren when they come on extended visits, or for guests in the duck-shooting season. There are also a swimming pool, tennis courts and a three-hole golf course, but I have a feeling they aren't used by anyone except children and guests, Claire and my father being too devoted to stock and the fruits of the earth to have time for such things. They cure their own pork, age their own beef, shear their own sheep and, according to Ma, weave their own tapestries. At least 50 percent of everything they put on their table comes from their own land, my father once told me at great length. Lewis's Landing is a farm. Clusters reminds me of something in the Argentine. It's a state-within-a-state, a community of virtually self-sustaining enterprises. Ma would have hated it.

She was still in Palm Beach when my ten-day spring vacation from St. Matthew's came around in March. Palm Beach never having been my favorite spot, certainly not at that time of year, Ma asked my father to take me in, about which I had no feelings one way or the other. It would, I thought, be a rest. I'd been studying hard, learning my lines for the play, behaving in comradely fashion to my peers, dismantling the pier on the river, and fucking my brains out. So much had happened so quickly I thought I could do with a little time out.

After two days at Clusters I was ready to return to St. Matthew's. It wasn't only that masturbation had lost a great deal of its original appeal and that the only potential fucks were the high-class Angora sheep Deke might have fancied, but I was completely out of the life there, not excluded yet not a part of it even in the way an ordinary guest might have been. Everyone tried to be nice but was instead elaborately self-conscious about me, as if I were already a cripple. My father—it was at this time that I realized I had nothing to call him and, in fact, never called him anything, "Dad" being too intimate for someone I'd seen only twice in five years, "Daddy" too childish, and "Father" too old-fashioned—my father now had other commitments. When I arrived one of Claire's married daughters was there with her children, aged ten, seven and three, each of whom called my father "Grandpa" and whom he treated with the patience and care he'd had with Tom. I didn't fit. I was an embarrassing souvenir; but he did try.

The first morning I was there he showed me around the place on horseback, always riding a little ahead of me, stopping for me to catch up, and then moving ahead of me again. Before turning back to the main house we stopped for a few minutes on the beach where we'd been riding. Without comment he offered me a cigarette, which I accepted, and then he held a light for me. His hands, burned a deep brown-red, shook slightly, but it was an awkward position as he leaned over in his saddle, held the match and tried to keep his horse quiet. The view was much like that from St. Matthew's along the river, as was the beach smell. I was aware of the sound of leather harnesses and straps rubbing together, also of his breathing. He was short of breath. "Are you happy, son?" He was looking out over the water. "I guess so," I said. His horse pawed at the sand and my father reined him in. "When I was your age," and he turned to look at me directly, "it was the happiest time of my life, until now. . . ." "Yes, sir," I said. It was the way one replied to masters at the private penal colonies I'd been attending. He smiled, shook his head. "I guess we don't know each other very well, do we?" "No," I said. "Well," he said, "let's try to correct that. Remember, you can come over here any time you want. I can pick you up or we can send the car for you. . . ." "That would be very nice," I said, feeling acutely uncomfortable. "I'd like us to be friends," he said, "you know, the way Tom and I always were. . . ."

My God! The way he and Tom always were! My father is a nice fellow, I suppose, but he is an idiot. He was very bucked up by our ride together, figuring that he'd at last made contact with his eccentric son. Before lunch, which was always the big meal of the day on the farm, he and Claire had drinks and he began acting very kittenish with her, just as he had once done with Ma. I was given a large bedroom whose windows faced the bay and were fitted with louvered shutters that folded back into the casements during the day. Claire said that from now on it would be "Marshall's room." Having been told about my fondness for the *Britannica*, she'd had the family's *Encyclopedia Americana* moved to the bookcase in my room that was otherwise stuffed with Ellery Queens, Crime Club selections and one mild Thorne Smith.

I went up to Baltimore with Claire one day to shop and she let me do the driving, but since she is a perfectly good driver herself, unlike Ma, she was inclined to get nervous and work the footbrake whenever we approached an intersection or a full-stop sign. One night Claire and my father took me into Crisfield, a small town nearby, to the movies, though movies, I suspected, bored Claire as much as they did my father, and this one bored even me. It was a laborious, romantic costume picture in which Tyrone Power, while digging the Suez Canal, fucked Annabella and dreamed of fucking Loretta Young, who was supposed to be the Empress Eugénie. I know he didn't really fuck Annabella in the movie but in my mind at that time all persons, even fictional characters as well as my father and Claire, were fucking everybody else. I was surrounded by people who, just as soon as my back was turned, flew into sexual union. Iron shavings going splat against magnets.

On the fourth or fifth day of my visit, on that drive to Baltimore, I briefly entertained the fantasy of showing Claire a hard-on while I drove. I got as far as the first faint stirrings of tumescence when I decided it would unnecessarily complicate matters, that I had as much as I could handle already and that I'd wait and jack off that night when I went to bed with a copy of something called *The Spaniard*, a comparatively dirty book I'd had the foresight to borrow from Ruddleston, W. before leaving school. I'd also brought along *Père Goriot*, which I would read after achieving sexual relief.

The one book I never opened during the ten-day respite from real life was a worn, stained copy of *Quentin Durward*, the flyleaf of which identified it as the fifth volume in the Immortal Literature Series published by Stevens & Hammer, Inc., Richmond, Virginia, edited and abridged by Henrietta Hawthright, with illustrations by Robin Starr, approved for secondary school use by the State of Virginia Department of Education. It had come to me in a plain brown wrapper the Friday night before the start of the spring vacation. I had descended from the school bus in Queen Anne and was walking toward Smith's Pharmacy when Gethsemane called me back. "Hey, boy." I turned. She motioned me over and, through the open door of the bus, handed me the package. "You forgot something," she said. "No, I didn't," I said. "Yes, you did," she said, displaying no interest whatsoever, no familiarity at all. If anything she was annoyed at the incon-

venience I'd put her to. I accepted the parcel and stepped away in
some surprise. She swung the bus door closed, revved the engine
and, grinding the gears, chugged away to wherever it was she went
to wait for us to get out of the movie. I never thought to ask. Now
that I reconstruct it I suppose she went to the movie too, and sat in
the Queen Anne Theater's tiny balcony that we knew to be Nigger
Heaven.

27

"How topping—to have played for England!" DeKoven Crozier
would approach that line as if it were something obscene he was
being forced to say in front of the mother who had a nose for
finding condoms. He clearly didn't have a thought about the play
or about his part in it. He could barely follow the plot. His lines
could have been Greek he was speaking phonetically. "How
topping—to have played for England!" Each time he said it in
Northern Neck—"Hah tahppin'—ta uh played fo' Ang-a-lan!"—
I'd break up, which would cause Ruddleston, W. to break up and,
eventually, anyone else who happened to be around with the exception of Mr. Devereaux. We were rehearsing in the St. Matthew's
Church Community House, on the other side of the highway from
the church, a grim, unheated building that even in April, when it
was warm outside, retained a November chill against which all of
us wore coats, scarfs and sometimes gloves. Mr. Devereaux sat on
the stage with us, on a collapsible wooden chair turned back to
front, leaning his arms on the back, smoking with his cigarette
holder and watching us as if we were members of the Old Vic instead of eleven acned misfits who could scarcely speak American
to say nothing of English with the appropriate English accents.

He took no notice of our hoots when DeKoven arrived at that
fatal line unless Stonewall Jackson, sprawled in a stupor at his
feet, was made anxious by the commotion. "Now, now, men," Mr.
Devereaux would say. Then to Deke: "Deke, boy, who's your favorite movie actor?" Deke: "I don't reckon I have one, sir." "Are
there any English movie actors you like?" Long pause. "The fella

who played Knute Rockne?" "Pat O'Brien," I say. Mr. Devereaux: "All right, Deke, try that line again and say it the way you think Pat O'Brien would say it. Be quiet for a minute and try to hear him saying it in your head." Deke would think hard, listening to Pat O'Brien, and then repeat the line exactly as he had said it before, only with more fear and desperation. "That's much better," Mr. Devereaux would say, and I'm sure he believed it. The hitch in Deke's successful use of Mr. Devereaux's method was that all of the voices he heard sounded exactly like his. Deke lived in a world inhabited entirely by Northern Neckers, except for Adolf Hitler who, he said one night after giving short attention to a radio broadcast, sounded to him like a goddamn foreigner. I said he was speaking German. "I know he's speaking German," said Deke. "That's why he sounds like a goddamn foreigner."

Deke was probably the least obnoxious and offensive member of the cast. He was genuine, always trying, which is, I assume, what endeared him to Mr. Devereaux. Whatever he did, he did with the total absorption of a character in a cartoon. He might not have had much upstairs but he used every ounce of what he had. The rest of us—Ruddleston, W., the others and I—must have been impossible, tossing around our conceptions of English accents which were not only terrible but, I'm sure, made even more unpleasant to the ear by our assurance that they were really not bad at all. If they were, Mr. Devereaux gave no notice of it. A dream was coming to life before eyes that saw but did not perceive.

"Now, men," he said to us the first day of rehearsal, "this is not an easy play to do. It helps, of course, that it has an all-male cast . . . no female roles. I don't think Deke Crozier here would look too good in a wig" (pleased guffaw from Deke) "and the sound effects are complicated, but we have several months to solve these problems. Philo Lumberton will be responsible for the set, the sound and lighting effects. . . . *Journey's End* is about why we're all here at St. Matthew's. It's an exciting play . . . more exciting than most of the movies you all sit through every Friday night over in Queen Anne; but it's also about growing up, learning to take responsibility, being true to oneself, going on reconnaissance missions when you'd much rather stay in bed. It's about honor, the kind of honor a man is guided by all his life, on the football field, in the classroom, in doing his duty, just as our Allies are now doing their duty in this new war. . . . I never had the privilege of meeting Mr. Sherriff, who wrote our play, but on the basis of this single work it's generally agreed that he's the greatest playwright of the English language since William Shakespeare. . . . I expect you men to honor his words, every comma and semicolon.

"It's a simple story on the face of it. The actual time elapsed is less than three days. Yet all of World War I takes place in this single dugout . . . all the courage, the sacrifice, the heroism, the fear, the senseless slaughter. You men will be going into your own battles soon. I wasn't much older than you men when I was sent to France" (ten-year-old Ruddleston, A., who's in charge of props, is following Mr. Devereaux's words so intently that he farts; no one dares to laugh). ". . . Things that seem important to you now will be forgotten when you get to the front lines. There ain't no Friday night movies at the front, I can promise you." "And no study hall," Deke says spontaneously, not attempting to be funny. "And no study hall," says Mr. Devereaux, who has been around boys long enough to incorporate such ad libs, ". . . and no clean sheets and no MacDougal making batter bread for Monday morning breakfasts. The men in this play value their world so much—value their traditions, their laws, their government, their king, their families, all those things that go to make the heritage of the English-speaking race the greatest man has ever known—they value these things so much they are ready to give their lives to save that world. You men are still young, barely boys. It's all very well for Ruddleston, A. here to say he's ready to die for his country" (Ruddleston, A., who has only recently mastered the mysteries of shoelace tying, nods in solemn agreement) "until that moment comes along and then, then that's when the real man must step forward. He ain't looking for glory. He does what must be done because he's the only man to do it. You can call him a hero . . . you can . . . he is, but in the final analysis he is simply the man he's met at the end of the road. This entire play is about the man you're going to meet at the end of the road in ten, twenty, thirty years. I've mentioned that man to you often enough so that I shouldn't have to remind you that the man at the end of the road is the man you're making yourself today. Stanhope is such a man. . . ."

I could see Deke's eyes going opaque as he tried to follow the Devereaux line but, as in morning assembly when Mr. Devereaux gave us essentially the same pep talk, the more Deke attempted to understand, the sleepier he became. He never understood the time sequences Mr. Devereaux used. Would one of us meet himself at the end of the road in ten years and someone else not for thirty? If so, why the discrimination? If one played the game, observed the rules, studied hard and fucked only one sheep a week, would one meet oneself sooner rather than later? Was there a possibility that one might get to the end of the road and, not recognizing oneself, walk right on by? What happened then? The way Deke's jaw clenched and the way he had started batting at his upstanding hair, as if trying to keep it quiet, usually meant that he was about to slip into deep, sudden sleep.

". . . and I can see," Mr. Devereaux was saying, "that our Raleigh is on the verge of leaving us so I will cut short my remarks. I would like to point out, as you will notice, that I've seen fit to make some slight alterations in the text. If you will open your scripts to page 2, the bottom of the page, you will see that when Hardy says 'damned annoying,' I've changed that to 'darned annoying.' On page 23, bottom of the page, when Stanhope says, 'Don't be a damn fool,' Henderson here will say, 'Don't be a darn fool.' On the next page, Stanhope has two 'damneds,' two 'hells' and a 'damn'; they are modified as noted. Now I realize that there's nothing wrong with a 'damn' or a 'hell' under certain circumstances, and at the front I was on, the men were sometimes heard to use a whole lot worse, but this is, after all, a play, an entertainment, and we're a church school, and we hope to sell a lot of tickets to the ladies of Tatterhummock County, so we ain't got any need to get up on this stage and use a lot of cuss words just because they're in the script. That sort of thing is all right in New York City but down here we're gentlemen and our women are ladies and we got to treat them as such."

After the first read-through, DeKoven Crozier said to me as if thinking out loud, "Didn't those guys in the English Army ever says words like 'fuck,' 'piss' or 'shit,' or anything like that?" I said

I didn't know. "Shee-ee-it," said Deke, "probably a bunch of fairies."

We were doing it lying down at my insistence and against Geth-semane's better judgment that was never as firm as my cock. We were in the bower of loblollies and new April honeysuckle, 50 feet removed from the path behind the church and the tennis courts. She lay back on my jacket as first I unbuttoned her shirt, opened it and brought forth those great shining black tits which, when she was prone like this, seemed to slide upward and settle somewhere close to her chin. I looked at them, stroked them, gently squeezed each nipple to make it hard, then sucked a minute on each, giving them equal time, stroking her thighs all the while through the heavy fabric of her trousers. The pleasure of unwrapping was new to me. She giggled and put her hands up to unbutton my shirt. I pushed them away. I didn't want interruptions. She giggled again. "I declare," she said, "you look so serious." "I am serious," I said, but to let her know I really did love her and not just that extraordinary body, I leaned up and kissed her hard on the mouth, though quickly. Then it was back to the principal dig. I unfastened her belt, her fly, the masculine disguise that guarded Sappho's treasure. She lifted her ass slightly to allow me to pull the trousers and panties down, but I couldn't get them off over those construction worker's boots. I untied each boot, loosened the laces and pulled off the shoes. Not until I had the trousers and panties completely off did I permit myself to observe the mons venus that I'd never really seen in all of our perpendicular encounters behind the counter. It looked tremendous and as virginal as a New World forest, as if no one in history had logged there before me.

I stared, enchanted, then quickly began to undo my shirt, my pants and shorts and shoes. Gethsemane still wore her shirt, though it was wide open to the breezes, and her socks. I was completely naked, wearing not even socks, sitting up on high viewing that vast new forest. If forests can also be seas, I was stout Cortez on a peak in Darien, discovering the Pacific, or did Cortez discover the Pacific?

"What's that?" I said.

"What's what?" said Gethsemane.

"I think I hear someone going by on the path. Don't make a sound. . . ."

With that I dove headfirst into her cunt, clutching her ass with both hands, roughly, as if to keep her quiet so that the imaginary hikers below wouldn't hear us. With my tongue I probed, charting that orifice and its immediate environs which, until that afternoon, had been to me only a clinical illustration, or, worse, something drawn in cross-section. This was the real thing. In three dimensions of flesh and color, as humid as the earth we lay against. She writhed and turned, holding my head in her hands in a bear's grip. Because her palms partially covered my ears I couldn't hear what she was saying but I assumed she was moaning, which she liked to do when we were standing up. The grip on my head intensified as she rocked me from side to side. I clung to her ass even more violently. If possible I would have crawled all the way into her, spelunking my way to heaven. Suddenly I became aware that she was trying to pull my head away from her. I looked up.

"For Christ's sake, boy, don't bite!"

She giggled and pulled me further up so that we were lying on our sides facing each other. My cock dangled erect just outside the main gate. She put her hand on it, squeezed it, pulled it closer, tickled its head with her pubic hairs. I leaned forward to kiss her, saying just before it was too late, "I love you . . ."

Doing it lying down! That was the only way. Joined at the mouth, cock enclosed by cunt. Pushing, pulling, hauling, shoving, biting, tonguing. Pulling that barge, toting that bale. "More, more, more!" "More?" Laughter. "Boy, you got all there is. There ain't any more!" It wasn't until after we'd both come that I remembered I hadn't used a rubber, but then I thought if she wasn't worried, I certainly wasn't but, as she'd said, that's how a girl gets knocked up—and worse.

Thus it was late each Thursday afternoon from early April until the end of May, on those days when she filled in for Jojo's regular nurse and one of her brothers minded the store. We had to synchronize our watches to make successful connections and on two occasions Mr. Devereaux screwed things up by driving Gethsemane home. One Friday night, after an especially instructive

Thursday afternoon, when I'd persuaded her to experiment with a sixty-nine, something that in those days was thought to be decadently French, even by liberated couples on New York's intellectual Upper West Side, I bought her a bottle of Coty perfume at Smith's Pharmacy.

When she began wearing dresses I knew, I thought, that she loved me. I especially liked all the underpinnings, though we agreed that not only did she not need a girdle, but that it was more of an impediment than its erotic content was worth. It wouldn't have contributed to my pleasure. A garter belt she never acquired, but she had everything else. She also began to take a direct interest in my welfare. "Boy, you're too thin. Look at those ribs. If I could play one of those things" (a xylophone) "I'd play 'Chop Sticks' on you." One afternoon I recited from Rimbaud's "Illuminations" for her. "C'est le repos éclairé, ni fièvre, ni languer, sur le lit ou sur le pré. . . ."

"Honey, I don't understand one word of it."

"Don't worry about understanding it. What do the sounds make you think of?"

She thinks, then says, "Skin . . . smooth, soft white skin. . . ." She rubs her hand along my back. "And . . . those ribs!"

28

Fifteen years ago during one of those periods when Miss Utah and I were having an unsuccessful trial separation (meaning that at the end of it we decided to give failure a second chance), I took off alone for the Caribbean with a desire to see what if any islands existed between Antigua and Barbados. It was late spring. After spending several days with Lake Forest friends at the Mill Reef in Antigua, I moved on to St. Constance (arid, ugly and so poor they sold postcards for the Virgin Islands), St. Martin (arid, ugly and anxious), Guadeloupe (hot, wet and dirty), the Saintes (small, beautiful but too primitive for me), Dominica (beautiful, primitive and menacing), Martinique (hot, wet, beautiful, troubled, good food) and, finally, St. Lucia where, more in boredom than in passion, I hired a sullen black waitress who worked at the airport hotel to accompany me on a weekend trip from Castries, the capital, to Soufrière, the tiny community on the southern tip of the island with a small, crude hotel that was used as a base for people wanting to climb to the crater of the volcano. It took most of the day to get from Castries to Soufrière on the old coastal boat that was packed with the usual Caribbean assortment of rowdy locals, animals and poultry. My mistress, who, when she cared to talk at all, whispered an unintelligible mixture of English and French patois, was so mortified by my crutches and braces and tropics-induced blood-red face that she declined to sit with me in the shade of the boat's saloon (a tarpaulin attached to four poles amidships), preferring to sit in the sun on the stern with the hoi polloi, though I noticed she didn't talk to them either. The Englishman who ran the hotel in Soufrière had no doubt about my relationship to the mute with me but he made no fuss since I booked two rooms. After a couple of drinks and an inedible supper of canned corn, macaroni with pimento and a dessert of fresh papaya, I elected to retire alone at 9:30.

The next morning I awoke completely refreshed, only to be told by the manager that my companion would have to vacate the premises as soon as it would be convenient. When I asked why, since we'd paid for the rooms for two nights in advance, and I could see no signs of an impending convention, he looked unhappy, then screwed up his courage to say, "Your friend . . ." "What's wrong with my friend?" I said. Through the door that opened onto a small dining terrace adjacent to the lobby I could see my friend, her hair pulled into a dozen tight little island-braids that stuck out from her head in all directions. She sat politely at a table picking at some scrambled eggs. "I suppose," I said, "that you don't like to have blacks at this Ritz Towers. That's ridiculous, cruel and short-sighted. The island is ninety-five percent black." "It's not that," said the Englishman, who was extraordinarily good-mannered under the circumstances. "It's just that last night, after you went to bed, she made proposals to my three other guests." "Who?" I said. "The German doctor," he said, referring to a fat little man of about sixty who, I suspected, was a Nazi war criminal on the run, "and the two young men from the University of California who are making studies of the volcano." "Are you sure?" I said. "Yes," he said. "She offered . . . well . . . 'to do' Dr. Franzblum for ten dollars Beewee." "Did she?" "I certainly don't think so," said the Englishman. "The doctor was, in fact, quite shocked. His wife has only been dead one month." "It don't rub off," I said. The Englishman smiled as if he'd just sat on a bad egg. "No, no, no," he said.

We returned to Castries by the morning boat and went our separate ways. It was, I thought, just more of the same.

Jackie returned this morning at ten. She called first, was very direct and crisp, a manner I used to like in her but have come to find objectionable. She asked if she could drop by to pick up some things. "Of course," I said. "I've been expecting you to come home," a not very subtle way of indicating that I was prepared to forgive and forget. I don't hold grudges without reason. Everyone is human. With one crutch I crab-walked around the living room collecting unfinished scotches, pouring them into one glass, emptying ashtrays, and was on my way to the kitchen, a full block away, carrying the debris of almost two months of isolation, when the doorbell rang in the dit-da-dit-dit each of us uses to let the other know who's coming in. She'd been telephoning from the goddamn corner phone booth so as not to give me time to prepare an attack.

I was in the hall, loaded with muck, when she rang and then began fiddling with keys that, of course, no longer worked. I put down the garbage and undid the bolts. Jackie barged in as if she'd never been away. I was not anxious or pushy. Very casually I picked up some of the debris I'd dropped. I smiled. She looked especially long-legged and slim and tan and chic, wearing some sort of couture slacks and shirt that she'd never have worn before she met me. Then it was blue jeans, T-shirts and pea jackets. Her hair was hanging loose down her back and she had on tinted aviator goggles I can do without. I leaned against the wall clutching my shit as she smiled, rather carefully, I thought. "Hi," she said. Hi! Not a word to me in almost two months and she says, "Hi!" I started to say something appropriate but I began to lose my grip on three stinking highball glasses. "Here," she said, taking the glasses from me and seeming to skip to the butler's pantry. "Where's Margaret?" she said. "Hasn't she been coming in?" "You don't seem to remember," I said, "she's on vacation." "But that was more than a month ago." "She's taking two months this time. You made the arrangements." "*You* made the arrangements," Jackie said. "You know she'd never deal with me." She was maintaining her calm with great effort, I know. Jackie: "You were always afraid that I'd say something rude to her that would make her quit. . . ."

I started the long hobble back up the hall to the living room, Jackie following, as she often did, ready to catch me if one knee didn't jerk far enough forward. I went across to the Eames chair she'd given me in more hopeful days and dropped into it the way Stonewall Jackson used to collapse at the feet of Mr. Devereaux. She sat on the couch under the Lautrec I'd given her. The best approach, I thought, was to assume that nothing had happened.

"Well?" I said. "Well?" "Would you like some coffee?" she said, and started to rise. "I know I'm dying for . . ." "Sit down," I said, "you goddamn bitch." She was determined not to cry but I detected a slight wobble in her lower lip. Force four, I thought. "Please, Marshall . . ." " 'Please, Marshall' what? I want an explanation. You go off to spend several days with those dreadful parents of yours and you're gone almost two months." She sighs, looks me in the eye in a way that bothers me, though I don't hesitate to return the look. Jackie: "I'm trying to do the right thing. I've been doing a lot of thinking. . . ." "Darling Jacqueline," I say, turning soft, "I have too. I've thought of nothing else in these last few weeks." "I've been thinking for a lot longer than the last few weeks," she says, not even noticing that I've called her Jacqueline.

Me: "You and that goddamn analyst! I finally figured out why you decided to go to Florida in July. You wouldn't be caught dead in Florida in July under ordinary circumstances, but that goddamn quack goes off to Martha's Vineyard for July and August so you are allowed to take your vacation. Jesus fucking Christ, Jackie, the amount of time and money you've wasted on that son-of-a-bitch. What did you buy him this year? A new boat?

A swimming pool? A Porsche?" Pause. Jackie: "Nothing." Me: "What do you mean, nothing? At fifty bucks an hour five days a week, you must have kept him in something." "The thing is, darling, I haven't been going to the analyst for over a year." "What are you talking about?" I say. It's so funny I have to laugh. "I know when you go to see your analyst." "No, you don't," says Jackie. "I stopped a year ago last July and you didn't even notice. . . ."

Things are not going at all well. I run around the ring a bit, sparring for time. Then, weakly, I ask, "Why didn't you tell me?" "You never asked." "Of course, I never asked. There was no goddamn reason to ask, for Christ's sake." "You always got so mad whenever I mentioned him." "I never got mad," I say, "just bored. All that stupid jargon. I've finally decided that analysis has done more to ruin the English language than all the pop singers and rock singers and ad writers in the world combined. . . ." "Oh, Marshall." "Anyway," I say, being, I think, very cool, "this has nothing to do with him. It has to do with us." "I know it," says Jackie who, I now see, is beginning to respond to me, to relate. "That's why I stopped the analysis. I knew that if I left you while I was still going to him you would blame it all on his influence. You'd never believe it was me talking." "Oh, shit," I say, "don't try to tell me that you sacrificed the pleasure of paying some quack fifty dollars an hour for the dubious achievement of telling me to go fuck myself." "I guess I am," says Jackie, "if that's the way you want to put it." I become conciliatory. "I don't want to put it any way," I say. "I love you. You love me. We should be together. That's all there is to it." "Not quite," says Jackie.

I still cannot believe she's not seeing that bastard. Maybe on the sly. Perhaps he's stopped charging her so that, technically, she's not lying when she says she's given him up. Pause while she stares at the floor and I look out the window. But that seems farfetched even to me in my present state. I borrow a line from Hollywood. It's a good time filler.

"You've found someone else," I say. "Yes," says Jackie. Pause. My chair spins a couple of revolutions. "Another doctor?" I say. "No," says Jackie, "another man." This is something else. I must be careful. I can't let her know what I'm feeling. Another

Hollywood line, said calmly: "Is it serious?" Jackie: "I'm afraid it is. . . ."

If she'd said absolutely anything else, but she didn't. The goddamn cunt.

"You're *afraid* it is. Why the fuck should you be *afraid* it is? If you love someone, why should you be *afraid*? You should be goddamn *happy*, not *afraid*! Don't give me any of your mother's martyr bullshit, you two-timing . . ." "Oh, Marshall, darling, this is just what I didn't want to happen. It's why I didn't call you or write to you." "You silly-assed cunt." I shake my head in disbelief. "You've found someone else to lay you, to fuck your brains out, and you're sad because you don't want to hurt *me*? Well, I must say. . . ." "What?" I sense she is becoming uncertain. "That you're acting very *dishonorably*." "Oh, for Christ's sake, Marshall!" I had made a mistake. She wasn't becoming uncertain, only impatient. "Let's keep calm," I say. Pause. Another approach is needed. I'd like to ask who the prick is but this is certainly not the time.

"Well," I say, "who the fuck is he?" "Who?" "Who? My God, are you stupid? The guy you're shacked up with. Mr. Right." "Somebody you don't know." "I don't give a fuck if I know him or not. Who is he?" "He's an editor at *Esquire*." "An editor at *Esquire*? I supposed he's not married?" "He's divorced." "And Jewish?" "Yes." "Well, that's a relief. Mom must be pleased. How long have you been fucking him?" "I've been 'fucking him' for about a week." "A week! How romantic! Was it a fuck at first sight?" "I've known him for three years." "And you never fucked him once in all that time?" "Oh, Marshall, stop putting it that way." "Oh, I'm sorry. I don't want to offend you. Good grief . . . I assume that he's in no way—well—disadvantaged, the way I am. . . ." "Oh, really," says Jackie, "if I'd had any doubts about what I was doing when I came over here this morning, I don't have any now. You're the goddamn bleeding end." "I'm also, as your mother so kindly put it not long ago, a cripple." "*One*," says Jackie, "she's sick she ever said anything like that." "I'm sure." "She called me in tears. She wanted to write you to apologize." "I hope she does," I say, "she should." Jackie: "I told her not to be ridiculous. It probably made your day. And, *Two*, you're no cripple. . . ."

"What do you mean?" "I mean . . . that it's no big deal. There are plenty of people worse off than you. You can get in and out of New York taxicabs better than I can. . . ."

I suddenly feel deflated. It's very early in the morning for this kind of go-round. How did Jackie ever manage to accomplish anything at those 8:00 A.M. sessions with her doctor? I think I'm actually sleepy. Then the panic returns. True, exquisite panic. A sudden awareness of a future in which there is no Jackie, in which there will never be any Jackie. Blank. I cannot look at her. I know the game is over.

Finally I say, seriously, "When did it start to—you know—go wrong?" "I'm not sure it was ever that right." "I don't believe that's true, not for me, anyway. We did have fun. We helped each other. . . ." "A lot of what you thought was fun wasn't fun for me." "What do you mean? We took this goddamn crummy apartment in the heart of the Jewish West Side intellectual community to please you, because you couldn't stand the high-class hookers and faggot antique dealers, the decent restaurants and all my friends who live on the East Side. . . . How's Alfred Kazin these days? Have you seen him recently? We were always going to have them to dinner. What happened?" "You're exactly right," she says furiously. "I know I am," I say. Jackie: "But it's not quite the way you think. Do you know why we've had fewer and fewer people to dinner, finally none at all, why we stopped going out together, I mean as a couple? Because you always behaved like an ass. Ridiculing people when half the time you don't come up to their ankles. People who do things, who care about things, who take each other seriously. What, really, have you ever done?" "I learned how to walk," I say. Jackie: "So has everyone else and, believe me, that's not enough." "I can fly a plane," I say. "I once found a gold mine in Alaska, not a very rich one, I admit, but it's a working gold mine, and I know more about the Albigensian heresy than Alfred fucking Kazin ever will. . . ." "And so fucking what?" "You asked me what I'd done. I'm answering your question." "And you still haven't the slightest idea of how to get along with people. Unless they're cooks or maids or taxi drivers or chauffeurs, you're rude. You have no feeling for anyone else. The thing is, dear, dear Marshall, you never really loved me." "That's analyst's crap," I say. "I did and I still do." "No, you don't, and right now, somewhere inside you, you're just the tiniest bit relieved." Me: "You're describing yourself, not me." Jackie: "Perhaps, but I also feel such loss . . . for what might have been. . . ."

We are approaching the goopy part, the platitudes, the noble sentiments, and I am exhausted. I wonder if Jackie will come back to bed with me now for a little while, the way we'd sometimes do in the early years, especially on a weekday, telling everyone else in the world to go to hell since we had each other. "You wouldn't . . ." I start to say, ". . . want to come. . . ." "No." She cuts me off but not sharply. She knows the rest of that sentence and, I suppose, that's something, isn't it? She looks around the room. "How's Therapy?" Jackie says. Me: "He's all right. He misses you. We're out of Kitty Litter and almost out of Meow Mix." Pause. I say, "I think you better take him with you." "No," says Jackie. Me: "I'm not going to turn into a lonely old man living in a rent-controlled home for the aged with a goddamned cat with the twee name of Therapy. If you don't take him, I'll throw him out the window." "Oh, darling. . . ." There was sorrow but no tears. "I mean," I say, "I couldn't . . . put up with having him around without you. I'd rather let him loose in the street."

At that moment the cat came ambling down the corridor into the living room, unhurried, stretching from a mid-morning snooze. He walked to Jackie with monumental lack of evident interest, rubbed against her left leg in a tentative pass, kept on going, turned, made another pass at her right leg and, thus reassured, he jumped onto the couch and settled in her lap. When Jackie left with the first installment of her possessions, she took Therapy, squawking and scratching at the interior of the carrying case, so noisily pissed off that I doubted any taxi driver would haul the two of them. The cat, I was sure, was ready to make life miserable for Mr. Right of *Esquire* who, if the gods were good, would be allergic. There would be an immediate showdown. Mr. Right would say to Jackie, it's either him or me, and Jackie, forced to make such a cruel decision, would pack up all her cares and woes and, with Therapy, return posthaste to West 88th Street. I waited. She never came.

29

By the second week in May things were becoming hectic. Ma returned from Palm Beach to Lewis's Landing and was, I gathered, in love again. She was anxious to get back to Chicago but was shamed into staying on to see our production of *Journey's End* in which Cousins Mary Lee and Annie Lee assured her I was bound to be an overnight star.

At this time I was beginning to become uneasy about the play. The set, designed by Philo Lumberton, looked less like a World War I dugout or trench than the storeroom in a dirty pillow factory. The set's three basic sides were left over from a production of *Dulcy* mounted some years earlier by the St. Matthew's Parish Women's Auxiliary and included a picture window and a fireplace that were disguised only after I persuaded Philo that they seemed out of place on the Western Front. What Philo did was to line the *Dulcy* set, in effect, with soiled pillows found in the dormitory attic. His sound effects were not much better, there being too much emphasis on the shaking of a sheet of tin, the breaking of bottles and the use of a cap pistol to be convincing as the sounds of trench warfare. A kettle drum, borrowed from the Queen Anne school band, was of immense help. The worst thing, though, was Deke Crozier, who knew only one line by heart, "How topping— to have played for England!"

We were to give two performances of the play. Opening night, Friday night, was to be for the school body and for families and friends of the students. Saturday night was for the public, and tickets, which had been offered for sale through the St. Matthew's Parish Women's Auxiliary, had been sold out for over a month. We'd gone clean with 150 tickets at $1 each, which would allow us to pay off Samuel French, and another firm in New York that had supplied us with eleven American doughboy uniforms that fitted none of us but which Mr. Devereaux said, when he saw us in full dress for the first time, wasn't really important. After all, we were supposed to be in the front lines and as there were no Friday night movies, batter bread or atheists in the front lines, there also were no Savile Row tailors. I was so busy that I couldn't meet Gethsemane in the bower on the Thursday afternoon the week before our opening. When I saw her the next afternoon, she said she hadn't been there either. I saw her briefly, but not to fuck, the following Wednesday to let her know that I'd be tied up the rest of the week preparing for my theatrical debut. She appeared to be bored, unconcerned, said she would be busy too. I remember resenting her self-interest. She didn't realize that, if things went badly, I would be making an epic fool of myself.

Our dress rehearsal Thursday afternoon was such a disaster we never got through the complete text of the play. Ruddleston, W. and I were letter-perfect and, I thought, fine, but Deke Crozier was beyond rational criticism. He made his first entrance late and only came onstage after his cue was repeated four times, and then in the manner of a blind man who expects to fall through old floorboards at any minute. Once on the stage he found it impossible to open his mouth. When he tried to talk, it was to see someone retching. While Deke remained mute, Ruddleston, W., who revealed himself to be a real trouper, played their entire first scene as if it were a remembered dialogue. Brilliant thinking. At the first-act intermission Deke had the balls to go horsing around backstage asking everyone what they thought and offering the opinion that he thought he was pretty fucking good even if he did say so himself. When the second act began he had thawed somewhat, reassured, I guess, by his own candid self-appraisal, but he was still hopelessly long in his responses and, once offstage, it was extremely difficult to persuade him to go back on.

Mr. Devereaux hadn't been able to get to the Community House for the start of the dress rehearsal. In his place he sent Mr. Twigg, who had never read the play but had the good sense to keep his mouth shut and follow the script to be able to feed us lines as needed. When Deke arrived at his "how topping" line, which he now read as if it were a warning to Ruddleston, W., Mr. Twigg shook with a series of interior quakes masked as burps.

But the whole thing was going at half-speed so that even I, who knew the entire play by heart, would lose my place. As Deke began to plow through a speech I'd know that we were in for several minutes of hesitations, returns to the first word, silences, dumb-stares, brow-furrowings and spasms of hair-beating. My mind would wander and then I'd find myself suddenly accused by the angry Deke of ruining his performance. Toward the end of the first scene of the second act Deke slipped into his death scene though, clearly, he hadn't yet been wounded, and at the beginning of the next scene a day student, who was playing the sergeant-major, on his entrance bumped against the door to the dugout and knocked over the back wall of the set composed of pillows, several of which burst open to fill the stage with small, swirling white feathers. That mess was still being cleaned up and *Dulcy's* fire-place hidden again when Mr. Devereaux arrived. He said nothing to us but sat in the back of the auditorium and allowed Mr. Twigg to carry on as best he could. He departed again before the start of the third act.

This act came to a halt when Philo Lumberton began his tin-shaking and glass-breaking at least two pages too soon, drowning the dialogue that Mr. Twigg suggested the audience might want to hear. By this time we'd missed evening chapel, which was no prob-lem, and were about to miss supper, which was. Mr. Twigg took it upon himself to call a break, saying that we could come back afterwards to finish the act if we liked. I would have. Also Rud-dleston, W. However, DeKoven was under the impression he was already so good that any further rehearsal would dull the edge of his performance. Because what Deke said automatically went for everyone else, the dress rehearsal was abandoned while all the members of the crew and all but two members of the cast left the Community House in lunatic high spirits.

On the Saturday afternoon of the week before, when Ma had driven over to take me to lunch, I'd grabbed the opportunity to buy several pints of Old Mr. Boston rye to have for what I hoped would be an opening night celebration. While Ma was in Smith's Pharmacy purchasing Kotex, I offered Queen Anne's single Low

Character, a gray-haired rummy of a black man who posted himself in the doorway next to the A.B.C. store, $1 to carry out my commission. It was what he was there to do and it kept him in Virginia Dare muscatel.

Deke became so strange the day of our opening that I began to fear we'd be able to get him to the Community House and onto the stage only if we fortified him with strong drink. He had awakened that day in great form but as the day progressed he melted into mush. In the afternoon, when we were supposed to be resting in anticipation of our premiere performance, Ruddleston, W., Deke and I had gathered in Deke's cubicle to go over lines that Deke claimed he knew better than either of us. Instead, as we went along, it appeared that he was forgetting those few he really did know. Finally he refused to say anything. He lay down on his cot and turned away from us. "I think you're a shit, DeKoven," Ruddleston, W. said as he and I departed. "It's not so bad you're screwing yourself, but you're screwing all the rest of us too." It was not the way one often talked to the school's most popular boy. Ruddleston, W. was trying shock treatment. I then told Ruddleston, W. about the booze I planned to break out after the show and suggested that we might use it to help get Deke over what promised to be opening night catatonia. He agreed and made the further suggestion that he and I, who were bearing the brunt of the disaster, might have a nip right now to calm our nerves. It was 3:30 in the afternoon. We sat on my cot, passing the Old Mr. Boston back and forth, actually swallowing a lot less of it than we were pretending to but still drinking enough to get as pleasantly high as is possible when drinking such stuff chased by tap water in a toothbrush glass. We relaxed.

Ruddleston, W., sitting next to the window, stared over at Mount Vernon. "You really like that nigger stuff?" he said. I said yes, that it was better than jacking off. Ruddleston, W. agreed, though he had a girl in Washington he was sure he could fuck this summer and he didn't want to get clapped up if he was going to be able to fuck a nice white girl. "Maybe," he said, "next year you can fix it up so that your nigger girl will take care of me and DeKoven too." "Sure," I said, "why not?" "We won't let anyone else in on it, though," said Ruddleston, W. "No," I said. "The

Three Musketeers," said Ruddleston, W. "Sure are," I said. Said Ruddleston, W., "It's time we got DeKoven away from sheep-fucking. It isn't good for him." When Ruddleston, W. returned to his cubicle, I had as restful a sleep as I'd had all year.

Ruddleston, W. woke me fifteen minutes before chapel to get one of my bottles to take in to DeKoven, who was still not talking. It seemed to work. Deke showed up for supper looking alive but not dangerously self-confident. He ate a hearty dinner, which was re-assuring, though Ruddleston, W. and I could get down nothing more than some milk and ice cream. The cast and crew of *Journey's End* ate together that evening, the understanding being that we could leave the dining hall as soon as we had finished, without waiting for the meal's official termination, to go to the Community House. The Devereaux family was not at its table but I didn't think that odd. They were probably entertaining parents at Mount Vernon.

Mr. Twigg was running things at the Community House when we arrived. One of MacDougal's helpers was in the foyer putting up card tables for the cake, coffee and punch that would be served after the performance. Backstage Philo Lumberton, who had not come to supper, was arranging his sound equipment in the order in which it was to be shaken, broken, rattled and rolled. He appeared to be more nervous than any member of the cast. Mrs. Boyleston, Bucktooth's wife, our cosmetician, made us up with lots of reassuring remarks ("I'm sure glad *I* don't have to go out there in front of all those people. I'm sure *I'd* like to die with embarrassment, trying to remember all those lines") and with more face powder and wrinkles than were needed by Sam Jaffe in *Lost Horizon*. Mrs. Boyleston, who was quite nice really, had a bite problem to match her husband's, which prompted me to fantasize that the only way they could kiss would be to start in a conventional sixty-nine position, then slide back until their jaws locked.

We were in costume and full makeup an hour before the eight o'clock curtain, which was not a good idea. DeKoven paced around the stage mumbling his lines, occasionally bumping into the wall of pillows at the back, at which he'd jump away as if he'd received an electric shock. He didn't want to be responsible for destroying the set. By 7:15 those students—mostly the younger ones—who were not in some way connected with the production were in their seats, some roughhousing in boredom, some staring intently at the curtain as if it were a movie screen that had gone unaccountably blank. The auditorium was almost full by 7:45 but still my mother and Cousins Mary Lee and Annie Lee hadn't arrived from Lewis's Landing. It would be the last straw, I thought, if Ma somehow found a way to miss the show. I couldn't find Mr. Devereaux, which now seemed definitely odd. When I asked Mr. Twigg about him, he said that Mr. Devereaux had been feeling unwell. "How unwell?" "Very unwell," he said, and moved on to talk to Philo. Ruddleston, W. gave DeKoven his last booster shot at 7:59. The way I sized up Deke, he could go either way— forget his lines completely or turn the show into *Three Men on a Horse*. But he did neither.

When the curtain went up at 8:10 there were at first some titters from the students who found the sight of disguised friends onstage hugely amusing, but within five minutes we had them. Even the youngest ones were grabbed. Ruddleston, W. was the Rock of Gibraltar all of us depended upon. I was so gallant, noble, handsome, thoughtful, kind, stern, romantic and lost that I almost brought tears to my own eyes as I put the character together. But DeKoven was a revelation. He entered on cue. He remembered every one of his lines and if not many of them were intelligible to the people out front, we and they knew what he meant. Though in rehearsal he moved like someone stricken, he now walked normally. He picked up his cues promptly. He was sailing through it, a sight that so moved Ruddleston, W. and me that I had the impression at one point we were almost laughing with pleasure and feared that our high spirits must be evident to the audience. Apparently not. When the first-act curtain came down there was a moment's pause followed by huge applause, whistles and feet-stamping. Ma and Cousin Mary Lee had come in near the end of the act and were in the last row. Fuck them, I thought.

I suggested to Ruddleston, W. that he make sure Deke didn't get so much booze he'd shoot beyond the crest we then had him on, but Ruddleston, W. knew what I meant even before I could finish saying it. The second act was even better than the first and when DeKoven died in Act III, his lifeless hand slipping silently to the floor, his eyes open but their senses shut, I could hear the sniffles down front where the second formers were.

The applause that met the final curtain was the sort one hears at the Metropolitan. It came at us in waves. It washed up and around us, bathing us in adoration. Deke, Ruddleston, W. and I took the last call together with much laughter and mutual poundings of the upper arms. In the wings Mr. Twigg congratulated us and smiled, though wanly, I thought, considering the magnitude of our triumph. Back in the dressing room, Deke kicked out the crew members who were hanging around and Ruddleston, W. brought out my bottle of Old Mr. Boston, which we polished off while removing our makeup. "My daddy's out there," said Deke. "He liked to die when he first saw me in this getup and by the end, do you know, he was bawling? I swear to God."

30

In mufti again, my head still clanging with applause, I made my way from the dressing room backstage to the foyer of the Community House, passing through little knots of suddenly awestricken adolescents I'd heretofore ignored as they had ignored me. I saw but did not acknowledge Gordon Felix who, I'm sure, would have gone for twenty bucks right then if he could have scraped it together. He looked at me as if Gary Cooper had just arrived. I saw my mother and Cousin Mary Lee, both appearing very strange, off to one side talking to Mr. Twigg. Ma held one of the St. Matthew's jelly jars that passed for punch glasses filled with MacDougal's mixture of canned cranberry juice, canned grapefruit juice, soda water, cinnamon and sugar. She looked like an apprehensive prune. She wasn't even smoking. She didn't face Mr.

Twigg as he talked and Cousin Mary Lee also was unnaturally subdued. He could have been telling them that General Lee had just surrendered at Appomattox.

These are reconstructed impressions. At the moment I was aware only of my own triumph. As I came up to the group, Mr. Twigg excused himself. Cousin Mary Lee, smashingly pretty in a white evening dress that probably dated from her Richmond coming-out party ten years earlier, pulled herself together enough to swoon at "our very own matinée idol," to kiss me, hug me and issue a series of belle-toned "I declares." Ma kissed me, patted me on the chest and said, as if to buck me up, "Dear, you were just fine." "What's wrong?" I said. "My God, what's wrong?" Cousin Mary Lee was on the verge of tears. My mother was as troubled as I was ever to see her, except when Tom committed suicide and, years later, when Lockie died. "Jesus," I said. "Now don't use that kind of language in here," said Ma. "It's not a church," I said. "It belongs to the church," said Ma. "Good grief," I said. Ma turned to Cousin Mary Lee and asked if she would mind if she took me outside for a few minutes. We walked out the front door of the Community House, off the path being used by people leaving to get into cars parked along the highway, and found ourselves standing up to our asses in Tatterhummock clover.

"What in good Christ's name is going on?" I said. "You look terrible." "Oh, darling," Ma said, "have you got a cigarette? We left the house in such a hurry I forgot mine." I knocked two from a package, gave her one, took one myself, and lit a match. Ma inhaled as if she were filling a blimp. I then realized she wasn't troubled. She was so excited she was coming apart at the seams.

"It's the most terrible thing," she began. "You'll never guess what's transpired. . . ." "Transpired? What, for heaven's sake?" "David's been run out of the county." "David Devereaux?" "Can you imagine?" "What do you mean, 'run out of the county'? By a posse? On a horse?" "In his Ford, I think." "Who ran him out?" "Well," said Ma, "I *suppose* he drove himself . . . and *that girl*." "What girl?" "That colored girl who worked for them. You know the one, the preacher's daughter?" "Gethsemane Shackleford? I don't believe it." "It *is* true. This afternoon. It was either that or the most *dreadful* scandal." "What sort of scandal?"

"She's pregnant." "Oh, my God. . . ." "On my word, it's true. We've just come from the house. That's why we were late. Odile telephoned Cousin Annie Lee just as we were sitting down to an early dinner . . . so we wouldn't be late for the play? We flew over . . . Odile's in a perfect state, I can tell you. Cousin Annie Lee's with her now, and David's father, Old Doctor Devereaux, and Dr. Perry? And Jojo's running around the house screaming for her daddy. Apparently yesterday the father of that girl . . ." "Gethsemane . . ." ". . . Whateverhername, the preacher's daughter, apparently yesterday he got her to admit to him she was pregnant and that David was responsible. The preacher went right over to Doctor Devereaux in Middlesex. It's been going on since the girl was fourteen. They say she's always been a very big girl." "Oh, shit," I said. The two-timing bitch.

". . . The preacher threatened to go to the sheriff, and if the sheriff wouldn't do anything he said he was going to Richmond. Can you imagine?" The thing was I could. Gethsemane and Mr. Devereaux made sense. It was consistent with his appreciation of things he thought authentic, with the way he idealized his precious county boys. Gethsemane represented something equally romantic. She would have appealed to the Delacroix in Devereaux. Like me he would have looked beyond the costume (*that* was why she had started to wear dresses!) into the impassive, unreflecting eyes to discover within them Something Other. Not Africa or jungles or tom-toms and all that exotic shit, but the woman who rocked the cradle of every Virginia gentleman for over 300 years. He also drove her back and forth to and from work more often than was necessary. All of the other slaves walked. "Since she was fourteen?" I said. "But that isn't all," said Ma, and she lowered her voice not to be discreet but to diminish somehow the reality of the next revelation, "there have been other—well—incidents." "What sort of incidents?" "Several years ago Odile received an anonymous letter warning her that David was a . . . pervert." "A pervert! Jesus, Ma!" ". . . that he was picking up colored girls in his car." "An anonymous letter?" "It was mailed from King and Queen County, Odile said, and written in pencil. She said the writing clearly was a colored person's. You know how they write. . . ." "With x's," I said. "Can you imagine?" said Ma. "Poor

David. Yet I think I've always known that he had a sort of *thing* for colored girls. I suspected way back, years ago, even before we were seriously engaged that time. I could tell by the way he might look at one of the serving girls or the maids—such an open look of interest, undisguised alertness, blatant lust, really—his face alive in a way it never was at any other time, not even with me. With me he was always a gentleman, always doing the proper thing a beau was supposed to do. But when he looked at one of those colored girls, I knew he was quite capable of being improper and, I suppose, I was jealous because I knew he'd never be improper with me. Isn't that strange? I mean, I had no idea at the time but now I can see it all so clearly. Poor Odile, this will absolutely kill her. She's so emotional, she's gone completely to pieces. . . ." I saw Odile's head on the dining room table where she'd left it when she came in from shopping, her torso in the laundry hamper, her legs thrown over the back of a chair, looking like stuffed stockings, wrinkled.

Gethsemane pregnant: *"Are you crazy?"* said Gethsemane. *"That's how a girl gets knocked up—and worse."* I wondered if she fucked Mr. Devereaux lying down or if they did it standing up. Obviously they must have done some fucking lying down, but where? In the kitchen? In his study when Odile and Jojo were out? In his Ford that had no back seat? In the woods? Ma: ". . . I mean, what can he have been thinking of? This isn't 1840. This isn't a Mississippi cotton plantation where such things happened all the time. This is 1940, Tatterhummock County. I don't think anything like this has ever happened here before, certainly not in my lifetime. And to think—I mean, David of all people, always so honorable, putting such store by his moral code, his honor. What kind of honor is that, I ask you?"

I had no idea how I felt so I assumed I wasn't feeling anything at all. I wasn't surprised. I accepted it. This was the way things were, always had been, always would be, and I thought of the last time Gethsemane and I had lain in the woods, eye-to-eye. I saw only her but somewhere over my shoulder she could have seen old Devereaux. I wondered if he took off his glasses before he fucked her or if, when they lay on their sides facing each other, she saw herself reflected in his lenses. "Honor," Ma was saying, "that's a sketch. Among other things, it seems, he took every cent of money from the sale of the tickets to the play." "That can't be very much," I said. "No," said Ma, "but it's all there is. Odile says she can't find their bankbook so she thinks he must have that too, though she says there was no more than sixty or seventy dollars at the most." "I wonder where they've gone," I said. I could picture myself searching through Catfish Row, asking the whereabouts of the beautiful solemn black girl who was keeping the eccentric white man by walking waterfront streets. "He telephoned Odile tonight . . . he wouldn't say where he was . . . just that he was going far away where he couldn't do any more harm to her and Jojo. Poor Jojo. Heaven knows what this will do to her. She's such a sweet child. . . ." "Oh, Ma," I said. "What?" "She's a brat and you know it." "But that's no excuse not to feel sorry for her in a time of stress. Do you think I should offer them some money? I don't know how to do it, though, without making it look like charity." "Just give it to her," I said. "She won't worry about the charity part." "Oh, darling, sometimes you are very unkind."

They didn't go to Catfish Row. They went to Washington. With money supplied by Old Doctor Devereaux, Gethsemane found a room in a black residential neighborhood while Mr. Devereaux moved in with the family of his younger half brother, who had a job with the Commerce Department and lived in Anacostia. He sold his car, applied for several teaching jobs that, not surprisingly, he didn't get, and finally became a clerk in a Florsheim Shoe Store near the Mayflower. A friend of Ma's saw him there about a year later. She said he looked like an ideal shoe salesman with his gray flannel suit, steel-gray hair, steel-rimmed spectacles and straight military posture. He seemed a shoe salesman one would trust. It was Old Doctor Devereaux who, when the time approached, arranged for Gethsemane's hospitalization and who was the only one in either family who hadn't urged her to get an abortion. Gethsemane had never before owned anything. She would not give up the child. Later Doctor Devereaux provided the references that enabled Gethsemane to obtain a position as nurse for the children of an attaché at the British embassy. When the attaché was transferred to Nassau during the reign of their R.H.'s, Gethsemane and the baby went too, and then on to Trinidad and, finally, to Jamaica. After Devereaux and Gethsemane fled the county she saw him once more, when she visited him at the VA hospital several months before he died. Because she had no one with whom to leave the baby, she took the squawking, chestnut-skinned Pru with her. Devereaux had no interest in the child. Being then loony on drugs, he spent most of the visit talking about the colonelcy he expected to receive any day from the Army, though he did have the wit (and the Old Manners) to treat her as if she were a treasured family retainer come to pay her respects to the Master. At one point he seemed to be expressing pleasure she'd named the baby Prud'homme. Even if Devereaux's mind had been straight he wouldn't have guessed the reason was she believed the name would haunt her father as well as the entire county, which, eventually, it did.

It seems not to have been true, as Ma had heard through the county grapevine, that Devereaux was once arrested for soliciting a minor. Minors would not have been for him unless they were minors in the way Gethsemane had been—big, black, strong, gentle, that pre-eminently fuckable mother-figure called Nurse. Less than two years after his flight from justice, David Prud'homme Devereaux died in a ward in the VA hospital near Baltimore. In his small intestine they'd found a tumor the size of a baseball, which subsequently reproduced itself in the liver, the kidneys, the spleen, the lungs, places where baseballs are not accommodated as readily as in the small intestine. Nearing victory, which would bring its own defeat, the invader became bold. Gelatinous baseballs appeared everywhere. When Gethsemane last saw him, one had begun to sprout on his left temple, as if to balance one on the right. Nature's boring symmetry. Devereaux was buried in a military cemetery in Maryland. I've no idea who—if anyone—attended. He may have been planted without witness. Gethsemane didn't know he was dead until there arrived in the mail a package containing his personal effects, which, for sentimental reasons, he wanted her to have. No love. No money. Just pocket items. Such was the man Devereaux met at the end of the road: a cancer-ridden salesman of hose, arch supports and shoes.

31

It was in the spring of the election year—a full-page ad in *The New York Times* in which 200 concerned women urged voters of all parties to support the Equal Rights Amendment. All the names you've ever read in such ads were represented, including Jacqueline Gold's, and a name I'd never before seen as a position-endorser. Since I'm the sort of *Times* reader who, when he comes upon such an ad while turning from page 1 to the inside jump, reads every name before continuing with the latest nondevelopments in the SALT talks, I knew that in all likelihood she was making her New York media debut as the signer of a sincere, pious, high-minded, utterly humorless, often self-promoting advertisement on behalf of a cause that I'd probably heard quite enough of by the time the ad appeared. The name was that of Gethsemane Shackleford, which came six ahead of Steinem's and eighty after Gold's. For one reason and another I'd never told Jackie more of the story than that I'd known Pru's mother when I went to St. Matthew's, and that I found Pru, for all of his over-reported, disciplined fury, to be someone totally at the mercy of events over which he exercised no control whatsoever. She didn't agree with me but she liked it when I said anything that indicated I'd come up for air from the twelfth century. She was more pleased than curious when I asked her if, by chance, her friends in the Mafia could give me Gethsemane's address. I thought, I said, that I'd like to write her. Suddenly Jackie's friends treated her as if she were an undercover agent for the FBI. She had to call someone in Flo Kennedy's office, who gave her the name of someone else to call, who gave her another number, which in turn led back to the first woman. It was evident after a time, even to Jackie, that what was being protected was not anyone's privacy but sources of supply for revenue to support ads like the one I'd read. Eventually Jackie was able to leave the name, number and address of the party who wanted to contact Mrs. Shackleford, and the information would be passed on to her. It would also, I knew from boring experience, be passed on to a master list of donors.

Late one afternoon three weeks later the telephone rang. "Mr. Henderson, please," said a voice that could have been the voice of someone from Anywhere, U.S.A., except for the trace of Gullah in the middle of Henderson. "Gethsemane?" I said. Pause. "Is this Marshall Lewis Henderson?" The voice is tentative, not friendly. "Yes," I say. "Gethsemane?" "Yes." Another pause, then, "Well, I'll be," which she says with a sort of sigh. Me: "It's been a long time. How are you?" "Fine." Pause. She says, "I live in Scarsdale." "Oh," I say. "But I've been on the West Coast for the last month. I got back yesterday so I just received your message." Pause. I say, "I saw your name in the *Times* ad. . . ." "What *Times* ad?" "The one that ran several weeks ago about the Equal Rights Amendment." "That must have been when I was away. . . ." "I guess it was," I say, and then, in desperation, "It was a very good ad, I thought." "In what way?" Now what could I say? It looked like a thousand other ads. "Well," I say, "it was quite far up front." "Up front of what?" Gethsemane says. "The paper," I say. "I mean, it was on page 5 or 9, where people would see it who don't go all the way through the paper." Gethsemane: "It was supposed to be on the back page. That's the page that gets the most readers. I guess they didn't have enough money." Pause. Me: "I was wondering if we could meet sometime." "What for?" she says. Me: "Well, I'm not really sure. I don't have any particular motive, but I've thought of you over the years and wondered about you. . . ." "Did you ever get my letter?" she says. Me: "What letter?" It's my turn to be suspicious. "Oh," she says, and she laughs like a normal, middle-aged woman, "years and years ago, when I was in Jamaica with Pru who wasn't even two yet, I was very homesick and you were the only person I could think of to write to." "No," I say, and I shake my head, "I didn't get it. I'm sorry." "It was a silly letter. I worked on it for days. If I made a mistake, I'd start over. I didn't want anything erased or crossed out. I wanted it to be a perfect letter." "Why perfect?" She laughs. "I didn't want you to think of me as just another dumb country nigger who couldn't write a decent letter." "You were never that," I say.

Now she laughs fully and heartily in a way I don't recognize. "Man, if I was anything in those days, I was that. I certainly was that." Me: "Could we have lunch together sometime?" Pause. "I don't know," she says. "I don't usually eat lunch when I come to town. If you want, you could come down to my office sometime. I'm in the city three days a week. I work with a community action group with offices on 14th Street. I have a desk and a phone here. If you come by toward the end of the day some day, maybe we could visit then." "Fine," I say, though I'd pictured myself taking her to "21" or the Caravelle. Would a woman disguised as a construction worker wearing a New York Yankees baseball cap be turned away for being out of uniform? Me: "Are you coming in tomorrow?" "Yes, but that wouldn't work out too good. I'm still very busy with paperwork to catch up on, and I must finish writing a report on my trip." "How about Friday then?" She laughs, and it's the laughter I remember. "All right," she says, "but don't come until four-thirty. I'll try to get in early on Friday so that I'll be through by then. It's called the Black Community Action Women's Volunteers and it's on the second floor of the building at 12 West 14th Street, between Fifth and Sixth but closer to Fifth. There's a luncheonette on the first floor." "Fine," I say, "and I'll be on time."

The window of my study faces east and north where, on the roof of the Barabbas & Ferrentino storage warehouse, a young man of a different color keeps his pigeons. Every morning at 6:45 he releases them from their cotes. For fifteen minutes, before he produces their feed, responding to his instructions by whistle and cry, they soar and dive and wheel around in changing formations, a disciplined cloud of white and gray and black that, at certain angles, becomes invisible against the early morning sky, immediately to become visible again when they switch direction. I think of my body that has to be so carefully tended to maintain circulation. I envy the simplest gesture. I'd like to rock back on my heels in boredom. Tales of retribution occupy my consciousness. There is a kind of aluminum wiring that shrinks with age, thus to cause short circuits within walls. Last night five children on Long Island were incinerated on the second floor of their modified ranch-style house while their mother and father, unable to help, watched them from the lawn. A woman driving up the FDR Highway is the victim when a thirteen-year-old boy, who lives with his parents on Delancey Street, stands on the pedestrian overpass and drops a cobblestone through the windshield of the car in which she's a passenger. It's a challenge, says the radio announcer, to make a tire for the American way of driving. If I should steal a ballpoint pen that's the property of the United States Post Office Department, I'd have to pay a $500 fine and/or spend a year in jail. It's right that Jackie left, but the pain is acute.

Last night's dream: I am my present age but my legs are strong, firm and shaped with flesh, not withered as if they were chicken bones. Through a revolving door I enter the lobby of a building that seems to be both a hotel and an office building. I carry, upended, a large, heavy, plain wooden desk, the sort that has drawers on the right, knee-space on the left. As I make my way to the bank of elevators, Therapy, the cat, sees me and in his pleasure wraps himself around my right ankle so that, as I step, I'm lifting him too. At the same time a dog I don't recognize happily recognizes me and climbs onto my left foot. I'm pleased too and remark to the strangers in the lobby that animals appear to like me as, I quickly add, I've always liked them. There are three elevators, two of which aren't working. The third, on the far left, has no guard door. The elevator car appears, empty and un-manned, waits for me to board, but I'm hesitant. Impatiently it shoots up and disappears. Someone says, "That thing's broken. I'd rather walk." "But I can't walk," I say, meaning the desk and animals. The elevator car comes zipping down again, still empty, waits a second or two, then goes flying out of sight. It reappears, a very insistent kind of empty elevator. I finally decide that I will have to take my chances. The next time it comes down I board it with all of my cargo and, to my surprise, so do several other people. We shoot up the shaft a couple of hundred feet, abruptly stop between two floors, hang there a minute, and then begin to fall. Because it is an open shaft the people on the adjacent floors can watch us falling at great speed. "We're falling," someone in the elevator says. Someone on a floor we pass yells, "You're falling!" I know goddamn well I'm falling. I don't need some jerk to tell me. I'm surprised, though, that we appear to be falling faster than is permitted by the 32-feet-per-second law of science. Suddenly but gently, the car stops next to the top of a marble arch that rises from the lobby. The top is a flat place 25 feet above the lobby floor. There's no way to get down from there but I've had enough of the elevator. I want off. I'm scared out of my wits. I quickly step out and onto the arch top. The elevator makes a now-normal, safe descent to the lobby. As my former fellow passengers disembark, they point at me and laugh. One calls up to me, "*Now* how are you going to get down?"

The door to the Black Community Action Women's Volunteers is locked so, after having pulled and swung myself up stairs too narrow and steep to be able to use crutches safely, I have to ring a bell and wait until some Marxist inside finishes a chatty phone call to Peking. There are messages written on the dirty cream-color wall, scribbled in pencil and various kinds of pen, mostly having to do with sexual aspiration (FUCK WHITEY AND ALL SPIKES TOO). The door is finally opened by a young black woman wearing a huge bush of hair, blue jeans and a blouse made of the flag of the National Liberation Front. "Yes?" she says, as if I were selling magazine subscriptions or were going to ask to use the toilet. "I'm here to see Mrs. Shackleford," I say. "I was supposed to be here at four-thirty and it was four-thirty exactly when I rang the bell." The girl turns and calls, "Mrs. Shackleford, there's a man here to see you. He says he has an appointment." Still the young woman doesn't allow me in. I hear the opening of an inner door, footsteps, then the front door is pulled wide open by Gethsemane.

She is a giantess to me now because I'm stooped on the crutches and have, over the years, lost a certain length in the legs. She too wears an Afro but it is a modified sort of suburban Afro of silver-tipped gray, not very becoming actually. Her face is as

fine and beautiful as ever, at least what I can see of it behind the
large harlequin-shaped glasses whose rims are inset with rhinestones. She is wearing what looks at first to be a surplus U.S.
Army blanket camouflaged for use in jungle warfare. It's a great
caftan sort of garment that hides her figure, flaring out from the
broad shoulders and not quite touching the floor. The pattern of
the material is not abstract but of leaves of various sizes and
shapes, in colors from deep blue-green to pale yellow. It's what the
Queen of Sheba might wear if she were in charge of the secretarial
pool. "Marshall Lewis Henderson," she says, smiling in a business-
like way, taking my paw, which, because I'm hung on my
crutches, I can't extend very far. "Come in, come in." She leads
the way across a large room filled with filing cabinets and a number of plain wooden desks that have drawers on the right and
knee-space on the left. She stops every few steps and turns, as if
waiting for a small dog to catch up. "We'll go into my office. . . ."
To the young woman: "Betty, if those letters are finished, why
don't you go home? I have keys. I'll lock up." She watches me
swing toward her. *"Don't look so worried. It'll still be there tomorrow. It's something I always carry with me."*

We go into her office, a cubbyhole just big enough for a plain
wooden desk, her chair behind it and one for me in front of it. No
windows, the light fluorescent. On the desk there is a pushbutton
telephone of the sort I believe to be a pointless convenience, a
neat stack of papers, an incoming basket sitting atop an outgoing
basket, both empty, everything overlooked by a huge poster on the
wall, the kind of poster sold in Broadway souvenir stores and joke
parlors, a close-up of Baby Pru's face in full, glorious color, passionately exhorting a crowd (in Havana, I think) but appearing to
smile too, showing teeth so perfect they seem capped. I flop into
the chair, prop the crutches against the wall. I nod toward the
poster. "He's a handsome man," I say. She smiles. "I've been on
the telephone all afternoon with his lecture bureau. He's scheduled
to give a series of lectures here this autumn and now they want
him to come over to go on the Tonight Show and do some other
things like that for publicity, but who's going to pay for the trans-
portation? The Tonight Show won't. Merv Griffin won't. Barbara
Walters might. I've been negotiating with the lecture bureau to

advance him the money out of the anticipated fees. He's very tight with a dollar. . . ." Pause. I say, "You look marvelous, more beautiful than ever. . . ." She really looks more butch than ever and I wonder briefly if she could have become a lesbian. She's built for it. "We've both changed," she says. "You have, I have. What happened to your legs?" "I had an accident a long time ago." "We both had, I guess—but you know?—now that the bad part is over I wouldn't have had it any other way." She looks down at the desk, then back to me. "But I'm sorry about your legs. I didn't know. I've read about you in the papers from time to time but nobody ever mentioned . . ." "It's not the sort of thing gossip columnists write about." "No," she says.

I offer her a cigarette, which she accepts. "You still smoke too much," she says, "but so do I. You're married?" "No." "Oh, I thought you were married to an actress." "She wasn't an actress. She was once Miss Utah. She called herself an actress but the only acting she ever did was flat on her back." There is a pause, then Gethsemane breaks into a loud, man-sized guffaw. "My gawd, you haven't changed! That's just the sort of thing you would have said when you were a little boy." "I was hardly a little boy." "Well, you didn't look like a little boy." "And you," I say, "are you married?" "My husband is an optometrist in White Plains. We've been married twenty-four years this Christmas, can you believe it? I met him not long after we got back, Pru and I. I was working during the day, housework, you know, and going to school at night, trying to finish college. So was my husband." "But everybody calls you Mrs. Shackleford. . . ." "That's what I had to call myself when we first got back. It'd be too much trouble to change it now, and besides, every time my name appears in the papers, or Pru's, or when he's on the TV, I know my father turns over in his grave and those two brothers of mine shit turnips. . . ." "I never knew your brothers," I say. "You must have met Reuben. He ran the store when I couldn't. You used to see him all the time. You just don't remember." "I think I remember everything, though sometimes I wish I didn't." Gethsemane: "You don't remember, you don't learn nothing, and that ain't good." I feel she's putting on a terrible act whenever she slips in an "ain't" or a double negative. Or maybe she's making fun of me.

I ask about her husband. "He's big and black and ugly, and he loves Pru almost as much as I do, though that don't always help his business . . . which is another reason I use the name of Shackleford. It protects Walter to a certain extent." "Have you ever gone back home?" "I sure as hell haven't. You know, when Pru and I came up from Jamaica I was crazy enough to want to go back? My daddy put a stop to that, though. . . ." She tells me about the arrival of her ship in Brooklyn, her father's meeting them, his implacability ("You been gathered, child, and I ain't about to have any *un*gathering going on"). I remember seeing him from time to time driving around the county in his big black Cadillac, always driving very slowly as if in a procession, ready to bless the passers-by, a big, deeply black man with large black-rimmed spectacles who, I now think, looked like God, whenever God is black.

". . . And he never knew the favor he did me. Can you imagine what my life would have been like back there? Or Pru's? If I'da been lucky they'da let me clean the rectory. Pru went back once, though. It was in '63 or '64—it must have been '64. It was after Alabama and after he graduated from Howard. He went down with a group to register black voters in the Tidewater. It was just a little *pissy*-assed drive. No real worry to it. Middlesex, Mathews, Gloucester, Tatterhummock . . . things weren't so bad there anyway, but do you know? That's as close as Pru ever came to assassination? In the south, I mean." "They did kill somebody, didn't they?" "Skinny, funny-looking little Roger Lonsdale, a young man from Utica. Sweetest tempered child you ever did see, with the flattest nose and the biggest ears. He was driving Pru's car and they ambushed him between Four Corners and Tatterhummock Court House, at that bend in the road where you have to slow down? And do you know who did it? Can you believe it? It was Reuben, my brother Reuben. He attempted to murder my son, his own flesh-and-blood, just because he was trying to give some poor county niggers their own right to vote. He got off— Reuben did. As I understand it, they didn't even charge him. He's now one of the richest businessmen in the county. That's progress, isn't it?"

She tells me about her work, about the complex interrelation-

ship of memberships on committees, committees-within-commit-
tees, steering committees, executive committees, ad hoc committees, about outside advisory boards, about attendance at
planning sessions, plenary sessions and joint sessions, of making
preliminary reports, interim reports and final reports. My mind
reels. "I'm probably boring you," says Gethsemane. "No," I say,
"I envy you your energy and your purpose. My life is very different. I'm still trying to catch up to where we are. I . . . I study."
"But you have all that money," says Gethsemane. "You can do
anything you want." "I do," I say. "I once spent a year looking for
a gold mine in Alaska and I found one. I learned how to fly and I
spent another year with my first wife going around the world in
our own plane. . . ." Now why had I said that? We hadn't flown
around the world in our own plane. Sometimes we chartered, but I
sure as hell hadn't flown one mile myself. "I've gone to the source
of the Nile. . . ." That was a most happy time, Higgenbotham at
her best, putting up with mosquitoes the size of bluebirds, dreadful
food and heat, followed by three glorious months in Luxor, tomb-
crawling in the morning, reading in the shade by the Winter Palace pool in the afternoons. Even Higgenbotham was content at
first, but then she kept getting interested in other tourists who
were passing through, envying their passages, but I had no interest
in people passing through, nor in the Egyptians themselves. Perhaps we could have made it if we'd kept the rest of the world
away. I'd have been willing, but not Higgenbotham. ". . . and
the source of the Amazon and the source of the Mississippi. . . ."
Also untrue, unless I've flown over it without being aware of the
fact. "I'm a perpetual student. I attended the Sorbonne for a
while. I've had two wives and now I'm living with another woman.
. . . And there isn't that much money any more."

"Are you stingy?" says Gethsemane. I laugh. "I don't know.
Perhaps I am. I suppose I was stingy as a boy. Was I?" Gethsemane: "It's not something of which I would have been aware." She
laughs. "You were just obsessed, like all little boys. You thought
the world began and ended with that thing between your legs."

"It was me, wasn't it?" I nod to the poster of Pru.

"No."

"I know it was."

For a second I think she might pull a gun on me. She scruti-
nizes me as if wondering how she might dispose of the body. She
sighs, relaxes. "Poor old Dee-Pee-Dee. I thought he was going to
beat hell out of me after I told my daddy and my daddy went to
Old Doctor Devereaux." "Why didn't you tell them it was me?"
She thinks. She looks me up and down. "Dee-Pee-Dee owed me
something, and he was ready to believe it. What a foolish man. He
always said that if people had sexual relations standing up, the
woman would never become pregnant—something about sperma-
tozoa not being able to swim upstream against the force of gravity,
I don't know." "He had a sense of honor," I say. "Honor? Listen,
if he hadn't gotten out of there—taken me to Washington—my
daddy would have had him put in jail for ninety-nine years.
Honor? Shit. He was running for his life. He even tried to get me
to have an abortion. That's how much honor he had. He was a
sick man. . . . Lordy, talk about your dumb county niggers. I won
first prize in that contest. Old Doctor Devereaux was the only one
who had any charity, not Dee-Pee-Dee, not nobody."

"But I am Pru's father."

"Shee-ee-it, man!"

"The thing is, I'd like to do something. . . ."

She howls with laughter. "Are you kidding? Oh my gawd!"
She nods at me. "Look at him!"

"I am that boy's father. He's my child too. He even looks like
me."

She stops laughing abruptly. "That *man* don't have no father,
do you understand? I let Dee-Pee-Dee think what he wanted, but
that child was all mine. *I* created him. *I* carried him. *I* fed him. *I*
made him. You're no more his father than a glass of milk I might
once have drunk. You have nothing to do with that person there.
Make no mistake about that."

"It's not that I want to take him away. . . ."

"Oh my gawd!" More laughter. "Are you sure you're all right
in the head, boy? That man is thirty-four years old. Nobody takes
him anywhere but he wants to go there."

"I know that," I say. I'd begun to realize that Gethsemane was
really none too bright for all of her efforts in night school, her

husband-the-optometrist, her reports, her committees, her silver-tipped Afro, her harlequin spectacles with the rhinestones, her filing cabinets, her pushbutton telephone.

"Is this a matter of conscience?" she says.

"No, but I have no children of my own—I mean, I might be able to help."

"The only way you can help, Marshall Lewis Henderson, is by going away." She laughs again, shakes her head in disbelief. "Man, you're out of date. You are one obsolete son-of-a-bitch."

I don't know what I'm feeling, so I think I'm not feeling anything, as usual, but there seems to be a kind of draft in the pockets under my eyes. I'm short of breath.

I say, "I think I'm aware of what I am."

"Are you sure?"

"Yes," I say, and I wonder what the fuck I thought I'd accomplish by coming here. I seem to be weeping, which is the worst part.

Neither of us says anything for a while. As discreetly as I can, as if scratching in thought, I remove the tears and wipe my finger on my trousers.

"Perhaps you are," she says at last.

Then she tells me about Mr. Devereaux's death and how she was sent his personal effects. "Maybe," she says, "you should have them. I could never throw them out but I don't want them. Pru, sure as hell, don't want them. I'll send them to you—kill two birds with one stone. . . ."

She glances at her watch. "Gawd," she says, "I gotta get out of here. I've got to make the 6:35 at Grand Central or I won't get home until after Walter, and he don't favor that."

I stand and by the time I've pulled my crutches in place, she's already in her coat, waiting for me at the office door, keys in hand.

"I can drop you off," I say. "I'm taking a cab uptown."

"I don't have time, honey," she says as she's throwing all sorts of elaborate bolts and locks and setting the alarm system. "The subway is quicker." Once done she looks at me, blinking a lazy Tatterhummock blink through her harlequins. "You don't mind,"

she says, "if I run? If I don't I'll never make my train." The reference is to my crutches and the business involved in my descending
a steep staircase.

She takes off down the stairs, peering carefully at the steps
through the bifocals. She stops halfway, turns without looking up,
and says, "I'll have Betty mail that material to you next week. All
right?"

"All right."

When she's on the bottom step I call her name. "What's that?"
she says.

"You and I," I say, "we had a baby and we never even danced
together."

She looks bewildered, then scoots out the door.

Once I'm at street level, I stop to catch my breath before
swinging my way down the sidewalk toward Sixth, looking for a
nice boringly anonymous bar. I have to telephone Jackie but I
also want a stiff double shot of the sort of rotgut I associate with
distress. There's no bar anywhere, only tacky stores selling things
like aprons and dungarees and potholders. Jesus, what a fucking
life. I finally locate an outside pay telephone that appears to work
and wait as a pretty Puerto Rican girl argues excitedly with her
boyfriend. When she slams down the receiver and leaves, she
avoids my eye. I step into the supposedly soundproofed chest
enclosure that today passes for a telephone booth. I dial and as the
phone rings I feel like an ostrich with my legs and crutches thus
exposed.

"Well," says Jackie, "what's she like?"

"Shirley Chisholm without the intelligence," I say, "and probably a dyke."

All these years I'd assumed the house to be vacant. Then that
afternoon as I looked through the windows again I found someone
looking out. How long had the creature been in there?

David Prud'homme Devereaux's personal effects fit neatly into a
worn imitation alligator-skin wallet of the kind he might have
purchased at Smith's Pharmacy in Queen Anne for $2.98 or it
could have been his Christmas present one year. There were his

driver's license, his social security card, a photocopy of his Army discharge paper, an engraved card of a certain Selwyn Rattner, Manager, Footwear for Gentlemen, 2983 First Street, Washington, D.C., a doctor's prescription for some sort of medication he'd never bothered to have filled, a snapshot of Odile looking pretty and pulled together, standing in front of a house I didn't recognize, holding a small baby who, I assume, grew up to be the odious toe-tapper. That was it.

Gethsemane also included, without comment, a Xerox of the following clipping from the Tatterhummock *Gazette* dated July 19, 1964:

LOCAL NEGRO LEADER CONDEMNS VIOLENCE FROM OUTSIDE: SEES NEED FOR HARD WORK, FAITH IN GOD

The Reverend Robert Shackleford, pastor of the All-Saints Christian Brotherhood Baptist Church, this county's most respected Negro leader, last week told the editor of the Tatterhummock *Gazette* that he roundly condemned the recent violence wherein two deputy sheriffs and eight demonstrators from outside the county were wounded, one fatally.

In an afternoon visit to the *Gazette* office, accompanied by his wife of 46 years, Naomi, who is president of the Ladies Gold Star Auxiliary of the All-Saints Christian Brotherhood Baptist Church, Rev. Shackleford called for "calm in this time of travail."

Commenting on the rock throwing and gunplay that erupted when a busload of 31 members of the self-styled Freedom Registration Party, with New Jersey license plates, attempted to persuade several Negro residents to enter the office of County Registrar Marion Jarrett, Rev. Shackleford said (we think wisely), "When you make an omelette some eggs must be broken."

Rev. Shackleford said, and again we agree, "Too many young folks today want something for nothing. They don't want to work like their daddies did."

Rev. Shackleford is living proof of what he preaches. In addition to being the pastor of the All-Saints Christian Brotherhood Baptist Church, a model for all Negro churches in the

Tidewater (and a church also served by both his late father and his late grandfather before him), Rev. Shackleford is proprietor of the Shackleford General Store on the Tatterhummock Trail (Route 3) and the Esso Service Station and Recreation Hall at Four Corners. That isn't all. In addition to his lovely home on Route 3, Rev. Shackleford farms 100 acres of corn, tobacco and peanuts on land he owns adjacent to St. Matthew's School for Boys.

Rev. Shackleford needs no credentials in this county. The Shacklefords are among the oldest living inhabitants of Tatterhummock County, his first ancestor having come here in 1653 as an indentured servant to one Leigh Shackleford, Gent., according to records that still exist at the county seat. Unlike most Negroes, many of the Shacklefords remained freemen during the slave years, a mark of the respect and high esteem in which the family was held throughout all those years. Rev. Shackleford's younger brother, Matthew, is a doctor residing in Richmond with his numerous children. His sister Mamie, who never married, is a teacher and religious worker in New York City and a visitor to her ancestral home on major holidays.

Rev. Shackleford and Mrs. Shackleford have had their share of troubles as we all know but they never let them get them down. When we asked the pastor who is about to celebrate his 70th birthday but he don't look a day over 40, what his recipe for success and happiness was, he said quickly, "Faith in God and in Jesus Christ His Only Son Our Lord." Who could be more living proof than our trusted friend Rev. Shackleford?

Asked about stories of racial tensions in Tatterhummock County and the rest of the South, as reported in newspapers in New York City and elsewhere, Rev. Shackleford came out strongly against "the communists and other hotheads, white and black alike, who are fostering all these stories of unrest and dissatisfaction on the part of the rank-and-file."

This subject makes Rev. Shackleford, ordinarily a peaceful man, hopping mad. "Whites and Negroes," he averred, "have lived in peace in this county for over 300 years and now some people who ain't even dry behind the ears yet want to tear it all down."

Rev. Shackleford told us after due consideration he has abandoned plans announced last year to open a bank for Negro clientele on property adjoining the Shackleford General Store and Gas Station on Route 3. He smiled as he told us, "I decided that I ain't no banker. I have enough trouble taking care of all the obligations and responsibilities I got now." That news will undoubtedly please Mr. Richard Warfield, president of the Queen Anne National Bank, and Mr. Holland Hartman, president of the Tatterhummock Court House Bank. They said last year they were afraid Rev. Shackleford "would get in over his head if he attempts to open a bank even for Negro clientele."

Rev. Shackleford added, "I'm not getting any younger and my sons Reuben (who has the Richland Farm Equipment Machinery franchise for this county) and Howard (who manages the family's businesses at Four Corners and on Route 3) are going to have their hands full as it is when I pass."

As you can tell we had a real good visit with Rev. and Mrs. Shackleford and we want to take this opportunity to make a suggestion we hope will not fall upon deaf ears. We propose that in the interests of our motto ("Pluck, Perseverance and Progress") the members of the Tatterhummock County Better Business Opportunities Commission ask Rev. Shackleford to join that body of civic-minded local businessmen in an advisory capacity. Now more than ever before we need dialogue between our two communities and who better than our old friend Rev. Shackleford can speak for the Negroes of Tatterhummock County?

32

Ten days ago Little Bob Carter scored what is described as a stunning upset in the elections in which he trounced the Democratic incumbent by a margin of 18 to 1 even though the Democratic presidential ticket carried the district easily. In his campaign speeches he came out firmly against amnesty for draft evaders and war resisters, against gun control, legalized abortion, busing and desegregation, though he took no stand on the League of Women Voters or the proposal to turn the United States Post Office Department over to the private sector. Little Bob's victory was so dramatic that he is already being mentioned as a possible vice-presidential candidate in 1980 and even presidential material for

1984. You can't beat all that machinery. For a computerized presidency, a transistorized man.

I went to hear Pru last night at Columbia. It was a well-attended performance but nowhere near sold out. From what I could gather by listening to people around me, as many people came to see Pru's wife, who never showed up, as to hear her husband. Gethsemane was there, sitting on the speaker's platform, and when she stood to acknowledge an introduction by Pru she looked like a great black hen arising from her nest to reveal that she had hatched a small wooden chair. The audience was about equally divided between blacks and whites, which, I suppose, is not unusual at a university but I find it odd when the issue that forced Baby Pru's retirement from the Reform Panthers, and contributed to his self-imposed exile, was the one of cooperation with members of the white radical movements. Pru has become increasingly obsessed with the subject in recent years, preaching an ever harder line at a time when his former associates were turning to policies of conciliation. He and Cleaver carried on a long-distance war of words between Cairo and Algiers before Cleaver decided to return to California and Jesus. Now, I understand, Pru and Cleaver don't even exchange press releases. In the question-and-answer period after his talk Pru denied that black nationalist leaders in Rhodesia and South Africa were no longer seeking his counsel. "The leaders of all black liberation movements are my brothers," he said. "The Third World is a black world, not brown or red or yellow or white." The crowd last night was hugely enthusiastic by the end, greeting every familiar piece of rhetoric ("And we won't hesitate to bring it all down in flames") with "right ons" that were the "amens" that half a century ago answered his Grandfather Shackleford when he described God's terrible beauty and wrath at Judgment Day. Passion is matter that cannot be destroyed—it simply takes another form.

It was a very depressing performance. Pru's metaphors have become familiar and by being familiar they no longer mean anything more than what they say. When he tells us again how he was fucked up the ass at age ten by two black brothers in the washroom of the Alfred E. Smith grammar school in the Bronx, the effect is not political but confessional. Poor, driven, beautiful

Baby Pru. I suspect that the fire next time will start not in our streets but in our parlors, from the simultaneous overheating of forty million color television sets.

I don't know exactly when it was that I made up my mind to do what I would do, but I'm sure it was before I went to Butler Library to hear Pru that night. Long, long before that something had been lying in my subconscious, for years maybe, a moth turning into a butterfly of destruction. I suppose it might have made slightly more initial sense if it had been Lewis's Landing I'd purchased. By stretching points Lewis's Landing could be said to be my family seat, though it really isn't. Lewis's Landing is the birthplace and the home of that Vietnamese-made appliance. It's not where he lives with his wife and child but it's his voting address. Although bought on the open market, Wicheley Hall is all mine, a piece of this nation I've acquired with the aid of a conglomerate that has recently become even more blue chip through an association with a Saudi-American petroleum combine. Wicheley is the oldest manor house in the county and one of the finest in the entire state. People feel responsible for it. Its survival reassures. Everyone recognizes that it is irreplaceable. Lewis's Landing would be judged private pique. I have need of a public act. The natives of Bed/Sty, Harlem, Newark, Detroit, Chicago and Watts no longer listen to Pru and Pru makes no efforts to reach them, preferring the high-paying lecture circuit that gives him access to minds in which all action has been distilled into theory.

Something has to be done, a gesture made. Constance of Defresney who, at twenty-four, had assassinated an associate of John of Puy, the heretic Bishop of Auvergne, was nutty as a fruitcake and could probably have used a good healthy fuck, among other things, but she possessed a will to act. Her act didn't change by one minute the timetable for the suppression and total annihilation of the Albigenses, but such an act should not be judged by the success or failure of a single campaign, rather by the splendor of its willfulness. That's what's remembered. For all the nimble nonsense concocted by Rome to make acceptable the mad, martyred Constance and to elevate her to the Communion of

Saints, she endures not for having been successful but for having
acted in all-consuming belief. Of course, some all-consuming be-
liefs are more important than others, just as (we must face that
fact) some people are. The children who blew themselves up in
that house on West 11th Street, making bombs as if they were
privileged mudpies, believed in something, I'm sure, but they were
woefully short of imagination and fatally lacking in the basic pre-
cautions required when handling explosives. They don't have to be
forgiven or even taken seriously. I certainly don't.

Jimmy Barnes is pleasant enough, not unintelligent in ordinary
affairs, but he's no one to raise a bit of Cain with. When we had
successfully negotiated the acquisition of Wicheley Hall in December of the Bicentennial Year, he and I flew to Richmond two
days before the closing to go over the property and buildings and
to inventory the furnishings and equipment. I'd had no advance
inkling how invigorating all this would be and when we returned
to the Walden's Point Inn the first night I was in a mood to celebrate and was, indeed, prepared to celebrate with two kittenish
ladies in their late thirties or early forties we met in the bar. They
looked like spinster schoolteachers en route to some deadly dull
all-state education conference of one sort or another at Virginia
Beach, which, it turned out, was exactly what they were. Neither
was my style. Both were short and on the dumpy side, every hair
glued into a perfect and uninteresting place, wearing single
strands of pearls and dark-printed dressy dresses that most likely
had deodorant stains under the arms. Yet they looked like the sort
of women who still wore stockings rather than one-piece panty-
hose, and the possibility of chancing upon a garter, to say nothing
of a real old-fashioned garter belt, contributed to my high spirits
as much as did the Jack Daniels we'd brought along. I was semi-
erect from the moment they accepted our invitation to join us at
our table.

Jimmy Barnes, though, behaved as if I'd taken him into a
Mexican whorehouse. He treated them with that elaborate Lake
Forest politeness that's about as rude as you can get, and he ig-
nored with pale smiles the double-entendres I began to lob across

the table and which they soon returned with spirit. Because I'd experienced no sexual desire since Jackie had walked out on me, I wasn't about to let this precious tumescence go to waste. It became very difficult since the schoolteachers both, obviously, preferred Jimmy as a one-night stand to me. I'm aware that though there are times when my crutches and leg braces can have an aphrodisiac effect on women, women of conventional tastes and habits shy away from all that machinery, as if the unscrewing of it would in some way fuse us into an intimacy that simple screwing would not. Finally when it was time to talk about nightcaps and ones-for-the-road, which would make necessary a clarification of who would be sleeping with whom, Jimmy botched all of the evening's preliminaries by saying that he'd pass this one up, old man, that he was bushed and had a long day ahead of him tomorrow. He stood to shake hands with each woman, his relief at getting away from them so great that he attempted to hide it by acting genuinely attracted to them. The sudden realization of what they were missing—not being able to go to bed with the even-featured nonentity—queered any chance that I might have had with either one. Before Jimmy had finished shaking hands, both Thelma Todd and Patsy Kelly were yawning too. I was soft again, and pissed off. "Don't linger too long over your *Penthouse*," I said to Jimmy, "or is it your *Hustler*?" Then, to our companions: "You know what they call those magazines, don't you? The masturbator's handbooks." Thelma and Patsy shrieked with appreciation and Jimmy Barnes turned crimson.

Two mornings later, after the formal closing ceremonies at the office of a Richmond attorney, Jimmy and I flew back north in a plane I chartered to take us directly to East Hampton where I would be formally rid of the house on the beach for about eight times what I'd paid for it twenty-odd years before. On the plane I explained to Jimmy the codicil I wanted added to my will concerning the disposition of Wicheley Hall. When I died, I told him, or if at some point I should be judged not competent to administer my estate, the title to Wicheley, its lands, furnishings, equipment, et cetera, as well as title to investments with an annual yield of not less than $60,000 were to go to Prud'homme Shackleford, my natural son by Gethsemane Shackleford, formerly of Tatterhummock County, Virginia. Sitting across the aisle from me in the pinched seat of the Lear jet, Jimmy was making notes on a legal pad resting on his Brooks Brothers attaché case.

"How do you spell 'Shackleford'?" he said. "With an 'e-l' or an 'l-e'?" " 'L-e,' " I said. He corrected his copy. "Can you spell 'Prud'homme'?" "No," he said, so I spelled that for him too. A few minutes later, looking at me, lawyer-to-client: "Is this something that's well known?" "I certainly don't think so," I said, "except to me and to the lady and maybe to her husband. She married him some years later. I'm sure the boy doesn't know anything about it. It will, I expect, create some surprise, but that's what I intend." "I assume," said Jimmy, "that you want this kept in confidence?" "The strictest confidence," I said. "You, your secretary and who-ever we have to have as witnesses. And I want you to be certain that you can come up with something that no members of my family—if there are any left by that time—or anyone else can break. Can you do that?" "I think so," said Jimmy Barnes, look-ing dubious. "Would it help things if I volunteered for a psychi-atric examination?" Jimmy, smiling slightly: "I'm sure that won't be necessary, but I'll look into it." Me, impatient but not dis-pleased to be startling Jimmy: "Haven't you ever dealt with some-thing like this before?" "Not exactly," said Jimmy. "No, to tell the truth, never." "Well," I said, "it involves a lot of money and a lot of property, so make sure you don't fuck it up."

A week later I decided on my own to get a clean psychiatric bill of health, which I finally received from a woman doctor, the wife of one of the quacks that Jackie had gone to three or four years back, and a panel of her associates. It wouldn't do, I thought, to go to any of the psychiatrists I'd seen in my youth, if any of them were still alive, which was doubtful. During the years I was in therapy for my legs, I was also seeing head doctors of various persuasions in case my paralysis might possibly have had psychosomatic as well as physical origins. Every third neurologist would think so and I'd be wheeled in to see some new quack who would either give up on me immediately or agree with me. Never once in all of those sessions did I ever mention Gethsemane, Devereaux or Pru, a baby whose name I didn't even know. In-stead I would talk about Tom. I didn't like to talk about Tom and, in fact, I didn't talk about him in any way that called up original feelings. I'd reported the same story, the same set of circumstances, the same associations and dreams so many times that they no longer seemed to be mine. They were history. They'd passed into the public domain.

33

Margaret and I drove down in February, shortly after my station wagon was delivered. We were due to leave at 8:30 in the morning and though Margaret had been up since four, clattering around the kitchen, we didn't actually get started until almost ten. In spite of the fact that neither of us ever breakfasts, Margaret had prepared bacon, eggs, pancakes, grits and, for good measure, cornbread, her way of placating the gods before we embarked on a journey she was sure would be fatal. Margaret doesn't believe that someone without the full use of his extremities should be allowed behind a wheel. In addition, Margaret wasn't keen about the move itself. Having originally come from Richmond she saw it as a kind of retreat to return to Virginia, especially since she is now used to Nelson Eddy and Jeanette MacDonald crowing their heads off in the elevators. Though I'm keeping the apartment on West 88th Street I've sold the East Side co-op, which depressed her; but she was pleased at the prospect of once again becoming a housekeeper in more than name, with a full staff to order about.

Our departure was delayed for an extra hour when I found that she had covered all the furniture in the drawing room with sheets. I had to tell her that I don't care about dust but I do care about walking into an apartment that looks like the city morgue. Since I plan to return to Manhattan at least once a month, I made her unwrap each piece of furniture and put the sheets back where they belong.

By 11:30 we were already beyond Philadelphia on a nearly empty thruway and I had to piss. Margaret, sitting in front with me, had a lap full of knitting she hadn't touched, being more intent on monitoring my driving. "Do let me know," I said, "when you want to go to the restroom." "Ah'm jes' fine," said Margaret, frowning at a trailer truck I was about to overtake. "I know you're not jes' fine," I said. Margaret: "Stop whenever you like. I can wait for you." Me: "For Christ's sake, stop playing the loyal slave. When you have to piss, say so. You do piss, don't you?" Margaret: "Ah declare, you did get out of the wrong side of the bed this morning, didn't you?" Me: "It has nothing to do with the wrong side of bed. I only want you to tell me when you have to piss." Margaret: "Well, that's a word I don't often use." Me (my kidneys about to burst): "I think it's about time you did. Piss. P-i-s-s." "All right," says Margaret, "in that case I think we better stop."

After that we got along fine. At lunch in Maryland we even had a cocktail and Margaret told me about the elderly Swede who'd proposed to her on her North Cape cruise. "Why the hell didn't you accept?" I said, but gently. "Oh, I don't rightly know," said Margaret, dunking her cherry into the manhattan. "I didn't admire all that attention. I guess I prefer . . . life as it is."

We were due to stay with Cousin Mary Lee for as long as a week but we moved to Wicheley the next day. One night was enough. Cousin Mary Lee never goes to bed—she rattles around the house all night looking for the General, and Margaret and Aunt Minnie spent their time circling each other like the city mouse and the country mouse. Later, of course, they became fast friends.

The preparations for our occupation of Wicheley were not easy. Cousin Mary Lee and Aunt Minnie supervised the refurbishing of the guest cottage, which is Margaret's permanent base. Cousin Mary Lee got so carried away in the excitement that she ordered nearly $1,000 worth of sheets, pillowcases, blankets and towels, which seemed an excessive sum, even to Margaret, who otherwise likes to travel luxe. More important, though, I found a seneschal. Through wheedling long-distance telephone calls and rash promises made in writing, I persuaded Carroll Tucker to come into my employ for a year as general estate manager but principally as chauffeur, with the understanding that he could have use of the farm manager's cottage and that I'd subsidize the rest of his college education when and if he resumed. By the time

Margaret and I arrived, Carroll had not only installed himself at Wicheley, but also his mother and father, a retired Miller & Rhoades maintenance engineer. I don't really mind. They stay out of sight but their presence increases Carroll's dependence on me, whether he knows it or not.

I sit at my desk in the Cornwallis Room, the huge master bedroom that occupies the entire second floor of the east wing. When I raise my eyes from my notebook I look north and east across my extraordinary river, so broad it seems not to be a river at all, more like a sea channel between one land and another. There's been no traffic on the river since I moved here from the guest house. On the low, flat ribbon of land that is the Northern Neck I see two small white buildings, houses, I suppose, about a mile distant from each other, but no movement, no signs of life. This must be what the view was like when old Wicheley began building the house. The color of the river at this time of year—mid-April—is a particular kind of temperate blue, pale and limpid, a single civilized hue from here to the far side, with no dramatic blotches of emerald or purple or royal that so enchant tired tourists on tropic seas. This is a blue for eyes that look and can perceive. I've grown very fond of the place but I will not lose sight of purpose.

Because the central heating system leaves a great deal to be desired (by everyone, of course, except me) I remained in the guest house with Margaret until the weather warmed enough for the fireplaces to be able to counteract twenty years of chill, which is how long it's been since anyone has occupied the main house. I've had the place thoroughly fumigated and cleaned, and the Pittsburgh-born stockbroker's family's personal rubbish removed, but I've not made any innovations except in my quarters. The insurance man from Richmond insists that a sprinkler system be installed, an operation that will take months, and I'm going to have the drawing room and kitchen spaces repainted, as well as the Adam ceiling restored, which will guarantee that there will be a lot of clumsy workmen cluttering up the place and is all part of my plan.

Ma and the now visibly ossifying Plyant were here last week, arriving in what looked like a one-car motorcade from Washington, being driven by a hired chauffeur in a black stretch-Cadillac of the sort that can transport twelve people from a downtown hotel to the airport. It poured rain both days they were here, which made the visit seem endless. They were a day late, having been held over in Washington by Cousin Mary Lee, who went north to greet them and who, according to Ma, is fast becoming Washington's most popular hostess as she presides over the household of Washington's most popular new junior congressman. Where this leaves Melanie I don't know, but I suspect she's been put in charge of the kid and its diapers while Cousin Mary Lee directs all traffic to the White House. This was Ma's introduction to the Washington scene, something that, until now, she'd always regarded as a bit vulgar, unstable and nouveau venu, all associations that had their roots in what Boo thought of politics in Chicago and especially about old Judge Henderson, the bagman. Ma has come late to the realization that politics can be, if not respectable, exciting, and that political power is sometimes more important than financial, subsuming social distinction. It's made her uneasy, a tiny bit dissatisfied, as if she'd missed something in her otherwise perfect life.

While Plyant napped in his bedroom, or sat in the first-floor library looking like an extremely tall mummy, a blanket over his lap and a hot water bottle under his feet, going through my Albigensian index, Ma inspected the house from top to bottom, at last coming forth with the conclusion I'd arrived at some time before, namely, that as far as original furnishings were concerned, I'd been screwed. "Everything in the house," said Ma, "is W & J Sloane 1925. There are some good Queen Anne reproductions— you can save them to put in the guest rooms—but everything else has to go. The hunt prints in the library aren't bad. Have you ever seen so much terrible chintz?"

The furnishings aren't exactly valueless but they don't do justice to the house, which, though the floors creak, is superb in design and construction. Everything second-rate about it—the bathrooms and bathroom fixtures, the wiring (including ugly ceiling fixtures and wall sconces) and kitchen equipment—are early twentieth-century contributions. The oak paneling in the entrance hall, library and Cornwallis Room has the patina of beige satin. The Adam ceiling and the chinoiserie wallpaper in the dining room are virtually worth what I paid for the whole place. There's not a room that doesn't have its own magnificent view. The swimming pool is apparently in good shape, though I'd like it to be heated and wish I could afford to enclose it in glass, so I could swim when the weather is cold; but who knows where I shall be next winter? To think such thoughts is to become sidetracked.

Ma insists that Mrs. Douglas Wormley of Philadelphia is an original and took her with her to be authenticated when she and Plyant departed in the stretch-Cadillac. Ma has also taken it upon herself to commission a New York photographer to come down to photograph the house in detail—he arrives next week—because, as she said cheerfully, "One simply never knows how much longer these old houses will last, and there should be records kept. This is one of the great houses in America and nobody knows about it." The next morning, before she and Plyant left, she was making plans to come back to spend Christmas here, conditioning that on my promise that I will come to London for the opening of Parliament. "The opening of Parliament?" I said. "The opening of Parliament? For Christ's sake, Ma, why would I want to attend the opening of Parliament?" Ma looked surprised at my surprise. "Well, darling, it's the Jubilee Year and if you've never seen the opening of Parliament, you should. It brings tears to my eyes every time I see the Queen in her coach riding down the Mall." "Bullshit," I said. "Ma, I think you've flipped." "Well, I declare," said Ma. "I simply don't understand you nor do I accept your language. I don't know where you learned it." "I'm fifty-fucking-three," I said. Ma looked grieved, but also relieved that Plyant had not yet come down to breakfast and had been spared this demonstration of filial pettishness that, try as she might, she would never comprehend.

Without remarkable changes spring has evolved into summer. The Peale portrait, authenticated, stays in an air-conditioned New York vault. In June Ma sent from London a letter written by Lord Cornwallis in his own hand in 1791 in which he recalls that on his way to Yorktown ten years earlier he had spent two nights in "a farm house typical of that county but more comfortable than most, said to have been built by Governeur Wicheley who, I believe, was kinsman to our family." It was Ma's birthday present some months late. The people who are to install the sprinkler system have begun their surveys and the painters are at work on the first floor. I take my meals downstairs and sleep and work in the Cornwallis Room, which I've made very comfortable with desk, stereo, bookcases and file cabinets.

Each day I am more addicted to the view across this great river. With summer there has been an increase in the river traffic, mostly small sailboats and more frivolous powercraft though, at the end of May, a large, fine old lumber schooner, of the sort we used to see from St. Matthew's, tacked its way upriver, remaining in my view for five hours. As far as I know, it's never come back. Or perhaps it sailed by at night and I missed it. I dine regularly with Cousin Mary Lee or with the Purdys at St. Matthew's and have them to dine here with some of the local gentry. Nice people in spite of an unreasonable passion for bridge. I have no idea what they think of me but I wouldn't like to embarrass them too much. I was called upon yesterday by a Mrs. Dabney Collins, the president of the Federated Garden Clubs of Western Virginia, who got through to me by using Cousin Mary Lee's name. She was making arrangements to bring a group of 150 ladies for a tour of the house and grounds next autumn. Well, we'll see about that.

34

The voice on the telephone was familiar but I couldn't immediately place it. "Hah!" it said. "Hah, Marshall Lewis Henderson?" "Yes." "I'm here," said Klein. "Where?" said I. "You always said," said Klein, "whenever you come to America, you must stay with me." That is probably the least likely thing I've ever said in my life. No matter how remote the possibility I never invite people to visit. "Where are you?" I said. If he were at Kennedy in New York I had a reasonable chance of escaping him. "In Richmond," he said, "hah." My heart sank. "At the Greyhound bus terminus on Broad Street. How do I find you?" Long pause. "I say," says Klein, "are you there?" "Yes," I say, "well . . ." (brightly) "what brings you to Richmond?" "Why you, my dear chap, to see you, my old colleague, to catch up on all the news. . . ." "Well," I flounder, "how nice. . . ." "Are you there? Are you there?" Then I'm saved by a few moments altercation with an operator, who sounds black. She accuses Klein of having put four 25-cent-sized slugs into the coin box. "Sloggs?" says Klein, so offended I suspect the operator must be correct. I hear Klein mumbling to someone, then an avalanche of apparently legitimate nickels dropping into the machine.

"Well," says Klein, "that's better. Can you hear me now?" I say I can. "What I wish for you to do," says Klein, "is to speak to a taxi driver I have here, and explain to him how to reach your house. Unfortunately I do not have the street name and number, only a postal box." Suddenly I'm talking to some troglodyte who's as surprised as I am. "Huh?" says the troglodyte. "Put Father Klein back on the telephone," I say. "He wants to speak to you, I guess," says the troglodyte, and the phone changes hands again. "I dare say there is no problem," says Klein. "You don't realize," I say, "that I live sixty miles outside Richmond. A taxi would cost a fortune." "Hah," says Klein, "in that case I follow your directions. I put myself in your hands completely. . . ." After considering one thing and another I decide that the simplest course is to send Carroll Tucker into Richmond to pick up Klein in the station wagon. It is then about one in the afternoon. I estimate that Carroll can be there in an hour and a half and return by 4:30 or five, which will give Margaret and her slaves a chance to prepare a guest room and me a chance to prepare excuses by which I can decently evict Klein after one night or, at the most, two.

This was mid-July. A hot, windless day. Patches of the tidal river had gone suddenly smooth as if to indicate that even gravitational impulses between planets had been temporarily suspended. I was at my desk in the Cornwallis Room when I at last heard the station wagon coming up the drive. Earlier I'd had the wit to call the Purdys, with whom I was supposed to dine that night at St. Matthew's, to announce my predicament and beg off. They fell all over themselves in the excitement of having a Jesuit priest for a guest, but I explained his age, his jet lag, his ignorance of bridge as a parlor game and the fact that he had to leave the next day. Susan Purdy was insistent. I was firm. Sometimes God is on my side. By the time Klein arrived I'd settled on a foolproof story about why he could remain only the one night. I was ready for Klein, but not for Fred.

Waiting for me in the entrance hall as I made my way down the great staircase, swinging myself with agility, one hand on the banister and both crutches nipped neatly under the other shoulder, were a puzzled, apprehensive, very spruce-looking Carroll Tucker, carrying two small, ancient valises, and Klein, still huge but very old and so thin he seemed to have lost all his feathers and fur. Though he wore baggy black slacks, sandals (without socks) and what appeared to be a black dashiki, the old gryphon seemed naked. With them was an exceedingly pale young man whose shaved head revealed a skull of most unusual color (light blue) and shape—it seemed to have been bound when he was an infant so that the back of it looked like an artificial extension. If it had been a dining table you would have said that all of the extra leaves had been inserted. The fellow—who carried a knapsack—wore dirty jeans, a new T-shirt with "69" on the front, sandals exactly like Klein's and an expression so vacant he seemed to be staring at a cornfield long after the harvest, seeing nothing but small, dead stumps. I wondered if he might be retarded or perhaps mute. While I made my way down the stairs the three regarded me as if I were giving some kind of performance, not an especially interesting one but the sort for which a certain respect is expected, like the playing of someone else's national anthem.

Once I was safely down on the hardwood floor, so highly polished by Margaret's minions that I could see my own upside down image, Klein lumbered over to me, hand outstretched, a large, toothy, insincere smile on his face. "My dear chap." We shook hands; then, as if overcome with emotion, he embraced me, his b.o. recalling for me what the Middle Ages must have smelt like in midsummer. His hands on my shoulders, he stood back, the better to see me. "My old friend," he said, "we meet again." "Yes," I said. "You look well," said Klein, which was not the sort of thing he was inclined to say under ordinary circumstances. "More gray, perhaps, but no older." Klein was not accustomed to acknowledging what people looked like. I'd always thought him to be above such fripperies. He stared at me intently with those fierce eyes that are so brown they appear to be black. It was his Fulton Sheen look. "I am so happy that you have me as your guest. God is good." "God is good, indeed," said the young man in the "69" T-shirt. Klein let me go. "Hah," he said, "hah, hah. You do not know my secretary? This is Fred." Fred looked sternly at the floor and then, as if he knew he had to do something to recognize our introduction, he slipped off his knapsack and dropped it to the floor. "I didn't know you had a traveling companion," I said, perhaps severely. "I'll have to ask the housekeeper to prepare another room." "No bother, old chap. No bother. Fred has his sleeping bag. He can put it on the floor in my room or perhaps he will decide to sleep outside, in your park."

I told Carroll to take Father Klein's bags up to the Rose Room and asked Klein and Fred if they cared to bathe after their long trip. Klein ignored me. "Fred," he said, "take the fish into the kitchen." For the first time Fred looked directly at me. I looked at Klein. "Fred prepares our food," said Klein. "We sup *with* you, but not *of* you. Hah!" I told Carroll to show the Rose Room to Fred and then to take him to the kitchen where, I was sure, he'd be as great a surprise to Margaret and her staff as to me.

Klein displayed absolutely no interest in the house so I steered him through the cavernous drawing room, shades drawn against the afternoon sun, to the Green Room, where the painters had stored their gear for the weekend (this was Friday), through the French doors to the screened-in veranda that has more or less the same commanding view of the river as the Cornwallis Room above. As I prepared the drinks at the bar—I didn't feel I had to ask him what he'd like, he'd drink scotch or nothing—Klein paced around the porch, poking cushions, looking out and down at the river a quarter of a mile away. With the first breezes of evening it was beginning to show some life again. Klein saw everything but appeared to take nothing in, or maybe he was just being himself once more. No small talk. Complete self-absorption. I handed him his glass and motioned for him to sit on a chaise, one of a dozen white plastic things Ma had sent down from New York, along with a colossal bill. I sat in a straight chair facing him and the glorious view.

"Here's to you," I said. We raised our glasses, then drank. "I didn't know you had a secretary," I said. "Secretary?" said Klein. "Oh, Fred? Well, old chap, Fred isn't exactly a secretary"—good grief, I thought, Klein has turned gay!—"more like a student, an apprentice. A nice boy. I think I can help him. He is a very religious young man, not, thank God, a Sodomite, like so many these days. Not that I have anything against Sodomites, but I could not work with one. They are very distracting, you know. Fred has become the companion to my mission. . . ." This was said so frankly that I was unable to respond. Silence. "Where are you going?" I said at last, with some impatience. "Tomorrow," said Klein. "Unfortunately we have to leave tomorrow night." I suppressed my disappointment. Silence. He noted the way I looked at his clothes. "And, really, where *have* you been?" Klein smiled his truly ugly smile that, this time, was totally sincere. "Do we seem to you so strange? So bizarre? Two poor travelers in search of shelter?" "No," I said, "but you do bounce around rather a lot. What was all that business last summer about Peter Weingarten and the London address?" Klein laughed, drank deeply and sighed with contentment. "Dear chap, everything in good time. Let's just sit here for a little while and enjoy all this tranquility, this beauty. . . ." "You should shift around," I said, "so you can have the view." "I have the view . . . here," he said, touching his heart. Silence. I could hear Carroll start the station wagon and drive off. I wondered what Fred might be up to in the kitchen.

Not once did Klein ask about Jackie, though she had been with me the last two times we'd met in Paris. Jackie was not the sort of woman to interest Klein. Too intelligent. Too independent. Too skeptical. Klein, I suspected, preferred poor, superstitious peasant women, kneeling before him, mouths at the ready to receive absolution as if from God's gasoline pump. Which briefly reminded me of the first pornographic film I'd ever seen, about a tiny priest, Mexican, I think, who ended each confession he heard by pulling up his cassock and whipping out a giant schlong (Jackie's word) to receive the blow job owed him. Because Klein was not forthcoming I sought to fill the silence by reporting to him about my work, which necessitated my telling him about my most recent failure with the Princeton University Press.

"What do these people know?" said Klein. Only later did it occur to me that he sounded suspicious.

"Nothing, I guess."

"If you want to publish," said Klein, "publish it yourself. I should think you could afford it. Augustine published his first works himself."

"I didn't know that," I said, but then I'd never before thought about the problems of publishing in fourth-century Carthage.

"Of course," said Klein. "Thomas Aquinas too. I have a friend in Lyons . . ." he pondered for a moment, thought better of the idea. "But maybe that wouldn't be practical."

It was at this time of day that I usually went to the pool to do my forty laps, but the drink removed my resolve and when Klein joined me in a second, I said to hell with it. Later, as the two of us huffed our way up the stairs, me to shower and change before dinner, Klein to hold a black mass, he said, "Why don't you have an elevator installed? You do have the money, don't you?" It was his second reference to my money in less than an hour. He was beginning to sound like the sort of Third World hooker one meets in places like Alexandria and Damascus, whores full of left-wing dialectics but not about to spread their legs, even to a good party member, until they've received some hard currency. I suspected that I might not find Klein interesting after all, and worse—that I couldn't afford him.

The only thing that Klein and I shared at dinner, in addition to the table, was a fine, smoky red wine. While Margaret, wearing her stiffly starched white uniform and a pained expression, served me my usual summer supper (cold soup, broiled chop, green salad), Fred (now barefoot) set before Klein a series of dishes that contained bits of marinated fish, brown rice, bean sprouts, raw vegetables. Though Fred's appearance was most disruptive in being riveting, he served Klein with the efficient grace of a Buddhist acolyte. On close inspection he was even more unattractive than he had seemed when I first saw him. Klein, reading my thoughts after Fred returned to the kitchen: "I agree. He has the most queerly shaped head, but one becomes accustomed to it. His father is a very important man. He owns Sear Rowbach of Trenton, New Jersey." Me: "How did you meet him?" Klein (tut-tutting): "Oh, I've never met him. Fred and his dad no longer communicate." Me: "Not the dad—Fred?" Klein: "On Fifth Avenue. The corner of 51st Street, I believe" (smiles at the memory) "he was with a large group of other young men and women, wearing the prettiest costumes, orange silk robes, dancing and chanting, clapping their hands and striking small brass cymbals. . . ." Me: "Hari Krishnas?" Klein: "It was so charming . . . you cannot believe. . . ." Me: "You mean he's a Hari Krishna?" I laugh. Klein: "He was but now he is—how should I put it?—a lapsed disciple. . . ."

It was still light after dinner when Klein expressed a desire to be shown around the house. If he had any knowledge of American history he gave no signs of it as I explained which parts of the house represented which eras. He was enchanted by the ballroom, though it was a mess—its plaster bubbled with mildew and the room a repository for pieces of furniture that hadn't yet been officially inventoried and certified. He was also charmed by the dormitory on the third floor. My bedroom-workroom—the huge Cornwallis Room with its grand fireplace and its beamed ceiling and bookcases—seemed not to impress him at all. "It's a great waste of space, old chap." Suddenly he noticed my particular treasure, the tiny, fragile Bible made by Herman of Valenciennes for the incinerated princess of Foix. I kept it on my desk inside a crystal belljar. "What's this?" said Klein. "I know," I said, "I'm indulging myself and not serving history. I should probably keep it in a vault somewhere, but I like having it near me when I work." "But what is it? Is it old?" Me: "It's the Valenciennes Bible. The one you obtained for me." Klein squinted at it, then frowned. "Oh yes," he said, "my, my. Hah."

As we were on our way down the stairs to the veranda and a nightcap, we met Fred on his way up. I continued down the stairs as the two conferred. When I reached the bottom, Klein called to me: "My dear chap, is there any chance that Fred could have the use of an automobile?" "I don't know," I said. "It's not here.

Carroll keeps it in the garage at his house. Why?" Klein (smiling with "Going My Way" kindliness): "He is young. He needs companionship." Me: "Companionship! What kind of companionship? It's eleven-thirty at night and this is Tatterhummock County. There's no companionship between here and Richmond . . ." (I pause) "except sheep." Fred whispers something else to Klein. Klein (still amused, to me): "He asks if you have anything to smoke—marijuana?" Me: "No, for Christ's sake, Father. Tell him there's booze in the butler's pantry. He's welcome to that." Fred shrugs sullenly. Klein to Fred: "God is good." Fred to Klein: "God is good, indeed." They kiss each other on each cheek and Fred continues up the stairs.

Klein (as he joins me on the veranda): "I hope you were not shocked." Me: "Just how long have you known Fred?" Klein (thinks a moment): "Let's see—eight days." Me: "Eight days! My God, Father, you don't even know him. He could be an ax murderer for all you know." Klein: "He is young. . . . He has his needs." Me: "He's so thin his only needs would appear to be food." Klein: "He has three children, two less than a year old." As we drank Klein told me about Fred's life in the commune in Brooklyn, which sounded quite unorthodox, even for a splinter group. "He is obsessed by two things," said Klein, "God and sexual intercourse. Until we met he was convinced they were incompatible." "They often are in this country," I said. Klein: "When we go to California I've promised to get him an operation —how do you say?—where they . . ." Klein made his fingers into scissors. "A vasectomy?" "Precisely," said Klein.

It was long after midnight. A waning moon had risen over the Northern Neck when Klein began his revelations. I'd been drinking slowly, so I wasn't drunk, but I was far from sober. I had stayed up beyond my usual bedtime because Klein, for the first time, appeared willing to talk about himself. Among the preliminary disclosures: Klein had been separated from the Society of Jesus for seven years. He'd never been a happy Jesuit, he said, not since the war anyway, and all his troubles stemmed from the war.

"You see, my dear chap—how should I put it?—I survived Auschwitz and lost . . . interest. How can one understand a prisoner, who is a priest, who despises the ill and infirm, the blind, the aged who are incontinent, the young who cannot speak in their terror? Especially those who gave in so . . . gratefully? I loathed the pitiful. . . ." (Then, brightly) "It was as simple as that. Yes it was. . . ." (Pause) "The ones who accepted their fates, do you know what we called them? The Muslims. I don't know why, perhaps because they seemed so . . . alien. I was strong and could work, so I was favored. After the first few months I made no attempts to bring Jesus Christ into it. That won me favors too. I became a member of a labor detail that met the trains. We were the élite, the chosen. We cleaned out the cars and searched the travelers. It was understood that we could keep all the food we found, and the drink. The gold and jewelry and clothing went to the guards. Our greatest fear was that they'd run out of people. You see, old chap, I understood the system and, by understanding, became a part of it. Oh God, oh God. . . ."

I thought Klein might be nearing a crying jag, but no. He was in high spirits. "You see, the curious thing—which you will appreciate, it's most amusing, really, to a Jesuit—is that I felt no guilt. If this was the way things were, and were meant to be, the possibility of guilt was eradicated, responsibility eliminated. Revulsion was pure, like love. I didn't want to live especially, but I had a great desire to avoid death. That was the ticket. Yes, that was the ticket. . . ." The memory amused him. "I was two kilos more heavy when I left the camp than when I went in." Long pause. "I shock you? You do not like my story, which, I emphasize, is not a confession?"

"It is very sad," I said. "I'm sorry. . . ."

"Sorry? Sorry?" said Klein. "It's a poor word but not to be sneezed at. Sometimes it's all that remains.

"The Jews say, 'never again,' but it will happen again. Maybe not to them, but certainly it will happen again to someone, if the world lasts long enough. 'Never again'? Always again. I know. It can never be any other way."

The veranda was in deep shadow. The moon, though eroding, lit the landscape so that we could clearly see the Northern Neck.

"You have noticed a change in me?" said Klein. I wasn't sure how he wanted me to answer, but I was prepared to give him any answer that suited him. In extreme cases I'm always prepared to do that. "Yes," I said. "You see," said Klein, "that I lead a new and different life."

"You are," I said, suppressing a burp, "the last man of Albi."

"Precisely," said Klein.

I slept until ten but fitfully, then awoke with a possibly malignant hangover, the first I'd had in years. All that poisonous brandy and loony talk had dehydrated my body and my mind. I felt depressed in a way that is unusual for me. It was like a hash-crash. Everything had come to a halt. There was no past, no future, only the wall opposite. I didn't want to get off my bed and for half an hour I didn't, not until my kidneys issued an ultimatum. It was a hot, sticky morning. I could feel the heat that had been accumulating for months in the grass, in the leaves of the trees. I was so dehydrated I didn't even sweat. I was as dry as someone in a fever. As I stood before the toilet, balanced on my crutches, relieving myself in pitiful spurts, I looked out the window and saw Klein, followed by pale, hairless Fred, coming toward the house on the flagstone path from the river bluff. Klein appeared to be no worse for the wear of last night, talking grandly to Believer Fred, whose expression was as mysteriously blank as ever. I shook my virtually retired cock, went to the wash basin and drank two tumblers of water in an attempt to lubricate my head and my tubes, then stepped into my shower, which, with the addition of several strategically located cross bars, can receive me if not as a lover, then as a practical nurse. The hot water soothed me, but I was on the brink of panic. I kept reassuring myself that Klein and his entire congregation would be gone by seven that evening. I didn't even have to see him if I didn't want to. Though I'd been dealing with Klein for over a quarter of a century I felt as if I'd just made an impetuous mistake, as if, late at night, I'd picked up the wrong hooker in a bar. I had to get rid of him as quietly and quickly as possible.

After I'd dressed, I rang the kitchen so that Margaret would send up one of her day-slaves with my juice and coffee, with that morning's Richmond paper and yesterday's *New York Times*. It takes longer to get *The New York Times* at Wicheley than it does

in Marrakesh. I was sitting under an awning on the terrace adjacent to the Cornwallis Room, staring somewhat resentfully at a
flotilla of tiny sailboats that was messing up my virgin view, deny-
ing myself the first cigarette of the day until I'd finished breakfast,
when my tray arrived carried by a pretty, no more than fifteen-
year-old black girl named Kitty, someone, I suspect, Carroll
Tucker has already tampered with, but discreetly. Unfortunately
Kitty was accompanied by Demon Klein who, in the morning
light, looked older and more stark than ever but seeming to be in
robust spirits. As Kitty set the small breakfast table, Klein seated
himself opposite me, breathing noisily and smelling, even in the
open air, of sweat, halitosis and garlic, which he seemed to have
chewed to start his day. He gave me no chance to tell him that my
routine is to breakfast alone when I'm in the midst of work. He
steamrollered me.

Klein: "What a magnificent spot. It's very European . . . a
family home like this." Me: "It's not my family home. . . ." Klein
(not listening): "What are your plans for it—when you die?"
Me: "I . . ." Klein: "You have no children, no close family. . . ."
Me: "Well . . ." Klein: "Old chap, do you know what I'm thinking?" Me: "You'd like to make this your See." Klein (roars with
laughter): "That's rich. Rich, rich, rich. . . ." (He becomes sober,
visionary) "We want to build a community, a place where young
people can come to study, to work. Nothing grand. We begin very
small. We learn from seeds. . . ." Me: "What about old people?
What about me?" Klein: "We want everyone, but the young people are more serious. There are so many who have the wish to
change. Now you know why I am in your country. It is why we
leave tonight for California. There, Mrs. Herbert Passmore of
Pasadena, California—do you know her by any chance?—will
discuss our future. She is very rich, very important, this Mrs. Herbert Passmore of Pasadena. Very influential. I cannot understand
that you do not know her? Well, no matter. I met her last autumn
when she came to Amalfi on a cruise on the *Oranjestad*. . . ." Me:
"It's of Panamanian registry, I believe." Klein: "I'm not sure. In
any case, we met at a café and now we correspond regularly. She
has offered me her services, hah." Me: "New religions do not
interest me." Klein: "This is hardly a new religion. It's a way of

living. What do you call this place?" Me: "Montségur West."
Klein: "A community with a school, a chapel, land to farm, a
great river to fish in. Oh, I tell you, dear chap, I could be young
again. . . ." Among other things, Klein possessed a network of
rich, obviously dotty American widows who were collectively
financing his mission.

Suddenly, from the general direction of the west wing, there
came a surprised cry, not quite a scream, more like the noise
evoked when someone wins a four-door Buick Masturbator, with
whitewall tires, radio, tape deck, vinyl seat covers and power
steering from the back seat. This was followed by either laughter
or tears, and the kind of commotion I still associate with the revels
of Ma, my father and Tom.

"What the hell was that?" I said.

Klein did not seem to have heard. He was giving me supple-
mentary information about a Mrs. Hastings Dotrice of Seattle,
Washington ("very fat but with many interests in a company that
makes airplanes") when Margaret, indignant and outraged, appeared in the doorway.

"Mr. Henderson," said Margaret, her small body shaking in
fury, "this must be stopped."

It was revealed that the Apostle Fred had tried to persuade
Kitty to meet his needs. When she went into Klein's room to make
the bed, Fred had cornered her, not to grab her, apparently, but so
that she might better regard him and his apparatus.

I did not have to speak to Fred again. Klein told him to stay out of
the house. The rest of the day Fred sat in the shade of an elm tree
on the front lawn, leaning against his knapsack, playing a recorder, which, because I am sometimes lucky, I could not hear.
Klein lunched alone downstairs while I remained at my desk and
worked. I was interrupted at two when Carroll came to ask me to
relieve him of having to drive our two ecclesiastics into Richmond. Carroll (politely): "I liked to bust that skinny white faggot's balls, if you know what I mean." "That's enough of that," I
said. "They'll sit in the back and won't bother you." "But they
smell," said Carroll, being as close to stubborn as he had ever

been with me. "The air conditioner makes it worse." "Then open all of the windows," I said. "How did people get along before there was air conditioning in cars?"

Ultimately Carroll accepted the assignment when I suggested that he could keep the car and spend the night in Richmond, where his parents were having a short vacation.

After two more showers, a quart of Perrier and six aspirin, my hangover lifted, and with it my spirits. I was focused on one thing, getting Klein out of Wicheley and off my back. Thus I was friendly when, at 5:30, the prophet appeared for a final interview. He was freshly bathed, wearing what appeared to be a clean black dashiki, his gospels in a neat little black leather sack on a chain around his neck, where the blunt instrument had once hung. I was not only cordial but festive. I rang Margaret to send up a bucket of ice, glasses and a bottle of scotch. As we sat in the cool of the Cornwallis Room I read Klein's subdued manner as chagrin over the morning's sex crime. Not at all. As I was pouring a dividend, Klein came out with it.

"I have something else I must say to you before I take leave."

"Yes?"

"I have not always been as honest as I might."

I laughed. "Father," I said, "I love you. You are completely crazy, but you are unique. You have helped to give my life meaning." I was feeling no pain but booze was not in charge of my tongue. Relief made me expansive. "Start your new church," I said. "I wish you well. I'd even like to make a contribution." I arose and swung myself over to my desk where I took out my checkbook. "Unfortunately for me" (laughter) "I assume you aren't yet tax deductible?" I started to write a check for $250 but thought, what the hell, why not $500? For old times. I had my back to Klein as I wrote. "God is good," said Klein. "God is good, indeed," I said. I tore the check from the pad, got up and went back to Klein to give him his little reward. He placed it on the table without looking at it.

"The thing is," said Klein, "you have already given me more than enough."

"Always for services rendered," I said, easing myself into my booze chair.

"They're all—how should I say it?—fake."

"What?"

"Everything."

"What, *everything*?"

"Everything."

I was aware that my stomach was slipping toward the floor but I wouldn't acknowledge what he had decided to tell me.

Klein: "All of the documents, the letters, the mementos you have purchased through me over the years. Not one of them is genuine."

"I don't believe you."

"It's true. God is my witness." He got up, went to my desk, where he picked up the belljar containing the nearly 1,000-year-old Valenciennes Bible. He brought it back and sat down again to look at it in its glass chamber.

"It's not true," I said.

He handed it to me. "Take it out. I'll show you." I broke the seal and removed the holy book, the vellum speckled with the tiny liver spots of age. He grabbed it from me as if reaching for a *Newsweek*. "Look, here"—he turned the ancient leaves as if seeking a telephone number. "Oh, good heavens," said Klein, "will you look at that?" He shifted around on the couch and pointed out a line in the text of St. Matthew's gospel. "E-p-i-s-t-o-l-e-a—e-a!—Otto is a competent scholar but he never could spell. Very sloppy about his cases, too."

The Valenciennes Bible was the work of Klein's brother-in-law, a fellow who, like Klein, had made a hobby of the history of the Cathars and who had supplemented his income by making reproductions of important artifacts. "Unfortunately," said Klein, adopting the manner of a comrade, "they weren't very good. Otto was never a first-class copyist." He now examined the volume very gently. "It *is* a pretty little thing, isn't it? But about half the text is from the Mecklenburg Bible of 1397. Otto liked the pictures."

"I've been dealing with a ring of forgers."

"No, dear chap," said Klein, "not a ring of forgers. Just Otto and me. And you were our only patron. The other things were always sold as reproductions."

"Where is Otto now?"

"He died last year—at the age of ninety-three."

Pause.

"The correspondence between Simon de Montfort and Edmund-Raymond of Thiers?"

"I wrote the original texts."

"The copy of the Epistola Ecclesiae Leodensis?"

"Handwritten, by Otto."

"The pornographic poems?"

"Copies of poems—adjusted here and there—written in the fifteenth century by Guilbert Rognons, one of Villon's contemporaries. Truly, those are things you should have recognized: 'The sainted abbess, wrapped in royal purple/Awaits the holy cross of her desire. . . .' You do not recognize that? Ah, well."

"The two letters from Prince Henry to Louis VII?"

"Composed by me, and in their way quite marvelous, I think."

"Herbert of Bosham's correspondence with the Abbot of Vézelay?"

"All copies of authenticated materials, much of which is available in the original in the collection of the current Count of Paris. He is a most liberal man in such matters."

"The Xeroxes . . . ?"

"Those *are* real but you could have had access to the originals in the Borghese Library in Rome. They can be obtained by anyone with the proper credentials."

"The material from the British Museum?"

"Copies of documents that were found to be forgeries in 1911."

"Why? I mean . . ."

"You wanted it so much—and you were always such a gullible scholar. So enthusiastic when you wanted to believe. And—perhaps I shouldn't say this—my dear chap, you are lazy and selfish. You are not one to share your discoveries, are you? Hah! You never bought anything on the open market. Traveling back and forth to Europe, with false-bottomed valises, you never announced your possessions. If you had, the fox would have been caught in the henhouse long before this."

I was completely calm. No outrage. "Before you go," I said at last, "you and I will go through all of the stuff you've sent me over

the years. You will separate the bogus material from the copies of
legitimate material."

"We must leave soon," said Klein.

Pause.

"Yes, yes," I said. "Of course."

Pause.

"It was time for me to clear the conscience," said Klein. He
looked away, anticipating California, I thought. Then, brightly,
"Look at it this way: You probably know more about the Albigenses than anyone else in this entire country, except, of course,
for me, now. Hah!"

I wondered what the people at the Princeton Press really
thought of the outline I'd submitted.

Klein: "My dear chap, what can I say? That I have regrets? I
suppose I have now, but I didn't have then, so how much are my
regrets worth? The money? It is gone, to some good causes, to
some not so good. Much of my life has been dishonorable, but as
they say, 'Never again.'" Another very long pause. I think I can
hear Fred's goddamn recorder. Flat. Klein reaches over and pats
my hand. "Well, well, I do feel better. Perhaps I have time for one
for the road?"

35

I was not going to surrender to this latest treachery. I had, after
all, designed my life as a monument that marks the betrayals by
others, the ruins of other lives. When I was sure that Klein and his
clergy had safely departed, I returned to my desk as if nothing had
happened. First I attended to the bills of the local tradesmen. The
others I slipped into a manila envelope and sent off to Louise for
her to deal with in New York. In the personal mail was a letter
from Ma in Michigan saying that Claire had written that my father was not recovering from his latest stroke as quickly as they'd
hoped (why the fuck hadn't she written me?), that Plyant was
well but depressed about the pound (great, I thought, just the sort
of shit one wants to read in a letter from home), plus news about

the social activities of a lot of people I'd never had any interest in. "We are expecting you in London in October," Ma ended. "What fun!" What fun, indeed. A letter from Claire was under Ma's. It was short and sweet, saying pretty much what Ma had reported, and then went on to ask me to come over to Maryland for Thanksgiving. There was also a note from my father, written in a hand that is the script-equivalent to a speech impediment. "Please plan ahead for Thanksgiving. If you want, we can send a car over for you. At least twenty children, grandchildren and great-grand-children are expected. Your presence would be a rare treat." And due to become more rare.

At the bottom of the pile was a legal envelope from Jimmy Barnes containing a long-ago requested photostat of my will and the unbreakable codicil. I could have a fatal heart attack, blow my brains out or go raving mad and Wicheley would pass safely on to Pru. At seven, fortified by another scotch, I went down to the dining room where, in the company of Margaret, I supped on a cold soup, which was green, a broiled pork chop that was brown, and a salad of bibb, which was also green. I asked for some red wine but Margaret somehow forgot. Instead she wheeled in her portable TV set that we might watch "The Newlyweds" and "Hollywood Squares," her two favorite programs. When it became apparent that I was not about to be given any wine, I arose from the table myself and fetched the scotch from the butler's pantry. Back at the table, I drank the contents of my water glass and refilled it with Chivas. Margaret sat stiffly on the edge of a chair at the far end of the table, under a terrible portrait of Sir William painted in the first decade of this century, pretending to be oc-cupied by the idiot small talk of a plump, androgynous man whose hair did not appear to be entirely his own.

There are times when I find watching dogshit pacifying, espe-cially with the sound turned off. I love identifying the pace of the hilarity by the way the camera cuts from one smiling face to an-other, interspersed with close-ups of totally mystifying words and phrases ("Princess Grace's shoe," "nine o'clock scholar," "PORT-LAND Mason"). In such an age, can there ever be a non sequitur? This night, however, I could not turn off the sound. I was beyond such games, anyway. Without saying anything to Margaret I abruptly got up from the table and began the journey back up to the Cornwallis Room, leaving behind the tumbler full of scotch, a gesture I thought would reassure her. It didn't. A half hour later she appeared in the door to my room carrying a demi-tasse, a most pathetic excuse to find out what I was up to since I never drink coffee at night. It was her second trip up the stairs that day, which was one above her limit, but she was not unrewarded. She discovered me in the process of emptying my file cabinets, first into the fireplace, which though huge, could not hold all the material, and then in the middle of the floor. She placed the tray on the table by the sofa where Klein had been sitting several hours earlier, while eyeing the scotch bottle and the glasses.

"Do you need any help?" she said, as if the sight of my turning the room into a garbage dump were the most ordinary sight in the world.

"The first thing in the morning," I said, "send up some people to clear out this shit. It can all be burned."

"There won't be anyone coming in tomorrow. It's Sunday. Everybody's off."

"Then find somebody," I said. "You don't expect me to live with all this crap, do you?"

"No," said Margaret.

"My God," I said.

"Why don't you stop now and finish in the morning? I'll help out then."

"What? And be responsible for your missing church? What would Minnie say?"

"I don't have to go."

"Margaret, for Christ's sake. . . ." Pause. The scene did look a little crazy. With a change of tone: "Now you go over to your house. Go to bed. Everything's all right."

"You're sure?"

"Yes."

"Maybe I should just pick up a bit. . . ." She headed toward the scotch bottle.

"Leave that! Leave everything. Now go. Please."

"Well, all right—I think it's turned a bit chilly all of a sudden. The wind has shifted. Will you be wanting a blanket?"

My patience was at an end.

"Go," I said with care. "Goodnight. Please close the door on your way out."

"Well," hopelessly, "goodnight."

"Goodnight."

Twenty minutes later the telephone rang. I allowed it to continue for some time before making my way to the desk to pick up the receiver.

"Yes?"

"Marshall?"

"Jacqueline?"

"Yes."

"Isn't this a pleasant surprise?"

"It's been a day for surprises," said Jackie.

"What's yours?"

"I've decided to leave David," said Jackie. "It wasn't working out."

"Tough shit," I said. "Now I suppose you want to come back?"

"No, that isn't why I called. I only wanted to hear how you were. It's been so long. You haven't answered my last two letters."

I reverted to type and lied. "I never received them. You probably misaddressed them."

Jackie pushed on, come what may. "What's your surprise?"

"I found Margaret humping the chauffeur in the kitchen. . . ."

"Oh—Marshall. . . ."

That was stupid but it wouldn't do to apologize. I pause to allow time to erase the memory. "Where are you? Why did you suddenly decide to call now? When I was in New York in May I telephoned you twice but all I got was that silly machine. I refuse to leave messages on machines. It's like giving up a sliver of one's soul." Jackie (laughs): "Now you sound better." Me: "Where are you?" Jackie: "At the apartment. I was just coming in the door when the phone was ringing." Me: "Oh? Where's Mr. Right. Has he left already?" Jackie: "He's still out at East Hampton. We were spending the weekend with Kurt and Jill when we had it out. . . ." Me: "Kurt and Jill? Kurt and Jill? Not Kurt and Jill Fond du Lac, the famous ballroom dance team, the stars of the Aragon-Trianon?" Jackie: "Shut up, Marshall. Try to behave decently for a change." Pause. Me: "Well, what are you working on these days?" Jackie: "I'm flying to California in the morning. I'm doing a piece about Patty Hearst."

Since I have no thoughts about Patty Hearst, one way or the other, there is another pause. I do want to be decent. Actually I often try. Me: "How's the cat?" Jackie: "Oh . . . darling. . . ." Me: "What?" I'm suddenly terrified that Jackie is about to cry. Me: "What is it?" Jackie (stifling a brief sniffle): "I had to have him put to sleep. It's absurd, I know, but I miss him." Me: "What happened?" Jackie: "He developed some kind of kidney disorder . . . I forget the name, but the vet said it's not unusual in cats who've been neutered, especially when they've been kept on those dry-food diets." Me: "When did it happen?" Jackie: "Early June." Me: "Why didn't you say anything about it in your letters?" It slipped out, just like that. Well, fuck it. Jackie knows I lie from time to time. I haven't been kidding her. She digests the wan deception. Jackie: "I felt so badly about it. Guilty, I think. I guess I felt it was a decision that you and I should have made together." Pause. Me: "Well, cats aren't people." Jackie: "No. Well, you *sound* all right. . . ." Now that's a rather strange emphasis to use with someone you haven't talked to in six or eight months. Me: "What do you mean, I *sound* all right? How did you think I'd *sound*?" Pause.

I start putting things together. Me: "Could it possibly be—I mean, am I completely insane—to suspect that when you came home tonight to find your telephone ringing . . . the party of the other part was none other than our own, live-in Miss Fixit, the ever-loyal Girl of the Limberlost, Mopey Margaret of Wicheley Hall?" Jackie: "Darling, she thought you might not be well. She also said she thought you might be lonely." Me: "Lonely? I've just had a houseful of guests!" Jackie: "Who?" Me: "Rasputin, among others. She has some nerve." Jackie: "Don't be nasty with her." Me: "For all she knew she might have been interrupting a splendid Saturday-night fuck." Jackie (frostily): "She didn't. . . ." Me: "I'll find out how much that call cost and dock it from her pay. I'm going to hang up now." Jackie: "Wait a minute. . . ." Me: "Why? You've found out that I'm of perfectly sound mind and body. You can call Margaret back at the guest house and tell her everything's fine. You can reverse the charges. I'll pay for both calls. I always do anyway." Jackie (angrily): "You can't buy everything." Me: "You're telling me? But let me tell you something. . . . It's not because there's anything wrong with using money. It's just that there's no *thing* and no *body* worth its purchase price. Do you understand that? Christ! Oh, fuck. . . ." Jackie: "What?" Me: "The thing is . . . I love you and I wish to fuck you'd hang up."

I didn't wait. I hung up on her. I went over to sit on the couch and drink from the bottle.

About midnight I decided that I wanted to talk to Pru. It seemed a most logical thing to do, but how to find him? I couldn't call Gethsemane. She wouldn't help even if I could reach her. If I had her number there would probably be no answer. Out bowling, most likely. Who does one call under such circumstances? *The New York Times*, of course. The first number I dialed was the subscription office, which apparently never sleeps. Near one o'clock I got through to someone in the newsroom, an elderly Clark Kent who sounded bored.

Me (being careful to enunciate clearly, since it wouldn't do to have him think he was talking to just another barroom drunk): "Perhaps you could help me, sir?"

C.K.: "What is it?"

Me: "I'm trying to locate Prud'homme Shackleford."

C.K.: "Who?"

Me: "Prud'homme Shackleford, the Black Power fellow?"

C.K.: "Oh, yeah. Why don't you try the N double-A CP?"

Me: "I suspect their main office is closed at this hour."

C.K.: "You're probably right."

Me: "I thought the *Times* might have some idea of his whereabouts."

C.K.: "His what?"

Me: "Where he is."

C.K.: "Can I ask who's calling?"

Me: "It's his father. . . ."

C.K.: "Why don't you ask his mother?"

Me: "I'm afraid she wouldn't tell me."

C.K.: "Oh, it's that sort of situation, is it?"

Me: "Yes."

C.K.: "She took the kid and the car and the house and now you haven't got anything, is that it?"

Me: "Not exactly. This is a legitimate call. I'm a subscriber to your newspaper."

C.K.: Well, I'll tell you, Mr. . . . Mr. Shackleford. There's really nobody here right now who can help you. Our Black Caucus has gone for the day. Perhaps if you called in the mornnig . . . ?"

Me: "This cannot wait."

C.K.: "Nothing at one in the morning can wait, but everything usually does, right?"

Me: "Right—does this sound like a crank call?"

C.K.: "Frankly, yes."

I hung up.

36

About 2:30 A.M. on July 17 the fire began, apparently in the Cornwallis Room where I was sleeping, though there were indications that something had ignited the paint-soaked rags in the Green Room on the first floor. Peculiarly, the flames spread almost immediately to the kitchen in the west wing but, as someone later said, you can't predict how fires will behave in these old houses. There are strange drafts as well as corridors within the walls that can suddenly transport flames from one end of a house to the other without appearing to damage intervening territory. I was lucky to escape with my life, more than one person said. As it was, in my haste to get out of the inferno I lost one crutch and both leg braces, though I had others in my room at the guest cottage, where I'd also left my steamer trunk. Everything else was lost— my priceless Albigensian manuscripts (won't Rome be pleased?), my library, my correspondence, my clothing and all my personal effects, to say nothing of the treasure that was the house itself. I'd smelled no smoke. I'd been alerted by the crackle of flames, as if kindling had been lit. The electricity had gone off so I had to make my blind way down the back stairs through the servants' dining room to the kitchen hall and out onto the rear gallery that faces the river. There were already flames climbing the central stairway. As best I could I raced to the guest cottage, where I called the operator who alerted the Tatterhummock County Volunteer Fire Department. In reply to the operator's question I said yes, that I thought we could use equipment from West Point as well as Middlesex County too, that the whole place was liable to go.

The first people to get there were neighbors who'd seen the unusual light in the sky. It took twenty minutes for the first members of the Tatterhummock Volunteers to arrive, but the hose truck and the truck with all of the pumping equipment were at least thirty minutes in coming. Warden Lewis (no kin), the fire chief, was in Cape May on a holiday with his family and it had taken some time before it could be learned who had duplicate keys. Once the entire first floor had caught, the fire took on a life of its own. Like a glorious fuck it couldn't have been stopped short of a heaven-invoked cataclysm, but it also took its time, working its way on, engulfing, then consuming at leisure. At one point that entire great house was in flames, from bottom to top, but still whole. It was so intact that it seemed as if we were watching some sort of display, a demonstration, one of those concrete mock-ups of buildings that can be set afire time and time again to teach trainee-firemen how to combat different sorts of blazes. Wicheley was burning everywhere, from every orifice flames shot forth, but nothing appeared to be damaged. I was almost afraid that it was magically impervious to the flames that were swallowing it.

It was brilliantly light. I'm told that at the height of the conflagration the red glow could be seen more than thirty miles away in West Point and Tappahannock. I stood as close as I could to the fire, 100 feet or so from the front door, in the center of a semicircle of firemen, neighbors and gawkers. One hose lazily poured water on the west wing but it was as effective as a small boy's peeing. At last, near 4:30, when the roof was outlined in flames, the interior began to collapse, room by room, each cave-in making a great impressive whooshing noise as a floor gave way, sending upward magnificent clouds of woody sparks but always miraculously free of smoke, which might have given discomfort to the spectators.

I suppose the age and dryness of the wood were the reasons there was so little potentially annoying smoke, but the scent was strong, unmistakable, the odor of over 300 years, and it would linger over the area into winter and, on warm days, into early spring. I stood there in my bathrobe, on one crutch, barefoot, and wept. On the perimeter of the crowd I could hear laughter, excitement. I suspected someone to be passing a bottle around but those near me were gentle and polite, people at the funeral of someone they didn't know. In deference to me, whose bereavement it was, they spoke in hushed voices. Someone offered to bring me some coffee or to get me a chair, but I declined. As much as it was possible for me, I stood at attention while sobbing without embarrassment. By 4:50 the east and center wings were gone, only a half dozen chimneys remained, a fire still burning in the second-floor fireplace that had warmed me in the Cornwallis Room. The west wing—the kitchen wing and the servants' quarters—was the hardiest. I wept but still the process of consumption and transformation of matter went on. The onlookers assumed I wept for my loss—everyone there knew how much I'd paid for the goddamned place. I was, in a way, but also in joy. I was thinking of Pru. He could start from scratch, build from a new beginning, turn the country around, put the nation on its feet again.

The last person to realize that anything was amiss was Margaret, a sound sleeper, who was awakened at five by the Queen Anne stringer for the Richmond *Times-Dispatch* as he shouted into the guest house telephone to a deaf rewrite man. Wearing an Yves St. Laurent bathrobe over a flannel nightdress, a black hairnet over her gray hair, and the woolly bedroom slippers of a child, she joined me at the pyre, the only other family member present. I was aware of total windlessness, of immense calm, when finally the last wall of the west wing sort of wobbled, unsure of which way to go, then politely caved into the rubble of the basement instead of littering the lawn. For another thirty minutes the firemen hosed down the charred ruins. Sometime before six, the sun rising into a cloudless sky over the Northern Neck—a strange view for, of course, I'd never before been able to see the Northern

Neck from the front drive, the house always having been in the way—the acting fire chief pronounced the body dead. As he left, each fireman came by to shake my hand and receive my thanks, which I gave with emotion. We shared a bond. When the last guests had departed, Margaret led me back to her cottage and put me to bed with the requested double shot of scotch and two of her sleeping pills. I would never have imagined that Margaret used sleeping pills. Sominex, I think.

It's not easy to burn down a house, even one that's almost 300 years old, largely made of wood and with wiring so faulty that you could blow a fuse simply by turning on a television set in the east wing while the Cuisinart was at work in the west. It doesn't much help, either, that you make no effort to conceal your activities. In May I'd flown to New York where I went to the main branch of the Public Library at 42nd Street and Fifth and, making more of a fuss than necessary, withdrew a dozen books about fire, celebrated arsonists and related topics. There are surprisingly few books on arson available and no more than a third of those listed in the card catalog were in the stacks. Back home at Wicheley I began stocking up on kerosene with regularity and in quantity, though no one appeared to find my purchases unusual. "I need five five-gallon cans," I said to Warden Lewis who, in addition to being the chief of the Tatterhummock County Volunteer Fire Department, also runs the general store in Tatterhummock Court House. "I want the most flammable kind you carry," I said. "I'd prefer gasoline but that's too difficult to control, gasoline fumes being so dangerously volatile. Better make that ten cans and put them on my account. I like to keep records. It must seem odd to you when someone like me comes into your store and places an order for such a large amount of kerosene." I didn't put it quite that way but my purchases surprised him not at all. He deals with arsonists every day. In the excitement of the fire no one took notice of the kerosene smell—there had been painters at work, after all.

Nobody has ever suspected the fire to be anything except an Act of God. It was not my intention to confess anything, just to be caught for the sake of Pru, though by the time it happened, Pru had nothing to do with it. Later I didn't wish to put myself into a position of defrauding anyone so I didn't file a claim with my insurers, the Old Dominion Casualty Company. Finally they sent a nice young man out to see me, in the course of which visit I was persuaded to file the claim, the young man apologizing all the while for the small amount I would get (about $18,000) but pointing out, too, that we all know that houses like Wicheley are beyond value even when they are equipped with suitable alarm systems and sprinklers. I shall probably use the money to enclose the swimming pool and add a heater.

I stay on at the guest house with Margaret and am most comfortable. I have neither the money nor the desire to rebuild the house itself, nor do I think it should be rebuilt. I want it to remain an open wound. If nothing is to come of my act—and I now realize that nothing will—I wish to preserve the wound as a reminder to me as well as to Pru. But it's not easy to keep a wound open. Nature asserts itself. This morning as I was showing a group of schoolchildren from Newport News around the place—my third tour this month and four more next month (the house that in life was ignored, virtually abandoned, is becoming a Tidewater site, with picture postcards on sale in Queen Anne and Tatterhummock Court House)—this morning as I was taking the visitors around the ruins I noticed that the wound seems to be healing. A scab is forming. Weeds have begun to sprout in the basement under what was once the dining room with the Adam ceiling. The landscape will not be denied. Do you understand that, Pru?

The night after the fire, an end-of-the world dream: I'm on some sort of tour of Winrock, the great experimental farm established by Winthrop Rockefeller when he moved to Arkansas and which I've never seen. I'm in the company of a group of men of various ages, most of them salesmen, I think. I know one of them to be Winthrop, but which one I'm not sure. I didn't even know him when he was alive. We are being shown through a house that rambles on various levels and is set upon a high plateau. It looks less like a house than a rundown country hotel. Walking down a

back staircase I see a poster showing a pretty black girl lying nude
on a bed, masturbating. The poster gives her room number and
says to call to make a reservation. One of the men with me says he
obtained her last free hour for that evening. Next we pass through
a darkened room in which there is a large round wooden bathtub
with three couples in it having sex. One man, who has the
physique of a weightlifter, stands on the far side of the tub facing
us but not seeing us, looking down dreamily at the head giving
him such a transporting blow job. The other couples seem to be
fucking under the soapy water, with only their heads and shoulders exposed. I realize with a shock that they all are men. We are
being shown the river—the Texarkana?—crossing by flatcar over
a railway bridge. Someone points to the center of a low dam
where there's a small, aged fieldstone house that looks as if it
might be a tollhouse on the Delaware Canal. "Isn't that too bad?"
the man says. "They're tearing down the Kennedy house."

It's Times Square. Though it's dark I think it is morning. The
street lights are on. I pass a junk-jewelry store that is being opened
for the day when several men I don't know stop me. "We were all
together at Winrock," one says. "Oh, yes," I say, and ask if they
know whether it's day or night. "It's eleven-thirty," says a man. I
say I know it's 11:30 but I don't know if it's 11:30 in the morning
or 11:30 at night. "The morning," he says. I'm relieved. I say I
thought it was morning but I was uncertain because it's so dark.
The others pass on but one man stays. I recognize him. I think he
must be someone I went to St. Matthew's with. He is older than I
am, taller, heavier set. We stand on the sidewalk side by side
talking. His name is Ken but that's not who he is. I move to get
out of the way of the other pedestrians and as I do my hand bumps
against his crotch. He has an erection. I hold it as my own. Briefly
El Greco clouds part to reveal a sunny morning sky beyond, then
come together again. Against the dark sky to the northeast I see
the silhouette of a gigantic atomic missile on a launching pad. It
might be twelve miles tall. It should have taken off but it isn't
moving. It's fizzling like a firecracker. Ken and I realize at the
same moment that it's in the process of detonating. "Something has
gone wrong," says Ken. "This is the end," I say. I'm aware of
violent explosions that sound small only because they are still far

off. I feel heat on my face. My eyes ache from the glare though it's
still dark. Ken and I are walking north on the West Side Highway.
A section ahead of us buckles and collapses. Automobiles slide
off. The people of the city have panicked. They run aimlessly. I
hear the sirens of fire engines going to the rescue but, I wonder,
why rescue if this is the end? A steel-and-glass skyscraper on Columbus Circle turns into a glowing forty-two-story ember. "Is this
a dream?" I ask Ken. "No," he says, and walks away.

Virginia State Historical Marker:

HENDERSON'S TREE

Three miles to the east on a bluff overlooking the Tatterhummock River grew Henderson's Tree, an old cherry tree so called
because it was the refuge in times of civil turmoil for Marshall
Lewis Henderson, the Rebel, Actor and Scholar. During the
night of May 29–30, 1940, Henderson sought privacy in its
upper branches having with him at that time a full pint of Old
Mr. Boston rye. It is thought he drank most of the contents and
was resting his eyes when Odile Devereaux, the well-known
Alabama beauty, and her daughter Jojo, a student of toe-tap,
being in the midst of certain domestic difficulties, left their house
situated some 50 feet northwest of Henderson's Tree to drive
home to Odile's mother in Montgomery, Ala., 519 miles south-
west. As was the custom in those days when Odile started her
car, a 1935 blue Buick four-door sedan, the journey began with
the backfiring of the motor, BANG, BANG, which so startled Henderson that he lost his perch and fell 18 feet to the ground. He
was discovered early in the morning by a yard slave named Bill
who treated him for a cracked spinal column and assisted him to
the infirmary. After a long illness Henderson's Tree died in 1955
and was chopped down. Some of its roots remain visible, however.

It was only the civilized sound of a car's backfiring, but for
most of my life I was convinced that Tom, at the last minute,
changed his mind and turned the gun on me.

He's been laid to rest. I'm finished with him and can now get on
with my own life. As I write this, for I've written everything down
and filed it in the steamer trunk (which, along with all I possess,

will one day go to Pru, who is not just a Henderson and a Shackle-ford but also a Lewis, and a Tatterhummock Lewis at that), I think, I can't be sure, but I have the sensation—I have the *feeling* —that I can move my right big toe.

The postcards being sold in Queen Anne and Tatterhummock Court House do not do justice to Wicheley as it really was. This morning I ordered some of my own to be made from the photographs taken by the man Ma sent down from New York. If people would like to know what the house looked like, they should be given an accurate representation. We will put them on sale here, along with a brief history of the house, which I will research. I've always been interested in postcards, not in the pictures which, God knows, are dead, insensitive things, but in the language. Postcards are the belles-lettres of transients. "It's rained every day this week." "No one speaks English." "We saw this on Thursday." "John has hives." "The people are friendly." "Prices are sky-high." "They hate Americans." And, of course, "Wish you were here," which means, "I am someplace else." They're all the same when boiled down: X marks the spot. For a short time, anyway.

A NOTE ON THE TYPE

The text of this book was set in a face
called Times Roman, designed by Stanley Morison for
The Times (London), and first introduced by that
newspaper in 1932.

Among typographers and designers of the twentieth century,
Stanley Morison has been a strong forming influence, as typo-
graphical adviser to the English Monotype Corporation, as a
director of two distinguished English publishing houses, and as
a writer of sensibility, erudition, and keen practical sense.

Composed by Maryland Linotype Composition Co.,
Baltimore, Maryland.
Printed and bound by American Book—Stratford Press, Inc.,
Saddle Brook, New Jersey.

Typography and binding design by
Virginia Tan.